FLIGHT OF THE STORKS

Also by Jean-Christophe Grangé
and published by The Harvill Press

BLOOD-RED RIVERS

Jean-Christophe Grangé

FLIGHT OF THE STORKS

Translated from the French by
Ian Monk

THE HARVILL PRESS
LONDON

First published with the title
Le Vol des cigognes by Éditions Albin Michel, 1994

First published in Great Britain in 2000 by
The Harvill Press
2 Aztec Row
Berners Road
London N1 0PW

www.harvill.com

1 3 5 7 9 8 6 4 2

© Éditions Albin Michel S.A., 1994
English translation © Ian Monk, 2000

Jean-Christophe Grangé asserts the moral right
to be identified as the author of this work

A CIP catalogue record for this book is available from the British Library

This edition is supported by the French Ministry for Foreign
Affairs, as part of the Burgess programme headed for the French
Embassy in London by the Institut Français du Royaume-Uni

ĭi institut français

This edition has also been published with the financial assistance
of the French Ministry of Culture

ISBN 1 86046 781 4 (hardback)
ISBN 1 86046 728 8 (paperback)

Text designed and typeset in Minion
at Libanus Press, Marlborough, Wiltshire

Printed and bound in Great Britain by
Butler & Tanner Ltd at Selwood Printing, Burgess Hill

For Virginie Luc

I
Sweet Europe

CHAPTER 1

Before setting off, I had promised to pay a final call on Max Böhm.

That day, a thunderstorm was brewing over the French-speaking part of Switzerland. The sky was scarred with deep blue and black marks, from which translucent beams emerged. A hot wind was blowing in all directions. In a hired convertible, I drove along the banks of Lake Geneva. Around a corner, Montreux appeared, looking hazy in the electric atmosphere. The waters of the lake were becoming turbulent and the hotels seemed condemned to an ominous silence, despite the tourist season. On reaching the centre, I slowed down and drove through the narrow streets that lead up to the top of the town.

When I arrived at Max Böhm's chalet, the sky was almost black. I glanced at my watch. It was 5 p.m. I rang, then waited. No answer. I tried again and pressed my ear to the door. Nothing was moving behind it. Strange. From what I had noticed during my initial visit, Böhm seemed to be the punctual sort. I went back to the car and waited. Dull rumblings racked the sky. I pulled down the roof of the convertible. At half past five, he had still not turned up. I decided to go and take a look around the enclosures. Maybe the ornithologist had decided to pay a call on his charges.

I entered German Switzerland via a town called Bulle. The rain was still holding off, but the wind had doubled in intensity, throwing clouds of dust under my wheels. One hour later, I reached the outskirts of Weissembach, just beside the enclosed plot of land.

I switched off the ignition then walked through the farmer's fields as far as the cages.

Behind the wiring, there were the storks, with their orange bills, black and white plumage and penetrating stares. They looked impatient. They were furiously beating their wings and snapping their bills. Presumably on account of the storm, but also because of their migratory instinct. Böhm's words came to mind: "Storks are instinctive migrants. Their departure is not triggered off by weather conditions or dietary variations, but by an inner clock. The day comes when it is time to go, it's that simple." It was the end of August and the storks must have been sensing that mysterious signal. Nearby, in some pastureland, other storks were coming and going, shaken by the wind. They too were attempting to take wing, but Böhm had "clipped" them, that is to say, plucked the feathers from the first phalanx of one of their wings, thus destabilizing them and preventing them from taking off. This "friend of nature" definitely had an odd way of looking at the natural order of things.

Suddenly, a scrawny man, doubled up by the wind, appeared in the nearby fields. The smell of cut grass was billowing at me and I felt a headache easing its way into my skull. From far off, the scare-crow was yelling something in German. I shouted back in French. He replied immediately in the same language: "Böhm hasn't been here today. Nor yesterday, for that matter." He was bald and a few locks of hair fluttered over his forehead. He kept plastering them back onto his scalp. He added: "He usually comes here every day to feed his creatures."

I went back to the car and headed for the Eco-Museum. It was a sort of wide-open space, not far from Montreux, where some traditional Swiss chalets had been reconstructed down to the very last detail. On each of the chimney pots, a pair of storks had been installed, under Max Böhm's supervision.

Before long, I had reached this artificial village. I set off on foot through the empty lanes. For some time, I wandered through the maze of brown and white houses, which looked as if they were totally deserted, and finally arrived at the belfry – a dark square tower that stood over twenty metres high. At its summit sat a nest of quite gargantuan dimensions, of which only the edges were visible. "Europe's biggest nest," Max Böhm had told me. The storks were up there, on their throne of twigs and mud. The clicking of their bills echoed down the empty streets, like the snapping of worn-down jaws. Böhm was nowhere to be seen.

Retracing my steps, I went in search of the janitor's house. I found him in front of his TV. He was eating a sandwich while his dog was munching up some meatballs from its bowl. "Böhm?" he said with his mouth full. "He came to the belfry the day before yesterday. We got the ladder out. (I remembered the infernal machine the ornithologist had used to gain access to the nest – an ancient, worm-eaten fireman's ladder.) But I haven't seen him since. He didn't even put his things away."

The man shrugged his shoulders then added:

"Böhm is at home here. He comes and goes as he likes."

Then he bit off another lump of his sandwich, to show that he was through.

"Could you get it out again?"

"What?"

"The ladder."

We set off in the storm, with the dog at our heels. The janitor walked in silence. As far as he was concerned, it was too late in the day for all this. At the foot of the belfry, he opened the doors of a barn that abutted on the tower. We took out the ladder, which was fixed on two cart wheels. The contraption looked more dangerous to me than ever. Nevertheless, with the janitor's help, I got the system of chains, pulleys and cables going and, slowly, the ladder extended its rungs. Its top wobbled in the wind.

I swallowed hard and gingerly started to climb. The higher I got, the more the altitude and the wind troubled my eyesight. My hands clung onto the rungs. I felt an abyss open up in my guts. Ten yards. I concentrated on the wall and climbed higher. Fifteen yards. The wood was damp and my feet kept slipping. The entire ladder was wobbling, sending shock waves into my knees. I risked a glance upwards. The nest was within arm's reach. I took a deep breath and clambered over the last rungs, putting my weight on the branches in the nest. The storks flew off. For a fleeting moment, all I could see was a cloud of feathers, then a vision of horror.

Böhm was there, lying on his back, his mouth agape. He had found his final resting place in that huge nest. His ghastly white stomach, dotted with mud, could be seen through his filthy shirt. His eyes were no more than empty bleeding sockets. I do not know if storks really bring babies, but they can certainly take care of the dead.

CHAPTER 2

Sterile whiteness, the clicking of metal, ghostly forms. At three in the morning, I was waiting in Montreux's little hospital. The doors of the emergency room opened and closed. Nurses scurried by. Masked faces appeared, indifferent to my presence.

The janitor had remained at the artificial village in a state of shock. As for me, I was in no great shape either. I could not stop shivering, and my head was empty. I had never seen a corpse before. And for a first experience, Böhm's body was quite something. The birds had started to devour his tongue and other parts of him, deeper down in his throat. Multiple wounds had been discovered on his abdomen and flanks: incisions, lacerations, cuts. In the end, they would have completely devoured him.

"You do know that storks are carnivorous, don't you?" Max Böhm had told me when first we met. There was no way I was going to forget that now.

The firemen had taken down the body from its perch, under the slow suspicious flight of the birds. For the last time I saw Böhm's flesh, back on earth, covered with scabs and mud, before it was wrapped up in a rustling body-bag. I had followed this moonlit show under the intermittent flashes of the ambulance's lights without uttering a word and, I must admit, without feeling the slightest emotion. Just a sort of absence, a terrified isolation.

Now I was waiting. And mulling over my existence during the previous few months – two months of ornithological enthusiasm, that had now finished with a funeral.

At the time, I was a thoroughly respectable young man. Aged thirty-two, I had just obtained a PhD in history. The culmination of eight years spent contemplating the "Concept of Culture in Oswald Spengler". When I had completed that thousand-page doorstopper, which was absolutely useless in practical terms, and rather a drain in personal terms, my only idea was to forget about academia. I was fed up with books, museums, and arty experimental films. I was fed up with that surrogate existence, the shadow-play of art and the vagueness of the social sciences. I wanted to live life to the full, to bite the apple of existence.

I knew young doctors who had gone into humanitarian work because they had a "year to kill", as they put it. Or up-and-coming lawyers who had wandered off to India and tried a little mysticism before embracing their careers. As for me, I had no vocation, and no taste for things exotic or for the misfortunes of others. So, once again, my adoptive parents came to my aid.

"Once again", because, ever since the accident in which my brother and my parents had died, twenty-five years earlier, those two elderly diplomats had always given me what I needed: first of all, the company of a nanny when I was a child; then a sizeable allowance, which allowed me to maintain a genuine distance from money worries.

Georges and Nelly Braesler had suggested that I contact Max Böhm, one of their Swiss friends, who was looking for someone like me. "Someone like me?" I asked, while noting down Böhm's address. They replied that it would probably be for several months. They would see about finding me a permanent position later.

Then, things took an unexpected turn. And my first, mysteriously unsettling meeting with Max Böhm will remain forever engraved in my memory down to the last detail.

That day, 17 May 1991, at about 4 p.m., I arrived at 3, Rue du Lac, after having wandered for ages through the tiny lanes around the heights of Montreux. At the end of a square, dotted with medieval lamps, I came across a chalet, which bore the name "Max Böhm" on its solid wooden door. I rang the bell. A long minute ticked by, then a live-wire aged about sixty opened it with a broad smile on his face.

"You must be Louis Antioch," he proclaimed. I nodded and went inside.

The interior of the chalet resembled the neighbourhood. The rooms were cramped, over-elaborate, full of nooks, crannies, shelves, and curtains that plainly did not conceal windows. The floor was a network of steps and daises. Böhm pulled aside a curtain and invited me down into his sanctuary in the basement. We entered a room with whitewashed walls, furnished with only an oak desk, on which stood a typewriter and piles of documents. Above it, hung a map of Europe and of Africa and numerous engravings of birds. I sat down. Böhm offered me some tea. I accepted with pleasure (all I drink is tea). In a series of rapid gestures, Böhm produced a thermos, cups, sugar and lemons. As he bustled about, I watched him more attentively.

He was short, thick-set and his crewcut hair was totally white. His round face was divided by a cropped moustache, which was also white. His corpulence made him look awkward, and his movements heavy, but his face imparted a curious friendliness.

Böhm carefully poured out the tea. His hands were chubby, his fingers graceless. "A wild man of the woods," I said to myself. There was something vaguely military about him – a past spent in the army or some other violent activity. At last he sat down, folded his hands and, in a soft voice, began:

"So, you are related to my friends, the Braeslers."

I cleared my throat.

"I'm their adopted son."

"I didn't think that they had any children."

"They don't. I mean, none of their own. (Böhm said nothing, so I went on:) My real parents were close friends of the Braeslers.

When I was seven, my mother, father and brother were killed in a fire. I had no other family. So Georges and Nelly adopted me."

"Nelly has told me about your intellectual capacities."

"I'm afraid she might have exaggerated them slightly. (I opened my briefcase.) I've brought you my curriculum vitae."

Böhm pushed the sheet of paper away with the flat of his hand. His hand was huge and powerful. It looked as though it could break your wrist with a simple twist of just two fingers. He replied:

"I'll trust Nelly's judgment. Has she told you about your 'mission'? Has she pointed out that this is a very special piece of business?"

"Nelly didn't tell me anything."

Böhm fell silent and stared at me. He seemed to be on the lookout for my slightest reaction.

"At my age, idle hands lead to the acquisition of fads. Certain beings now mean much more to me than they did before."

"Who is that?" I asked.

"Not human beings."

Böhm fell silent again. He clearly liked working up the suspense. He finally murmured:

"I'm talking about storks."

"Storks?"

"You see, I'm a nature lover. I've been interested in birds for the last forty years. When I was young I read everything I could find about ornithology. I spent hours in the forest, clutching my binoculars, observing each species. I was particularly fond of the white stork. The reason why I loved them more than the rest is because they are wonderful migrants, capable of covering more than twelve thousand miles each year. At the end of summer, when the storks set off for Africa, my soul would fly off alongside them. So it was that I later chose a career which allowed me to travel and follow those birds. I am a retired civil engineer, Monsieur Antioch. Throughout my life, I managed to find work on large building projects in the Middle East, or Africa, on the birds' migration paths. Nowadays, I stay put here, but I am still studying migration. I have written several books on the subject.

7

"I know nothing about storks. What is it you expect from me?"

"I'm coming to that. (Böhm sipped his tea.) Since I retired here, in Montreux, the storks have been thriving. Each spring, my pairs come back and find exactly the same nests again. It all runs like clockwork. But, this year, the storks from the east have not returned."

"What do you mean?"

"Of the seven hundred migratory pairs counted in Germany and Poland, fewer than fifty reappeared in their skies during March and April. I waited for several weeks. I went there myself. But there was nothing to be done. The birds did not come back."

The ornithologist suddenly seemed older and lonelier to me. I asked:

"And do you know why?"

"Perhaps because of some ecological catastrophe. Or the effects of a new insecticide. But these are only 'maybes'. What I want is proof."

"How can I help you?"

"Next August, dozens of juvenile storks will set off, as they do every year, on their migration paths. I want you to follow them. Day after day. I want you to take exactly the same route as they do. I want you to observe all the difficulties they come up against. To question local inhabitants, the police, each region's ornithologists. I want you to find out why my storks disappeared."

Max Böhm's plan amazed me.

"Wouldn't you be far more qualified than me to . . . "

"I swore never to set foot in Africa again. In any case, I am now fifty-seven. I have a weak heart. It would be impossible for me to do the fieldwork."

"Don't you have an assistant, a young ornithologist who could do the job?"

"I don't like specialists. I want a man with no preconceived opinions, no previous knowledge, someone with an open mind who would go to the heart of the mystery. So are you going to accept, or are you not?"

"I accept," I answered without any hesitation. "When do I leave?"

"When the storks do, at the end of August. The journey will take about two months. In October, the birds will be in Sudan. If anything is going to happen, then I imagine that it will be before that date. Otherwise, you then come home and the mystery will remain unsolved. Your salary will be 15,000 Swiss francs per month, plus expenses. It will be paid by our association, the SPES – The Society for the Protection of the European Stork. We are not particularly well-endowed, but I have arranged the most comfortable ways to travel: first-class flights, hire cars, luxury hotels. The first instalment will be paid in mid-August, along with your plane tickets and reservations. Does my offer seem reasonable?"

"I'm your man. But tell me something first. How did you meet the Braeslers?"

"It was in 1987, at an ornithological symposium in Metz. The main theme was 'Storks: an endangered species in Western Europe'. Georges also gave an interesting lecture about the common crane."

Later, Max Böhm took me round Switzerland to visit some of the enclosures where he raised domestic storks, whose young became migratory birds – the very ones that I was to follow. As we travelled, the ornithologist explained the guiding principles of my journey. Firstly, the paths storks follow have for the most part already been traced out. Secondly, storks cover only about sixty miles per day. Finally, Böhm had an infallible way of identifying the European storks. He had ringed them. Each spring, he fixed rings on the storks' feet, which bore their date of birth and identification number. With a pair of binoculars, it would thus be possible to pick out "his" birds each evening. Added to all this was the fact that Böhm corresponded with ornithologists in each country along the path, who would be able to help me and answer my questions. In these circumstances, Böhm was sure that I would be able to find out what had happened last spring on the birds' migration paths.

Three months later, on 17 August 1991, Max Böhm telephoned me in a highly excited state. He was just back from Germany where he had noticed that the storks were about to depart. Böhm had credited my account with an advance payment of 50,000 francs (two months' salary, plus an initial contribution to my expenses) and sent me, by

DHL, the plane tickets, vouchers for hiring cars and a list of hotel reservations. The ornithologist had added in a "Paris–Lausanne" ticket. He wanted to see me one last time so that we could check the details of the project.

So, at 7 a.m. on 19 August, I set off, well supplied with guide books, visas and medicines. I had decided to travel light. My entire belongings – computer included – fitted into a medium-sized suitcase, as well as a small rucksack. Everything was in order. On the other hand, my heart was beating chaotically, full of a burning confusion of hope, excitement and apprehension.

CHAPTER 3

Yet now, it was all over. Before it had even begun. Max Böhm would never know why his storks had disappeared. And neither would I, for that matter. Because his death meant that my investigations had come to an end. I would pay the money back to the association and return to my studies. My life as a traveller had been extremely brief. And I was not even surprised at this aborted career. After all, I had never been anything more than an idle student. There was no reason at all why I should now suddenly become a swashbuckling adventurer.

But still I waited there. In the hospital. For the arrival of the Federal Inspector and the result of the postmortem. Yes, there had been a postmortem. The doctor on night duty had begun it at once, as soon as he had received police permission – Max Böhm apparently had no family. So what had happened to old Max? A heart attack? A stork attack? These questions needed answering, and that was no doubt why the ornithologist's body was now being dissected.

"Are you Louis Antioch?"

Lost in my thoughts, I had not noticed the man who had just sat down beside me. His voice was kind, his features too. A long face,

10

with a polite expression, under an agitated mop of hair. He gazed at me with sleepy eyes, still half in dreamland. He was unshaven, and I clearly sensed that this was exceptional. He was wearing light, neatly tailored cotton trousers and a lavender blue Lacoste shirt. We were dressed almost identically, except my shirt was black and had a skull emblazoned on it instead of a crocodile.

"Yes. Are you from the police?" I answered.

He nodded and put his hands together, as though he was going to pray.

"I'm Inspector Dumaz. I'm on night duty. A nasty business. So you found the body?"

"Yes."

"What was it like?"

"Dead."

Dumaz shrugged and produced a note pad.

"In what circumstances did you find it?"

I told him about the trail that had led me to Böhm. Dumaz slowly noted it all down, then asked:

"Are you French?"

"Yes. I live in Paris."

The inspector carefully jotted down my address.

"Had you known Max Böhm for long?"

"No."

"What was the nature of your relationship?"

I decided to lie.

"I'm an amateur ornithologist. He and I were planning to put together an educational programme concerning various species of birds."

"Which ones?"

"Mainly the white stork."

"What's your job?"

"I've just completed my studies."

"What sort of studies? Ornithology?"

"No, history and philosophy."

"And how old are you?"

"Thirty-two."

The inspector whistled softly.

"You're lucky to have been able to pursue your interests for so long. I'm the same age as you, and I've been in the police force for thirteen years."

"History doesn't interest me," I said coldly.

Dumaz stared at the wall in front of us. A dreamy smile drifted over his face once more.

"My job doesn't interest me either, I can promise you that."

He turned his eyes to me again.

"How long do you think Max Böhm had been dead for?"

"Since the day before yesterday. The evening of the seventeenth. The janitor saw him climb up to the nest, but didn't see him come down again."

"And what do you think he died of?"

"I've no idea. A heart attack, maybe. The storks had started to . . . eat him."

"I saw the body before the postmortem. Do you have anything to add?"

"No."

"You'll have to sign a statement at police headquarters in the town centre. It will be ready at the end of the morning. Here's the address. (Dumaz sighed.) This death is going to make tongues wag. Böhm was a celebrity. I suppose you know that he reintroduced storks into Switzerland. Things like that mean a lot to us Swiss."

He came to a halt, then gave a short laugh.

"You're wearing an unusual shirt . . . It's rather appropriate, don't you think?"

I had been waiting for this since the start. I was saved by the arrival of a short, forthright woman with dark-brown hair. Her white coat was blood-stained, her face blotchy and covered with wrinkles. The sort who has been around a bit. Oddly enough, in that cotton wool atmosphere, she was wearing high-heels, which clicked at each step she took. She came over to us. Her breath stank of tobacco.

"You're here for Böhm?" she asked in a hoarse voice.

We stood up. Dumaz dealt with the introductions.

"This is Louis Antioch, a student, and Max Böhm's friend. (I sensed a tone of irony in his voice.) He's the one who discovered the body tonight. I'm Inspector Dumaz, from the Federal Police."

"Catherine Warel, heart surgeon. The postmortem took a long time," she said, wiping her forehead, which was running with sweat. "It was a more complicated case than expected. Firstly, because of the wounds. All those lumps that had been pecked out of him. Apparently he was found in a stork's nest. What was he doing up there, for heaven's sake?"

"Max Böhm was an ornithologist," Dumaz explained stiffly. "I'm surprised you've never heard of him. He was extremely famous. He protected Switzerland's storks."

"Ah, did he?" the woman said, unconvinced.

She took out a packet of French cigarettes and lit one. I noticed the no-smoking sign and realized that she was not Swiss. After blowing out a long puff of smoke, she went on:

"Let's get back to the postmortem. Despite all of the injuries – you'll receive a typed description of them later this morning – it is clear that he died of a heart attack on the evening of August 17, at about eight o'clock. (She turned towards me.) If it hadn't been for you, the smell would have ended up alerting the tourists. But there is something surprising. Did you know that Böhm had had a heart transplant?"

Dumaz stared round at me quizzically. The doctor went on:

"When the team found a long scar on his sternum they called me in so that I could supervise the postmortem. There is no doubt about the transplant. First of all there's the scar typical of a sternotomy, then abnormal adhesions in the pericardiac cavity, which are signs of a previous operation. I also found the sutures of the graft around the aorta, the pulmonary artery and the left and right auricles, which were done with non-reabsorbent thread."

Dr Warel took another drag, and continued.

"The operation evidently occurred several years ago, but the new organ was remarkably well accepted – normally we find a large number of white scars on a transplanted heart, which correspond to points of rejection, or, to put it another way, muscular cells with necrosis. Böhm's transplant is therefore extremely interesting. And, from what I could see, the transplant was performed by someone who knew what they were doing. Now, I asked around and Max Böhm was not being treated by any of our doctors. There's a little mystery to solve, gentlemen. I'll look into it myself. But there's nothing original about the cause of death. A classic coronary thrombosis, which occurred about fifty hours ago. From the effort of climbing up to the nest, presumably. If it's any consolation to you, Böhm didn't suffer."

"What do you mean?" I asked.

Warel blew out a long puff of nicotine in the aseptic air.

"A transplanted heart is independent from the host nervous system. So a heart attack doesn't cause any particular pain. Max Böhm didn't feel himself die. That's all, gentlemen." She turned towards me. "Are you going to deal with the funeral?"

I hesitated for a second.

"Unfortunately, I have to go away and . . . " I replied.

"Okay," she cut in. "We'll sort things out. The death certificate will be ready later this morning. (And then, to Dumaz:) Can I speak to you for a minute?"

The inspector and the doctor nodded to me in farewell. Dumaz added:

"Don't forget to come in and sign your statement at the end of the morning."

Then they left me in the corridor, him with his dreamy face, and her with her heels clicking. Though not loud enough to drown out what she whispered to him:

"There's a problem . . . "

CHAPTER 4

Outside, dawn was making metallic shadows, and casting a grey light through the sleepy streets. Ignoring the traffic lights, I crossed Montreux and drove directly to Böhm's house. I did not know why, but I was terrified of the idea of the police investigating him. I wanted to destroy all the documents that concerned me, and quietly pay back the SPES, without the police becoming involved. No trace, no problems.

I parked at a discreet distance from the chalet. First of all, I checked that the front door was not bolted, then went back to the car and fetched a flexible plastic divider from my bag. I slid it in between the door and the frame. Playing with the lock, I tried to slip the plastic sheet under the latch. At last, after I had given it a good shoulder thrust, the door silently opened. I entered the residence of Monsieur Böhm, deceased. The half-light made the interior of the chalet look smaller and more cramped than ever. It was already a dead man's house.

I went down to the study in the basement and had no difficulty in finding the file marked "Louis Antioch", which was lying on the desk. It contained the receipt of the bank transfer, bills for the plane tickets and rental agreements. I also read the notes that Böhm had taken about me from what Nelly Braesler had told him:

> "Louis Antioch. Age thirty-two. Adopted by the Braeslers at the age of ten.
> Intelligent, brilliant and sensitive. But indolent and disillusioned. To be handled with caution.
> Watch out for traumas from the accident. Partial amnesia."

So, as far as the Braeslers were concerned, even after all those years I was still in a critical condition – a nutcase. I turned over the page. There was nothing more. Nelly had told him nothing about my family tragedy. Just as well. I kept the file and continued looking.

In the drawers, I found a file entitled "Storks", similar to the one Max had prepared for me that first day, with contact addresses and a ream of information. I hung onto that one, too.

It was time to go. But, gripped by a strange curiosity, I continued searching in a random manner. In a metal filing cabinet, as tall as I was, I found thousands of index cards for his birds. They were crammed in together, vertically, with different coloured edges. Böhm had explained this colour coding to me. For each event or piece of information a different shade was given: red – female; blue – male; green – migratory; pink – accident involving electrocution; yellow – illness; black – death, and so on. Thus, by just looking at the edges of the cards, Böhm could pick out those that concerned any given research subject.

An idea occurred to me. I looked through the list of storks that had disappeared, then dug out some of the cards concerning them from the drawer. Böhm used an indecipherable coded language. All I could figure out was that the storks that had vanished were all adults, more than seven years old. I pocketed the cards. I was beginning to become a kleptomaniac. Still in the throes of an irresistible impulse, I went right through the desk, this time in search of a medical file. "Böhm is a textbook case." Dr Warel had said. Where had he been operated on? Who was the surgeon? I found nothing.

In desperation, I turned to a small recess that was adjacent to the study. There, Max Böhm soldered his rings and kept his ornithological equipment. On the work surface lay a pair of binoculars, some photographic filters and myriad rings of every sort and every description. I also found some surgical instruments, some hypodermic syringes, dressings, splints and disinfectants. In his spare time, Max Böhm had obviously also played at being an amateur vet. That old man's universe now seemed increasingly lonely, centred on his incomprehensible obsessions. At last, I put everything back into place and returned to the ground floor.

I strode across the main sitting-room, the dining-room and the kitchen. All they contained were Swiss knick-knacks, junk mail and old newspapers. I went up to the bedrooms. There were three of them. The one where I had slept that first night was still just as anonymous, with its narrow bed and cramped furniture. Böhm's room smelt damp and sad. The decor was faded and the furniture piled up, without any apparent rhyme or reason. I searched the lot: wardrobe, desk and chests-of-drawers. They were all practically empty. I looked under the bed and the rugs. I pulled up the corners of the wallpaper. Nothing. Apart from a cardboard box at the bottom of a wardrobe containing some old photographs of a woman. I looked at these snapshots for a moment. She was small, with vague features and a fragile face, against a background of tropical scenery. This had to be Madame Böhm. In the more recent photos – with the outdated colours of the 1970s – she looked about forty. I went into the third bedroom. All I found was the same antiquated atmosphere, nothing more. Brushing the dust off my clothes, I went back down the narrow staircase.

Through the windows, the sun was coming up. A golden ray of light stroked the backs of the furniture and the edges of the daises, which rose up for no apparent reason in each corner of the room. I sat down on one of them. This house was definitely missing several things: Max Böhm's medical file (someone with a heart transplant must have endless prescriptions, scans, electrocardiograms, and so on); the classical souvenirs of a life spent travelling, such as African bric-à-brac, Oriental rugs, hunting trophies and what have you; the remnants of a professional career – I had not even found a file dealing with his pension, let alone bank statements or tax returns. If Böhm had decided to obliterate his past, then he could hardly have gone about it more thoroughly. And yet, there just had to be a hiding place somewhere.

I glanced at my watch. It was 7.15. If there was going to be an investigation, the police would be there soon, to set seals on the door, if nothing else. With a feeling of regret, I stood up and went to the door. I opened it, then thought about all those steps. Those daises in the main living-room were ideal hiding places. I retraced my steps and tapped on their sides. They were hollow. I ran down-stairs to the recess, fetched a few tools and dashed back up. Twenty minutes later, I had opened up the seven steps in Böhm's sitting-room while doing a minimum of damage. In front of me were three brown, dusty, anonymous envelopes.

I went back to the car and, in search of a quiet place, drove off to the hills that overlook Montreux. Six miles further on, down an isolated lane, I pulled up beside a wood that was still wet with dew. My hands trembled as I opened the first envelope.

It contained the medical file of Irène Böhm, née Fogel, born in Geneva in 1942, died at Bellevue Hospital, Lausanne, in August 1977, of a generalized cancer. The file contained a few x-rays, diagrams and prescriptions, then a death certificate, with an attached telegram addressed to Max Böhm plus a letter of condolence from Dr Lierbaüm, who had treated Irène. I looked at the little envelope. It bore Max Böhm's address in 1977: 66, avenue Bokassa, Bangui, Central African Republic. My heart was racing. The Central African Republic had been Böhm's last address in Africa. That country so tragically famous for the lunacy of its short-lived dictator, Emperor Bokassa. That glistening jungle, sweltering and humid, hidden in the heart of Africa – and also hidden in the depths of my own past.

I rolled down the window to breathe the fresh air outside, then continued looking through the file. I found some more photographs of his frail wife, then some other snapshots showing Max Böhm with a boy of about thirteen, who looked extraordinarily like him. The same squat build, blond hair in a crewcut, brown eyes and an ox-like muscular neck. But, the boy's eyes had a dreamy nonchalance about them which did not match Böhm's stiffness. These photos also apparently came from the same period, the 1970s. There was one of the entire family: father, mother and son. But why had Böhm hidden these extremely ordinary photos under a dais? And where was his son now?

The second envelope contained only a chest x-ray, without any dates, name, or observations. But one thing was sure. A heart could be made out on that dark image. And, in the centre of that organ, a white mark shone out very precisely, which looked to me as though it was some imperfection in the image, or a white clot inside the heart. I thought about Böhm's transplant. This x-ray must show one of his two hearts. The first, or the second? I carefully put it back.

Finally, I opened the third envelope, and froze in terror. In front of me were the most ghastly scenes imaginable. Black and white photographs of a sort of human abattoir, with the bodies of children hung up on meat hooks – flesh puppets, with red gashes instead of arms or genitals; faces with lacerated lips and empty eye sockets; arms, legs and assorted limbs piled up on the corner of a stall; heads covered with brown scabs rolled out across long tables, staring at me with their dry eyes. All of these corpses, without exception, were Blacks.

This terrible place was not simply a death chamber. The walls were covered with white tiles, like a clinic or a morgue, and a collection of gleaming surgical instruments could be seen. It was more like a diabolical laboratory or horrific torture chamber. The secret den of a monster who indulged in the most terrifying practices. I got out of the car. My body was racked with disgust and nausea. Long minutes ticked by in the cool of the morning. From time to time I glanced back at the photos. I tried to drink in their reality, to overcome them, the better to master them. It was impossible. The crudity of the pictures and the grain of the photographs gave that legion of corpses a hallucinatory presence. Who could have committed such horrors? And why?

I got back into the car, closed the three envelopes and promised myself not to open them again for some time. I turned the key and drove back down to Montreux with tears clouding my eyes.

CHAPTER 5

I headed for the town centre, then took the avenue that runs alongside the lake. I found an empty space in the car park of the bright and majestic Hôtel de la Terrasse. The sun was already beaming down on the colourless waters of Lake Geneva. The scenery seemed to be surrounded by a golden halo of fire. I sat down in the hotel garden, facing the lake and the misty mountains that framed the landscape.

A few minutes later, a waiter appeared. I decided to go for some iced Chinese tea. I tried to think. Böhm's death. The mysteries concerning his heart. That morning's search and my terrifying discoveries. It was all a bit much for a simple student employed to follow storks.

"A last bit of tourism before leaving?"

I turned round. Inspector Dumaz, immaculately shaven, was standing behind me. He was wearing a light, brown cotton jacket and pale linen trousers.

"How did you find me?"

"Easy. You all come here. It's as if all of Montreux's roads led to the lake."

"What do you mean, 'you all'?"

"Visitors. Tourists. (He nodded towards the first people out that morning, walking along the banks.) It's a very romantic spot, you know. There's an air of eternity about it, like something out of Jean-Jacques Rousseau's *La Nouvelle Héloïse*. But I'll tell you a secret. All those clichés piss me off. And I reckon that most Swiss feel the same way."

I forced a smile. "You're being very cynical all of a sudden. Can I offer you anything?"

"Some coffee. Some very strong coffee."

I called over the waiter and ordered an espresso. Dumaz sat down next to me. He put on his sunglasses and waited in silence, staring intently at the landscape. When the coffee arrived, he drank it in one gulp, then sighed:

"I haven't stopped since we went our separate ways. First of all, there was that conversation with Dr Warel. You know, the little chain-smoker in the blood-stained white coat. She's new here. I don't think she was expecting anything like this. (Dumaz giggled nervously.) Two weeks in Montreux, and they bring you an ornithologist, who's been discovered in a stork's nest, half eaten by his own birds! Then, on leaving the hospital, I went home to change. After that, I dropped into the station to type out what you'd told me. (Dumaz tapped his jacket.) I've got your statement here. You can sign it now. That way, you won't have to go to the station. Then I decided to take a look round Max Böhm's house. What I found there led me to make a few phone calls. Within half an hour, I had all the answers to my questions. And here I am!"

"What's your conclusion?"

"That's just it. There isn't any conclusion."

"I don't understand."

Dumaz put his hands together again, leant on the table, then turned towards me.

"I told you, Böhm was a celebrity. So what we need is a plain and simple death. Something clear and straightforward."

"And that isn't what you've got?"

"It is and it isn't. His death, leaving aside the exceptional setting, poses no problem at all. A heart attack. No doubt about it. But when you look around, nothing else fits. And I don't want to sully the memory of a great man. Follow me?"

"Do you want to tell me what's so odd about it?"

Dumaz stared at me from behind his dark glasses.

"It's more up to you to fill me in."

"What do you mean?"

"Why did you really visit Max Böhm?"

"I told you last night."

"You were lying. I checked a few things out. I can now prove that what you said isn't true."

I did not answer. Dumaz went on:

"When I searched Böhm's chalet, I noticed that someone had beaten me to it. I'd even say that they'd been through the place a few minutes before I got there. I immediately called the Eco-Museum, where Böhm has another office. A man like him presumably kept a second copy of certain documents. His secretary, who's obviously an early riser, agreed to take a look and came across an amazing file

21

concerning some storks that had disappeared. She then faxed me the most important documents it contained. Do I need to go on?"

It was my turn to stare at the waters of the lake. Tiny yachts could be made out against the gleaming horizon.

"Then, there was the bank. I phoned Böhm's branch. The ornithologist had just made a large bank transfer. I have the beneficiary's name, his address and bank account number."

The silence between us deepened. A crystal silence, like the morning air, that could shatter in numerous different directions. I seized the initiative.

"This time, there is a conclusion."

Dumaz smiled, then took off his glasses.

"What I reckon is that you panicked. Böhm's death isn't as straightforward as all that. There's going to be an inquest. Now, he had just paid you a large sum of money to undertake a specific task, and, for some inexplicable reason, you got scared. You broke into his house to steal your file and wipe out all trace of your relationship. I don't suspect you of wanting to keep the money. You were presumably about to pay it back. But the break-in is a serious offence . . . "

I thought about the three envelopes and hastily replied:

"Inspector, the work Max Böhm offered me was just to do with storks. I don't see that there's anything suspicious about it. I'll pay the money back to the association and . . . "

"There isn't any association."

"Sorry?"

"There is no association, or at least not what you imagine. Böhm worked alone and was the sole member of the SPES. He paid a few employees, supplied material and rented offices. Böhm didn't need other people's money. He was incredibly rich."

I was lost for words. Dumaz pressed on:

"His current account contains over 100,000 Swiss francs. And he must have had a numbered account in one or other of our banks. At some time in his life, our ornithologist did some extremely lucrative work.

"What are you going to do?"

"For the moment, nothing. He's dead. He doesn't seem to have any family. I'm sure that he's left his fortune to some international environmental protection association, such as the WWF or Greenpeace. And so the case is closed. And yet, I'd really like to look into it more deeply. And I need your help."

"My help?"

"Did you find anything in Böhm's chalet this morning?"

Those three envelopes sprang into my mind's eye, like burning meteors.

"Nothing, apart from my file."

Dumaz smiled in disbelief. He stood up.

"Shall we go for a stroll?"

I followed him along the lake shore.

"Let's just suppose that you found nothing," he said. "After all, our man was secretive. I've already done some investigating this morning and haven't learnt much. Neither about his past, nor about his mysterious operation. You remember, his heart transplant. Another puzzle. Do you know what Dr Warel discovered? Böhm's new heart had something odd about it. Something that shouldn't be there. A tiny capsule of titanium, the metal used to manufacture certain sorts of artificial organs, was sewn onto its tip. Normally, they graft a clip there to allow biopsies to be made more easily. But this is quite different. According to Warel, it had no obvious use."

I remained silent. I was thinking about that white patch on the x-ray. So the image I had was of the second heart. In the hope of getting the business over with I asked:

"So how can I be of help?"

"Böhm was going to pay you to follow the migration of the storks. Are you going to do so?"

"No. I'm going to pay back the money. What do I care if the storks have decided to abandon Switzerland and Germany, or been sucked up by some gigantic typhoon?"

"Shame. This trip would have been of great use. I have started to map out, rather approximately, Böhm's career as an engineer. Your journey would have allowed us to retrace his steps across Africa and the Middle East."

"What's your plan?"

"A partnership. With me here, and you on your travels. I'll find out about his money and his operation. I'll dig out the dates and locations of his various jobs. And you'll do the fieldwork, while following the storks' migration paths. We'll stay in close contact. And in a few weeks, we'll know everything about Max Böhm's life. His mysteries, his good deeds, and his smuggling activities."

"Smuggling?"

"For example."

"What's in it for me?"

"A beautiful trip. And the proverbial secrecy of the Swiss. (He tapped his jacket pocket.) We'll sign your statement together, then we'll forget about it."

"And what's in it for you?"

"A lot. Anyway, it's a change from stolen traveller's cheques and lost poodles. Believe me, Monsieur Antioch, the daily round in Montreux during August is not particularly thrilling. I didn't believe you this morning when you told me about your studies. Nobody spends ten years of his life on a subject that doesn't interest him. I lied as well. I love my job. But it isn't living up to my expectations. The days go by, and boredom mounts. I want to work on something solid. Böhm's life gives us the possibility of conducting a special investigation, and working as a team. Such an enigma must tickle your intellectual curiosity. Think about it."

"I'm going back to France. I'll phone you tomorrow. My statement can wait a day or two, can't it?"

The inspector smiled and nodded. He walked back to the car with me then held out his hand. I avoided shaking it and clambered into the convertible. Dumaz smiled again, then blocked the half-open door. After a moment's silence, he asked:

"Can I ask you a personal question?"

I nodded curtly.

"What happened to your hands?"

The question took me aback. I looked at my fingers, that had been deformed for so long, the skin a network of tiny scars. Then I shrugged.

"An accident I had when I was a kid. I was living with a nanny who dyed clothes. One day, a vat full of acid spilt on to my hands. That's all I know. The shock and the pain made me forget the rest."

Dumaz scrutinized my hands. He had clearly noticed my infirmity the night before and was now able to satisfy his desire to examine my old burns. I slammed the door. Dumaz stared at me, then coolly asked:

"And these scars have nothing to do with your parents' accident?"

"How do you know my parents had an accident?"

"Böhm's file is full of information."

I pulled off and drove along the lake shore without looking back in my rear-view mirror. A few miles further on, I had forgotten the inspector's indiscreet question. I drove in silence towards Lausanne.

Soon, in a sunny field, I noticed a group of black and white shapes. I parked the car and cautiously approached them. I took out my binoculars. The storks were there. With their bills in the earth, they were calmly eating their breakfast. I went nearer. In the golden light, their plumage looked like velvet. Shiny, thick and silken. I had no natural interest in animals, but those birds, and the way they stared like an offended duchess, had something special about them.

I thought of Böhm, in the fields of Weissembach. He had seemed pleased to introduce me to his creatures. He had silently pushed his bulky frame through the crops towards the enclosures. Despite his size, he moved lightly and easily. With his short-sleeved shirt, his canvas trousers and the binoculars round his neck, he looked like a retired colonel out on some imaginary manoeuvres. Once inside the enclosure, Böhm had spoken softly to the storks in a voice full of tenderness. The birds had initially backed off, glancing at us furtively.

Then Böhm reached the nest, which stood three feet off the ground. It was a crown of branches and mud, more than three feet in diameter, its surface flat and immaculately clean. The stork shuffled away unwillingly, and Böhm showed me the young which were sitting in the middle. "Six little ones, just imagine it!" The tiny nestlings' plumage was a greenish grey. They opened their eyes wide, and nestled against one another. It was a curiously intimate scene; the heart of a quiet family life. The evening sunlight added a weird and ghostly dimension to the sight. Böhm had suddenly whispered: "You're hooked now, aren't you?" I stared back at him and silently nodded.

The next morning, after Böhm had given me a thick file containing contacts, maps and photographs, and while we were going back up the stairs from his study, he stopped me and abruptly said: "I hope you've understood me correctly, Louis. This business is of vital importance to me. You absolutely must find my storks and discover why they are disappearing. It's a matter of life and death!" In the weak light on the top steps I made out an expression on his face that terrified me. A white, rigid mask that was about to crack. Böhm had definitely been scared to death.

In the distance, the birds languidly took wing. I watched their slow movements rip into the morning light. With a smile on my lips, I wished them a good flight and set off once more.

I arrived at the train station in Lausanne at 12.30. A high-speed express was leaving for Paris in twenty minutes. I found a phone box and, by force of habit, checked my answering machine. There was a message from Ulrich Wagner, a German biologist I had met one month before during my ornithological preparations. Ulrich and his team were getting ready to follow the storks by satellite. They had equipped about twenty birds with miniature Japanese transmitters and would thus be able to locate them precisely each day thanks to Argos map coordinates. They had suggested that I consult their satellite data. This idea would be of great use, preventing me from running after those tiny rings that were hard to spot. The message read: "That's it, Louis! They're off! The system's working perfectly. Call me back. I'll give you the storks' numbers and their locations. Good luck!"

So, those birds refused to leave me alone. I left the phone booth. Families were walking round the station with ruddy faces and huge suitcases bouncing off their legs. Tourists were strolling about with expressions of determined curiosity. I glanced at my watch and went to the taxi rank. This time, I headed for the airport.

II
Sofia in Wartime

CHAPTER 6

After taking the Lausanne–Vienna flight, then hiring a car at the airport, I reached Bratislava at the end of the day.

Max Böhm had decided that this town would be my first port of call. The German and Polish storks passed that way every year. From there, I could travel around as necessary, using Wagner's information to find and observe them. What is more, I had the address of Joro Grybinski, a Slovak ornithologist who spoke French. So I was not completely out on my own.

Bratislava was a grey, neutral city, criss-crossed with sharply angled blocks of flats and long avenues, where small red or pastel blue cars drove around, seemingly trying to choke the town with their dense black clouds of smoke. Intense heat added to this stifling atmosphere. All the same, I lapped up each image, each detail of my new surroundings. Böhm's death and the horrors of that morning already seemed light years away from me.

In his notes, Max Böhm explained that Joro Grybinski was a cab driver at Bratislava's central station. I found his taxi rank easily enough. The drivers of the Skodas and Trabants informed me that Joro knocked off at 7 p.m. They advised me to wait for him in a small café, over the road from the station. I sat down on the terrace, next to a horde of German tourists and pretty secretaries. I ordered some tea, asked the waiter to tell me when Joro arrived, then continued lapping up everything that was in my line of vision. I was savouring the distance that had suddenly separated me from my former life. In Paris, I lived in a huge flat on the fourth floor of a plush block on Boulevard Raspail. I used only three of its six rooms: living-room, bedroom and study. But I loved pacing round that vast area, full of emptiness and silence. This flat was a gift from my adoptive parents. Another example of that generosity that simplified my daily existence, but which did not make me feel in the slightest bit grateful. I hated those two old people.

So far as I was concerned, they were an anonymous upper-middle class couple that had watched over me, but from a distance. In twenty-five years, they had written a mere handful of letters to me and had seen me a grand total of four or five times. It was as if they were keeping some obscure promise to my dead parents, and going about it with great circumspection by sending cheques and presents. I had long ago given up hope of their showing any affection for me. I had blocked them out from my thoughts, while still taking advantage of their money, with a secret bitterness.

The last time I had seen the Braeslers was in 1982, when they gave me the keys to the flat. They were not looking in great shape. Nelly was fifty. Small and dry as a mouthful of salt, she was wearing a blue-rinse wig and kept laughing spasmodically like a cage bird. She was drunk from morning to night. Georges was hardly any better. This former French ambassador, and friend of André Gide and Valéry Larbaud, now seemed to prefer the company of his common cranes to that of his fellow humans. All anybody got out of him were monosyllables and nods.

I, too, led a solitary existence. No women, few friends, no night-life. I had been through all of that in abundance when I was twenty. I thought I had exhausted those possibilities. At the age when most people burn up their lives in excess and partying, I plunged into solitude, asceticism and books. For nearly a decade, I lived in libraries, researching, writing and maturing almost a thousand pages of reflections. I gave myself up to the abstract greatness of thought and the daily solitude of my existence in front of my computer's glistening screen.

My only extravagance was dressing expensively. I have always had difficulty in describing myself physically. My face is an amalgam. On the one hand, it is rather distinguished, my features sculpted by premature wrinkles, angular cheekbones and a high forehead. On the other, I have low eyebrows, a heavy chin and a boxer's nose. My body is similarly contrasted. While I am tall and rather elegant, I am also squat and muscular. This is why I was choosy about my clothes. I always wore finely tailored jackets and immaculately pressed trousers. At the same time, I enjoyed being daring in my choice of colours, patterns and small details. I was one of those who thought that wearing a red shirt or a jacket with five buttons was a truly existential act. How far away all that seems to me now!

The sun was going down over Bratislava and I was loving every minute of it, overhearing snatches of an unknown language and breathing in the pollution from the fuming cars.

At 7.30, a small man appeared in front of me.

"Louis Antioch?"

Sticking my hands in my pockets, I stood up to greet him. Joro did not offer his to be shaken either.

"Joro Grybinski, I presume?"

With a sullen expression, he nodded. He looked like a tempest. Grey curls slapped at his forehead. His eyes shone in their deep sockets. Joro appeared to be about fifty. He was wearing dreadful clothes, but nothing could detract from the nobility of his features and gestures.

I explained the reason for my visit to Bratislava and my wish to see the birds as they migrated. His face brightened. He immediately told me that he had been watching white storks for the last twenty years and he knew all of their stop-over points in the region. His French came out in chopped-up sentences, like final judgments. I then spoke to him about the idea of the satellite experiment and the exact positions I was going to receive. When he had heard me out, a smile flickered over his lips. "No need for a satellite to find the storks. Come with me."

We took his car, a brightly polished Skoda. On the way out of Bratislava, we drove through industrial areas, dotted with the brick chimneys that figure as Communist icons. A terrible stench, acidic, nauseous, worrying, dogged us. Then we saw huge quarries inhabited by metallic monsters. Finally, the countryside appeared, deserted and bare. The odour of fertilizers replaced the stench of industry. It smelt as if those fields had been given over to excessive productivity, which would wear out the earth's heart.

We drove past fields of wheat, rape and corn. In the distance, heavy tractors were spraying up a cloud of chaff and dust. The sunlight softened, the atmosphere grew deeper. As he drove, Joro kept one eye on the horizon, seeing what I had missed, stopping in places where nothing seemed different.

At last, he turned down a rocky track, where silence and calm reigned. We drove alongside a green, motionless lagoon. A large number of birds were fluttering about. Herons, cranes, kites and ox-peckers which shot up in formation. But no black and white birds. Joro grimaced. This lack of storks was clearly exceptional. We waited. Joro, as impassive as a statue, clasping his binoculars. Me by his side, sitting on the scorched earth. I decided to question him.

"Do you ring the storks?"

Joro put down his binoculars.

"What for? They come, then they go. Why number them? I know where they nest, that's all. Every year, each stork returns to its nest. Like clockwork."

"Do you see ringed storks go by during the migration?"

"Of course I do. I even register them."

"Register them?"

"I note down the numbers I've spotted. The place. The day. The time. This Swiss guy pays me to do it."

"Max Böhm?"

"That's him."

The ornithologist had not told me that Joro was one of his "sentinels".

"How long has he been paying you?"

"About ten years now."

"And what's the reason, do you think?"

"Because he's mad."

Joro repeated: "He's mad," while tapping his index finger against his temple.

"In spring, when the storks come back, Böhm phones me every day: 'Have you seen such-and-such number go by? And this one? And that one?' At times like that, he seems out of his mind. In May, when all the birds are back, he finally calms down and stops phoning me. This year, it was terrible. Hardly any of them returned. I thought he was going to drop dead on me. But, he pays, so I do the job."

I felt I could trust Joro. I explained how I, too, was working for Max Böhm, but omitted to tell him that the ornithologist was dead. This brought us closer together. So far as Joro had been concerned, I was French, and thus a rich Westerner to be looked down on. The fact that he knew we were both working for the same man took away his complex. His tone at once grew friendlier. I took out the photographs of the storks and went straight to the point:

"Do you have any idea why the birds disappeared?"

"Only a certain type of stork disappeared."

"What do you mean?"

"Only birds that had been ringed failed to come back. And, in particular, those with two rings."

This was vital information. Joro gazed at the photographs.

"Look," he said, handing me some of them. "Most of these birds have two rings. Two rings, both on the right leg, above the joint. That means that they were once caught on the ground."

"Meaning?"

"In Europe, the first ring is fitted when the chicks can't fly yet. To put the second one on, the bird has to be immobilized in some way, wounded perhaps, or ill. That's when they put the second ring on, with the date of the treatment. You can see that clearly here."

Joro gave me the picture. The dates on the two rings could, indeed, be clearly made out: April 1984 and July 1987. Three years after its birth, this bird had been nursed by Böhm.

"I've made some calculations," Joro added. "Seventy per cent of

32

the birds that vanished were specimens with two rings. Ones that had been injured."

"So what's your opinion?"

Joro shrugged.

"Maybe there's a disease going round in Africa, Israel or Turkey. Maybe these storks were less resistant than the others. Maybe the rings stop them from hunting effectively in the bush. I don't know."

"Did you speak to Böhm about this?"

Joro was not listening any more. He had picked up his binoculars and was mumbling in his teeth: "There. There. Over there . . . "

A couple of seconds later, I saw a group of elegant, undulating birds burst into the still clear sky. They were heading our way. Joro swore in Slovak. He was mistaken. They were not storks, but kites, which glided up high above our heads. Nevertheless, Joro continued to follow them just for the pleasure of it. I watched those raptors in the bewitching silence of that summer evening. I was suddenly struck by their exquisite lightness, which was unknown to man. While looking at them I understood that there was nothing more magical in the world than birds, than that natural grace which was swooping away from us.

Joro finally sat down on the ground beside me and put down his binoculars. He started to roll a cigarette. I looked at his hands and realized why he had not presented his right hand to be shaken earlier. It was racked with rheumatism. His fingers were bent at right-angles to the palm. Like the actor Jules Berry, who had made great play of the fact in his pre-war movies. Or like John Carradine, the horror film actor, who could no longer rattle a pair of castanets. All the same, Joro's cigarette was rolled in a few seconds. Before lighting it, he asked:

"How old are you?"

"Thirty-two."

"Where are you from in France?"

"Paris."

"Ah, Paris, Paris . . . "

This cliché sounded curiously profound in that old man's mouth.

Staring at the horizon, he lit his cigarette.

"Böhm is paying you to follow the storks?"

"Exactly."

"Nice work. You think you'll find out what happened to them?"

"I hope so."

"Me too. For Böhm's sake. Otherwise it'll be the death of him."

I waited a few seconds, then confessed:

"Max Böhm is already dead, Joro."

"Dead? That really doesn't surprise me, kid."

I explained the circumstances of Böhm's death. Joro did not look particularly upset. Except, that is, for his wages. I sensed that he did not like the Swiss gentleman, nor ornithologists in general. He scorned the sort of people who considered the storks to be their property, almost their pets, and yet remained a million miles away from those thousands of birds winging their way across the eastern skies in complete freedom.

As an epitaph, Joro told me how Max Böhm had come to Bratislava in 1982 to offer him this responsible position. When the Swiss had said he would pay him several thousand Czech crowns just to watch the storks go by each year, Joro had thought that the man was nuts, but accepted the job without hesitating.

"It's funny," he said, taking a drag from his cigarette, "that you're here asking me about those birds."

"Why?"

"Because you're not the first. Last April, two men came to see me and asked exactly the same questions."

"Who were they?"

"I don't know. They weren't like you, kid. They were Bulgarians, I reckon. Two brutes, one tall, the other stocky. I wouldn't have trusted them with my shirt. Bulgarians are bastards, everyone knows that."

"Why were they interested in storks? Were they ornithologists?"

"They told me they belonged to an international organization, called One World, and that they were carrying out an ecological survey. I didn't believe a word of it. Those two buggers looked like spies to me."

34

One World. The name rang bells. It was an international body which carried out humanitarian projects all over the planet, and especially in countries at war.

"What did you tell them?"

"Nothing," Joro grinned. "Then they went on their way. That's all."

"Did they mention Max Böhm?"

"No. They didn't seem to know much about the world of ornithology. I'm telling you, they were spies."

At 9.30, night fell. We had not seen a single stork, but I had learnt a few things. The evening ended in Sarovar, Joro's village, over Czech Budweisers and loud stories in Slovak. The men wore felt caps and the women were wrapped up in long aprons. They were all talking at the top of their voices, especially Joro, who had forgotten his usual reserve. The night was cool and, despite the occasional smell of burnt fat, I enjoyed those hours spent with joyous people who welcomed me with warmth and simplicity. Later, Joro took me to the Bratislava Hilton, where Böhm had booked me a room. I suggested paying him for the next few days, so that we could look for the storks together. Joro accepted with a grin. All we had to hope for now was that the birds would keep their usual appointment.

CHAPTER 7

Each morning, at 5 a.m., Joro came to pick me up, then we drank tea together on Sarovar's little square, which seemed fluorescent in the blue of the night. We then headed straight off. First, across the hills that overlooked Bratislava and its acid fumes. Then through the meadows, in storms of fertilizer and dust. There were not many storks. Sometimes, at around 11 a.m., a large group of them appeared in the sky, but so high that the birds were barely visible. Five hundred black and white birds circling through the azure sky, guided by their infallible instincts. That spiral motion was remarkable. I had been expecting a straight flight, with wings out and bills up. But then I remembered what Böhm had told me: "The white stork does not actively fly during migration, but rather glides along the thermals which keep it in the air. They are, in a way, invisible canals produced by chemical reactions in the atmosphere." And so the birds were slipping away to the south, sliding on the scorched air.

In the evening, I consulted the information from the satellite. I received the exact degrees of latitude and longitude, down to the last minute, for the position of each stork. By using a road map, I had no difficulty following their path. On my laptop, their positions were indicated on a digital map of Europe and Africa. It was a delight to watch them moving across my screen.

There are two types of migrant storks. Those from Western Europe cross Spain and the straits of Gibraltar and thus reach North Africa. They pick up more and more birds on the way, until they arrive in Mali, Senegal, the Central African Republic or the Congo. But the storks from the east, which are ten times more numerous, leave Poland, Germany and Russia, cross the Bosporus, arrive in the Middle East then go to Egypt via the Suez Canal. They then fly down to Sudan, Kenya or even as far as South Africa. Such a journey can cover twelve thousand miles.

Of the twenty specimens equipped with transmitters, twelve had taken the eastern route, and the others the western flight paths. The eastern storks were following their usual itinerary: from Berlin, they had crossed East Germany, passed by Dresden, then skirted Poland to enter Czechoslovakia and reach Bratislava, where I was waiting for them. This satellite surveillance was working excellently. Ulrich Wagner was ecstatic. On the third evening, he phoned me and said: "It's fantastic! It has taken us decades, using rings, to trace out an approximate route. Now, with these transmitters, in just one month we'll pinpoint the storks' precise itinerary!"

During those days, Switzerland and its mysteries seemed never to have existed. But then, on the evening of 23 August, I received a fax from Hervé Dumaz at my hotel. I had told him that I had decided to leave after all, but had pointed out that for the moment all I was

36

worried about were the storks, and not Max Böhm's past. The Federal Inspector, on the other hand, was obsessed by the old man. His first fax read like a novel, written in a nervy, harsh style, which contrasted with his dreamy appearance. The whole thing was couched in a friendly tone, so unlike the tenor of our last meeting.

From: Hervé Dumaz
To: Louis Antioch
Hilton Hotel, Bratislava
Montreux, 23 August 1991, 8 p.m.

My dear Louis,

How's your trip going? As for me, I'm making great strides forward. Four days of inquiries have allowed me to establish the following facts:

Max Böhm was born in 1934 in Montreux. The only son of a couple of antiques dealers, he studied at Lausanne University and passed his engineering degree at the age of twenty-six. Three years later, he set off for Mali, to work for SOGEP, a civil engineering company. He took part in preliminary studies for the construction of dikes in the Niger delta. Political troubles forced him to return to Switzerland in 1964. Böhm then left for Egypt, still with SOGEP, to work on the Aswan dam. In 1967, the Six Days' War meant that he had to return home again. In 1969, after one year spent in Switzerland, Böhm went to South Africa, where he stayed for two years. This time, he worked for De Beers, the international diamond empire. He supervised the construction of infrastructures for their mines. Next, he moved to the Central African Republic in 1972. The country was then in the hands of Jean-Bedel Bokassa.

Böhm became the president's technical adviser. He simultaneously organized several projects: building work, coffee plantations and diamond mines. In 1977, my inquiries came up against a black hole, which lasts about one year. The next trace of Max Böhm is to be found at the beginning of 1979, back in Montreux, Switzerland. He was exhausted and broken by his years in Africa. Now forty-five, Böhm concentrated entirely on storks. All the people I have contacted, who worked with him in the field, describe him in the same way: he was intransigent, rigorous and cruel. Many of them mentioned his love of birds, which was almost obsessive.

As for his family, I've made some interesting discoveries. Max Böhm met his wife, Irène, in 1962 when he was twenty-eight. They married at once. A few months later, they had a son, Philippe. The engineer was a passionate family man, and his wife and his son followed him everywhere, adapting to different climates and cultures. However, Irène began to run out of steam in the early 1970s. She often came back to Switzerland, made fewer and fewer trips to Africa, but wrote regularly to her husband and son. In 1976, she returned to Montreux for good. A year later, she died of generalized cancer, and Max disappeared at about the same time. From that moment on, I have also lost track of their son, Philippe, who was fifteen. No news of him since then. Philippe Böhm did not come forward when his father died. Is he dead, too? Does he live abroad? Another enigma.

As for Max Böhm's fortune, I have nothing new to add. According to his personal bank accounts, and that of his association, he possessed almost 800,000 francs. So far, I've found no trace of a numbered account (but there is one, I'm sure of it). When and how did Böhm get hold of all this money? During his life as a traveller, he must have carried out some illegal activities. There were certainly plenty of opportunities. My guess, of course, is that he was in cahoots with Bokassa – gold, diamonds, ivory etc. I am now waiting for a summary of the dictator's two trials. Perhaps there will be some mention of Max Böhm.

Right now, the biggest enigma is still the heart transplant. Dr Catherine Warel agreed to undertake an investigation of Switzerland's clinics and hospitals. She found nothing. Nor anything in France or in the rest of Europe. So where and when did it happen? In Africa? That's not as unlikely as it sounds. The first heart transplant on a man was carried out by Christiaan Barnard in Cape Town, South Africa, in 1967. He successfully performed a second one a year later. Böhm arrived in South Africa in 1969. Did Barnard operate on him? I checked. The Swiss does not appear in the records of Groote Schuur Hospital.

Another oddity is that Max Böhm seemed to be in perfect health. I searched his chalet again looking for prescriptions, tests, or a medical file. Nothing. I went through his bank accounts and telephone bills. Not a single cheque nor a single call that is in any way connected with a heart specialist or a clinic. But a heart transplant is no common condition. He should have seen a doctor regularly, had electrocardiograms, biopsies and a host of other tests. Did he have them done abroad? Böhm travelled widely in Europe, and the storks gave him excellent reasons to visit Belgium, France, Germany and so on. There, too, we are up against a brick wall.

That's where I'm at. As you can see, Max Böhm is quite a mystery man. Believe me, Louis, there is a Böhm scandal somewhere. Here in Montreux, the case is closed. The press is in mourning and paying homage to the 'stork man'. How ironic! He was buried in Montreux cemetery. All the Great and the Good from the town were there, seeing who could come up with the finest sounding claptrap.

One last thing. Böhm made a will leaving his entire fortune to a humanitarian organization that is well known here in Switzerland: One World. This could be a new lead. I'm continuing my investigations.

Keep in touch,
Hervé Dumaz.

The inspector rather took me aback. In just a few days, he had unearthed reams of solid information. I immediately faxed him back a reply. I did not tell him about Max Böhm's documents. This made me feel a bit guilty, but for some reason I just could not bring myself to mention them. My instincts told me to be wary of appearances, and to distrust those documents with their overly blatant violence.

It was two in the morning. I turned off the light and watched the shadows drift across the semi-darkness. What was Max Böhm's real secret? And what part did the storks play in all of this, since they seemed to interest so many people? Did they conceal some incomprehensibly violent secret? More than ever, I was determined to follow them. To the end of their conundrum.

CHAPTER 8

The next day, I got up late with a pounding migraine. Joro was waiting for me in the hall. We set off at once. During the course of that day, Joro questioned me about my life in Paris, my background and my studies. We were on a hillside. The earth crackled in the heat and a few sheep grazed in the dry bushes.

"And what about women, Louis? Do you have a woman in Paris?"

"I did. Several of them. But I'm a bit of a loner. And the girls don't seem to want to make me change my ways."

"Don't they? I would have thought that a snappy dresser like you would appeal to the ladies of Paris."

"It's a problem of contact," I joked, showing him my hands. Those hideous hands, with their horny nails, which belonged to my non-existent past.

Joro approached and carefully examined my scars. He whistled gently between his teeth, midway between admiration and compassion.

"How did that happen, kid?" he murmured.

"It was when I was little, in the countryside," I lied. "A petrol lamp exploded between my hands."

Joro sat down beside me, repeating the words: "Good God." I had become used to varying my lies concerning the accident. It had turned into a nervous tic, a way of responding to others' curiosity and of hiding my own embarrassment. But Joro then quietly added:

"I, too, have my scars."

He then turned over his paralysed hands. His palms were crisscrossed with ghastly swollen weals. With difficulty he opened the top buttons of his shirt. The same lacerations covered his torso, like trails of suffering, regularly punctuated by larger bright pink dots. I looked at him questioningly. I realized that he had decided to tell me his story – the story of his tortured flesh. He narrated it in a dull voice, and in perfect French, which he seemed to have improved for the sole purpose of revealing his past.

"When the Warsaw Pact forces invaded the country in 1968, I was thirty-two. Just like you. For me that invasion spelt the end of the dream of socialism with a human face. At the time, I was living in Prague with my family. I can still remember the way the earth trembled when the tanks arrived. A terrible clanking noise, like roots of iron shooting up from the ground. I can remember the first gunshots, the blows from rifle butts, the arrests. I couldn't believe it. Our town, our lives suddenly had no meaning any more. People took refuge in their houses. Death and fear stalked our streets and our thoughts. We started to resist, especially the young. But the tanks made mincemeat of our bodies and of our rebellion. So, one night, my family and I decided to escape to the West, via Bratislava. It seemed possible to us. We were so near Austria!

"My two sisters were gunned down after crossing the barbed wire on the border. My father was shot in the head. Half of his face was blown off with his cap. As for my mother, she got stuck on the barbed wire. I tried to free her, but it was impossible. She was screaming and wriggling like a mad woman. And the more she moved, the more she pushed the spikes through her coat into her flesh, while the bullets were whistling above our heads. I was covered in blood, I was tugging at that fucking barbed wire with my bare hands. Her screams will stay with me to my dying day."

Joro lit a cigarette. He had not brought these ghosts back to life for some time.

"We were arrested by Russians. I never saw my mother again. As for me, I spent four years in a forced labour camp in Piodv. Four years spent freezing to death in the mud, with a pickaxe stuck in my hands. I kept thinking about my mother and the barbed wire. I walked around the wire that fenced off the camp and touched that steel which had torn into my mother. It was my fault, I thought. Then I would grip those spikes until my hands bled. One day, I stole some lengths of wire. I made them into a harness which I wore under my coat. With each blow of the pickaxe, with each gesture, they ripped into my muscles. It was a sort of expiation. After a few months, I had barbed wire wrapped all round me. I couldn't work any more.

Every time I moved, it dug into me and the wounds were becoming infected. In the end, I collapsed. I was no more than an open wound, gangrenous, dripping with blood and pus.

"I woke up a few days later in the infirmary. My limbs were shot through with agony and my body was one big scar. That's when I noticed them. Half conscious, I saw some white birds through the filthy window panes. I thought they were angels. I believed I was in heaven and that the angels had come to welcome me. I was wrong. I was still in the same hell-hole. It was quite simply spring, and the storks were coming back. I watched them during my convalescence. There were several pairs nesting on top of the watchtowers. How can I put it? Those gleaming creatures, above all that misery and cruelty, were a vision that gave me courage. I observed their daily lives, each bird taking its turn to sit on the eggs, then the nestlings' little black bills, their first attempts at flying, then the great departure . . . For four years, each spring, those storks gave me the strength to go on. My nightmares were still lurking there, but those bright birds against the blue of the sky were a rope ladder for me to cling to. Not much of a ladder, you might say. But I served my sentence, working like a dog at the feet of the Russians, hearing the screams of tortured men, eating mud and shivering in the frost. That's when I learnt French, from a member of the French Communist Party who was there for some reason. When I was released, I joined the Party and bought a pair of binoculars."

Night had fallen. The storks had not arrived, except in Joro's story. We drove back in silence. Along the fields, barbed wire swayed between the twisted stakes in elaborate arabesques.

*

On 25 August, the first of the storks with transmitters arrived in Bratislava. At the end of the afternoon, I consulted Argos and saw that two of them were nine miles to the west of Sarovar. Joro looked sceptical, but he agreed to study the map. He knew the place – a valley where, according to him, no storks ever landed. At about 7 p.m. we arrived near the lagoon. As we drove, we examined the sky and the surroundings. There was no trace of any birds. Joro could not resist smiling. We had now been on the lookout for five days, but had spotted only a few groups that were so distant that they could easily have been kites, or other raptors. If my computer had helped us to find the storks that evening, then Joro would have been distinctly put out.

But then he suddenly mumbled: "There they are." I looked up. In the purple sky, a group was rotating. About a hundred birds then came to rest on the shallow waters of the swamp. Joro lent me his binoculars. I observed those birds gliding, bills extended, as though listening to the sky. It was marvellous. I then began to realize how long their flight to Africa was going to be. So, among that airy, wild flock two birds were wearing transmitters. A shiver of joy ran through me. The satellite system was working. Accurate to the last feather.

On 27 August, I received another fax from Hervé Dumaz. He had not made any progress. He had had to go back to his routine job as an inspector, but was still contacting France, looking for retired engineers who might have known Max Böhm in the Central African Republic. Dumaz was obstinately pursuing this lead, convinced that Böhm had been up to no good over there. In conclusion, he mentioned an agricultural engineer who had, apparently, worked in Central Africa from 1973 to 1977. The inspector intended to go to France and see him, as soon as he was back from holiday.

By 28 August, it was time for me to leave. Ten of the storks had already passed Bratislava and the quickest ones – which were covering ninety miles per day – were already in Bulgaria. The problem I now had was how to follow their exact path by car. This would mean crossing former Yugoslavia, where the crisis had started to erupt. I studied my map and decided to avoid that powder keg by following the border round to Romania – after all, I did have a Romanian visa. Then I would drive to Bulgaria via a small town called Calafat, and head straight for Sofia. This meant covering about six hundred and fifty miles. I reckoned it would take me about one and a half days, bearing in mind border controls and the state of the roads. So, that morning I booked a room in the Sofia Sheraton for the following evening, then contacted a certain Marcel Minaüs, another person on Böhm's list. Minaüs was not an ornithologist, but a linguist who would help me contact Rajko Nicolich, who was Bulgaria's stork specialist. After several unsuccessful attempts, I at last got through to my compatriot in Sofia. He sounded very friendly and I arranged to meet him downstairs in the Sheraton at 10 p.m. the following evening. I hung up, faxed my new address to Dumaz and packed. As soon as I had paid the hotel bill, I set off for Sarovar to say good-bye to Joro Grybinski. Neither of us was effusive. We swapped addresses. I promised to send him an invitation, which would allow him to enter France.

A few hours later, I was in Hungary and nearing Budapest. At noon, I stopped at a motorway service station and lunched on a revolting salad beside the petrol pump. Some young blonde girls, as light as corn husks, stared at me with their majestic proud eyes. These adolescents, with their serious brows, wide jaws and fair hair, looked just like the stereotype I had always had of Eastern European beauties. And that coincidence disturbed me. I had ever been a bitter enemy of received opinions and commonplace ideas. I did not then know that the world is often plainer than people imagine and that the truth, no matter how banal, is always alive and glowing. For some reason, I experienced a shudder of profound joy. At 1 p.m., I set off again.

CHAPTER 9

The next evening, it was pouring with rain when I reached Sofia. Old dirty brick buildings surrounded the irregular paving stones of the streets. Ladas slithered and bounded across them, like old-fashioned toy cars, narrowly avoiding the relentless trams. Trams were the real heroes of Sofia. They sprang from nowhere in a deafening din, spitting blue sparks through the torrential rain. Between the streetlights,

I saw their yellowish gleam waver then spread over the expressionless faces of their passengers. These strange wagons looked like the theatre for some novel experiment – the generalized electrocution of bloodless guinea pigs.

I drove around randomly, not knowing where I was going. The street signs were written in Cyrillic. With my right hand, I removed the guide book I had bought in Paris from my bag. As I was flicking through it, I stumbled by chance on Lenin Square. I looked up. The architecture was like a celebration of the rain storm. Austere, powerful buildings rose up on all sides, dotted with narrow windows. Square towers rising up to sharpened peaks were covered with a multitude of arrow slits. Their unnatural colours stood out bizarrely as night fell. To my right, stood a hunched, blackened church. To my left, the Balkan Sofia Sheraton Hotel sat plumply, like a precursor of all-conquering capitalism. This was where American, European and Japanese businessmen stayed, in quarantine from the surrounding Communist gloom.

Marcel Minaüs was waiting for me under the huge candelabra of the hall. I recognized him at once. He had told me: "I have a beard and a pointed skull." But Marcel had far more than that. He was a walking icon. Extremely tall and bulky, he stood there like a bear, back bent, feet pointing inwards, arms flapping. A mountain, topped off by the head of an Orthodox patriarch, with a long beard and regal nose. His eyes were masterpieces of lightish green, rimmed with shadows, as though burning with some ancient Balkan beliefs. And then, like a mitre, came his skull, completely bald and pointing to the sky like a dolmen.

"Did you have a good trip?"

"Not so bad," I replied, avoiding shaking hands with him. "It's been raining since I crossed the border. I tried to keep up a good average speed, but what with the mountain passes and ruined roads, I had to slow down and . . . "

"You know, I always take the bus."

I gave my luggage to the porter and went with my new companion to the hotel's main restaurant. Marcel had already

45

dined, but tucked heartily into a second meal.

Marcel Minaüs was forty. He had French nationality, but was a sort of wandering scholar, a polyglot who spoke fluent Polish, Bulgarian, Hungarian, Czech, Serbo-Croat, Macedonian, Albanian and Greek, among others, and of course Romany, the language of the gypsies. Romany was his speciality. He had written several books on the subject, as well as a handbook for children, of which he was especially proud. As an eminent member of numerous learned societies from Finland to Turkey, he travelled from one symposium to another and accordingly managed to live the life of Riley in cities such as Warsaw and Bucharest.

The meal came to an end at about 11.30. We had hardly mentioned storks. Minaüs had simply asked me to explain how the satellite worked. He knew nothing about the subject, but promised to introduce me to Rajko Nicolich the next day. "The best ornithologist in the Balkans," he claimed.

Midnight chimed. I made an appointment with Marcel for 7 a.m. the next morning in the hall. We would hire another car and drive to Sliven, where Rajko Nicolich lived. Minaüs seemed delighted at the idea of this excursion. I went up to my bedroom. A message had been slipped under my door. Another fax from Dumaz.

From: Hervé Dumaz
To: Louis Antioch
Balkan Sofia Sheraton Hotel
Montreux, 29 August 1991, 10 p.m.

Dear Louis,

A hard day's trip to France, but certainly worthwhile. I at last met the man I was looking for. Michel Guillard, an agricultural engineer, aged fifty-six. Four solid years in the Central African Republic. Four years of humid forests, coffee plantations and . . . Max Böhm! I dropped in on Guillard in Poitiers, just as he was coming back from holiday with his family. Thanks to him, I can piece together Böhm's career in Africa. Here are the facts:

– August 1972: Max Böhm arrived in Bangui, the capital of the Central African Republic. His wife and son were with him, and he appeared indifferent to the political situation in the country, which was under the control of Bokassa, who had just declared himself "President for Life". Böhm had seen it all before. He had just come from the diamond mines of South Africa, where the miners worked naked and were x-rayed on their way home, to make certain that they hadn't swallowed any gems. Max Böhm set up home in a colonial mansion and started work. His first task was to oversee work on a large building, one of Bokassa's projects called "Pacific 2". Bokassa was impressed and offered him more work. Böhm accepted.

– 1973: for a few months, he put together a security team to watch over the coffee fields of Lobaye – a densely wooded province in the extreme south. The greatest problem with farming was apparently the amount of grains the villagers stole before the harvest. It was during this period that Guillard, who was working on a farming project in the same region, met Böhm. His memories are of a brutal man, with a military bearing, but who was honest and sincere. Later, Böhm played the role of the Central African Republic's spokesman to the government of South Africa (a country he knew well) in order to secure a loan for the construction of two hundred villas. He obtained it. Bokassa then offered him another job in the diamond mining sector. Diamonds were the dictator's obsession. They constituted the lion's share of his personal fortune (I am sure you remember such tales as the famous "jam pot", where he kept his jewels, and which he loved showing to his guests, the fantastic "Catherine Bokassa" diamond, shaped like a mango, that was inserted into the imperial crown, the scandal of the "presents" he gave to the French President Giscard d'Estaing, and so on). So, Bokassa asked Böhm to visit the mines and supervise the prospecting in the northern semi-desert savannas, and in the heart of the jungle in the south. He was hoping that this engineer would rationalize activities and wipe out any clandestine prospecting.

Böhm visited all the mines, from the sands of the north, to the jungles of the south. His cruelty terrified the miners and he became famous for a punishment he had invented. In South Africa, they broke thieves' ankles to punish them, then forced them to continue working. Böhm came up with something new: by means of a cable cutter he severed robbers' Achilles tendons. It was a quick, effective method but, in the jungle, the wounds became infected. Guillard saw several men die this way.

At the time, he was supervising the activities of various companies, including Centramines, SCAD and Diadème and Sicamine, all official enterprises concealing Bokassa's no less official smuggling. Max Böhm, as the dictator's emissary, did not interfere in such fraud. According to Guillard, the engineer stood out distinctly from the con-men and sycophants that surrounded the emperor. He never worked directly for any of Bokassa's companies, which explains why his name was not mentioned at either of the dictator's trials. I've checked this.

– 1974: Böhm stood up to Bokassa, whose illegal activities, rackets and downright thefts from the state coffers were escalating. One of these embezzlements directly affected Böhm. Once the loan from South Africa had been obtained, Bokassa built only half of the planned number of villas, allotted the business to himself, then demanded to be paid for all two hundred of them. Böhm, who was implicated in this deal, made no bones about showing his anger. He was immediately imprisoned, then released. Bokassa needed him. Since his takeover of the supervision of the diamond mines, they had become far more productive.

Later, the engineer also complained to Bokassa about the massive trade in ivory and the resulting massacre of elephants. Quite unexpectedly, he obtained what he wanted. The dictator carried on trading, but agreed to open up a natural reserve at Bayanga, near Nola, in the extreme south-west of the country. This park still exists. The last wild elephants of Central Africa can be seen there.

According to Guillard, Böhm's personality was paradoxical. He was extremely cruel to Africans (and killed several illegal prospectors with his own hands), but at the same time he lived only with Blacks. He detested the European community in Bangui, the diplomatic receptions and parties in clubs. Böhm was a misanthropist who was softened only by contact with the jungle, with animals and, of course, with storks.

In October 1974, Guillard happened upon Max Böhm, who was

camping out with his guide in the grasses of the eastern savanna. Clutching his binoculars, he was waiting for the storks. He then told the young agriculturalist how he had saved the storks of Switzerland and how he returned home each year to admire them on their return from migration. "What's so special about them, then?" Guillard asked. Böhm simply replied: "They soothe me."

Guillard does not know much about the Böhm family. By 1974, Irène Böhm no longer lived in Africa very much. He vaguely remembers a small, shy woman, with a yellowish hue, who was left alone in her colonial mansion. But he did get to know the son, Philippe, a bit better because he sometimes accompanied his father during his expeditions. Apparently, father and son were strikingly similar: same stocky build, same round face, same crewcut. But Philippe had inherited his mother's character. He was shy, indolent and a daydreamer. He was ruled by his father and suffered his brutal education in silence. Böhm wanted to "make a man of him". He took him to hostile regions, taught him how to use weapons and entrusted him with missions in order to toughen him up.

– 1977: in August, Böhm went prospecting beyond Mbaïki, in the deep jungle towards the SCAD sawmill. This is where Pygmy territory begins. The engineer set up his base camp in the jungle. He was accompanied by a Belgian geologist, called Niels van Dötten, two guides (a 'tall Black' and a Pygmy) and some porters. One morning, a Pygmy messenger brought him a telegram. It announced that his wife had died. Now, Böhm had no idea that his wife had been suffering from cancer. He collapsed in the mud. Max Böhm had just had a heart attack. Van Dötten tried to save him with the means to hand – cardiac massage, mouth to mouth resuscitation, first aid medication and so on. He immediately ordered his men to carry the unconscious man to Mbaiki Hospital, which is several days' march away. Then Böhm came to. He stammered out that there was a mission nearby, to the south just over the Congolese border (here, such territorial limits are just invisible lines through jungles). He wanted to be taken for treatment there. Van Dötten hesitated. Böhm pulled rank and ordered the geologist back to Bangui to fetch help. "All will be well," he reassured him.

Dumbfounded, Van Dötten set off and reached the capital six days later. The French army immediately laid on a helicopter which flew back, guided by the geologist. But, once there, they found no trace of any mission, or of Böhm. Everything had vanished. Or had never existed. The Swiss was reported missing and the Belgian didn't hang around long in Bangui.

One year later Max Böhm, as large as life, reappeared in Bangui. He explained that a helicopter from a Congolese lumber company had flown him to Brazzaville and that he had then taken the plane back to Switzerland, still miraculously alive. Once there, the excellent treatment he had received in a clinic in Geneva had allowed him to make a full recovery. But he was a mere shadow of himself, and constantly talked about his wife. This was in October 1978. Max Böhm left shortly afterwards. He never returned to the Central African Republic. Since then, a former mercenary soldier from Czechoslovakia called Otto Kiefer, has taken over supervision of the mines.

There's the entire story, Louis. This commentary allows us to clarify certain points. But it casts an even greater shadow over others. For example, after Irène Böhm's death, we lose all trace of the son. The heart transplant remains just as mysterious, except perhaps for its date, which must have been some time in autumn 1977. But the business about convalescing in Geneva is a lie. Böhm appears on no Swiss medical records over the last twenty years.

Then there is the diamond lead. I am sure that Böhm's fortune came from precious stones. It's a real pity that your journey won't take you to the Central African Republic so that you can cast some light on this mystery. Maybe you'll find out something in Egypt or Sudan? As for me, I'm taking a week off as of 7 September. I intend to go to Antwerp and pay a call on the Diamond Exchange. I'm sure I'll find some trace of Max Böhm there. All of this information is hot off the press. Think it over and get back to me quickly.

Keep in touch,
Hervé

As I read, my ideas flew off in all directions. I was trying to fit my own pieces into the puzzle: the pictures of Irène and Philippe, Böhm's heart scan and, above all, those unbearable photographs of mutilated black bodies.

There was something else Dumaz did not know. I knew all about the history of the Central African Republic. I had personal reasons for that. The name of Bokassa's lieutenant, Otto Kiefer, was not unknown to me. That obsessively violent Czech refugee was notorious for his intimidation methods. He put grenades in the mouths of his prisoners and blew them up if they refused to talk. This technique had given him the grotesque nickname of Papa Grenade. Böhm and Kiefer were thus two sides of the same cruelty: the cable cutter and the grenade.

I turned off the light. Although I was tired, I could not sleep. Finally, without switching on the lamp, I called the Argos centre. Sofia's telephone lines were less busy at that time of night and the connection was perfect. In the gloomy light of my bedroom, the paths the storks were taking gleamed out, black on white, on the digital map of Eastern Europe. There was only one thing of interest. One of the storks had reached Bulgaria. It had landed on a wide plain not far from Sliven, the town where Rajko Nicolich lived.

CHAPTER 10

"Everything's changing in Sofia. The great 'American dream' has arrived. Since Bulgarians have no clear future inside Europe, they're turning to the United States. Nowadays, speaking English in Sofia opens doors. It is even said that Americans no longer have to pay for their visas. Incredible! Just two years ago, they used to call Bulgaria the sixteenth republic of the Soviet Union."

Marcel Minaüs was speaking loudly, in a mixture of irritation and irony. It was 10 a.m. We were driving alongside the mountains in brilliant sunshine. The fields displayed unexpected colours: vibrant yellows, soft blues and pale greens shimmered as the light stroked them. Pale, chalk-like villages with their roughcast houses appeared.

I was following Marcel's directions. He had brought along his "fiancée", a strange gypsy woman called Yeta, who was dressed in a fake Chanel suit made of gingham. She was short and plump, a little past her best and had a huge mane of grey hair, framing a pointed face with dark eyes. She closely resembled a hedgehog. She spoke only Romany and sat quietly on the back seat.

Marcel was now singing Rajko Nicolich's praises.

"You're going to the right place," he repeated. "Rajko is very young, but has exceptional qualities. In fact, he's starting to participate in international symposia. The Bulgarians are furious because he refuses to fly their flag."

"You mean Rajko Nicolich isn't Bulgarian?" I asked, astonished. Marcel chuckled.

"No, Louis. He's a Romany – a gypsy. And pig-headed with it. He comes from a family of gatherers. In springtime, the gypsies leave the Sliven ghetto for the forests around the plain. They gather lime blossom, camomile, dogwood, cherry stalks. (I stared at him, Marcel was surprised.) You mean you don't know? Cherry stalks are a well-known diuretic. Only Roms ('men' as they call themselves) know where wild plants grow. They supply the Bulgarian pharmaceutical industry, which is the largest one in Eastern Europe. They're incredible, as you'll see. They feed on hedgehogs, otters, frogs, stinging nettles, wild sorrel . . . everything that nature puts their way. (Marcel was exultant.) I haven't seen Rajko for at least six months!"

My companion then treated me to a quarter of an hour of Albanian jokes. In the Balkans, Albanians are Britain's Irish or France's Belgians, the butt of jokes that play on their naivety, or their lack of means or ideas. Minaüs loved this sort of humour.

"Stop me if you've heard it. One morning, a press release appears in *Pravda*: 'During sea manoeuvres, a serious accident destroyed half the Albanian fleet. Their left-hand paddle got broken!' (Marcel laughed into his beard.) Or this one: the Albanians launch a space programme in collaboration with the Russians – they plan to send an animal into orbit. They send a telegram to the USSR: 'Have dog, please send rocket.'"

I burst out laughing. Marcel added:

"Obviously, it's not very topical any more. But Albanian jokes are still my favourites."

The linguist then launched into a long celebration of gypsy cooking (his pipe dream was to open up a specialized restaurant in Paris). The linchpin of this cuisine was the hedgehog. It was hunted down in the evening with a stick, then bloated to allow its spines to be removed easily. When cooked in *zumi*, a special sort of flour, then sliced into six equal portions it was, according to Marcel, a real delicacy.

"So we'll have to keep our eyes peeled on the way there."

"No way," Marcel replied in a professorial tone. "Hedgehogs never go out during the day."

Suddenly, as though to contradict him deliberately, one of those spiny creatures appeared on the hillside. Marcel pouted sceptically.

"It must be ill. Or else a pregnant female."

I burst out laughing again. What had become of the cold countries of the East, full of greyness and depression? Marcel seemed possessed of some special magic that transformed the Balkans into an ideal destination, a place of fantasy and pleasure that was full of human warmth and humour.

But we were now nearing the Sliven region. The roads became narrower and more winding. Dark forests closed in around us. We drove past a few *vardoes* – nomad gypsy caravans. On these wobbly carts, entire families stared at us with their dark eyes. Black faces, dishevelled hair, figures in rags. These gypsies did not look like Yeta. We were now with the Romanies, real ones who travel and pilfer, with just the tips of their fingers, in scorn and condescension.

Before long, Marcel pointed out a path to our right. It was an earth track, which ran down from the road towards a stream. We came to a clearing in the undergrowth and, through the trees, I could make out a camp: four garish tents, a few horses and women sitting on the grass making bunches of white flowers.

Marcel got out of the car and yelled something to the gypsies in his most singsong voice. The women gave him an icy glare. Marcel turned back towards us: "There's a problem. Wait for me here." I watched his skull push its way through the leaves, then his tall form re-emerge again among the women. One of them had stood up and was talking to him heatedly. She was wearing a sunflower yellow sweater squeezed over her flaccid breasts. Her face was brown and rough, as though carved from wood bark. Under her multi-coloured scarf, she looked ageless, with an appearance of intense hardness and ever-present violence. Beside her another, smaller gypsy woman was nodding. She too had stood up. Her hooked nose was crooked, as though broken in a fight. Heavy silver earrings dangled from her lobes. Her turquoise pullover had holes in its elbows. A third female remained seated with a baby in her arms. She looked about fifteen or sixteen and was gazing in my direction, her eyes glistening under her shiny black mop of hair.

I approached them. The sunflower woman was screaming, pointing in turn at the depths of the forest and the young mother sitting on the grass. When I was only a few paces from the group, she fell silent and stared at me. Marcel had gone pale. "I don't understand, Louis . . . I don't understand. Rajko is dead. In the spring he was . . . he was murdered. We'll have to go and see Marin', the boss, in the forest." Feeling my heart jolting, I nodded. The women moved off and we followed them through the trees.

The forest air was cooler. The tips of the spruces swayed in the wind and the bushes rustled as we passed. Sunbeams fell sweetly down into the clearings. The millions of motes gave them the velvety look of peach skin. We were following a sort of path, which had recently been traced out. The gypsies walked on with no hesitation. Suddenly, voices echoed off the heights of that emerald dome. Men's voices, being exchanged over a long distance. The sunflower woman turned round and said something to Marcel, who nodded in reply and walked on.

The first of the men we met was young, and wearing a blue cotton suit – or rather a set of shreds held together by dense threads. He was up to his elbows in a thick shrub, from which he was cutting a tiny branch topped by a pale flower. He spoke to Marcel, then looked at me. "Costa," he said. His dark face was young, but the slightest smile gave it the ambiguous beauty of a knife blade. Costa accompanied us. Soon, we found ourselves in another clearing. The men were there. Some of them were asleep, or apparently so, under their lowered hats. Others were playing cards. One was seated on a stump. Leather faces, gleams of silver from their belts and hats, a power ready to leap out at the slightest attack. By the trees, canvas sacks were already full of freshly harvested plants.

Marcel spoke to the man on the stump. They appeared to be old acquaintants. After a long palaver, he introduced me, then said in French:

"This is Marin', Mariana's father. She's the one with the baby. She was Rajko's wife." The young woman was standing back from us in the undergrowth. Marin' stared at me. His dark skin was dotted with needle holes, as though he had been encased in an iron mask of nails. His eyes were narrow, his hair wavy. A thin moustache crossed his face. He was wearing a torn jacket, under which a filthy T-shirt could be seen.

I greeted him, then bowed to the other men. Some of them stared back at me. Marin' spoke to me in Romany and Marcel translated.

"He's asking what you want."

"Tell him I'm trying to find out why so many storks disappeared last year. Explain that I was counting on Rajko's help. How he died is no business of mine. But the disappearance of those birds is linked to other puzzles. Maybe Rajko knew some Westerners who were interested in storks. I think he was in contact with a certain Max Böhm."

As I spoke, Marcel looked more and more dazed. He did not understand at all what I was on about. However, he translated what I said, then Marin' slightly bowed his head, but without taking the slits of his eyes off me. Silence fell. For another minute, Marin' continued to size me up. Then he spoke. For a long time.

Unhurriedly. In that voice which is typical of tired souls that have been worn down by the cruelty of others.

"Rajko was a shit-stirrer," said Marin'. "But he was like a son to me. He didn't work, and that didn't matter. He didn't take care of his family, and that did matter. But I didn't hold it against him. That was his nature. The world never left him in peace."

He removed a flower from one of the sacks.

"You see this flower? For us, it's just a way to earn a few leva. For him, it was an open mystery. So he studied, he read, he observed. Rajko was incredibly knowledgeable. He knew the names and the virtues of every tree and every plant. The same went for birds. Especially the ones that migrate in spring and autumn. Like storks, for instance. He counted them. He wrote to Gorgios in Europe. So far as I remember, the man you mentioned, Böhm, was one of them."

So Rajko had been another of Böhm's sentinels. Max had not told me that. I was feeling my way forward blindly. Marin' went on:

"That's why I'm telling you this story. You're the same sort as Rajko – the intellectual sort."

I looked at Mariana through the branches. She was keeping her distance from her father.

"But my son's death has nothing to do with those birds. It was a racist murder. Part of another world. Part of the hatred for gypsies.

"It happened in spring, at the end of April when we set off as usual. Rajko had his own habits. From the beginning of March, he would ride as far as the edge of the plain here and watch for storks. At that time, he would live alone in the forest. He ate roots and slept rough. Then he waited for us to arrive. But this year, there was no one to welcome us. We searched the plain, wandered through the woods, then one of us found Rajko in the depths of the forest. His body was already cold. Animals had started to devour it. I'd never seen anything like it. Rajko was naked. His chest had been cut open, his entire body lacerated, one arm and his genitals almost sliced off and wounds everywhere."

Mariana, a delicate form in the shadows of the leaves, crossed herself.

56

"You have to go back a long way to understand atrocities like this, young man. I could tell you endless stories. People say that we come from India, that we are descended from a caste of dancers, or such like. It's all utter nonsense. I'll tell you where we come from. From manhunts in Bavaria, from slave markets in Romania, from concentration camps in Poland, from the Nazis, who sliced us up like laboratory rats. I'll tell you, kid. I know an old gypsy woman who suffered terribly during the war. The Nazis sterilized her. But she survived. A few years ago, she heard that the German government was paying compensation to the victims of the death camps. To get a pension, all you had to do was have a medical examination – to prove the suffering, if you like. She went to the nearest clinic to have her examination and get her certificate. The door opened and who should she see? The doctor who operated in the camps. This is a true story, kid. It happened in Leipzig, four years ago. That woman was my mother. She died shortly afterwards without receiving a penny."

"But," I asked, "what has that got to do with Rajko's death?"

Marcel translated. Marin' replied:

"What's it got to do with it?" He stared at me with his arrow-slit eyes. "It means that Evil is back amongst us." He pointed down at the ground. "It means Evil is once more walking the Earth."

Then, beating his breast, Marin' spoke to Marcel. He hesitated before translating. He asked Marin' to repeat what he had said. Their voices rose. Marcel failed to understand the leader's last words. Finally, he turned towards me with tears in his eyes and whispered:

"Louis, the murderers . . . the murderers stole Rajko's heart."

CHAPTER 11

Nobody said anything on the way back to Sliven. Marin' had provided us with additional details: after finding the body, the gypsies had informed Dr Djuric, a Romany practitioner who was on a tour of duty in the suburbs of Sliven. Milan Djuric had asked the hospital to provide him with a theatre in order to carry out a post-mortem. They had refused. There was no room for a gypsy. Even when dead. The caravan drove to a clinic. Another refusal. Finally, the convoy reached a dilapidated gymnasium, set aside for gypsies. There, under the basketball nets, in the bitter smell of a sports hall, Djuric carried out the postmortem. It was then that the theft of the heart was discovered. He wrote up a detailed report and informed the police, who failed to undertake any investigations. None of the gypsies was shocked by such indifference. They were used to it. No, what bothered the old leader was his desire to know who had killed his son-in-law. The day when he found out the names of his killers, the sun would glint on the blades of their knives.

Something peculiar occurred while we were leaving. Mariana came over to me and slipped a dog-eared notebook into my hands. She did not utter a word, but all I needed to do was glance at it to work out what it was: Rajko's personal notes. The pages on which he jotted down his observations and theories concerning storks. I immediately hid the document in the glove compartment.

At noon, we arrived in Sliven. It was a bland, standard version of an industrial town. Average size, average buildings, average sadness. This mediocrity seemed to float down its streets like dust from minerals, covering the façades and the people's faces. Marcel had an appointment with Markus Lasarevich, a personality in the Romany world. We were due to have lunch with him and, despite the recent events, it was now too late to cancel.

We lunched with no appetite and no desire to remain at the table. Markus Lasarevich was a dandy, over six foot tall, with a very dark complexion, wearing an identity bracelet and a gold chain. The perfect image of a successful gypsy, up to his ears in suspect deals and millions of leva. An insidious man, steeped in velvet-like cunning.

"You understand," he said in English, while smoking a long cigarette with a golden filter, "I was very sad about Rajko's death. But there's nothing we can do. Always the same violence, the same shady affairs."

"In your opinion," I asked him, "was this a settling of scores between gypsies?"

"That's not what I said. Maybe the Bulgarians are behind it. But gypsies still do have their law of the vendetta and their old grudges. There's always another house to be burnt, or another bad reputation to pick up. I'm telling you all this quite openly. I'm a Rom myself."

"Jesus Christ, how can you talk like that?" Marcel butted in. "You do know how Rajko died, don't you?"

"That's just it, Marcel." He dropped a little grey ash from his cigarette. "A Bulgarian hood would have been found down a back alley with a knife in his guts. Period. But not a gypsy. They have to be discovered in the middle of a forest with their hearts torn out. In a country which is still obsessed with superstitions and witchcraft, this sort of murder works dangerously on people's imaginations."

"Rajko wasn't a hood," Marcel barked back.

The "salad bowls" arrived – raw vegetables sprinkled with grated cheese. Nobody touched them. We were in a large empty room, decked with a brown carpet and containing tables covered with white cloths, without cutlery or decorations. Fake crystal chandeliers dangled down sadly, sending dull glints back to the exterior daylight. Everything seemed ready for a party which would presumably never happen. Markus went on:

"There were no traces, no clues discovered around the body. Only the theft of his heart was confirmed. The local press got hold of the story. They wrote a lot of old nonsense. Business about magic and witchcraft. And even worse than that. (He stubbed out his cigarette and looked straight into Marcel's eyes.) You know what I mean."

As I did not understand what he was getting at, Marcel explained to me in French that, for many centuries, gypsies had been reputed to be cannibals.

"It's only an old horror story," said Marcel. "The one about the ogre that eats children applied to Roms. But the disappearance of Rajko's heart definitely had them all shivering in their cottages."

I glanced across at Markus. His large frame remained motionless. He had lit another cigarette.

"For many years now," he continued, "I have been fighting to improve our image. And this has put us back into the Middle Ages! What is more, everybody is in part responsible. You do understand, Monsieur Antioch. I'm not being sarcastic. I'm quite simply thinking about the future." He laid his octopus fingers down on the table-cloth. "I'm struggling to improve our living conditions and for the right to work."

Markus Lasarevich was a political figure in the Sliven region. He was the gypsies' *only* candidate, which gave him considerable power. Marcel had told me how Lasarevich swaggered through the ghettos of Sliven in his checked suits, being pursued by a horde of dark grimy paupers, who joyfully grabbed hold of the tails of his pricey jackets. I imagined his forced smiles when confronted by his dirty, smelly potential voters. But, despite this repugnance, Markus had to flatter the gypsies. It was the price he had to pay for his political ambitions – and Rajko's death was a serious stumbling block. He put it his way:

"This murder has undermined many of our efforts, specially at a social level. So, I have set up some health care centres in the ghettos with the help of a humanitarian organization."

"Which one?" I asked nervously.

"Monde Unique." Markus pronounced its name in French, then gave the English version: "One World."

One World. This was the third time in a few days and over a distance of a few hundred miles that I had heard that name. Markus went on:

"Then their young doctors left. On an urgent mission, or so they told me. But I wouldn't be surprised if they were not fed up with our continual infighting, with our refusal to adapt and our scorn for the Gorgios. In my opinion, Rajko's death was the last nail in the coffin."

"The doctors left straight after Rajko was murdered?"

"Not exactly. They left Bulgaria in July."

"What precisely did they do here?"

"They took care of the ill, vaccinated children, handed out medicines. They had a laboratory for conducting tests and some equipment for carrying out minor operations." Markus rubbed his thumb and index finger together in a knowing way. "There's plenty of money behind One World. Plenty of it."

Markus paid the bill, then talked of the failed coup d'état in Moscow ten days before. In his mind, everything apparently was part of one vast political programme, in which each element had its respective role. The gypsies' poverty, Rajko's murder and the decadence of socialism formed in his eyes a logical whole, which would result, of course, in his being elected.

Finally, on the steps of the restaurant, he fingered the lapel of my jacket and asked me how much my Volkswagen cost in dollars. I hit him with some enormous sum, just for the pleasure of watching him take the blow. It was the first time he twitched nervously. I slammed the car door. He bade us farewell once more and bent his huge frame down until his head was level with my window. He asked: "I don't get it. What on earth are you doing in Bulgaria?" I switched on the ignition and briefly summed up the business with the storks. "Oh, really?" he remarked in an American accent, full of condescension. I pulled away rapidly.

CHAPTER 12

We were back in Sofia at 6 p.m. I immediately phoned Dr Milan Djuric. He was consulting in Podliv until the following afternoon. His wife spoke a little English, so I introduced myself and said that I would be calling by tomorrow evening. I added that it was vital for me to meet Milan Djuric. After a moment's hesitation, his wife gave me their address, adding a few directions as to the best way to get there. I hung up and then began studying my next port of call: Istanbul.

Max Böhm's envelope contained a Sofia–Istanbul train ticket, together with a timetable. Each night, a train left for Turkey at about eleven o'clock. He certainly had thought of everything. I weighed up the bizarre Swiss ornithologist for a while. I knew somebody who might be able to tell me more about him. Nelly Braesler. After all, she was the one who had put me Böhm's way. I picked up the phone and dialled the number of my adoptive mother in France.

At the tenth attempt, I got through. I heard the distant ringing tone, then Nelly's dry voice, which sounded even more distant.

"Hello?"

"It's Louis," I said coldly.

"Louis? My little Louis? Where are you?"

I at once recognized her oily, falsely friendly tone and felt my nerves stiffen under my skin.

"In Bulgaria."

"Bulgaria! Whatever are you doing there?"

"I'm working for Max Böhm."

"Poor old Max. I've just heard the news. I didn't know that you had in fact gone . . . "

"Böhm paid me to do the job. So I'm carrying out my obligations. To the dead."

"You might have told us."

"You're the one who should have warned me. Who was Max Böhm? What did you know about the job he was going to offer me?"

"Now, now, Louis. You're scaring me! Max Böhm was just an ornithologist. We met him during an ornithological symposium. You know that Georges is interested in that kind of thing. Max seemed very nice. What's more, he had travelled widely. We'd been to the same countries, and . . . "

"To the Central African Republic for instance?" I butted in.

Nelly paused for a moment, then replied more quietly:

"Yes, the Central African Republic for instance . . . "

"What did you know about the job he wanted to give me?"

"Nothing, or practically nothing. In May, Max wrote to us saying that he was looking for a student to go on a short mission abroad. So we quite naturally thought of you."

"Did you know that this mission was about storks?"

"Yes, so far as I remember."

"Did you know that this mission was going to be dangerous?"

"Dangerous? Good heavens, no . . . "

I changed tack.

"What do you know about Max Böhm's family and his past?"

"Nothing. Max was an extremely solitary sort."

"Did he ever mention his wife to you?"

The line crackled horribly.

"Vaguely," Nelly answered in a muffled voice.

"He never spoke about his son?"

"His son? I didn't even know that he had a son. What are all these questions about, Louis?"

The crackling burst out again. I yelled:

"One last question, Nelly. Did you know that Max Böhm had had a heart transplant?"

"No!" Nelly's voice was trembling. "All I knew was that he had heart problems. He died of a coronary, didn't he? Louis, there's no reason to continue your trip now. It's all over."

"No it isn't, Nelly. It's only just begun. I'll call you back later."

"Louis, my little Louis, when are you coming home?"

The line was plagued with more interference.

"I don't know. Give Georges a kiss from me. And take care of yourself."

I hung up. I was in a state, as I was each time I spoke to my adoptive mother. Nelly did not know anything. The Braeslers were definitely too rich to be dishonest.

It was 8 p.m. I hastily wrote a fax to Hervé Dumaz informing him of that day's horrific revelations. In conclusion, I promised him that I would make my own investigations into Max Böhm's past.

That evening, Marcel decided to take Yeta and me out to dinner. This seemed a strange idea after the day we had just spent. But Minaüs liked contrasts, and his idea was that we needed to relax.

The restaurant was on Rouski Boulevard. Marcel played at being the master of ceremonies and asked the man on reception, who was dressed in a dirty white dinner jacket, whether we could sit outside on the terrace. The man nodded and pointed upstairs. The terrace was on the first floor.

It was a long room with open windows that overlooked the wide boulevard. I found the smells of grilled meat, sausages and smoked bacon that were wafting up there distinctly unappetizing. We sat down, and I glanced around at the decor. Imitation woodwork, brown carpet, copper chandeliers. Families talking in hushed tones. The only din came from a far corner, where some Bulgarians had been overdoing the *arkhi*, the local vodka. I picked up a menu, which was translated into English, while Marcel was dictating Yeta's meal in a professorial voice. I glanced round at them. He, with his long beard and sharpened skull; she, sitting bolt upright, staring around nervously, her pointed mammal's face looking distrustful beneath her mop of grey hair. I just could not work out what had brought these two odd birds together. The woman had not uttered a single word since the previous evening.

The waiter arrived. And trouble started at once. They were out of "salad bowls". Out of aubergine caviar. Even out of *tourchia* (a dish of vegetables). And totally out of fish. Growing short of patience, I asked the waiter what was left in the kitchen. "Just meat," he replied in Bulgarian, with an unpleasant grin on his face. So I fell back on the accompaniments to a steak – green beans and potatoes – and emphasized that I did not want any meat. Marcel criticized my lack of appetite and launched into a train of highly specific physiological arguments.

Half an hour later, my vegetables arrived. Beside them, lay a lump of bloody, scarcely cooked meat. Disgust rose in my throat. I grabbed the waiter by his jacket and told him to take back my plate at once. He fought me off. The cutlery went flying and glasses smashed. The waiter insulted me, then seized me as well. He were standing, on the point of having a fight, when Marcel managed to separate us. Muttering insults, the waiter took back the plate, while the drunkards at the back lifted their glasses to encourage me. I was livid, and trembling from head to foot. I straightened my shirt and went out onto the balcony to calm down.

The cool of the evening was now covering Sofia. The balcony overlooked Naradno-Sabranie Square, the seat of the government. From there, I could admire a large part of the city, which was softly illuminated.

Sofia lies at the bottom of a valley. In the evening, the mountains around it become a tender blue. But the red and brown city seems to draw in on itself. Lofty, tortured and extravagant, Sofia looked to me like a city of pride, in the midst of the Balkans, with its fiery buildings and chalky walls. I was surprised by its vivacity and diversity, which did not fit the usual dull image of Eastern European countries. The city did of course have its share of grey blocks, petrol stations with lines of waiting cars and empty shops, but it was also clear and airy, full of sweetness and craziness. Its improvised skyline, its orange trams and its brightly coloured stores made it look like some strange Luna Park, with attractions wavering between the amusing and the disconcerting.

Marcel joined me outside.

"Feeling better?" he asked, slapping me on the shoulder.

"Yes, I feel better."

He laughed nervously.

"Well, you're not the partner I'm going to open my gypsy restaurant with."

"I'm sorry, Marcel." I answered. "I should have warned you. The very sight of a steak makes me run a mile."

"You're vegetarian?"

"That's right."

"It doesn't matter." He gazed round at the brightly lit city, then repeated: "It doesn't matter. I wasn't hungry, either. This restaurant was a bad idea."

He fell silent for a moment.

"Rajko was a friend of mine, Louis. A true and tender friend, a marvellous young man who knew the forest better than anybody else and who could find out the best places for each plant. He was the brains of the Nicolich clan. He played an essential role in their harvests."

"Why hadn't you seen Rajko for six months? Why hadn't anybody told you he'd been killed?"

"In spring, I was in Albania. There's going to be a terrible famine there, and I was trying to alert the French authorities. As for Marin' and the others, why should they have told me? They were terrified. And, after all, I am only a Gorgio."

"What do you think about Rajko's death?"

Marcel shrugged his shoulders, then paused for a moment to put his thoughts in order.

"I don't have any explanation. The world of gypsies is one of violence. Firstly to one another. They are quick with their knives and even quicker with their fists. They think like little pimps. But the worst violence comes from the outside. The insidious, relentless violence of the Gorgios. It follows them everywhere and has been hunting them down for centuries. I have seen so many shanty towns on the outskirts of big cities in Bulgaria, Yugoslavia and Turkey. Ramshackle huts built on mud, where families survive without jobs or futures, constantly struggling against an implacable racism. Sometimes the attacks are brutally direct. On other occasions, the system is more refined, with its laws and legal measures. But the result is always the same: out with the gypsies! I have witnessed all sorts of exclusion, police raids, bulldozers, arson . . . I have seen children die like that, Louis, in the wrecks of their homes, in their blazing caravans. Gypsies are the plague, an illness to be stamped out. So, what happened to Rajko? Honestly, I don't know. Maybe it was a racist murder. Or a warning, to frighten the gypsies out of the region. Or even a strategy to discredit them. Whatever the truth, Rajko was the innocent victim of some horrible machination."

I drank in this information. After all, maybe this "horrible machination" really did have nothing to do with Max Böhm and his secrets. I changed the subject.

"What's your opinion of One World?"

"The ghetto medics? They're wonderful. Understanding and devoted. It's the first time anybody has really come to help Bulgaria's gypsies."

Marcel turned towards me.

"And you, Louis. What do you make of all this? Are you really an ornithologist? What is this serious business you mentioned to Marin'? And what do storks have to do with it all?"

"I've no idea, either. But I have been hiding something from you, Marcel. It was Max Böhm who paid me to follow the storks. Meanwhile, he died and since his death the riddles have been piling up. The only sure thing I can tell you is that the ornithologist was not what he seemed."

"Why did you accept the job?"

"I've just spent ten years studying hard, which has completely put me off academic occupations. For ten years I saw nothing, experienced nothing. I wanted to put an end to that intellectual masturbation, which leaves an aching void in your guts and such a hunger for existence that you feel like banging your head against the wall. It became an obsession for me. To break my solitude, Marcel, and go out into the unknown. When old Max asked me to cross Europe, the Middle East and Africa in pursuit of his storks, I didn't hesitate for a second."

Yeta also joined us. She was getting impatient. The waiter had refused to serve her. In the end, none of us had eaten. As night fell, black woolly clouds were blowing across the sky.

"Let's go back," said Marcel. "A storm's brewing."

*

My room was anonymous. The light anaemic. Thunder was booming outside, but the rain refused to fall. The heat was suffocating and there was no air conditioning. The temperature came as a surprise. I had always imagined Eastern Europe to be miserably cold, in need of central heating and chapkas.

At ten thirty, I consulted the Argos data. The first two of the Sliven storks were heading for the Bosporus. The markers indicated that they had come to rest that evening, at 6.15, in Svilengrad, near the Turkish border. Another stork had reached Sliven that evening. The others were imperturbably following. I also took a look at the other route, to the west – the eight storks that were flying via

Spain and Morocco. Most of them had already crossed the straits of Gibraltar and were heading for the Sahara.

The storm was still rumbling. I lay down on the bed, switched off the lamp and put on my reading light. Only then did I open Rajko's notebook.

It was an anthem in praise of storks. Rajko took down everything: the birds' movements, the numbers of nests and of young, any accidents . . . He calculated averages and did his best to exploit analytic systems. His notebook was crammed with columns and elaborate figures which would have appealed to Max Böhm. In the margins, he had jotted down commentaries in his awkward English. Observations that were serious, affectionate or even humorous. He had given nicknames to the pairs that nested in Sliven and explained their meanings in an index. Thus, I learnt that "Silver Ashes" nested on a bed of moss, the male of the "Charmed Bills" had an asymmetric beak and that "Purple Springs" arrived during a crimson sunset.

Rajko also punctuated these observations with technical diagrams and anatomical studies. Another set of sketches depicted the different sorts of ring used in France, Germany, Holland and, of course, by Böhm. By each picture, Rajko had noted the date and place of his observation. One detail that had struck him was that storks with two rings always wore different sorts. The ones that indicated their date of birth were thin and cast in one piece. While the ones that Böhm had added later were thicker and seemed to open like a bracelet with a catch. I fetched my photos and examined the birds' feet. Rajko had been right. The two rings were not the same. I thought over this detail. However, the inscriptions on the rings were of the same kind: where and when they were put on, nothing more.

Outside, it had at last started to rain. I opened the windows to let the cool air flood in. Far away, Sofia was a mass of lights, like a galaxy lost in a silver storm. I returned to the notebook.

The final pages dealt with the 1991 storks. It was Rajko's last spring. During the months of February and March he, like Joro, noticed that

Böhm's storks were not reappearing. Also like Joro, he supposed that this was because the birds were ill or had been wounded. There was nothing more Rajko could tell me. I followed his last days through his diary. On 22 April, the page was blank.

CHAPTER 13

"Historically, the nomadic nature of gypsies seems rather to be a consequence of persecutions, of the Gorgios' unrelenting racism."

At 6 a.m., in the pallid dawn of the Bulgarian countryside, Marcel was already lecturing while I drove:

"Those gypsies that continue to travel are the poorest and most unfortunate ones. Each spring, they set off dreaming of large well-heated houses. But, at the same time, and here comes the paradox, the nomadic life remains firmly rooted in Romany tradition. Even sedentary Roms continue to travel from time to time. This is how husbands meet their wives and families become associated. This tradition transcends mere geographic mobility. It is a mind-set, a way of life. A Rom's house is always set out like a tent: one large room, which is the essential ingredient for a community lifestyle, in which the furnishings, ornaments and knick-knacks are reminiscent of the interior of a caravan."

On the back seat, Yeta was asleep. It was 31 August. Just sixteen more hours to be spent in Bulgaria. I had made up my mind to go back to Sliven in order to question Marin' once more and to look through the local papers of 23 and 24 April 1991. If the police were not interested, perhaps some journalists may have picked up some interesting details. I knew that this was only a slim chance, but it would keep me busy until my meeting with Dr Djuric at the end of the afternoon. What is more, I wanted to observe the storks on the open plain at the moment when they woke up.

We learnt nothing from our visits to the newspapers. The articles about Rajko's murder were just torrents of racist abuse. Markus Lasarevich was right. This killing had played on their minds.

The *Atkitno* believed that it had been a gypsy gangland murder. According to the article, two clans of Roms had been fighting over the gathering of herbs. The piece ended with an indictment accusing the gypsies of playing a central role in several scandals that had shaken Sliven over the previous few months. Rajko's murder was the final straw. It was no longer possible to allow the forests to become battlegrounds, thus endangering the lives of Bulgarian country folk and especially those of their children when playing there. Marcel fumed as he translated the article.

The *Koutba*, the main newspaper of the UDF – the opposition party – went more for the superstition angle. The article dwelt on the absence of any clues, then rattled off a list of suppositions based on magic and witchcraft. Rajko had obviously committed a "crime". As a punishment, his heart had been ripped out and offered to the greedy maw of some predator. The piece finished up with an apocalyptic warning to the inhabitants of Sliven against the diabolical dangers posed by such vermin as the gypsies.

As for the *Hunter's Union*, its brief article simply gave a potted history of Romany cruelty. Arson, murder, thefts, fights and general disorder were described in an off-hand tone, even down to evidence of cannibalism. As proof, the writer mentioned a series of events that had occurred in Hungary during the nineteenth century, when similar accusations had been made against gypsies.

"What they don't say," Marcel boomed, "is that these accusations were shown to be unfounded. But it was too late by then. Over a hundred Roms had already been lynched in the backwaters of the marshes."

This was too much to bear. Minaüs started to bellow in the old printing works. He screamed after the editor-in-chief, sent reams of paper flying, knocked over the ink and shook the old man who had allowed us to consult the archives. I managed to talk him round. We left. Yeta trotted behind us, not having understood a word.

I spotted a prefabricated bar near the train station in Sliven and suggested that we have some Turkish coffee. For half an hour, Marcel grumbled in Romany, then finally calmed down. Behind us, some gypsies were crunching almonds in hostile silence. Minaüs could not resist addressing them in his best ceremonial Romany. They smiled and spoke back. Soon, Marcel burst out laughing. His good mood had resurfaced. It was 10 a.m. I suggested that, for a change of scene, we head off into the country in search of the storks. Marcel enthusiastically agreed. I started to understand more clearly the way his mind worked. My companion was a nomad not only spatially, but also temporally. He lived purely in the present. His moods were radically different from one moment to the next.

At first we crossed the vineyards. Cohorts of Romanies were picking the grapes, bent double over the twisted shrubs. A heavy scent of fruit hung in the air. As we drove by, the women stood up to hail us. They all had the same mat dark faces, and brightly coloured rags. Some of them wore scarlet nail varnish. Then we reached the immense deserted plain with a scattering of flowers. But generally all we saw were patches of dark marshland gleaming between the shining grasses.

Suddenly, a long white crest appeared in the landscape.

"There they are," I murmured.

Marcel took my binoculars and directed them at the group.

"Go that way," he said, pointing at a path to our right.

I drove through the muddy furrows. We were slowly approaching the storks. Several hundred of them were there, drowsy, silent, standing on one leg.

"Turn off the engine," Marcel whispered.

We got out and advanced on foot. Some of the birds trembled, beat their wings and then took off. We stopped. Thirty seconds. A minute. The birds went back to their activities, pecking at the soil, moving on with their delicate gait. We took another few steps forward. The birds were now thirty yards away. Marcel said: "Let's stop here. This is as near as we'll get." I took back my binoculars and observed the storks. None of them was ringed.

The morning ended in Marin's clearing. This time, the Roms were more friendly. I was introduced to the women: Sultana, Marin's wife, the giantess in the sunflower sweater; Mermet's wife, Zainepo, the one with the broken nose; and Katio, Costa's wife, with her hands on her hips and her head of red hair. Rajko's widow, Mariana, was cuddling Denke, her three-month-old baby. The sun was up. An effervescence rose from the grasses, underscored by the hum of the insects.

"I want to talk to the person who discovered the body," I said at last.

Marcel grimaced. But still he translated my request. Then it was Marin's turn to look at me in disgust, before calling over Mermet. He was a colossus with brown skin and a sharp face beneath gleaming locks of hair. He was in no mood to talk. He picked a grass stalk and started chewing at it absentmindedly while muttering to himself.

"There's nothing to be said," Marcel translated. "Mermet found Rajko in the woods. The entire family was scouring the countryside after him. Mermet wandered into an area where nobody ever goes. People say there are bears there. And he discovered the body."

"Where exactly? In the undergrowth? In a clearing?"

Marcel translated my questions. Then relayed Mermet's answers:

"In a clearing. The grass was extremely short, as if it had been flattened."

"And there were no traces on this grass?"

"No, none."

"And nearby, there were no tyre marks, no footprints?"

"No. The clearing is deep inside the forest. No car could ever get there."

"What about the body?" I went on. "What was it like? Did it look as if there had been a struggle?"

"Hard to say," Marcel interpreted after hearing Mermet out. "Rajko was lying flat, arms beside his body. His skin had been lacerated all over. His innards were pouring out of a dark gash which started here." Mermet struck his heart. "The strangest thing was his face. It seemed to have two different halves. His eyes were wide open. Completely white. Panic-stricken. But his mouth was closed

72

and placid, his lips relaxed."

"Is that all? Nothing else that was striking?"

"No."

Mermet fell silent for a moment, still chewing at his stalk, then added:

"There must have been one hell of a storm the day before. Because, all around, the trees had been blown flat and their leaves were all over the place."

"One last question. Had Rajko mentioned anything, some discovery he might have made? Did he seem worried in any way?"

Mermet, with Marcel interpreting, had the last word:

"Nobody had seen him for two months."

I jotted this information down in my notebook, then thanked Mermet. He responded with a slight nod of his head. He looked like a wolf being offered a saucer of milk. We went back to the camp. The children insisted on playing some of their cassettes on the car hi-fi. In a flash, the Volkswagen was transformed into a gypsy orchestra, with clarinets, accordions and drums pursuing one other frantically. I was rather surprised. Like everybody else, I had thought that gypsy music consisted of languid violins. But this sounded more like the obsessive rhythms of a dervish dance.

Sultana gave us some Turkish coffee, a bitter liquid swimming above its grounds. I barely sipped at mine. But Marcel drank his slowly, like a true connoisseur, while holding an animated conversation with the sunflower lady. I guessed that he was talking about how to make and prepare coffee. Then he tipped over his cup. After waiting a few minutes, he examined the result with an expert eye and commented on it, with Sultana's help. I realized that he was learning how to read the future in coffee grounds.

As for me, feeling agitated, I glanced round at people, smiling haphazardly. As far as Marin' and the others were concerned, Rajko's death was a thing of the past (Marcel had explained to me that, after one year, the name of the dead person is freed; they can then give it to a newborn baby, organize a banquet and sleep in peace, for the spirit of the deceased will henceforth no longer trouble its brothers' dreams). As for me, this murder was eating its way into the present. And no doubt even more so into the future.

At 2 p.m., the clouds drifted back. It was time to head off to Sofia for my appointment with Milan Djuric at the end of the afternoon. We bade farewell to the *kumpania* and left in a volley of hugs and smiles.

On the way, we drove through the suburbs of Sliven. Dusty shanty towns, criss-crossed with unmade tracks, and dotted with the occasional burnt-out wreck of a car. I slowed down. "I have a lot of friends here," said Marcel, "but I'd best spare you that ordeal. Let's go." By the side of the road, children yelled after us: "Gorgio! Gorgio! Gorgio!" They were walking barefoot. Their faces were filthy and lumps of dirt stuck out of their hair. I put my foot down. After a while, I broke the silence:

"Tell me something, Marcel. Why are Romany children so dirty?"

"It's not from negligence, Louis. It's an old tradition. According to the Roms, children are so beautiful that they can attract the jealousy of adults, who may cast an evil eye on them. So they are never washed. It's a sort of disguise. To hide their beauty and purity from others."

CHAPTER 14

While we drove back, Marcel told me about Milan Djuric.

"He's an oddball. A solitary gypsy. Nobody knows exactly where he comes from. He speaks perfect French. Some people say that he studied medicine in Paris. He turned up in the Balkans in the 1970s. Since then, he's been touring around Bulgaria, Yugoslavia, Romania and Albania giving free consultations. He treats the Roms with whatever's to hand, uniting modern medicine with a gypsy's knowledge of plants. For example, he has saved several women who were haemorrhaging badly after being sterilized in Hungary or Czechoslovakia. And yet Djuric has been accused of carrying out back-street abortions. He's even been imprisoned on two occasions, I think. But these charges are totally false. As soon as he was released, he started touring round again. Djuric is a celebrity, almost a myth, in the Romany world. He's supposed to have magical powers. I suggest you go and see him alone. Maybe he'll talk to one Gorgio. Two would definitely be too much for him."

An hour later, at about six o'clock, we reached the outskirts of Sofia. First we drove through some run-down neighbourhoods, bordered by deep ditches, then we passed the wastelands where the gypsies camp and eke out an existence. Their drenched tents seemed about to be swallowed up by the mud. I carried away the sad image of little gypsy girls, wearing baggy oriental trousers, hanging out washing in that quagmire of slime and rain. They were staring nervously, yet also smiling furtively. Once more, I was deeply touched by the beauty and pride of the Romany people.

I turned into Lenin Boulevard and dropped off Marcel and Yeta on Naradno-Sabranie Square. Their two-room flat was just nearby. Marcel tried to explain where Djuric lived. He produced an ancient note pad and covered an entire page of it with maps and Cyrillic inscriptions.

"You can't miss it," he said, reeling off a list of street names, detours and pointless details.

Finally, he wrote down Djuric's exact address in Roman letters. Marcel and Yeta then insisted that they would see me off at the station. We arranged to meet again on the same square at eight o'clock.

I returned to the Sheraton, packed and paid the bill with several thick wads of leva. By 6.30, I was driving once more through the beautiful streets of Sofia.

I headed back down Rouski Boulevard, then turned left into General Vladimir Zaimov Avenue. Illuminated street signs glittered reflections in the puddles. I reached the top of a hill. On the far side lay a veritable forest. "Drive across the park," Marcel had said. So I pressed on through several miles of thick woodland, which gave way to dull blocks of flats along a grey boulevard. Finally, I found the street. I turned, hesitated, banging my chassis on the churned-up road, then wove my way past the anonymous buildings. The doctor lived in Block 3 C. I could not find this number anywhere. I showed my notebook to some Romany children, who were playing in the rain. They pointed out the building, which was just in front of me, then burst out laughing.

Once inside, the temperature doubled. The atmosphere reeked of frying smells, cabbage and rubbish. At the back, two men were pulling at the door of the lift. Sweating hulks, whose muscles gleamed in the harsh light of the electric lamp. "Dr Djuric?" I asked them. They pointed at the number 2. I leapt up the stairs and spotted the doctor's brass plate. An incredible racket was going on inside. I rang. Several times. Someone opened the door. Music ripped into my ears. An extremely plump, dark woman was standing in front of me. I repeated my name and that of Dr Djuric. She eventually let me in and left me standing in a narrow corridor, amid a powerful stench of garlic and a legion of shoes. My face running with sweat, I took off my Docksiders and waited.

Doors slammed, the noise grew louder, then more distant. A couple of seconds later, over the din of conversation, I made out the music which Marin' and his tribe had played on my car stereo. The same flurries, the same wild peels of clarinets and accordions. But here, a voice was entering into the fray. An ear-splittingly raucous woman's voice.

"She's got a lovely voice, hasn't she?"

I screwed up my eyes in the direction of the shadow. At the end of the corridor, a man was standing motionless. Dr Milan Djuric. With his usual obsessive attention to detail, Marcel had omitted the main point. Milan Djuric was a dwarf. Not a minuscule one (he must have measured four foot eight), but someone who bore certain typical signs of that infirmity. His head looked enormous. He was barrel-chested, and his bandy legs stood out in the shadows like pincers. I could not see his face. In a deep voice, Djuric spoke once more in his impeccable French:

"It's Esma. The Romanies' diva. In Albania, it was her concerts that set off the first riots. Who are you, sir?"

"My name's Louis Antioch," I replied. "I'm French. Marcel Minaüs advised me to come and see you. Could you spare me a few minutes?"

"Step this way."

The doctor turned and vanished through a door to his right. I followed him. We crossed a living-room containing a furiously barking television. On the screen, a huge redhead, dressed as a peasant woman, was spinning round and singing like a red and white top, accompanied by an old accordionist in a mujik costume. Their appearance was decidedly off-putting, but the music was superb. In the room, some gypsies were chattering even more loudly. They were eating, drinking, gesticulating wildly and bursting into laughter. The women wore sombre earrings under their long black locks of hair. The men had small felt hats.

We went into Djuric's office. He closed the door and drew a heavy curtain over it, which deadened the noise to some extent. I glanced round the room. The carpet was threadbare and the furniture looked as though it was made of cardboard. In one corner stood a bed with iron bars and leather straps. Beside it, some rusty surgical instruments lay on glass shelves. I had the fleeting impression of being in the surgery of some back-street abortionist, or quack practitioner. The thought at once made me feel ashamed. Djuric had already been imprisoned several times because of that sort of prejudice. Milan Djuric was quite simply a Romany doctor who treated other Roms.

"Take a seat," he said.

I chose a red desk chair, with cracked arms. For a moment, Djuric remained standing in front of me. This gave me time to observe him. His face was fascinating. His features were supple and regular, as though beautifully carved in tree-bark. His green eyes stared out, surrounded by horn-rimmed spectacles. He was about forty, but prematurely aged. The lines of his wrinkles could be clearly made out in his olive skin and his dense hair was a metallic grey. However, a certain unexpected force and vitality could also be read in his features. His muscular arms stretched the sleeves of his shirt and a closer look revealed that the upper part of his body was normally proportioned. Milan Djuric went and sat behind his desk. Outside, the rain doubled in intensity. I began by complimenting him on his perfect French.

"I studied in Paris. At the faculty on Rue des Saints-Pères."

He fell silent, then said:

"Forget the polite chitchat, Monsieur Antioch. What do you want?"

"I came here to talk to you about Rajko Nicolich, the gypsy who was killed in April in the forest of Sliven. I know that you carried out a postmortem. I'd like to ask you a few questions."

"Are you from the French police?"

"No. But this murder may be connected to an investigation I am currently working on. You aren't at all obliged to answer my questions. Just let me tell you my story. Then you can decide for yourself if you want to help me."

"Go ahead."

I told him everything that had happened: the initial task which Max Böhm had given me, the ornithologist's death, the mysteries that shrouded his past, the bizarre details that cropped up on my travels – the two Bulgarians also investigating the storks, the recurrent presence of One World, and so on.

While I spoke, his face remained expressionless. Then he finally asked me:

"What has all this to do with Rajko's death?"

"Rajko was an ornithologist. He used to watch out for migrating storks. I am sure that these birds hide a secret. From observing them, Rajko may have discovered what that secret was. And this may have cost him his life. I fully realize, Dr Djuric, that my suppositions probably sound absurd to you. But you carried out the postmortem on the body. You can give me valuable additional information. In ten days, I have covered nearly a thousand miles. I have about another four thousand to go. At eleven o'clock tonight, I'm taking the train to Istanbul. You are the only person in Sofia who might know anything else of importance."

Djuric stared at me for a few seconds, then took out a packet of cigarettes. After offering me one, which I refused, he lit up using a large chrome-plated lighter which gave off a strong smell of petrol. A cloud of blue smoke separated us for a moment then, in a neutral tone of voice, he asked:

"Is that really all?"

Anger rose up into my throat.

"No, Dr Djuric, it isn't. There is another coincidence in this business, which apparently has nothing to do with the storks, but still remains disturbing. Max Böhm had had a heart transplant. But he had no medical file or records."

"So that's it," Djuric said, flicking his ash into a large bowl. "You have obviously been told that Rajko's heart was stolen, and you have deduced that people are smuggling organs, or something along those lines."

"Well, yes . . ."

"Stuff and nonsense, Monsieur Antioch. Listen, I have no intention of helping you. Nor any other Gorgio, for that matter. But a few words of explanation will ease my conscience. (Djuric opened a drawer and laid some stapled pages onto the desk.) Here is the postmortem report which I drew up on the 23rd of April 1991, in the gymnasium of Sliven, after four hours spent observing and working on Rajko Nicolich's body. At my age, memories such as this count double. I made a point of writing the report in Bulgarian, but I might as well have written it in Romany, or Esperanto for that matter. Nobody has ever read it. You don't understand Bulgarian, I suppose? In that case, I'll try to sum it up for you."

He picked up the papers and took off his glasses. His eyes magically halved in dimension.

"Let's begin by setting it in context. On the morning of the 23rd of April I was carrying out a routine tour of duty in the Sliven ghetto. Costa and Mermet Nicolich, two herb gatherers I know well, came to see me. They had just found Rajko's corpse and were convinced that their cousin had been attacked by a bear. As soon as I saw the body in that clearing, I knew that they were wrong. The terrible wounds that covered Rajko's body fell into two distinct categories. There were indeed bites caused by animals, but these were subsequent to other incisions that had been made by surgical instruments. In any case, there was far too little blood around the scene. From the number of injuries, Rajko should have been awash in a pool of gore. But this was not the case. Finally, the body was naked, and I do not think that wild animals bother to undress their victims. I asked the Nicolich family to take the body to Sliven for a postmortem. We looked for a hospital. But in vain. We therefore fell back on the gymnasium, where I was able to do my job and at last work out approximately what happened during the last hours of Rajko's life. Listen carefully:

"*Extracts from the postmortem report of 23/4/91:*

"Subject: Rajko Nicolich. Sex: male. Naked. Born in about 1963 in Iskenderum, Turkey. Probable date of death 22/4/91 in the Clear Water Forest, near Sliven, Bulgaria, between 20.00 and 23.00 hours, following a deep wound to the cardiac region."

Djuric looked up, then remarked:
"I shall pass over the general presentation of the deceased. Listen to the description of the wounds.

"Upper part of the body. Face intact, except for signs of having been gagged. Tongue severed (the victim probably bit straight through it). No visible signs of bruising to the nape. Examination of the front of the thorax revealed a straight longitudinal wound running from the collarbones to the navel. The incision was perfect, carried out by some sharp, presumably surgical instrument – perhaps an electric lancet, given the small amount of haemorrhaging on the edges of the wound. We also observed multiple lacerations made by another sharp instrument to the neck, the front of the thorax and the arms. Partial amputation of the right arm at the shoulder. Numerous marks of scratches around the thoraco-abdominal wound. Probably made by bears or lynxes. Multiple bites on the torso, shoulders, sides and arms. We counted about twenty-five oval bites with teeth marks around them, but the skin was much too lacerated for moulds to be made. Back intact. Strap marks on the shoulders and wrists."

Djuric paused, took a drag of his cigarette, then proceeded:

"An examination of the upper half of the thoracic cavity revealed the absence of the heart. The connecting arteries and veins had been carefully severed, as far away as possible from the organ – a classic technique to avoid any heart traumatism. Other organs had been mutilated: the lungs, liver, stomach and gall-bladder. They were half eaten, but presumably by wild animals. Scraps of dry organic fibres, found inside and outside the body. No moulds could be made. No sign of haemorrhaging in the thoracic cavity.

"Lower half of the body. Deep wounds to the right of the groin, exposing the femoral artery. Multiple lacerations on the penis, the testicles and upper thighs. The sharp instrument seems to have been used repeatedly on this region. The penis remained attached only by a few strands of tissue. Numerous traces of scratches on the thighs. Animal bite marks on both legs. Inner side of thigh completely eaten through. Strap marks on the thighs, knees and ankles."

Djuric looked up and said:
"So much for the postmortem, Monsieur Antioch. I carried out a few toxicological tests, then returned the body, duly cleaned up, to the family. I had learnt all I needed to know about the death of a Rom, which would in any case never be investigated."

I was chilled to the bone, and my breathing came in gasps. Djuric put his glasses back on and lit another cigarette. His craggy features danced through the clouds of smoke.

"In my opinion, this is what happened. Rajko was attacked in the middle of the woods during the evening of the 22nd of April. He was tied up, then gagged. A long incision was then made in his thorax. His heart was removed with great precision by an experienced surgeon. I would call this Phase One of the murder. And Rajko died during that phase, there is no doubt about that. Up until then, everything had gone smoothly and professionally. The murderer had removed the organ with great care and skill. Then something snapped. The murderer (or someone else equipped with a surgical instrument) went crazy, ripping into the body left, right and centre, but paying particular attention to the pubic region, digging his blade in and using it as a saw on the penis. This was Phase Two of the carnage. Finally, the wild animals in the forest finished off the work. From this point of view, given that the body spent a night out among predators, it was in a relatively good condition. I would explain this fact by the coat of antiseptic which the murderer or murderers applied to the thorax before operating. The smell must have kept the animals at bay for several hours.

"That is my summary of the facts, Monsieur Antioch. As to the scene of the crime, I should say that the entire thing took place just where the body was found, lying on a plastic sheet or something of that kind. The absence of any traces in the clearing confirms this hypothesis. There is no need for me to tell you that this is the most atrocious murder I have ever seen. I told the Nicolich family the truth. They had to know. This atrocity then spread like a pool of blood through the region, giving rise to the sort of rumours that you no doubt read in the local press. As for me, I have no comments to make. All I want to do is forget this nightmare."

The noise of a door opening. The voices of the gypsies, the tumult of sounds and the smell of garlic returned. The turquoise woman entered, carrying a tray with a bottle of vodka and some soft drinks on it. Her earrings clunked together when she put it down on the small table near my chair. I refused the spirits. So she served me a glass of yellowish liquid, the colour of urine. Djuric poured out a shot of vodka. My throat was as dry as leather. I swallowed the fizzy drink in one gulp. I waited for the woman to close the door again, then said:

"So, despite the barbarity of the murder, you would agree that it could have been a surgical operation with the aim of removing Rajko's heart."

82

"Yes and no. Yes, because surgical techniques and a certain degree of asepsis seem to have been respected. No, because certain details do not gel. It all happened in a forest, and the ablation of a heart requires extremely rigorous antiseptic conditions, which can hardly be respected in the middle of nowhere. But, above all, because the 'patient' should normally have been anaesthetized. And Rajko was still conscious."

"What do you mean?"

"I took a blood sample. There was no trace of any sedative. The sternotomy was performed without anaesthetic. Rajko died in agony."

Sweat ran down my spine. Djuric's eyes stared at me fixedly from behind his glasses. He seemed to be savouring the effect of his last revelation.

"Please explain yourself, doctor."

"Apart from the lack of any anaesthetic in the blood, the marks speak for themselves. I mentioned the traces of strapping around the shoulders, wrists, thighs and ankles. They were bands of rubber and were so tight that they dug ever further into the flesh as the body contorted in agony. The gag, too, was remarkable. It had an extremely strong adhesive. When I carried out the postmortem about eighteen hours after Rajko's death, his beard had grown back (hair continues to grow for about three days after death), except around his lips which had remained completely smooth. Why? Because when the murderers tore off the gag, they brutally depilated that part of his face. The body had thus been made perfectly immobile and silent. As though the killers had wanted to have their hands free to enjoy his suffering, to take their time over digging around in his still-living flesh. Then, I could also mention Rajko's mouth. He was in such pain, that he bit right through his own tongue. He choked on those lumps of tissue and the blood that was spurting down his throat. That's the truth of it, Monsieur Antioch. This operation was a monstrous piece of sadism that could only have been cooked up by sick minds, drunk on madness and racism."

I pressed on:

"Does the fact that the 'donor' was still conscious make the heart useless? I mean, would the spasms caused by the suffering have stopped the heart working normally?"

"You are tenacious, Antioch. But, oddly enough, no. Even such extreme pain does not damage the heart. It simply makes it beat more rapidly, start racing and no longer irrigate the body correctly. But it still remains in perfect condition. What I cannot understand, apart from the sadistic aspect, is the technical absurdity. Why operate on a living, writhing body when an anaesthetic would have given them the immobility they required?"

I changed tack:

"Do you think such a murder could have been committed by a Bulgarian?"

"No way."

"What about a gangland killing, as suggested in some of the papers I read?"

Djuric shrugged. Smoke wafted between us.

"That's ridiculous. It was far too sophisticated for Roms. I am the only doctor they have in all of Bulgaria. What is more, there was no motive. I knew Rajko. He lived a completely pure life."

"Pure?"

"He lived as a Rom. In the precise way in which a Rom should. In our culture, our daily existence is governed by a series of laws. An extremely strict code of conduct. The notion of purity is central to what is and is not allowed. Rajko obeyed our laws."

"So there was no reason to kill him?"

"No, none."

"Could he perhaps have discovered something dangerous?"

"What could he have discovered? Rajko was interested only in plants and birds."

"Exactly."

"Are you referring to your storks? Absolute nonsense. No one in any country has ever been killed for the sake of a few birds. And especially not in that way."

Djuric was right. This upsurge of violence could have nothing to do with the storks. We were more in the realm of Max Böhm's photographs or of the mystery surrounding his heart. The dwarf ran his hand through his hair. His grey locks looked like a doll's synthetic wig. He emptied his glass then slammed it down, as a sign that our talk was over. I slipped in one more question.

"Were the teams from One World in this region in April?"

"I think so."

"They had the sort of equipment you mentioned."

"You are barking up the wrong tree there, Antioch. One World are good people. They understand nothing about Roms, but they are devoted doctors. Do not let your suspicions lead you by the nose. You will not find out anything that way."

"And what's your opinion?"

"Rajko's murder is a complete enigma. No witnesses, no clues, no motive. Not to mention the perfect technical skill. After the postmortem, I feared for the worst. I thought there was some racist machination at work aimed against us Roms. I imagined that the Nazis were back. That other murders would be committed. I was wrong. Nothing has happened since April. Neither here, nor elsewhere in the Balkans. I felt relieved. So I decided to write this murder off as one of our losses.

"I may sound sceptical to you. But you have no idea of a Rom's daily existence. Our past, present and future are a concatenation of persecution, hostility and negation. I have travelled widely, Antioch. Everywhere I go, I see the same hatred, the same fear of the nomad. I struggle against that. As much as I can, I alleviate the sufferings of my people. Paradoxically, the fact that I am infirm has given me enormous strength. In your world, a dwarf is nothing but a monster, bent under the burden of indifference. But I am first and foremost a Rom. My origin is a blessing to me, a second chance. Do you understand that? My fight against being different has expanded into a larger, more noble struggle. That of my people. So, let me follow my path. If some sadists have started disembowelling their victims, then that's all right by me – so long as they choose Gorgios."

I stood up. Djuric wriggled round on his chair to get a foot on the floor. He strode in front of me with his crooked gait. In the corridor, still echoing with music, I put on my Docksiders without saying a word. Just as he was about to bid me farewell in the stifling half-light, Djuric sized me up for a few seconds.

"How odd. Your face seems familiar. Maybe I knew a member of your family while I was living in France."

"I doubt that. My family never lived in mainland France. What's more, my parents both died when I was six. I don't have any other relatives."

Djuric was not listening to my answer. His bulging eyes remained fixed on my face, like the beam of light from a watchtower. At last, he lowered his head, massaged the nape of his head and murmured:

"How odd! Strange, the impression I had."

I opened the door to avoid shaking his hand. Djuric said in conclusion:

"Good luck, Antioch. But keep to your study of birds. Humans do not deserve your attention. Whether they be Roms or Gorgios."

CHAPTER 15

At half past nine, I arrived at Sofia station, accompanied by Marcel and Yeta. There was a sort of golden, shifting, fairy-like mist in the air. A metal, spiral-shaped clock looked down on the huge concourse from a great height. Its hands turned in jolts as the trains arrived and departed. A crush of people swarmed below. Tourists, trailing their suitcases, pressed on in panicked herds. Workers covered in mud or oil looked on vacantly. Mothers wrapped up in coloured headscarfs dragged their shabbily dressed offspring in shorts and sandals. Khaki-clad soldiers staggered around, drunk and guffawing. But, above all, there were gypsies. Asleep on the benches. In large groups on the platforms. On the tracks, eating sausages and drinking vodka. Everywhere, women in gold-braided scarfs, men the colour of oak and half-naked children, all indifferent to the trains and to all those who were dashing about chasing their business or their pleasure.

More discreetly, other details emerged. The bright colours, the felt hats, the whirling music broadcast by the radios, the peanuts being sold on the platforms. Sofia station was already part of the Orient. Here began the seething world of the Byzantine Empire, with its hammams, golden domes, chasings and arabesques. Here began the perfumed incense and the supple bellies of dancers. Here began Islam, with its high minarets and the incessant call of the muezzins. From Venice or Belgrade, it was necessary to go via Sofia in order to reach Turkey. This was the great crossroads, the decisive bend in the tracks for the Orient Express.

"Antioch . . . Antioch . . . Funny name for a Frenchman. In fact, it's the name of an old Turkish town," Marcel exclaimed as he followed my hasty steps.

Hardly listening to him, I answered:

"My origins are shrouded in darkness."

"Antioch . . . Since you're going to Turkey, you ought to drop in there. The town's called Antakya now, and it's near the border with Syria. During Antiquity it was huge. The third city in the Roman Empire, after Rome and Alexandria. Today, it has lost its brilliance, but there are still many things worth seeing there . . ."

I did not answer. Marcel was becoming tedious. I looked for platform 18 and the Istanbul train. It lay at the far side of the station, beyond the main concourse.

"I'll have to give you the keys," I said to Marcel. "So you can take the car back."

"No problem. On the way, I'll give Yeta a little tour of 'Sofia by Night'."

Platform 18 was deserted. My train had not arrived yet. We were more than one hour early. Old trains on the nearby tracks blocked off the view. But to our right, behind the dusty coaches, I noticed two men. They seemed to be walking in the same direction as us, but they were not carrying any luggage. Marcel said:

"We can meet up again in Paris when I come to France next October."

Then he said something to a Romany woman, who was waiting there alone with her baby. I put my bag down. My head was seething with what Djuric had told me, and I was looking forward to getting onto the train – in order to be alone and think over everything I had just learnt.

Behind the motionless coaches I spotted the two men again. The taller one was wearing a dark blue acrylic tracksuit. His spiky hair looked like shards of broken glass. The other was a sort of squat muscleman, with a pale mask for a face, covered with a three-day growth. Two ugly mugs, of the sort to be found in all train stations. Marcel was still talking with the gypsy woman. He finally turned towards me and explained:

"She'd like to travel in your compartment. She's never taken the train before. She's going to Istanbul to meet her family there."

I looked at the two men, who were now less than fifty yards away, right in front of us, in the space between the coaches. The squat one had turned round. It looked as though he was looking for something in his raincoat. A large patch of sweat darkened his back. The tall one was still staring at us with feverish eyes. Marcel went on jokingly:

"But remember, hands off her till you're out of Bulgaria! You know what the Roms are like!"

The short one spun round. I said:

"Let's not wait here."

I bent down to pick up my bag. I was just gripping the handle when I heard a small blast. A second later, I was rolling on the ground and screaming: "Marcel!" But it was too late. His head had just been blown to pieces.

I heard another "phut" through a shower of blood. Yeta's shrill cry rang out – it was the first time I had heard her speak. One, two, three, four muffled gunshots followed. I saw Yeta being blown off her feet. A minuscule beam of red light was darting about. "A laser sight," I thought and crawled through the blood that was sticking to the

88

asphalt. I glanced to my right. The Romany woman was doubled up over her child, her hands black with blood. I glanced to my left. The hitmen were running, bending down to spot me between the steel train wheels. The man in the raincoat was carrying an assault rifle equipped with a silencer. I slipped down onto the tracks, just opposite the two of them. I stumbled over Yeta's body. Red and pink guts were spilling out from the folds of her jacket. Then I ran, my ankles banging on the rails.

Still down on the track, I reached the buffers. I looked round the concourse. The crowd was still there, indifferent. The clock read 9.55 p.m.

After scrutinizing the faces of the people nearest me, I got up and marched off through the crowds, elbowing my way forwards and hugging my blood-stained bag in front of me. At last I reached the exit. There was no sign of the hitmen.

I ran to the car park and dived into my car. Luckily, I still had the keys. I pulled away rapidly, slithering and skidding on the wet asphalt. I had no idea where to go, so I put my foot down and drove. Images exploded in my mind. Marcel's face turning into a mess of gore, Yeta's body slumping down onto the tracks, the gypsy woman gripping her child. Red everywhere.

I had been driving for five minutes when a shiver ran down my spine. A dark saloon was following every move I made. I accelerated and turned left, then right. The saloon was still there. It was driving with its headlights off at an incredible speed. In the furtive light of the street lamps I caught a glimpse of the killers. The tall one was at the wheel and the squat one was no longer bothering to conceal his weapon – a stocky rifle with a wide barrel. On their heads, they were wearing night vision devices. I turned left down a long deserted street and accelerated. The saloon kept up with me. Gripping the wheel, I tried to put my thoughts in order. I was losing ground. The straight road even enabled the killers to get alongside me, wing against wing. Our bodywork touched, sliding together with a damp hiss. I swerved right, so abruptly that the saloon kept going straight. I was hitting one hundred and twenty-five miles per hour.

On the avenue, the sodium lights twinkled in the storm. Suddenly, I was bouncing over a level crossing. My chassis crashed against the asphalt in a metallic screech. From having two lanes, the avenue was now a one-way street.

My headlamps revealed another intersection. I opted for the right turning, and found a black gleam blocking my way. The saloon was parked sideways across the road. I heard the first bullets hit the bonnet. The rain was playing in my favour. At the first side turning, I backed up to my left – just in time to see the saloon drive off in front of me – then headed down the deserted avenue facing me. I bombed down it, losing speed as I became lost in a maze of bumpy streets, of dark detached houses and trains in sidings. Then I arrived in an area of unlit warehouses. I turned off my headlamps and, leaving the road, bounced over the humps. I slid between the wagons, jolted on, then came to a skidding halt beside a railway line. I got out of the car. It had stopped raining. Two hundred yards away, a disused warehouse rose up in the shadows. I tip-toed inside.

The windows were gaping holes, the walls gutted, ripped up cables lay everywhere. There had been no human presence here for quite some time. The floor was a nest of cooings – a moving bed of feathers and droppings. Thousands of pigeons had set up home here. I advanced gingerly. It was as if the night had shattered. Countless bodies rose up, their clacking wings deafening me. Feathers blew around me in the foul-smelling air. I slipped along a corridor. A stink of petrol and oil filled the damp atmosphere. My eyes were now getting used to the dark. To my right, I could see a series of offices with smashed windows. The floor was covered with shards of glass. I shuffled alongside them, clambering over the broken chairs, tipped-over cupboards and pulverized telephones. A staircase appeared.

I went up the steps under a white arch of bird excrement. It felt as though I were entering the rectum of some monstrous pigeon. On the first floor, I found a huge room. Four hundred yards of absolute nothingness, open to the four winds, except for a regularly spaced row of rectangular pillars that crossed it. On the floor there was another mass of broken glass, glistening in the night. I listened. No sound. No breathing. Slowly, I crossed the room, finally reaching a metal door that was locked with heavy chains. I was stuck, but nobody would ever find me there. I decided to wait for dawn. I brushed away the shards behind the last pillar and sat down. My body was shattered, but I did not feel the slightest bit afraid. I stayed there, crouching at the foot of the column and soon fell asleep.

The crunching of broken glass woke me up. I opened my eyes and looked at my watch. It was 2.45 a.m. It had taken the bastards over four hours to find me. I heard their footsteps screeching on the floor behind me. They must have spotted my car and were now after me – like two beasts hunting down their prey. The occasional beating of wings echoed round the room. High above me, rain could be heard beating down again. I glanced round rapidly. The two hitmen were using neither torches nor any other light source – just their night vision devices. Trembling, I suddenly remembered that that sort of gadgetry is sometimes equipped with heat detectors. If that was the case, then my body was going to generate a nice red shadow behind the pillar. The door in front of me was locked. The hitmen were between me and the exit.

The crunching advanced at regular intervals. First, a series of footsteps, a pause lasting ten to fifteen seconds, then more footfalls. My pursuers were moving along together, pillar by pillar. They clearly did not know I was there. They were walking quietly, but without taking any particular precautions. Sooner or later, they were going to pluck me out from behind that last pillar. How many columns could there still be between them and me? I wiped away the veil of sweat that was clouding my eyesight. Slowly, I pulled off my shoes, then hung them by their laces round my neck. Even more slowly, I took off my shirt, tore it into shreds with my teeth, and wrapped them round my feet. The footsteps were getting closer.

I was half-naked, haggard and sweating with fear. I glanced behind the pillar, then leapt out to my right, hiding behind the next one. My feet had touched the ground just once, protected from the broken glass by the layer of cotton. No noise. No breathing. Then, in front of me, I heard their feet on the shards once more. I immediately slid behind the next pillar. There were about five or six of them left between us. I heard them move again and threw myself behind the next pillar. My plan was simple. In a few seconds' time, the killers and I would be either side of the same pillar. I would then slip by to the right, as they moved to the left. It was a crazy, almost childish idea. But it was the only chance I had. I slowly bent down and, with two fingers, picked up a lump of plaster topped with a piece of glass. I advanced another three columns. The sound of breathing made me freeze. They were there. On the other side. I counted ten seconds then, when the crunching sound started again, leapt out to the right, flattening my back against the pillar.

My heart jumped in astonishment. In front of me stood the monster in the tracksuit, a metal object gleaming in his hand. It took him a tenth of a second to realize what was happening. A tenth of a second later, the shard of glass was sticking in his throat. The blood spurted out between my clenched fingers. I dropped my weapon and opened my arms to receive the body that now sank down heavily. I crouched and slid the giant onto my back. This horrific manoeuvre was made smoother thanks to the blood that was gushing out of him. I knelt down, hands on the ground. My numb, burnt palms pressed down onto the broken glass insensibly. It was the first time that my infirmity had saved my life. Hot blood was still spurting from the body. My eyes staring, my throat agape in a silent scream, I heard the second hitman move on without suspecting a thing. I allowed that inert mass to slide noiselessly down from my shoulders, then I set off as light as fear itself. It was only when I was going down the stairs, white with droppings, that I realized what weapon the killer had been holding – a high frequency lancet connected to a battery on his belt.

I ran to my car, pulled off at once and steered it between the damp bushes until I was on the tarmac again. After half an hour of one-way streets and dark lanes, I turned onto the motorway and headed for Istanbul. I drove for a long time at over a hundred and forty miles per hour, headlamps full on, into the darkness.

I was soon nearing the border. Realizing that my face must be red and my hands clammy with blood, I stopped. In the rear-view mirror I saw my eyelids, besmirched with clots, and my matted hair – all covered with his blood. My hands started to shake. This shaking then spread in jolts to my arms and my jaws. I got out of the car. The rain had grown heavier. I got undressed and stood there, upright and naked in the downpour, feeling the fresh mud rise up round my ankles. I stayed like that for five, ten, twenty minutes, being rinsed by the raindrops, and washed clean of my crime. Then I took shelter again in the car, found some dry clothes and put them on. My wounds were shallow. I dug out my first-aid kit, disinfected my palms then bandaged them.

Despite having gone over the permitted forty-eight-hour stay, I crossed the border without any difficulty. Then I shot off once more. The sun was coming up. A signpost indicated that Istanbul was now fifty miles away. I slowed down. Three quarters of an hour later, I was nearing the city's suburbs and, without stopping, searched for a particular location in my papers. The map was clear. By ringing round and asking while still in Paris, I had managed to pinpoint this "strategic" position. Finally, after missing my way a couple of times, I reached the summit of the Büyük Küçük Canlyca hills, above the Bosporus.

From these heights, the straits looked like a motionless giant made of ashes. In the distance, Istanbul rose up through the mist with its tall minarets and sleepy domes. I stopped. It was 6.30. The silence was vast, pure, full of the details that I love – bird calls, distant bleating, the sighing of the wind in swaying grasses. The gold of the sun progressively lit up the waters. I stayed there, staring into the sky with my binoculars. Not a single bird. Not a single shadow. An hour went by then, suddenly, way up yonder, a seething rippling cloud appeared. Sometimes black, sometimes white. It was them. A group of one thousand storks was about to cross the straits. I had never seen anything like it before. A sumptuous winged ballet, their bills extended, propelled by the same force, the same tenacity. A light airy wave, its foam made of feathers and its energy pure wind . . .

In front of me, the storks rose ever higher in the immaculate sky until they became minuscule. Then they rapidly crossed the straits. I thought of those juvenile storks that had set off from Germany, guided only by their instincts. For the first time in their lives, they were triumphing over the sea. I suddenly lowered my binoculars and stared down at the waters of the Bosporus.

For the first time in my life, I had killed a man.

III
The Stork Kibbutz

CHAPTER 16

From Istanbul, I drove down to Izmir in south-west Turkey. There, I gave the Volkswagen back to the hire company's agent. He seemed a bit put out by the state it was in but, as the brochure had promised, he made no fuss. I then took a taxi to Kusadasi, a tiny port from which ferries leave for Rhodes. It was the first day of September. I boarded at 7.30 p.m. after taking a shower and changing my shirt in a hotel room. I now opted for an inconspicuous outfit – T-shirt, cotton trousers and yellow safari jacket – and kept on my Goretex cap and sunglasses as two further guarantees of anonymity. My bag had emerged unscathed, my laptop too. As for my hands, the wounds were already healing. At the stroke of eight, I left the Turkish coast. At dawn the next day, at the foot of the fortress of Rhodes, I boarded a ship for Haifa, Israel. Crossing the Mediterranean would take about twenty-four hours. During my enforced cruise, I whiled away the time by drinking black tea.

Marcel's face, shattered by the first blast, Yeta's body, riddled with holes, the gypsy child, presumably shot dead by one of the bullets that had been meant for me – these images continued to torment my memory. I had caused the death of three innocent people. And I was still alive. This injustice obsessed me. I was haunted by the desire for revenge. Curiously enough, in the sway of this sort of logic, the fact that I had already killed a man did not seem to matter. I was a moving target, someone advancing into the unknown, ready to kill or be killed.

I meant to follow the storks to the bitter end. Their migration might seem rather futile compared with what had just happened. But, after all, it was those birds that had placed me on this trail of violence. And I was now more certain than ever that they played a vital role in this story. Weren't the two men who had tried to kill me the pair of Bulgarians that Joro had mentioned? And wasn't my victim's weapon – a high-frequency lancet – directly related to Rajko's murder?

Before embarking, I had called up the Argos Centre from a hotel. The storks were still on track. A leading group had reached Dörtyol in the gulf of Iskenderun, near the border with Syria. Their average rate of progress was exceeding the ornithologists' estimates. They were easily covering a hundred and twenty-five miles per day. Now exhausted, they were probably going to rest around Damascus, before setting off on their inevitable route, to the ponds of Beyt Shean, in Galilee, where they poached off the fish farms. That was my destination.

During the voyage, other questions bugged me. What had I discovered that meant I must now be killed? And who had tipped off the hitmen? Milan Djuric? Markus Lasarevich? The Sliven gypsies? Had I been followed from the start? And what had One World got to do with all this? When these spiralling questions gave me a moment's respite, I tried to sleep. I dozed off on the deck, lulled by the slapping of the waves, only to wake up again at once with another round of persistent questions.

At 9 a.m. on the morning of 3 September, Haifa appeared in the dust-filled air. The port was separated into an industrial centre and a residential area. The upper town lay on the bright, serene slopes of Mount Carmel. In the furnace of the quays, with their noisy jostling crowds, I encountered that highly scented overpowering fragrance that reminded me of Oriental markets in adventure stories. Reality was less romantic.

Israel was at war. An uneasy underground war of nerves and attrition. A war with no truces, punctuated by furious outbreaks of violence. As soon as I set foot there, that tension hit me. First, I was searched. Every minute detail of my luggage was examined. Then I had to go through the usual interrogation in a small recess, behind a white curtain. A uniformed woman assailed me with questions in English. Always the same ones. First put one way. Then another. "Why have you come to Israel?" "Who are you going to see?" "What do you mean to do here?" "Is this your first visit?" "What have you brought with you?" "Do you know any Israelis?" and so on. My case was a difficult one. She did not believe this business about storks. What is more, all I had was a one-way ticket. "Why did you come via Turkey?" she asked nervously. "How do you intend to leave?" another woman added, who had arrived to back her up.

After three hours of body searches and repetitive questioning, I was allowed through customs and into Israeli territory. I changed $500 into shekels and hired a small Rover. Once again, I used Max Böhm's vouchers. With great precision, the receptionist showed me the best route to Beyt Shean, then strongly advised me to stick to it. "You know, it's very dangerous to drive through the occupied territories with Israeli number plates. The Palestinian children will throw stones at you and attack you." I thanked her for her help and promised not to make any detours.

Outside, far from the sea breezes, the heat was stifling. The car park was ablaze with torrid light. Everything seemed petrified in the morning brightness. Armed soldiers, in heavy helmets and camouflaged combat uniforms, strolled along the pavements weighed down with walky-talkies and ammunition. I showed them my rental contract, crossed the car park and found my car. The steering-wheel and the seats were scorching. I closed the windows, turned on the air conditioning, then checked my route in my French guide book. Haifa was to the west, and Beyt Shean to the east, near the border with Jordan. I thus had to cross the entirety of Galilee, meaning about sixty miles. Galilee . . . In other circumstances this name would have plunged me into a long meditation. I would have delighted in the charm of such a legendary place, that mythical land so central to the Bible. I put the key in the ignition and headed east.

I had two contacts: Iddo Gabbor, a young ornithologist who

nursed injured birds in the Newe-Eitan kibbutz, near Beyt Shean; and Yossé Lenfeld, the head of the Nature Protection Society, a large laboratory which had been set up near Ben-Gurion Airport.

Around me, the scenery alternated between arid deserts and the artificial hospitality of recently built towns. Sometimes I spotted a camel-keeper amid his charges. In the blinding light, his brown tunic would meld in with the colour of their herds. On other occasions, I drove through bright modern towns, whose whiteness stung my eyes. So far, the landscape did not really appeal to me. What amazed me most was the light. Vast, pure and oscillating, it seemed like a huge breath of fire that had scorched the countryside, while keeping it in a state of extraordinarily dazzling fusion.

At around noon, I stopped at a roadside café. In the shade, I drank tea, nibbled at some over-sweet biscuits and tried calling Gabbor several times. No answer. At 1.30 p.m., I decided to continue in the hope of finding him once I had arrived.

An hour later, I had reached the Beyt Shean kibbutzim. Three perfectly arranged villages surrounded by vast agricultural fields. My guide book had plenty to say about kibbutzim and explained that they were "communities based on the collective ownership of the means of production, and a collective consumption, given that wages had no direct link to the work done". The chapter ended as follows: "Because of their efficiency, the agricultural techniques of the kibbutzim have been admired and studied throughout the world." I drove on aimlessly along those green expanses.

Finally, I found Newe-Eitan kibbutz. I recognized it thanks to its farms with their fishponds, their briny surfaces reflecting back occasional flashes of sunlight. It was three o'clock and the heat was not letting up. I entered a village made up of carefully aligned white houses. The streets had been decorated with patches of flowers. Blue glints of swimming pools could be seen behind some of the hedges. But everything was deserted. Not a soul about. Not even a dog crossing the road.

I decided to check out the fishponds. I took a small lane which ran alongside a narrow valley. Below lay the dark waters of the ponds.

Men and women were working in the sunlight. I went down on foot. I was struck by the bitter, sensual smell of the fish, mingled with the ashen fragrances of the dry trees. The dull sound of an engine rose up into the sky. Two men on a tractor were loading crates full of fish.

"Shalom," I called out, smiling. They stared back at me with their pale eyes, without uttering a word. One of them had a leather holster on his belt, from which the brown stock of a revolver poked up. I introduced myself in English and asked them if they knew Iddo Gabbor. Their faces grew even harder, the man's right hand moved towards his gun. Still not a word. Raising my voice to speak over the tractor engine, I explained why I was there. I was fascinated by storks, had covered nearly two thousand miles to watch them here, and I wanted Iddo to take me to see them in the places where they generally landed. The two men looked at each other, still in silence. Finally, the unarmed man pointed at a woman who was working beside a pond, about two hundred yards away. I thanked them and went to speak to her. I sensed their eyes on my back, like the sights of an automatic rifle.

When I reached her, I said "Shalom" again. The woman stood up. She was quite young, looked about thirty and was approximately six feet tall. Her body was dry and harsh, like a leather hide that had hardened in the sun. Her long blond hair fluttered around her dark, pointed features. She fixed her eyes on me. They were full of fear and scorn. I was incapable of saying what colour they were, but the shape of her eyebrows gave them the shimmering beauty of the sun flashing on the backs of the waves, the clear glint from jars of water being poured out onto the parched earth in the heat of the dusk. She was wearing rubber boots and a mud-stained T-shirt.

"What do you want?" she asked in English.

I repeated my story of storks and told her about my travels and Iddo. Without responding, she abruptly went back to her work and plunged a heavy net into the dark pond. Her gestures were awkward. Her bird-like bone structure caused a tingle to run down my spine. I waited a few seconds then tried again:

"What's the matter?"

99

She stood up once more, then answered in French:

"Iddo's dead."

The storks' migration path was a trail of blood. My heart sank and I stammered out:

"Dead? When did it happen?"

"About four months ago. When the storks came back."

"How did he die?"

"He was killed. I don't want to talk about it."

"I'm sorry. Were you his wife?"

"His sister."

She bent down once more, following the fish with her net. Iddo Gabbor had been murdered, shortly after Rajko. Another corpse. Another puzzle. But with the certainty that the path of the storks was a one-way trip to hell. I looked at the Israeli woman: the wind was blowing through her hair. This time, she stopped of her own accord and asked:

"You want to see the storks?"

"Well . . . (my request now seemed grotesque amid all that carnage) . . . Yes, I would."

"Iddo used to nurse them."

"I know. That's why I'm here."

"They arrive in the evening. On the other side of the hills."

She stared at the horizon, then murmured:

"Wait for me at the kibbutz at six o'clock. I'll take you there."

"I don't know the kibbutz."

"Near the little square. There's a fountain. The birdwatchers stay in that neighbourhood."

"Thank you, um . . ."

"Sarah."

"Thank you, Sarah. My name's Louis. Louis Antioch."

"Shalom, Louis."

I walked back under the hostile glares of the two men. I trudged on like a sleepwalker, dazzled by the sun, devastated by this news of another death. But there was something else now in my mind. Sarah's sun-bleached hair was running across my skin like fire.

The click of the safety catch woke me up with a jump. I opened my eyes. I had fallen asleep in my car on the small square in the kibbutz. All around me, men in civvies were pointing a veritable arsenal of weapons at me. Some of the men were huge, with brown beards, others were fair-haired with rosy cheeks. They were conversing in an Oriental language devoid of gutturals – Hebrew – and most of them were wearing skullcaps. Looking into the car with inquisitive stares, they started yelling in English: "Who are you? What are you doing here?" One of the giants banged on my window and shouted: "Open your window! Passport!" As though reinforcing his request, he loaded a bullet into the breech of his rifle. I slowly wound down the window and handed over my papers. Keeping his gun on me, he snatched them and gave them to one of his followers. My papers were then handed round the group. Suddenly the harsh, fragile tones of a woman's voice intervened. The group made way for her. Sarah appeared, elbowing her way through the hulks. She screamed at them and pushed them aside, slapping their weapons, with a volley of cries, insults and grunts. She grabbed my passport and, still yelling at my attackers, returned it to me at once. Finally, the men backed away, cursing and dragging their heels. Sarah turned towards me and said, in French:

"Everybody's a bit nervy here. A week ago, four Arabs killed three of our men in a military camp near the kibbutz. They stuck garden forks into them while they were asleep. Can I get in?"

We drove for ten minutes. There were more dark fishponds, concealed among the high grasses as green as paddy fields. We then reached the edge of another valley and I had to rub my eyes to make them believe what they were seeing.

Marshland, entirely covered with storks, stretched as far as the eye could see. Everywhere, the whiteness of their plumage. Everywhere, their pointed bills were busy dipping up and down. There were tens of thousands of them. The trees groaned under their weight. The waters were invisible beneath their drenched bodies, their diving necks and their seething activity, as each bird fed hungrily. Half flying, half paddling, the storks caught the fish in their sharpened bills swiftly and precisely. They did not look like the birds from Alsace. They were dark and emaciated. There was no question of them smoothing down their feathers or carefully preparing the contours of their nests. Their only concern now was to reach Africa in good time. On a scientific level, I had stumbled across a discovery, because certain European ornithologists had told me that storks never fished, and ate only meat.

The car was beginning to get bogged down in the ruts. We got out. Sarah said simply:

"This is the stork kibbutz. Each day, thousands of them arrive here. They are building up their strength before confronting the Negev desert."

Through my binoculars I took a long look at them. It was impossible to see if any of them were ringed. Above us, I heard a sustained, heady swoosh. I looked up. Without any break, entire flocks were passing at low altitude. Each stork, as though propped up in the azure, was following its path along the thermals. We were at the heart of the storks' kingdom. We sat down on a hollow patch of dry grass. Sarah wrapped her arms round her bent legs, then leant her chin on her knees. She was less pretty than I had thought. Her face was too hard, dried by the sun. Her cheekbones jutted out like pebbles. But her stare was that of a bird, and it fluttered into my heart.

"Each evening," Sarah went on, "Iddo would come here. He set off on foot and crossed the marshes. He would pick up the injured or exhausted storks then either take care of them here, or else take them home. He had turned the garage into a sort of bird clinic."

"All the storks pass by here?"

"All of them, without exception. They've altered their path so as to feed from the fishponds."

"Last spring, did Iddo mention anything about storks disappearing?"

"What do you mean?"

"This year, when they came back from Africa, there were fewer of them than usual. Iddo must have noticed that."

"He didn't mention it to me."

I wondered if Iddo, like Rajko, had kept records. And whether he, too, had worked for Max Böhm.

"Your French is excellent."

"My grandparents were born in your country. After the war, they didn't want to go back to France. They were the founders of the Beyt Shean kibbutzim."

"It's a magnificent region."

"That depends. I've always lived here, except when I was a student in Tel Aviv. I speak Hebrew, French and English. I got my master's degree in physics in 1987. And all that to end up in this shit-heap, getting up at three in the morning to splash around in smelly water six days a week."

"You'd like to leave?"

"What with? This is a community system we have here. Everybody earns the same money, precisely nothing."

Sarah looked up at the birds as they flew through the reddening sky, her hand sheltering her eyes from the last gleams of the sun. In that light, her eyes glistened like water at the bottom of a well.

"The stork is part of our ancient traditions. In the Bible, Jeremiah encourage the people to leave, by saying:

> Everyone turned to his course,
> as the horse rusheth into battle.
> Yea, the stork in the heaven
> knoweth her appointed times;
> and the turtle and the crane and the swallow
> observe the time of their coming."

"What does that all mean?"

Still scrutinizing the birds, Sarah shrugged.

"It means that I, too, am waiting for my time to come."

CHAPTER 17

We had a delicious dinner. Sarah had invited me back for the evening. My mind emptied, rocked by the sweetness of this unexpected moment.

We ate in the garden of her house, gazing at the red and pink streamers of the sunset. She kept offering me more pittas, each one opening to reveal fresh delicacies. My mouth full, I accepted each time. I was famished, and the Israeli diet suited me down to the ground. Meat was extremely expensive, so people generally ate dairy products and vegetables. What is more, Sarah had made me some pure, scented Chinese tea.

Sarah was twenty-eight, with violent ideas and the gestures of an elf. She spoke to me about Israel. The softness of her voice contrasted with her disgust. The dream of the Promised Land meant nothing to Sarah. She criticized the excesses of the Jewish people, its hunger for more land, justified by laws, which led to so much injustice, so much violence in that war-torn country. She told me about the atrocities committed by each side. The broken limbs of the Arabs, the stabbing of Israeli children, the clashes with the Intifada. She also painted a strange portrait of Israel. According to her, the Hebrew state was in fact a war laboratory, always in advance with its spying methods, technological weapons and means of oppression.

She told me about her life in the kibbutz, with its hard labour, its communal meals, its Saturday evening meetings where decisions were made that "concerned one and all". That totally shared existence, where each succeeding day was increasingly similar. She mentioned the jealousy, the boredom and insidious hypocrisy of community life. Sarah was sick with loneliness.

However, she also insisted on how efficient kibbutz farming was, mentioning her grandparents, those Sephardic pioneers who had founded the first communities after the Second World War. She spoke of her parents' courage and of how, in their fervent determination, they had worked themselves to death. At times like that, she talked as though the Jewess in her was struggling with the woman in her; ideals confronting individuality. And her long hands gesticulated wildly in the evening air, emphasizing the ideas that were seething in her mind.

Later, she asked me about my activities, my past, my life in Paris. I summed up my long years of study, then explained that I was now going to concentrate on ornithology. I recounted my travels and reaffirmed my wish to see the storks as they passed over Israel. She did not find this obsession surprising. The Beyt Shean kibbutzim attracted numerous birdwatchers from all over Europe and the United States. They stayed there during the migration periods and spent all day observing those inaccessible flights through binoculars, telescopes and zoom lenses.

Eleven o'clock chimed. I at last risked mentioning Iddo's death. Sarah looked at me icily, then said in a neutral tone of voice:

"Iddo was killed four months ago. He was murdered while he was out nursing the storks in the marshes. Some Arabs jumped him. They tied him to a tree, then tortured him. They beat his face with stones until they smashed his jaws. His throat was full of scraps of bone and teeth. They also broke his fingers and ankles. They undressed him and flayed him with a sheep shearer. When his body was found, the only skin left on him was his face, which looked like an ill-fitting mask. His guts had spilt down to his feet. The birds had started to devour his body."

The night was completely still.

"You say it was Arabs. Were they caught?"

"We think it was the four Arabs I mentioned earlier. The ones that killed the soldiers."

"Have they been arrested?"

"They're dead. On our territory, we settle our own scores."

"Do Arabs often attack civilians?"

"Not in this region. Or only if they're active militants, like the settlers you saw this evening."

"Was Iddo a militant?"

"Not at all. All the same, he had changed recently. He'd got hold of some weapons, assault rifles, hand guns and, strangest of all, silencers. He used to go off armed and would vanish for days on end. He'd stopped going to the ponds. He had become violent and irritable. One moment he was jubilant, then the next he would stay silent for hours."

"Did Iddo like kibbutz life?"

Sarah laughed bitterly.

"Iddo wasn't like me, Louis. He loved the fish and the ponds. He loved the marshes and the storks. He loved coming home at night, covered in mud, and locking himself up in his clinic with a few featherless birds." Sarah gave another joyless laugh. "But above all he loved me. And he was looking for a way to get us out of this fucking shit-hole."

Sarah paused, shrugged, then started gathering up the plates and cutlery.

"In fact," she went on, "I don't think Iddo ever would have left. He was truly happy here. With the sky, the storks, and then me. In his opinion, this was the best thing about the kibbutz – he had me to himself."

"What do you mean?"

"What I said. He had me to himself."

With her hands full, Sarah went back into the house. I helped her clear the table. While she was finishing tidying up the kitchen, I strolled into the living-room. Sarah's house was small and white. From what I could see, there was this large room, and then, along a corridor, two bedrooms. One for Sarah, one for Iddo. On a table, I saw a photograph of a young man with broad shoulders. His sun-tanned face was lively, and his features were brimming with health and sweetness. Iddo looked like Sarah. The same eyebrows, same cheekbones but, while his sister was thin and built on tension, Iddo appeared full of vitality. In the photo he looked younger than Sarah, maybe twenty-two or twenty-three years old.

Sarah came out of the kitchen. We went back to the terrace. She opened a little metal box that she had brought with her.

"Do you smoke?"

"Cigarettes?"

"No, grass."

"No, never."

"That doesn't surprise me. You're a strange guy, Louis."

"But don't let me stop you, if you want."

"It's only worth it if it's shared," Sarah pronounced, closing the box.

She fell silent, then glanced at me for a moment.

"Now, Louis, you're going to explain what you're really doing here. You don't look like a birdwatcher to me. I know their sort. They're crazy about birds, and that's all they ever talk about, with their heads up in the clouds. You know nothing about the subject, except for storks. And you have the eyes of someone who is as much pursued as the pursuer. Who are you, Louis? A cop? A journalist? We don't trust goys around here. (She lowered her voice.) But I'm ready to help you. Tell me what you're looking for."

I thought for a couple of seconds then, with no hesitation, told her everything. What did I have to lose? Opening my heart was a relief. I explained the strange mission that Max Böhm had sent me on, just before he died. I spoke to her about the storks and that sublimely pure pursuit through the winds and the sky, which had abruptly become a nightmare. I told her about my last forty-eight hours in Bulgaria. I described the death of Rajko Nicolich. How Marcel, Yeta and presumably a little child had been killed. Then, how I had slit a stranger's throat with a shard of broken glass in a warehouse. I declared my intention to search out the other bastard, and those who were behind him. Finally, I mentioned One World, Dumaz, Djuric and Joro. The high-frequency lancet, the theft of Rajko's heart, Max Böhm's mysterious transplant. Everything became mixed up in my mind.

"It may sound odd," I concluded, "but I'm sure that the key to this whole affair lies with the storks. Right from the start, I sensed that Böhm had another motive for finding his storks. And murders are now happening all along their route."

"Does my brother's death have anything to do with all this?"

"Maybe. I'll have to find out more about it."

"The Shin-bet have the file. There's no chance you'll be able to see it."

"What about the people who found the body?"

"They won't tell you anything."

"I'm sorry to ask, Sarah, but did you see the body?"

"No, I didn't."

"Do you know . . ." I hesitated for a second, ". . . do you know if there were any organs missing?"

"What do you mean?"

"Was the interior of his thorax intact?"

Sarah's face clouded over.

"Most of his innards had been gobbled up by the birds. That's all I know. His body was discovered at dawn. On the 16th of May."

I stood up and paced round the garden. Iddo's death was certainly another link in the chain, another addition to the horror. But, more than ever, I was in the dark. Totally in the dark.

"I don't understand what you're on about, Louis, but there are things I can tell you."

I sat down again and removed my notebook from my pocket.

"To begin with, Iddo had discovered something. I don't know what exactly, but on several occasions he told me that we were going to be rich and so be able to leave for Europe. At the beginning I paid no attention. I thought he was making it up to please me."

"When did this start?"

"At the beginning of March, I think. One evening, he came home completely overexcited. He took me in his arms and told me I could pack my bags. I spat in his face. I don't like to be made fun of."

"Where had he been?"

Sarah shrugged.

"In the marshes, as usual."

"Did Iddo leave any papers, or notes?"

"Everything is in his den at the back of the garden. One other thing. One World has a strong presence here. They cooperate with the United Nations and work in the Palestinian camps."

"What do they do there?"

"They look after Arab kids, hand out food and medicine. That organization has an excellent reputation in Israel. It's one of the few that people are unanimous in supporting."

I jotted down each detail. With her head to one side, Sarah was staring at me again.

"Louis, why are you doing this? Why don't you go to the police?"

"Which police? In which country? And for what crime? I have no proof. Anyway, one cop is already working on the case. Hervé Dumaz. He's a strange guy, and I've never been able to work out his real motivations. But in the field, I am alone. Alone and determined."

Suddenly, before I had had time to avoid it, Sarah took my hands. I felt nothing. Neither disgust, nor apprehension. No more than I felt the softness of her fingers on my dead tissue. She undid the bandages and gazed at my long scars. A strange, perverse smile crossed her face, then she stared hard at me, her eyes gliding under our thoughts. The time for words was over.

CHAPTER 18

We were wrapped up in darkness, but everything suddenly became drenched in sunlight. There was something harsh, brutal and intransigent in our jolting movements. Our kisses were long, tormented and passionate. Sarah's body was almost a man's. No breasts. Almost no hips. Long muscles, as taut as cables. Our mouths remained silent, concentrated on breathing. My tongue explored every corner of her body. I did not use my hands, which felt more dead than ever. I crawled, turned, advanced in a spiral until I reached her centre, which was burning like a crater. At that moment, I rose up and entered her. Sarah squirmed. She roared softly and seized my shoulders. I stayed bolt upright. Sarah beat my torso, accentuating the movement of our hips. This had nothing to do with sweetness and care. We were two wild beasts, locked together in a kiss of death. Nervy shocks, moments of absence. Cliffs where you graze your fingertips. Kisses murdering each other. As my eyes blinked, I saw her blond locks, soaked with sweat, the folds of the sheets, torn by our nails, the twisting of veins swelling our flesh. Suddenly, Sarah murmured something in Hebrew. A groan rose up from her throat, then an icy blast erupted from my belly. We stayed like that, motionless. As though dazzled by the night, astonished at the violence of what we had done. There had been neither pleasure, nor sharing. Just a solitary relief that was bestial and selfish. Two beings grappling with their own flesh. I did not feel bitter about this emptiness. Our sensual war would no doubt become calmer and more tempered, would finally turn into unison. But that would take time. Some night. Some other night. Then love would become pleasure. An hour passed. The first light of dawn appeared. Sarah's voice returned.

"Tell me about your hands, Louis."

Could I lie to Sarah after what had just happened? Our faces were still plunged in the shadows. For the first time, I was going to be able to recount that tragedy, without fear or shame.

"I was born in Africa. In Niger, or Mali. I don't know exactly. My parents emigrated to Black Africa in the 1950s. My father was a doctor. He treated the local inhabitants. In 1963, Paul and Marthe Antioch moved to the Central African Republic. One of that continent's most remote countries. There, they resolutely continued their work. My elder brother and I were growing up, dividing our time between air-conditioned classrooms and the heat of the bush.

"At that time, the Central African Republic was governed by David Dacko who, amidst great public rejoicing, had been sworn in by André Malraux himself. The situation was neither brilliant, nor catastrophic. The inhabitants certainly did not want a change of government. But, in 1965, Colonel Jean-Bedel Bokassa decided that nothing was going to be the same again.

"He was then merely an obscure soldier, but he was the Central African Republic's only officer, a member of the President's family and one of the Mbaka tribe. Naturally enough, he was given command of the army, which consisted of just one small battalion of infantry. Once he had been made head of the Republic's armed forces, Bokassa began to become more powerful. During official parades, he would push his way to the front, tread on Dacko's toes and puff out his bemedalled chest in front of the ministers. He publicly proclaimed that power was rightfully his and that he was older than the President. Nobody took any notice, because they all underestimated his intelligence. He was thought to be just a vindictive drunk. However, at the end of 1965, with the help of Lieutenant Banza – who had become his blood brother – Bokassa decided to act. On New Year's Eve, to be precise.

"On the 31st of December, at three in the afternoon, he assembled the few hundred men that made up his battalion and told them that an exercise had been planned for that very evening. The men were rather surprised. After all, going on manoeuvres on New Year's Eve did seem a strange idea. Bokassa brushed aside their protests. At seven o'clock, the troops from the Kassai camp formed up. Some of them discovered that the ammunition cases contained real bullets and demanded an explanation. Banza pressed his pistol to their heads and told them to shut up. They got ready. In Bangui, the festivities were starting.

"Picture the scene, Sarah. In that poorly lit town of red clay, full of ghost-like buildings, music rose up and alcohol began to flow. The President's allies in the police headquarters suspected nothing. They danced, drank, had fun. At half past eight, Bokassa and Banza led Henri Izamo, the chief of the brigade, into a trap. He was summoned alone to Roux camp, another strategic point. Bokassa welcomed him effusively and explained his planned putsch. He was trembling with excitement. Izamo didn't understand what he was talking about and abruptly burst out laughing. Banza at once slit his throat with a sword. The two accomplices then handcuffed him and dragged him down to the cellar. The tension was rising. They now had to find David Dacko.

"The column of soldiers set off in forty camouflaged trucks, full of uneasy men who were only now beginning to catch on. At the head of that macabre parade, Bokassa and Banza lorded it in a white Peugeot 404. That evening, it rained on the red earth. A light seasonal shower, which is known as the 'mango rain', because people say that it allows that succulent fruit to grow. On the way, the trucks ran into Commandant Sana, another one of Dacko's allies, who was taking his parents home. Sana was petrified. 'This time, it's a coup d'état,' he thought. When they reached the Palais de la Renaissance, the Colonel looked for the President in vain. Dacko was nowhere to be found. Bokassa became worried. He nervously ran about screaming, ordering his men to see if there were any cellars or hiding places. Then they moved on again. This time, the troops went to different strategic points: Radio Bangui, the prison, ministers' residences, and so on.

"In the city there was total chaos. The pleasantly tipsy men and women heard the first gunshots. They panicked. Everyone ran to take shelter. The main streets were blocked. The first victims fell. Bokassa went crazy, hitting his prisoners and bawling out his men while staying hidden in Roux camp. He was scared to death. His plan might still fail. He had not captured Dacko, or his more dangerous counsellors.

"Meanwhile, the President had no idea what was going on. When he was returning to Bangui at one in the morning, he came across some terrified groups of people, who announced the news of the coup d'état and of his own death. Half an hour later, he was arrested. As soon as he saw him, Bokassa ran into his arms, kissed him and said: 'I did warn you. It was time for a change.'

"The battalion moved on at once, this time to Ngaragba Prison. Bokassa woke up the governor who, thinking this was a Congolese offensive, met him with grenades in his hands. Bokassa ordered him to open the prison gates and release all the prisoners. The governor refused. Banza then pointed his gun at him, and the governor noticed that Dacko was in the back of the car, with a rifle held against his neck. 'This is a coup d'état,' Bokassa murmured. 'I need to free them, for my own popularity. Understand?' The governor obeyed. Thieves, con-men and murderers flooded out into the town, yelling: 'Glory to Bokassa!' Among them was a group of particularly dangerous killers. Men from the Kara tribe, who were due to be executed in a few days' time. Blood-thirsty murderers. These were the people who knocked on the door of our house, on Avenue de France, at about two in the morning.

"Our drowsy steward went to the door with a gun in his hand. But those madmen had already broken it down. They overcame Mohamed and disarmed him. The Karas then undressed him and pinned him to the floor. Beating him with sticks and pistol-whipping him, they smashed his nose, his jaws and his ribs. His wife Azzora ran up to discover this scene. Her children also appeared. She pushed them away. Mohamed's body slumped down into a pool of blood, then the men's fury reached fever-pitch. They hacked at him with picks and axes. Not once did Mohamed cry out. Not once did he beg their mercy. Making the most of their frenzy, Azzora tried to escape with the children. The family hid in a half-submerged concrete shaft. The man who had taken Mohamed's gun followed them down there. The gunshots barely echoed in that water-logged conduit. When the murderer re-emerged, his crazed features were awash with a mixture of rain and blood. A few seconds later, the tiny bodies of the children floated out after him, then Azzora herself, who was pregnant.

"How long had my father been watching this scene? He rushed into the house and loaded his gun, a large-calibre Mauser. He positioned himself behind a window and waited for the assailants to arrive. My mother woke up and, still slightly groggy from the New Year's champagne, went up to our bedrooms. But the house was already burning. The men had broken in through the back door, ransacked each room, knocking over the furniture and the lamps, and thus starting a fire in their madness.

"There is no official version of the massacre of my family. It is thought that my father was shot dead with his own gun, at point-blank range. My mother was presumably attacked at the top of the staircase. She must have been hacked to death with axes, just a few yards from our bedrooms. Her charred limbs were found scattered about in the cinders. As for my brother, who was two years older than me, he died in the flames, a prisoner of his blazing mosquito net. Most of our attackers perished too, surprised by the violence of the fire they had set off.

"I don't know by what miracle I survived. My hands were on fire and I ran, screaming and stumbling through the rain. Finally I passed out by the gates of the French embassy, where my parents' friends Nelly and Georges Braesler lived. As soon as they found me, had grasped the horror of that genocide and realized that Colonel Bokassa had seized power, they went to Bangui airport and left in a biplane belonging to the French air force. We took off in a thunderstorm, leaving the Central African Republic to the madness of one man.

"For several days, nothing much was said about this 'incident'. The French government was rather embarrassed by the turn of events. Totally unprepared, they ended up recognizing the new regime. Reports were made concerning the victims of the New Year massacre. Little Louis Antioch was given a handsome state pension. As for the Braeslers, they moved heaven and earth in the attempt to see that justice was done. But what sort of justice was possible? The murderers were already dead and the person principally responsible had become the Central African Republic's head of state."

My words lingered in the silence of the dawn. Sarah murmured: "I'm sorry."

"Don't be, Sarah. I was six. I can't remember anything about it. It's a long white void in my existence. Anyway, who can remember much about their first five years? All I know is what the Braeslers told me."

Our bodies interlaced once more. In shades of pink, red and mauve, the dawn sweetened our violence and rage. But pleasure still did not come. We said nothing. Words can do nothing for bodies.

Later, delightfully naked, Sarah sat down in front of me and took hold of my hands. She scrutinized my superficial wounds, running her fingers along the still-pink scars from that warehouse of broken glass.

"Do your hands hurt?"

"Not a bit. They're completely insensitive."

114

She stroked them again.

"You're my first goy, Louis."

"I could always convert."

Still feeling my palms, Sarah shrugged.

"No, no you couldn't."

"A little snip with the scissors in the right place and . . . "

"You could never be an Israeli citizen."

"Why not?"

Grimacing, Sarah released my hands and looked out the window.

"You're nobody Louis. You don't have any fingerprints."

CHAPTER 19

The next day I woke up late. I forced my eyes open and fixed them on Sarah's bedroom, with its white sun-splashed walls, the small wooden chest of drawers, pinned-up posters of Einstein sticking his tongue out and Stephen Hawking in his wheelchair. Paperbacks were piled up on the floor. The bedroom of a lonely girl.

I looked at my watch. It was 11.20 a.m. on 4 September. Sarah had already gone to the fishponds. I got up and had a shower. In the mirror hung above the basin I took a long look at my face. My features had become drawn. My forehead was gleaming dully and my eyes, under their weary lids, still had their playful blueness. It was perhaps only an impression, but it seemed to me that I had aged, and acquired an expression of cruelty. A few minutes later, I had shaved and dressed. In the kitchen, I found a note from Sarah stuck under the tea caddy.

Louis,

The fish won't wait. I'll be back at the end of the day. Make yourself at home with the tea, telephone and washing machine.

Take care of yourself and wait for me.

Have a nice day, little goy,

Sarah

I made some tea, then sipped it while gazing out of the window at the Promised Land. The countryside facing me was a strange mixture of aridness and fertility, of dry patches and verdant expanses. In that intense light, the glinting surfaces of the fishponds were scratches in the earth.

I took the teapot and went to sit outside under the trees. I pulled the telephone over to me and dialled my answering machine. It was a bad line, but I managed to catch my messages. Dumaz was desperate for my news. Wagner impatiently wanted me to call him back. The third call was the most surprising. It was Nelly Braesler. She was worried about me. "My little Louis, it's Nelly. Your call has made me fret terribly. Whatever are you doing? Please call me back."

I dialled Hervé Dumaz's number at the Montreux police station. It was 9 a.m., local time. After several unsuccessful attempts, I was finally put through to the inspector.

"Dumaz? It's Antioch here."

"At last. Where are you? In Istanbul?"

"I didn't have time to stop in Turkey. I'm in Israel. Can I talk?"

"Of course."

"I mean, is anybody listening to our conversation?"

Dumaz gave one of his weak chuckles.

"What's happening?"

"Someone tried to kill me."

I could almost hear Dumaz's face disintegrating.

"How?"

"Two men. Four days ago in the train station in Sofia. They had assault rifles and night vision devices."

"How did you escape?"

"Miraculously. But three innocent people were killed."

Dumaz remained silent, so I added:

"I killed one of the hitmen, Hervé. Then I drove to Istanbul and took a ferry to Israel."

"So what have you found out?"

"I've no idea. But the storks are definitely central to the whole business. First of all there was Rajko Nicolich, an ornithologist who was brutally murdered. Then they tried to kill me, even though I was only investigating birds. And now there's a third victim. I've just learnt that an Israeli ornithologist was murdered four months ago. It's part of the same series. I'm sure of that. Like Rajko, Iddo had discovered something."

"Who were the hitmen that attacked you?"

"Perhaps the two Bulgarians who questioned Joro Grybinski in April."

"What are you going to do?"

"Continue."

Dumaz panicked.

"What do you mean 'continue'? You must contact the Israeli police, and tell Interpol!"

"Definitely not. Here, Iddo's murder is a closed case. In Sofia, nobody is interested in Rajko's death. There will be a bit more of a stink about Marcel, because he was French. But it's all part of the overall chaos. No proof. A tangle of details. It's too early to go to any international body. My only chance is to keep on going alone."

The inspector sighed.

"Are you armed?"

"No. But here in Israel, it isn't very difficult to procure that sort of equipment."

Dumaz said nothing. I could hear him panting.

"What about you? Anything new?"

"Nothing solid. I'm still digging into Böhm's past. For the moment, the only link I can see are the diamond mines. First in South Africa, then in the Central African Republic. So I'll keep looking. None of the other leads has turned up anything of interest."

"What have you found out about One World?"

"Nothing. One World is irreproachable. Its management is transparent, and its actions efficient and universally acclaimed."

"When was it set up?"

"One World was founded at the end of the 1970s by Pierre Doisneau, a French doctor practising in Calcutta in the north of India. He was treating outcasts, sick children and lepers, and he decided to get organized. He set up open clinics on the pavements, and these became highly important. Doisneau began to be talked about. His reputation spread. Other Western doctors came to help him, he was allotted funding which allowed thousands of men and women to be treated."

"And then?"

"Then Pierre Doisneau founded One World and, after that, the 1001 Club, which consists of about 1,001 members – companies, VIPs etc – who each contributed ten thousand dollars. The entire sum, over ten million dollars, was then invested so that each year it generates a large income."

"What was the idea?"

"The interest is enough to finance One World's administrative costs. In that way, the organization can guarantee its contributors that their money will go directly to where it's needed and not to pay for some luxurious suite of offices. This transparency has greatly contributed to OW's success. Today, it has health care centres all over the world. OW is at the head of a positive humanitarian army. It's a reference in the field."

Interference crackled over the line.

"Could you get me a list of their centres throughout the world?"

"Of course, but I don't see what . . . "

"And a list of the members of the club?"

"You're barking up the wrong tree, Louis. Pierre Doisneau is a celebrity. He almost got the Nobel Peace Prize last year and . . . "

"Can you, or can't you?"

"I'll try."

Another outburst of crackling.

"I'm counting on you, Hervé. I'll call you back tomorrow, or the next day."

"Where can I contact you?"

"I'll call you."

Dumaz sounded out of his depth. I hung up and dialled Wagner's number. He was pleased to hear from me.

"Where are you?" he exclaimed.

"In Israel."

"Excellent. Have you seen the storks?"

"I'm waiting for them here. I'm right on their path, at Beyt Shean."

"At the fishpools?"

"Exactly."

"Did you see them in Bulgaria, and over the Bosporus?"

"I'm not sure. But I certainly saw some storks over the straits. It was magnificent. Ulrich, I can't stay on for long. Do you have the new positions?"

"I have them here right in front of me."

"Go on."

"The largest group is in front. They passed Damascus yesterday and are heading for Beyt Shean. I think you'll see them tomorrow."

Ulrich then gave me their positions. I noted them down on my map.

"What about the west route?"

"The west? Hang on a moment . . . The quickest ones are now crossing the Sahara. They'll soon be in Mali, in the Niger delta."

I also jotted down this information.

"Very good," I said in conclusion. "I'll call you back in two days."

"Where are you exactly, Louis? We could maybe send you a fax. We've started doing some statistical analysis and . . ."

"Sorry, Ulrich. There's no fax here."

"You sound odd. Are you all right?"

"I'm fine, Ulrich. It was nice talking to you."

Finally, I rang Yossé Lenfeld, the director of the Nature Protection Society. Yossé spoke English with such a gravelly accent and shouted so loudly that the receiver trembled in my hand. I sensed that this ornithologist was yet another 'character'. We made an appointment for 8.30 the next morning at Ben-Gurion Airport.

I stood up, nibbled at a few pittas in the kitchen, and then went to explore Iddo's den in the garden. He had not left any notes, statistics or any other information. Just the same sort of dressings and instruments that I had found in Böhm's study.

On the other hand, I did find the washing machine. While my entire wardrobe was spinning in the drum, I continued to search. All I found was some more old dressings, with feathers stuck to them. This was obviously not going to be a productive day. But right there and then, all I wanted to do was see Sarah.

An hour later, I was hanging out my washing in the sun, when she appeared between two shirts.

"Finished work?"

In reply, Sarah winked and took me by the arm.

CHAPTER 20

Through the window, the sun was gently setting. Sarah rolled away from me. Sweat glistened on her body. She was staring at the fan, which was limping round on the ceiling above us. Her body was long and firm, her dark skin burnt and dry. At each gesture, her muscles rippled like hunted beasts, ready to attack.

"Do you want some tea?"

"I'd love some," I replied.

Sarah got up and went to the kitchen. Her limbs were slightly bowed. I began to become aroused again. My desire for Sarah was inexhaustible. Two hours of love-making had done nothing to appease me. It was not a question of pleasure or of orgasms, but a bodily alchemy, attraction and arousal, as though we were made to burn for each other. And forever.

Sarah returned carrying a small copper tray with a metal teapot, two small cups and some biscuits. She sat down on the edge of the bed and poured the tea out in Oriental fashion – raising the pot high up above the cups.

"Louis," she said, "I've been thinking. I reckon you've got it all wrong."

"What do you mean?"

"The birds, their migration, the ornithologists. This is about murder. And no one kills for a few birds."

I had already been told that. I replied:

"There's only one common factor in all this business, Sarah. The storks. I don't know where they are leading me. Nor do I know why this path has become scattered with corpses. But there must be some logic behind this multinational violence."

"There's money behind it all. Some illegal business between the various countries."

"Definitely," I replied. "Max Böhm was involved in some shady dealings."

"What sort?"

"I don't know yet. Diamonds maybe? Ivory? Gold? The riches of Africa, in any case. Dumaz, the Swiss inspector who's investigating this affair, is convinced that it was gemstones. I think he's right. Böhm was incapable of smuggling ivory. He was violently opposed to the slaughtering of elephants in the Central African Republic. As for gold, there isn't that much of it on the storks' path. So we come back to diamonds, in the Central African Republic, and in South Africa. Max Böhm was an engineer and used to work in that field. But the whole thing still remains a mystery. He retired in 1977. He never returned to Africa. All he did was look after his storks. I really don't get it, Sarah."

Sarah lit a cigarette and shrugged.

"I'm sure you have an idea."

I smiled.

"You're right. I think this smuggling is still going on and the storks are the couriers. Or messengers, if you prefer. Like homing pigeons. They carry their messages in their rings."

"What rings?"

"In Europe, ornithologists put rings on the birds' legs, indicating their date and place of birth or, in the case of wild birds, when and where they were captured. I think that the rings on Böhm's birds have a tale to tell."

"What?"

"Something that it's worth killing for. Rajko found the answer. Your brother, too, I think. Iddo must also have deciphered the meaning of the messages. Which explains why he was so excited and thought he was going to be rich."

A light flickered across Sarah's eyes. She exhaled some more smoke, but said nothing. For a moment, I thought that she'd forgotten all about me. Then she stood up.

"Right now, Louis, your problems are not up in the sky. So come down to earth. If you keep your head in the clouds like that, you're going to end up getting shot down like a jackal."

She slipped on her jeans and T-shirt.

"Come with me."

Outside, the sun was receding. On the horizon, the hills were shimmering in the cool air. Sarah crossed the garden then stopped halfway between the house and the shed. She pushed aside the branches of an olive tree and swept away the dust. A plastic sheet appeared. She grabbed it and told me to help her. We pulled away the material, to reveal a trap-door. I must have walked past the spot a dozen times that day. Sarah lifted it. There was a veritable arsenal inside – assault rifles, hand guns and boxes of ammunition. "The Gabbor family's reserve." Sarah explained. "We've always had weapons, but Iddo got some more. Assault rifles with silencers." She knelt down and pulled out an old dusty golf bag. She brushed it down then loaded it with guns and ammunition. "Come on," she said.

We took my car and crossed the fishponds. Half an hour later we reached a desert dotted with black rocks and scrawny vegetation. We marched through piles of litter and household waste; rank smells floated in the wind. It was the kibbutzim's rubbish tip. A clicking noise made me turn round. Sarah was kneeling down and examining the guns laid out before her.

She smiled and began:

"These two assault rifles are Israeli weapons. An Uzi machine-gun and a Galil model. Classics. There's no better equipment in the world. They're streets ahead of Kalashnikovs and your M16s." Sarah took out a box of ammunition and showed me some long, pointed shells. "These guns use .22 ammo, like traditional .22 long rifle hunting guns. But the bullets contain more powder and have full-metal jackets." She slid a curved magazine into the Galil and showed me its side. "Here, you have two positions. Normal or automatic. On automatic you can fire off fifty bullets in a few seconds." Sarah pretended to spray the surrounding space, then put the Galil down again.

"Now let's look at the hand guns. The two monsters you can see there are the biggest calibre automatics on the market – a 357 Magnum and a 44 Magnum." She picked up the silvery gun and fitted a magazine into its ivory-covered grip. The gun was almost as long as her forearm. "The 44 fires sixteen Magnum rounds. It's the most powerful hand gun in the world. With it, you can stop a car that's going at seventy miles an hour." She effortlessly straightened her arm and aimed at some imaginary point. Her strength astonished me. "The problem is that it jams all the time."

"The guns you can see here are much easier to use. The 9mm Beretta is the automatic pistol most American policemen use." She ejected the magazine from that black, perfectly proportioned gun, which seemed to fit the hand perfectly. "Over there, this Italian piece has supplanted the good old .38 Smith and Wesson. It's a reference. Accurate, light and rapid. The .38 fired six rounds, the Beretta fires sixteen." She kissed the grip. "It's a real companion in arms. But these are even better – the Glock 17 and the Glock 21, made in Austria. These are the guns of the future, which will probably supplant the Beretta." She picked up a gun which looked like an ill-made, badly finished Beretta. "It's seventy per cent polymer. Incredibly light." She gave it to me to weigh up. It was no heavier than a handful of feathers. "A phosphorescent sight for shooting at night, a trigger which is totally secure and a sixteen-round magazine. Aesthetes criticize it because it's far from beautiful. But in my opinion, this 'toy' is the best thing on the market. The Glock 17 uses 9mm parabellum, the 21 fires 45mm. The 21 is less accurate, but with cartridges like these you stop your target wherever you hit it."

Sarah gave me a handful of heavy, squat, threatening bullets.

"These two Glocks are mine," she went on. "I'll give you the 21. But be careful. The trigger was especially adjusted to my index finger. It'll be too supple for you."

I looked at the gun incredulously, then stared up at her.

"How do you know all that, Sarah?"

Another grin.

"We're at war, Louis. Don't forget that. In case of an alert at the fishponds, we each have twenty minutes to reach a secret meeting point. Everybody who works in a kibbutz is a virtual soldier. We've all been trained and conditioned and are ready to fight. At the beginning of this year, there were still Scuds whistling over our heads." She picked up the 9mm, pressed it to her ear, then loaded a bullet into its breech. "But you shouldn't keep gawping at me like that. Right now, I'm sure you're in more danger than the whole of Israel put together."

I gritted my teeth, grabbed the Glock, then asked:

"The hitmen who attacked me in Bulgaria had pretty sophisticated equipment. An assault rifle, a laser sight and night vision devices. What do you reckon about that?"

"Nothing. There's nothing very sophisticated about any of that. All the armies of the industrialized world have that kind of thing."

"You mean, the two hitmen might have been soldiers in mufti?"

"Soldiers, or mercenaries."

Sarah walked away through the dust to set up some improvised targets. Lumps of plastic hanging off shrubs, tin cans positioned on roots. Bending under the wind, she came back to teach me the rudiments of marksmanship.

"Brace your legs," she said. "Arm taut, index placed laterally along the barrel. You look through the notch in the sight. Each time you fire, you take the recoil with your wrist, backwards and forwards. And above all not with your arm in the air, as you would naturally do. If you do, the rear end of the barrel will touch your wrist, and you'll end up jamming your gun. Got all that, little goy?"

I nodded and adopted the position Sarah had showed me.

"Okay, Sarah, I'm ready."

She stretched out her arms, gripped her gun, took off the safety catch, waited a few seconds and then yelled: "Go on!"

A din of battle broke out. Sarah shot incredibly well. Even I hit a few targets. Silence returned, laden with a smell of cordite. Thirty-two rounds had been emptied into the evening air.

"Reload!" Sarah shouted. The used magazines were ejected in unison and we started again. Another volley. More tin cans sent reeling. "Reload!" Sarah repeated. Everything accelerated. The bullets being pushed onto the spring in the magazine, the click of the breech as it was loaded, the aim through the sight. We emptied one, two, three, four magazines like this. The cartridge cases flew up into our faces. I couldn't hear anything. My Glock was smoking and I realized that it was red-hot, but my numb hands allowed me to keep on firing unaffected by the heat.

"Reload!" Sarah screamed. Each sensation became a hidden delight. The weapon that kicked, jumped and sprang in my hands. The thunderous noise, which was at once brief, all-embracing and deafening. The compact bluish fire full of acrid smoke. And the terrifying, unreal damage that our guns were causing a hundred yards or so away.

"Reload!" Sarah was trembling all over. She fumbled with her cartridges. Her horizon was a devastated battlefield. I was suddenly filled with a terrible feeling of tenderness for that young woman. I lowered my gun and walked towards her. She seemed more alone than ever, drunk on violence, lost in the smoke from the empty cartridge cases.

Then, suddenly, three storks passed above us. I saw them, pale and beautiful in the dusk. I saw Sarah turn round, her eyes shining, her hair flapping in the wind. And I understood. She immediately slipped a magazine into her Glock, loaded the breech and aimed at the sky. Three shots rang out, followed by perfect silence. As though in slow motion, I saw the birds being blown to pieces, floating in the air, then flopping down in the distance with a discreetly sad crash. I stared at Sarah, but could say nothing. She returned my stare then, throwing her head back, she burst out laughing. Her laughter was too strong, too serious, too terrifying.

"The rings!" I ran over to the dead birds. A hundred yards away, I found their bodies. The sand had already drunk their blood. I looked at their legs. They were not wearing rings. They were just another set of anonymous birds. As I slowly paced back, I saw Sarah. She was now doubled up, crying and moaning like a rock of sorrows in those desert sands.

That night, we made love again. Our hands smelt of gunpowder and, with pathetic fury, we sought our pleasure. Then, in the darkness of night, we came together. We were lifted up on a crashing wave of blindness, as our senses sank and drowned.

CHAPTER 21

The next morning, we got up at 3 a.m. We drank our tea without saying a word. Outside, the heavy tread of the kibbutzniks could already be heard. Sarah refused to let me go to the fishponds with her. A young Jewess could not be seen publicly with a goy. I kissed her and left in the opposite direction. Towards Ben-Gurion Airport.

I had about two hundred miles to cover. As the day slowly dawned, I gradually accelerated. On the outskirts of Naplouse, I was confronted by Israel's other reality. A military roadblock barred my way. Passport. Interrogation. With the assault rifles inches away, I once again explained the reason for my journey. "Storks? What are you on about?" I had to answer further questions in a dimly lit hut. Soldiers were dozing in their helmets and bullet-proof jackets. Others were looking at one another incredulously. Finally, I produced Böhm's snaps and showed them the black and white birds. The soldiers burst out laughing. So did I. They gave me some tea, which I drank rapidly. Then I left at once, with cold shivers running down my spine.

At eight o'clock in the morning, I reached the huge warehouses of Ben-Gurion Airport, where Yossé Lenfeld's laboratories had been set up. Lenfeld was already waiting for me impatiently, pacing up and down in front of the corrugated iron door.

This ornithologist, the director of the Nature Protection Society, was quite a specimen. Another one. But even though Yossé Lenfeld talked at the top of his voice (presumably to drown out the planes that were flying over our heads), spoke staccato English at an incredible speed, wore his skullcap askew and a mafioso's Ray-Bans, he did not intimidate me. Nothing intimidated me any more. I was now passing myself off as a journalist and, to my mind, this little grey-haired man, as concentrated on his ideas as a juggler on his skittles, was there to answer my questions. Period.

Yossé began by explaining Israel's ornithological problem. Each year, fifteen million migrating birds, belonging to two hundred and eighty different species, crossed the country thus occupying its airspace with a seething mass. In recent years, there had been numerous accidents involving birds and civil and military aircraft. Several pilots had been killed and many planes completely destroyed. The cost of each accident had been estimated to be five hundred thousand dollars. The Israeli Air Force had decided to take steps and requested his help in 1986. Yossé now had unlimited means to organize an "anti-bird HQ" and to allow air traffic to return to its usual intensity without any risks. My visit started with the surveillance section, situated in the civil airport's flight control tower. Beside the usual radars, two female soldiers were watching another radar, specialized in following migrating birds. Its screen regularly showed long flights of them.

"This is how we avoid the worst," Yossé explained. "In case of an unexpected flight, we can avoid a catastrophe. These flocks of birds are sometimes incredibly huge."

Lenfeld bent down over his computer, tapped at its keyboard and brought up a map of Israel on which immense groups of birds could be seen covering the entire territory.

"Which birds?" I asked.

"Storks," Lenfeld replied. "From Beyt Shean to the Negev, they can cross Israel in less than six hours. In fact, the airport runways are equipped with loudspeakers which reproduce the calls of certain birds of prey, so as to avoid any concentration of them over this area. If the worst comes to the worst, we have a few trained raptors – our 'assault' unit – which we can release."

While continuing to speak, Lenfeld headed off again. We crossed the runways through the purring of the jet engines lodged beneath the giant wings. Yossé was making my head spin with explanations, which wavered between fear of catastrophes and national pride at being "the first country, after Panama, when it comes to migrating birds".

We had now reached the laboratories. With a swipecard, Lenfeld opened a metal door. We went inside a sort of glass cage, equipped with a computer terminal, which overlooked the huge aeronautic workshop.

"Here, we recreate the exact conditions of accidents," Lenfeld explained. "We project birds' bodies onto our prototypes at speeds exceeding six hundred miles per hour. We then analyse the impact points, the resistance and damage."

"What sort of birds?"

Lenfeld chuckled in his gravelly way.

"Chickens, Monsieur Antioch. Supermarket chickens!"

The next room was full of computers, their screens covered with columns of figures, maps marked out in squares, graphs and displays.

"This is our research department. Here, we determine each species' trajectory. We assemble thousands of observations and notes taken by birdwatchers. In exchange for this information, we give them certain advantages, such as accommodation during their stay, the possibility of observing the birds on specific strategic sites, and so on."

This point interested me.

"So you know exactly where the storks go as they cross Israel?"

Yossé grinned and went over to one of the unused computers. The map of Israel flashed up once again, and paths of dotted lines appeared over it. They were relatively close, and all of them came together over Beyt Shean.

"We have each species' trajectories and annual migration dates. As far as possible, our planes avoid those corridors. Here, in red, you can see the storks' main pathways. You will notice that they all, without exception, go via Beyt Shean. That's the . . . "

"I know Beyt Shean. And you're sure these routes never change?"

"Absolutely," Lenfeld replied, still speaking at the top of his voice. "What you see here is a synthesis of hundreds of observations made over the last five years."

"Do you have quantitative data dealing with how many birds come and go?"

"Of course. Four hundred and fifty thousand storks cross Israel each year, in spring and then again in autumn. We know their rate of arrival. We know everything about their habits. We have the exact dates, the periods of high concentration, the averages . . . everything. Storks are as regular as clockwork."

"Are you interested in the ringed storks that come from Europe?"

"Not especially, why?"

"It seems that the ringed birds didn't make it back last spring."

Yossé Lenfeld observed me from behind his Ray-Bans. Despite the tinted lenses, I could see that he was peering at me incredulously. He simply said:

"I didn't know. But as regards the number . . . You're not looking very well, old chap. Come on. I'll offer you something to drink."

I followed him through a maze of corridors. The air conditioning was ice-cold. We arrived at a drinks machine. I chose a sparkling mineral water, and its fresh bubbliness made me feel better. Then the tour got going again.

We entered the biological laboratory, with its draining boards, test-tubes and microscopes. The researchers here were dressed in white coats and looked as though they were involved in some germ warfare. Yossé explained:

"This is the brains of the programme. Here we study the slightest details of aeroplane accidents and their consequences on our military equipment. The debris is brought to the lab then examined under a microscope down to the tiniest feather, or trace of blood, so as to determine the speed of impact and the violence of the shock. Here is where we evaluate hazards and come up with real security measures. You won't believe me when I tell you that this lab is an independent unit in our armed forces. Migrating birds are, in a way, enemies of the Israeli cause."

"After the Six Days' War, the million bird war?"

Yossé Lenfeld chuckled.

"Exactly! I can show you only a part of our research. The rest is classified. But I do have something here that will interest you."

We went into a small studio, full of video players and high-definition screens. On one of them could be seen an Israeli Air Force pilot, with his helmet on and visor down. In fact, the only thing visible was his mouth. It was saying, in English: "I felt an explosion, something extremely powerful had hit my shoulder. I passed out for a few seconds, then came round. But I couldn't see anything. My helmet was completely covered with blood and lumps of flesh."

Lenfeld commented:

"He's one of our pilots. Two years ago, he collided with a stork at full speed. It was in March, when they were returning to Europe. He was incredibly lucky. The bird hit him straight on and his cockpit exploded. But he was still able to land. It took them hours to remove all the shards of broken glass and bird feathers from his face."

"Why is he wearing his helmet on the screen?"

"Because the identity of an IAF pilot is top secret."

"So I can't meet him?"

"No," Yossé said. "But I've got something even better."

We left the studio. Lenfeld picked up a wall phone, entered a code, then spoke in Hebrew. Almost at once, a little man with a frog face appeared. His eyelids were heavy, but they slid down rapidly over his bulging eyeballs.

"Shalom Wilm," said Yossé for my information. "He's in charge of the analytical work carried out in this lab. He personally researched the accident I've just mentioned."

In English, Lenfeld told him the reasons for my visit. He grinned at me and invited me into his office. Oddly enough, he told Yossé to leave us alone.

I followed him down another set of corridors and doors. Finally, we entered a small recess, like a safe, whose door had to be opened with a combination.

"This is your office?" I asked in amazement.

"I lied to Yossé. I want to show you something."

Wilm closed the door and turned on the light. He then looked me up and down seriously for a long minute.

"I didn't imagine you'd be like this."

"Sorry?"

"I've been expecting you since the 1989 accident."

"Expecting me?"

"You or someone else. I was expecting a visitor who was particularly interested in storks going back towards Europe."

Silence. My blood was pounding in my temples. Softly, I asked: "What do you mean?"

Wilm started searching around in the recess, which was a junk shop full of metal, samples of synthetic fibres and other material. He uncovered a little door at head height and entered the combination.

"When analysing the various parts of the damaged plane, I made a strange discovery. I realized that my find was not down to pure chance and supposed that it must be connected to a larger chain, of which you are presumably one of the links."

He opened the door, plunged his head into the wall safe and continued speaking – his voice echoing as though from the depths of a cave:

"My intuition tells me that I can trust you."

Wilm re-emerged from the safe. He was holding two small transparent sachets in his hand.

"What's more, I've been dying to get rid of this burden," he added.

I was losing my cool.

"What are you talking about? Explain yourself!"

Wilm calmly replied:

"When we searched the interior of the damaged plane's cockpit, as well as the pilot's equipment and in particular his helmet, we were able to pick out various particles among the wreckage. For example, we collected the broken glass of the cockpit."

Shalom put one of the sachets, with a label written in Hebrew, down onto the table. It contained minuscule shards of tinted glass.

"We also gathered the remains of the shattered visor."

He put down another sachet containing lumps of clearer glass.

"The pilot was very lucky to escape."

Wilm was keeping his hand clenched.

"But, when I examined these fragments under a microscope, I found something else. (His fingers were still closed.) Something which should definitely not have been there."

With a rush of adrenaline, I suddenly realized what Wilm was going to say. But still I yelled out:

"What, for Christ's sake?"

He slowly opened his hand and whispered:

"A diamond."

CHAPTER 22

I left the Lenfeld laboratories feeling worn out. So, Shalom Wilm's revelations had led me directly where my imagination had not yet dared to go.

Max Böhm was a diamond smuggler and the storks were his couriers. His strategy was exceptional, astonishing and daring. I now knew enough to be able to piece it together accurately. According to Dumaz, Max had worked on two occasions in the diamond industry – from 1969 to 1972 in South Africa and from 1972 to 1977 in the Central African Republic. At the same time, he used to observe the migration of storks, which traced out a direct air link to Europe.

When had he had the idea of using these birds as porters? Impossible to say, but his network had definitely already been set up by the time he left the Central African Republic in 1977, at least as regards the western route. All he needed were a few accomplices in the Republic who, unbeknown to the management of the diamond mines, made off with the most beautiful gems and fixed them to the feet of the ringed birds. The stones then vanished across the frontiers.

After that it was child's play for Böhm to recover the diamonds. He had the numbers of the rings and knew the nest of each stork in Switzerland, Belgium, Holland, Poland and Germany. Then, covered by the pretext of having to ring the nestlings, off he would go to anaesthetize the adults and collect his gems.

The system did have a few weak links. If a stork had an accident, then this would cause a loss but, given the fact that several hundred birds were used each year, the profits still remained huge and the risk of discovery practically nil. His interest in ornithology had been a perfect cover. What is more, over the years Böhm had presumably put together special 'troops' of birds, selecting the strongest and most experienced specimens. As an additional precaution, he had employed various sentinels along the migration paths to ensure that everything went normally. In this way, he had been successfully smuggling diamonds for over ten years.

Other points confirmed this hypothesis. Given what they were carrying – gems worth millions of Swiss francs each migration – it was not surprising that Böhm had panicked when the eastern storks had not returned last spring. He had then sent those two Bulgarians after the birds. They had questioned Joro Grybinski and thought him innocent. Then they pursued Iddo and, finding him more suspect, they had killed him and then dumped his body in the marshes.

From what Sarah had told me, it was obvious that the young ornithologist had found out about this business. One evening, when nursing one of Böhm's storks, he must have happened upon a diamond hidden in the ring. He had then equipped himself with an assault rifle and, each evening, had shot down the ringed birds as they arrived in the marshes so he could collect the gems. In spring

1991, then, Iddo must have laid his hands on most of the storks' consignment. This led to two further possibilities: either Iddo had been made to talk under torture and the Bulgarians had recovered the diamonds; or he had remained silent and his treasure was still hidden somewhere. The second seemed more likely. Otherwise, why would Max Böhm have sent me to follow the storks?

But this revelation about the birds did not explain everything. How long had this smuggling been going on? Who were Max Böhm's accomplices in Africa? What part did One World play in this set-up? And, last but not least, what was the connection between diamond smuggling and the horrific removal of Rajko's heart? Had the two Bulgarians also killed Rajko? Were they the virtuoso surgeons Milan Djuric had mentioned? Finally, there also remained a basic point above and beyond all these questions: why had Max Böhm chosen me to conduct this inquiry? Why me? I knew nothing about storks, did not belong to his network and could well end up working out was going on.

I was driving at top speed back to Beyt Shean. I left the deserts of the occupied territories at about 7 p.m. In the distance, I could make out the army camps, with their lights flickering on the top of the hills. On the outskirts of Naplouse, I was stopped by an army roadblock once more. The diamond Wilm had given me was hidden in a piece of folded paper in the depths of one of my pockets. My Glock 21 was concealed under the mat. Once again, I trotted out my speech about birds. They finally let me through.

At 10 p.m., Beyt Shean appeared. The scent of dusk was rising, feeding that strange sense of compassion which dominates the evening air after the sun has gone down. I parked and walked over to Sarah's house. The lights were all off. When I knocked on the door, it swung open. I got out my Glock and took the safety catch off – a gunman's reflexes are quickly acquired – and went into the living-room. Nobody there. I rushed into the garden, lifted up the plastic sheet which hid the trap-door, then pulled it open. A Galil and the Glock 17 had vanished. Sarah had gone. In her own way. Armed like a soldier going to battle. Light as a bird.

CHAPTER 23

As on the previous day, I woke up at 3 a.m. in the morning. It was 6 September. I had crashed out on Sarah's bed and fallen asleep still fully dressed. The kibbutz was waking up. In the purple darkness, I melded in with the men and women who were heading for the fishponds and tried to ask them about Sarah. All I got in reply were hostile glares or evasive answers.

I went to talk to the birdwatchers. They, too, got up extremely early so as to observe the birds as soon as they awoke. At four o'clock, they were already checking their equipment, loading films and preparing their packed lunches. On the doorsteps of the houses, I risked a few questions in English. After several unsuccessful attempts, a young Dutchman affirmed that he had seen her the day before, at about 8 a.m. in the morning, in the streets of Newe-Eitan. She was getting onto a 133 bus travelling west in the direction of Netanya. He had been particularly struck by the fact that she was carrying a golf bag.

A few seconds later, I was driving westwards with my foot down. At 5 a.m., daylight was already flooding over the plains of Galilee. I stopped at a service station near Caesarea to fill up the tank. While drinking some black tea, I flicked through my guide book looking for information about Netanya, Sarah's destination. What I discovered almost made me drop my scalding cup: "Netanya. Population: 107,200 inhabitants. This seaside resort, famous for its splendid sandy beaches and its tranquillity, is also a large industrial centre specializing in diamond cutting. In the Herzl Street quarter, cutters and polishers can be seen at work."

My tyres screeched as I pulled away. Sarah had understood the entire system. And now she obviously also had the diamonds.

At 9 a.m., Netanya appeared on the horizon. A large bright city, huddled up beside the sea. As I followed the coast road, which contained a succession of hotels and clinics, I grasped Netanya's true nature. Behind its appearance of being a seaside resort, it was in fact a lair for elderly rich people who wanted to laze in the sun. Shuffling steps, dry faces, trembling hands. What could all these old people be thinking about? Their youth, all those Yom Kippurs that had, year after year, marked out their exiled existences? All those wars, the horror of the concentration camps, that relentless struggle to possess their own land? In Israel, Netanya was the final resting-place for the living. A cemetery of memories.

Soon, the road widened to the right, opening out into Atzma'ut Square, where Herzl Street and its numerous diamond-cutting establishments began. I parked my car and walked. After about a hundred yards, I entered a denser neighbourhood that had the scented, crowded atmosphere of a souk. In the dark streets, occasional beams of daylight forced their way through, drifting under the shopkeepers' displays and the closed shutters of the houses. The smell of fruit mingled with sweat and spices. Shoulders collided in an incessant toing and froing. Skullcaps bounced up and down in the crowd, like a galaxy of black suns.

Running with sweat, I could not take off my jacket because under it I was wearing my Glock 21 in the Velcro holster that Sarah had given me. I thought of that young Jewess who had walked the same streets a few hours earlier, carrying diamonds and state-of-the-art weaponry. At the end of Smilasky Street, I found what I was looking for. The diamond-cutters' quarter.

In the dusty air, workshops clustered together. The air was humming with the high-pitched sound of the cutters' wheels. Artisanship was still thriving there. Outside each door a man sat in patient concentration. At the first shop, I asked my first questions: "Have you seen a tall young blonde woman? Did she offer you some highly valuable rough diamonds? Did she try to get the stones valued, or to sell them to you?" Each time, the same denials and the same incredulous stare behind their thick lenses or magnifying glasses. The quarter was becoming palpably hostile. Diamond-cutters dislike questions and stories. Their job starts with the glistening of the gem. It does not matter what happened before or around the object in question. By 12.30, I had gone round almost the entire area and had learnt precisely nothing. A few more workshops, and my visit would be over. At 12.45, I put my questions for the last time to an old man who spoke perfect French. He stopped his wheel and asked: "And did the young lady have a golf bag?"

Sarah had been there the evening before. She had placed a diamond on his desk and asked: "How much?" Isaac Knicklevitz had examined the stone in the light, observing its reflections on a piece of paper, then under a magnifying glass. He had compared it with other diamonds and come to the conclusion that, in terms of colour and purity, this diamond was a masterpiece. The old man had named a price and, without haggling, Sarah had accepted at once. Isaac had emptied his safe, thus doing, he had to admit, an excellent bit of business. However, Isaac was no fool. He knew that that meeting was only the first step in the adventure. According to him, selling a stone without a certificate was going to be extremely risky. He knew that a man like me, or else a more official person, would knock on his door sooner or later. He also knew that he might have to give the stone back, unless he had had time to cut it.

Isaac was an old man, with aquiline features and short, cropped hair. His square head and broad shoulders made him look like a cubist portrait. He finally stood up – though remaining bent over as the ceiling was so low that I too had been doubled up ever since our conversation began – and suggested that we had lunch. Isaac apparently had more to tell me. And Sarah was long gone. I wiped my face and followed the diamond-cutter through the maze of alleyways.

Soon we reached a small square in the shade of a grove of stunted trees. Under this roof of coolness stood the tables of a restaurant. All around, the market was in full flow. Men yelling from behind their stalls. Passers-by shoving past one another. Along the walls of light green wattle, other shops lodged in the shadows were seething, surrounding that busy centre with a crown of even greater agitation. Isaac made his way through the crush and sat down at a table. A sickening smell of blood surged up just to the right of us. Amid stinking cages and a cloud of feathers, a man was systematically cutting the heads off hundreds of hens. Blood was pouring everywhere. Near the butcher, a huge rabbi dressed in black was mumbling, Torah in hand, and constantly bowing. Isaac smiled.

"You don't seem very familiar with the Jewish world, young man. Never heard of kosher? All of our food is blessed like that. Now, tell me your story."

I played it by ear.

"I can't tell you anything, Isaac. The woman you saw yesterday is in danger. I'm in danger, too. This entire business is one long menace for whoever approaches it. Trust me. Just answer my questions and keep well clear of all this."

"Are you in love with her?"

"That's not where I'd have started, Isaac. But yes, I must admit that I do love her. Madly. Let's just say that this whole business is a love story, full of chaos, desire and violence. Will that do you?"

Isaac smiled again and, in Hebrew, ordered the day's special. As for me, the smell of poultry had made me lose my appetite, so I requested some tea.

The diamond-cutter then asked:

"So, how can I help you?"

"Tell me about the diamond she had."

"It's a sumptuous stone. Not very big – just a few carats – but extraordinarily white and pure. A diamond's value is based on four unvarying criteria: weight, purity, colour and shape. Your lady friend's diamond is absolutely colourless and perfectly pure. Without the slightest inclusion. It's a little miracle."

"If you were suspicious about where it came from, why did you buy it?"

Isaac's face brightened.

"Because that's my job. I'm a diamond-cutter. For the last forty years, I've been cutting, splitting and polishing gems. The one we're talking about is a real challenge for somebody like me. The cutter is a determining factor in a stone's beauty. One false move, and it's all over, the treasure has been destroyed. On the other hand, a successful cutting can magnify a stone, make it richer and even more sublime. When I saw that diamond, I realized that heaven was giving me my one and only chance to produce a masterpiece."

"How much is a stone like that worth, before being cut?"

Isaac twitched nervously.

"It isn't a question of money."

"Please answer. I need to have an idea of its worth."

"It's hard to say. Between five and ten thousands dollars, maybe."

In my mind's eye, I saw Böhm's storks, swooping through the sky with their precious load. Every year they had come back to Europe, then landed on their nests on the tops of roofs in Germany, Belgium and Switzerland. Millions of dollars each springtime.

"Do you have any idea where such a diamond came from?"

"In the diamond exchanges, the most beautiful stones change hands all through the year wrapped up in little envelopes. Nobody can say where they come from. Or even if they have been taken from the earth or from water. Diamonds are completely anonymous."

"Stones of such high quality are rare. Is it known which mines are capable of producing such diamonds?"

"Yes, it is. But nowadays the market is opening up. Of course, there is still South and Central Africa. But Angola and Russia are becoming increasingly fertile."

"Once they have been mined, where can uncut stones like that be sold?"

"There's only one place in the world. Antwerp. Everything that does not go through De Beers, that is about twenty to thirty per cent of the market, is sold on the Antwerp diamond exchanges."

"Did you tell the young woman that?"

"I certainly did."

So, my Alice was on her way to Antwerp. The speciality of the day arrived: fried bean croquettes, with mashed chick peas and olive oil. Isaac, as imperturbably as ever, tucked into his pittas.

I watched him for a moment. He seemed willing to tell me everything I needed to know, but with nothing in return. In his slanted stare, all I could read was patience and concentration. I realized that nothing could amaze him any more. His experience as a diamond-cutter was a thorough education in worldly wisdom. He had seen so many desperados, lost souls and lunatics of my sort.

"How are things run in Antwerp?"

"It's really something. The exchanges are as well protected as the Pentagon. You can feel invisible cameras filming you from every angle. Over there, politics and rivalries count for nothing. All that matters is the quality of the stones."

"What are the main difficulties in selling such a diamond? What about smuggling? Are there any networks?"

Isaac smiled ironically.

"Networks? Yes, of course there are. But uncut diamonds are a world apart, Monsieur Antioch. It is the planet's best protected citadel. Supply and demand are strictly controlled by De Beers. Structures for buying, sorting and stocking diamonds have been set up and most of the ones on the market are sold via the same system. Its role is to distribute a predetermined number of stones at regular intervals. It turns on and off the flow of diamonds at a world level, if you like, in order to avoid uncontrollable fluctuations."

"So you mean that illegal dealing in uncut stones is impossible? That De Beers runs the entire diamond market?"

"There are still the stones that are bought and sold in Antwerp. But it was the word 'networks' that made me smile. The regular arrival of high-quality specimens would destabilize the market and be noticed at once."

I took out my piece of folded paper and slipped Wilm's diamond out into my hand.

"Specimens like this one?"

Isaac wiped his mouth, lowered his glasses and looked at it with his expert eye. All around, the market was in full swing.

"Yes, exactly like this one," Isaac nodded and stared at me in disbelief. "A certain number of them would cause a reaction, then prices would fluctuate. (He frowned and stared again at the stone.) This is incredible. In all of my life, I have seen only five such stones. Then in two days, I get to see two more, as though they were as common as children's marbles. Is this one for sale?"

"No. Another question: if I understand you correctly, a smuggler's biggest enemy is De Beers."

"Exactly. But nor should you underestimate customs. They have some excellent specialists. All of the world's police forces keep their eyes out for these little stones that are so easy to hide."

"What's in it for a diamond smuggler?"

"The same as for any other smuggler. To avoid taxes and get round the legislation of countries that produce and distribute the articles."

Max Böhm had managed to evade those obstacles by means of a system that nobody had thought of before. There were two other points that needed confirmation. I put the precious stone away and took out from my bag one of Max Böhm's index cards. Those cards covered with figures that I had been incapable of deciphering, but the meaning of which I was now beginning to guess.

"Could you take a glance at these figures, and tell me if they mean anything to you?"

Isaac lowered his glasses once more and read them in silence.

"Yes, this is perfectly clear," he replied. "It is all about the characteristics of diamonds. I have already told you about the four criteria – weight, purity, colour and shape. They are also called the Four Cs – carat, colour, clarity and cut. Here, each line corresponds to one of the criteria. Take this one for example. First we have a date, 13/4/87, then we find 'VVSI', which stands for 'very very small inclusions'. In other words, an extremely pure stone, whose impurities cannot be seen under a magnifying glass that enlarges ten times. Then we have '10 C', that's the weight, ten carats (one carat equals 0.2 grams). After that comes the letter 'D', which means 'exceptional white +', i.e. the finest colour of all. This is the description of a unique stone. And from a glance at the other lines and dates, I can say that the owner of these treasures is quite incredibly rich."

My throat was as dry as the desert. The fortune that Isaac was talking about was based on the record of just one stork, during its years of migration. My head spun when I thought of the large number of similar cards I had in my bag, which themselves represented just a few of Böhm's deliveries. Year after year. For a final confirmation, I asked:

"And this, Isaac. Can you tell me what it is?"

I handed him a map of Europe and Africa, covered with dotted lines. He leant over and, after a few seconds, said:

"It could be the journeys diamonds make from the countries in Africa where they are mined, to the countries in Europe where they are bought and cut. What is it?" he added mockingly. "Your 'network'?"

"Yes, in a way," I answered.

What I had shown him was quite simply a map of the storks' migration paths. A photocopy from a children's book which Böhm had given me. I got to my feet. The slaughterer of poultry was still swimming in a sea of blood.

Isaac also stood up and tried his luck again.

"What are you going to do with your stone?"

"I can't sell it to you, Isaac. I need it."

"Shame. Anyway, such stones are too dangerous."

I paid the bill and said:

"Isaac, only two people know that you have that diamond. Me and the young lady. So now we can say it's yours."

"We'll see, Monsieur Antioch. But, whatever happens, these stones have given me a new lease of life. A sudden flash of beauty in my old age."

Isaac bade me farewell with a vague gesture.

"Shalom, Louis."

I slipped away into the crowd. I walked along the narrow streets, past the shops and tried to find my way back to my car. My head was racing and I had trouble concentrating. What is more, something else was now on my mind. A feeling that had been nagging me ever since I left the restaurant: the impression that I was being followed.

CHAPTER 24

I finally got back to Herzl Street and Atzma'ut Square. I was close to my car, but decided to wait a little longer in the shelter of the crowd. I edged towards the beach. The sea wind was blowing in long salty gusts. I spun round to look at the passers-by and scrutinize their faces. Nobody looked suspect. A few cars slipped by in the white light. The high façades of the buildings rose up, as clear as a mirror. On the other side of the street bordering the sea, old people shivered on deckchairs. I stared with amazement at that row of stiff, arched backs and their absurd clothes – different varieties of thick and heavy material, even though the temperature must have been over 35°C. Sweaters, jackets, a raincoat, cardigans. A raincoat! I observed that shape as it moved along the promenade. The man's collar was turned up and a large sweat stain covered his back. My head swam. I had just recognized one of the Sofia hitmen.

I dashed across the road towards him.

The man turned round. He opened his mouth, then immediately took to his heels, weaving between the old folk on their chairs. I accelerated, scattering the chairs and the veterans. In a few strides, I caught up with him. He stuffed his hand into his raincoat. I grabbed him by his collar and punched him in the stomach. An Uzi sub-machine gun dropped to the ground. I kicked the gun away and grabbed his neck with both hands. I smashed his face against my knee. His nose broke with a clean snap. Behind me, I was aware of the frightened geriatrics whining, getting to their feet amid the toppled chairs.

"Who are you?" I yelled in English, then head-butted him between the eyes. The man fell backwards. His skull cracked against the concrete. I grabbed him again at once. His mucous membranes and cartilage were gushing blood. "Who are you, for Christ's sake?" I punched him repeatedly in the face. My numb fingers crashed into his bones. I hit him again and again, splitting his lips. "Who's paying you, you mother-fucker?" I asked, holding him down with my right hand, while going through his pockets with the left. I found his wallet. I took his passport out from the other papers. A metallic blue, glittering in the sunlight. My mouth opened wide as I recognized that familiar symbol – the UNO. The hitman had a United Nations passport.

My second of astonishment lasted too long.

The Bulgarian kneed me in the balls, then shot up like a jack-in-the-box. I was doubled over and panting. He pushed me back and aimed a steel-capped kick at my jaws. I just dodged it in time but felt my lip split. A spray of blood shot across the sun. I put my hands to my face and held my skin in place with my left hand, while clumsily trying to draw my Glock with my right. The killer was already disappearing at high speed.

In another town, I would have had several minutes to escape. But in Israel I had only a maximum of a few seconds before the police force or army arrived. I waved my gun in front of me to make the old folk step back. Then, groaning, I staggered as fast as I could to my car on Atzma'ut Square.

My hand shook as I slipped the key into the lock. I was bleeding profusely. I had tears in my eyes and my crotch was in agony. I opened the door and slumped down onto the seat. At once, a wave of nausea passed over me, as though my head was going to split in two. "Start the car," I thought. "Start the car before you pass out." As I turned the key in the ignition, Sarah's face flashed into my mind. Never had I needed her so much. Never had I felt so lonely. The car screamed across the asphalt as it pulled away.

I drove for twenty miles. I was losing a lot of blood and my eyesight was beginning to dim. It felt as though someone was playing cymbals in my head. My jaws were clacking together. The houses began to thin out and soon I was back in the desert. Realizing that I was bound to hit a police or army roadblock sooner or later, I spotted a tall rock and parked in its shade. I pointed the rear-view mirror at my face. Half of my face was a mess of blood, its features no longer discernible. A long scrap of flesh hung down below my chin. It was my lower lip. Mastering another wave of nausea, I got out my first-aid kit. I disinfected the wound, took some painkillers and wrapped a plaster around my lips. I put on my sunglasses and checked the effect in the mirror. I looked just like the Invisible Man.

I closed my eyes for a moment and tried to still my racing mind. So, I had been followed all the way from Bulgaria. Or else, they knew the path I was taking so well that they had simply picked up my trace again there in Israel. There was nothing very surprising about that. After all, they just had to follow the storks to find me. But what did surprise me was that United Nations passport. I took it out of my pocket and flicked through it. The man was called Miklos Sikkov. Country of origin: Bulgaria. Age: 38. Profession: escort. The hitman, if he really worked for One World, looked after the transportation of humanitarian cargoes of medicines, food and equipment. But it also meant something else. Sikkov was one of Böhm's agents. One of those who, along the storks' migration routes, watched out for them and, in Africa, stopped them from being hunted. I looked through the pages of visas. Bulgaria, Turkey, Israel, Egypt, Mali, the Central African Republic, South Africa. These stamps clearly confirmed my hypothesis. For the last five years, this United Nations employee had been constantly patrolling the storks' routes – both in the east and the west. I slipped Sikkov's passport into the torn cover of my filofax, then set off again towards Jerusalem.

For half an hour, I drove through a landscape of rock. The pain eased off. The coolness of the air conditioning was soothing. All I wanted to do was leap on a plane and get out of that land of fire.

In my panic, I had missed the most direct route and was now going to have to make a long detour via the Occupied Territories. At 4 p.m., I reached the outskirts of Naplouse. I knew that trying to cross the army roadblocks in my present state was hardly a brilliant idea. But Jerusalem was still over sixty miles away. Then I noticed a black car; it had been behind me for some time. I stared at it through my rear-view mirror. It seemed to be floating in the torrid air. I slowed down and it neared me. It was a Renault 25, with Israeli number plates. I slowed down even more. A one thousand volt shudder ran through me. In the mirror I saw Sikkov, his face red with blood, like a crimson monster crouched over its steering-wheel. I changed up into third and put my foot down. A few seconds later, I was doing over one hundred and twenty miles an hour. The car kept up with me.

We drove on like that for ten minutes. Sikkov tried to overtake me. All the time, I was expecting shots to hit the rear window. I had lain the Glock on the passenger seat. Suddenly, I saw Naplouse rise up on the horizon, grey and shimmering in the heavy atmosphere. Nearer, on the right, a Palestinian camp loomed up. The sign read "Balatakamp". I thought of my Israeli number plates. I turned off and left the motorway. Dust billowed up from under my wheels. I accelerated again. I was now only a few yards from the camp, and Sikkov was still behind me. I spotted an Israeli lookout with a pair of binoculars on a roof. Elsewhere, the Palestinian women on the terraces were bustled around pointing at me. Hordes of children were scampering about in all directions, picking up stones. My plan was going to work.

I drove straight through the gates of hell.

The first stones hit me as I reached the main road. My windscreen shattered. On my left, Sikkov was still trying to slip in between me and the adjacent wall, which was covered with graffiti. A first shock. Our two cars bounced off the walls that surrounded us. Right in front of us, the children carried on throwing stones. The Renault attacked again. Sikkov, daubed in blood, was looking daggers at me. Everywhere, women were screaming on the rooftops, spinning round between their laundered sheets. Some Israeli soldiers came running up in a state of alert, loading tear-gas canisters into their guns and forming up along the terraces.

Suddenly, a small square opened up. I turned abruptly and skidded round, my chassis scraping on the earth as stones rained down on the car. The windows shattered. Sikkov drew up beside me, and blocked the way. I saw the hitman point his gun at me, threw myself down onto the passenger seat then heard the dull sound of my door breaking up under the gunfire. At the same moment, tear-gas canisters whistled over us. I looked up. I was staring straight down the Bulgarian's barrel. I felt for my Glock, which had slipped off the seat as I fell. Too late. However, Sikkov did not have time to press his trigger. As he was aiming at me, a stone hit him in the back of the neck. He arched his back, screamed, then vanished. The gas was beginning to spread, clouding my eyes and clawing at my throat. The din around us was ear-splitting.

I drew back and crawled through the dust. I groped around for my Glock. The gas whistled, the women bawled, men came running. From the four corners of the square, the warriors of the Intifada continued throwing stones. But they were no longer aiming at our cars. Instead, they were now concentrating on the soldiers who were arriving in large numbers. Jeeps accumulated in the dust. Green-uniformed men in gas masks clambered out. Some of the guns fired more of that white poison, others shot rubber bullets, while others still were blasting real bullets at real children. The square was like an erupting volcano. My eyes were burning and my throat was on fire. The noise from the running feet and weapons was enough to make the earth shake. Suddenly, another sound rose up from the ground, like a massive, deep and magnificent roll of thunder. A wave of mingled voices. Then I saw Palestinian teenagers standing on the walls, singing their song of rebellion, their fingers shaped in a 'V' for victory.

At that moment, Sikkov's steel-capped shoes passed in front of me, running through the thick smoke. I got up and ran after him. Down the little streets, I was at that bastard's heels. He was losing blood, which the sand immediately drank up. A few seconds later, I tore off my dressings and pulled back the Glock's breech. We were still running between a series of whitewashed walls. Neither of us could go very fast because of all that gas in our lungs. Sikkov's raincoat was now just a few paces from me. I was about to grab him, when he spun round and pointed his 44 Magnum at me. The flash of the gun blinded me. I kicked out towards him. Sikkov fell back against a wall, then raised his pistol again. I heard the first shot. I closed my eyes and emptied my Glock in front of me. A few seconds of eternity, weighted with suspense. When I opened my eyes, Sikkov's head was no more than a gaping mass of blood and fibres. His blackened flesh spat out tiny red geysers. The wall, covered with brains and bone, contained a hole of over one metre in diameter. I instinctively put my gun away. In the distance, the Palestinian children could still be heard singing, braving the Israeli guns.

CHAPTER 25

Two Israeli soldiers found me on that little square. My face was pouring with blood and my mind was wandering. I no longer knew where I was exactly or what I was doing. Some orderlies took me away. My Glock was still hidden snugly under my jacket. A few minutes later, I was being given a blood transfusion on a metal bed, under the baking canvas of a tent.

Some doctors arrived and examined my face. They spoke in French, mentioning clips, an anaesthetic and an operation. They thought I was an innocent tourist, a victim of an Intifada attack. I realized that I was in a One World clinic, situated about three hundred yards from Balatakamp. If my lips had been more than just shattered mush, then I would have smiled. I discreetly slipped my Glock under the mattress and closed my eyes. The night immediately swept me away.

When I woke up, everything was silent and dark. I could not even make out how big the tent was. I was shivering with cold and bathed in sweat. I closed my eyes again and returned to my nightmares. I dreamt of a man with long, wiry arms, who was coolly and methodically slicing up a child's body. From time to time he dipped his black lips into the palpitating entrails. I could not see his face, because he was standing amid a forest of limbs and torsos, hanging up on meat hooks, which had the gleaming ochre colour of pieces of lacquered meat in Chinese restaurants.

I dreamt of an explosion of flesh under a tent with puffed-out sides. Of Rajko's face, as he agonized, his stomach slit open, innards quivering. Of Iddo, totally flayed, his organs exposed, like some terrible Prometheus being devoured by storks.

The sun rose. The vast tent was full of beds and there was a smell of camphor. Young Palestinians were lying there, injured. The distant humming of generators could be heard. Three times during that day, my dressings were removed and I was given a sort of aubergine stew, washed down by extremely black tea. My mouth was like a slab of concrete and my body as stiff as a rake. I was constantly expecting the UN soldiers or the Israeli army to burst in and take me away. But nobody came and, despite listening attentively, I heard no mention of Sikkov's death.

Slowly, I drank in the reality that surrounded me. The Intifada was a children's war and this was a children's hospital. On the neighbouring beds, young kids were suffering and dying in proud silence. Above their beds, x-rays displayed the damage done to those shattered bodies: broken limbs, perforated flesh, infected lungs. There were also a lot of children who were simply ill. The lack of hygiene in the camps provoked all sorts of infection.

At the end of the afternoon, another attack broke out. In the distance could be heard the ringing of gunshots, the whistling of tear-gas canisters and the cries of wild children, drunk on fury, running for protection through the little streets of Balatakamp. Shortly afterwards, the cortege of the wounded arrived. Mothers in tears, hysterical beneath their veils, carrying their bruised children as they coughed and choked. Other wounded children with wan faces, their clothes drenched with blood, lying curled up on stretchers. Fathers sobbing, holding their sons' hands, waiting for the operation, or else outside, screaming their lust for revenge.

On the third day, an Israeli ambulance came for me. They wanted to put me in a comfortable room in Jerusalem, before sending me back to France. I refused. An hour later, a delegation from the tourist board arrived to offer me better standard food, a more comfortable mattress and various other advantages. Once again I refused. Not

149

from solidarity with the Arabs, but because that tent was the only possible refuge for me. My Glock, fully loaded, was still hidden under my mattress. The Israelis made me sign a form which declared that everything that had already happened to me, or yet might, on the West Bank was entirely my own responsibility. I signed. In exchange, I asked them for another hire car.

When they had gone, I had a wash and examined my face in the filthy mirror. My skin had become even darker and I had lost a lot of weight. My cheekbones were almost sticking through my skin.

Gingerly, I raised the dressings that were covering my mouth. Just beneath my lower lip a long scar formed a second smile, as though woven from barbed wire. I considered my new face. Then I thought about my personality, and how it was continuing to change. This gave me a strange feeling of feverish, even suicidal optimism. My departure on 19 August now seemed like a private apocalypse. Within a few weeks, I had become an Anonymous Traveller, rootless, taking terrible risks, but knowing that the recompense lay in each day's discoveries. Indeed, Sarah had already said it. I was "nobody". My hands with no fingerprints had become the symbols of that new freedom.

That evening, I thought about One World. My suspicions now seemed absurd. The few days I had spent there had allowed me to evaluate that organization. There was absolutely no sign of any manipulations, suspect operations or smuggling of organs. The members of One World were volunteer doctors practising their art with zeal and devotion. Even if the organization constantly cropped up on my path, even if Sikkov was supposed to have worked for it, even if Max Böhm had, for some mysterious reason, bequeathed his entire fortune to it, my idea that they were involved in selling organs was a blind alley. But a link did exist. Of that much I was certain.

CHAPTER 26

On 10 September, Christian Lodemberg, a Swiss doctor in One World whom I had got to know in the camp, took my clips out. I immediately spoke a few words. Unexpectedly, the sounds that issued from my parched mouth were perfectly clear and intelligible. I could speak again. That evening, I explained to Christian that I was an ornithologist following the storks. He seemed sceptical.

"Are there any storks round here?" I asked.

"Storks?"

"Yes, black and white birds."

"Ah . . . (Christian, with his blue eyes, was trying to find a double meaning in my words.) No, there are none of them in Naplouse. You'll have to go back up towards Beyt Shean, in the Jordan valley."

I told him about my travels and the satellite surveillance throughout Europe and Africa.

"Do you know someone called Miklos Sikkov?" I asked him. "A guy with the UN."

"His name doesn't ring any bells."

I handed Christian the hitman's passport.

"Yes, I do know this chap," he said, looking at the photo. "How did you get hold of his papers?"

"What do you know about him?"

"Not a lot. He used to hang about round here. A rather shifty character. (Christian fell silent and stared at me.) He was killed the same day as your accident."

He handed me back the metallic passport.

"His face had been blown away. He'd taken sixteen 45mm rounds at point-blank range. I've never seen such a massacre. You don't get many 45s round here. In fact, the only 45 I know of is the one hidden under your mattress."

"How do you know that?"

"A little private investigation."

"What about Sikkov?" I went on. "When was he found?"

"Just after you. A few streets further on. In all that chaos, nobody connected his presence and yours. We first thought that it was Palestinians settling a score. Then we recognized his clothes and his gun. His fingerprints confirmed his identity. There are files kept on all of us here in One World. A postmortem was carried out and several bullets were found lodged in his skull. I read the report, which is a confidential document, with no name or number. I immediately realized that something was wrong. First, the circumstances of his death were mysterious. Second, the dead man was that shifty Bulgarian. So we told the Shin-bet that there had simply been an accident, that the corpse belonged to a member of our organization and that it had nothing at all to do with the Israeli police. We are protected by the United Nations. The Israelis shut up. So nobody talks any more about a murder and a 45mm. The case is closed."

"Who was Sikkov?"

"I don't know. A sort of mercenary sent by Geneva to protect us from possible pillage. Sikkov was a weird guy. Last year, he only showed up on a few occasions, on particular dates."

"When?"

"I can't remember. September, I think, and in February."

The periods when the storks pass through Israel. A further confirmation that Sikkov had been one of Böhm's "pawns".

"What have you done with the body?"

Christian shrugged.

"We quite simply buried him. Sikkov wasn't the sort who would have a family claiming the body."

"And nobody wondered who killed him?"

"No, Sikkov was a shady character who is not going to be missed. You killed him?"

"Yes," I whispered. "But I can't tell you much more. I mentioned how I've been following the storks. I think Sikkov was doing so, too. In Sofia, he and another Bulgarian tried to kill me. They murdered several innocent people. In the fray, I managed to kill his accomplice and escape. Then Sikkov caught up with me here. In fact, he already knew my next port of call."

"How did he know that?"

"Because of the storks. So, you really don't know what Sikkov got up to in the camp?"

"Nothing medical, that much is sure. This year, he arrived about two weeks ago, then left again almost at once. The next time we saw him, he was dead."

So, Sikkov had been waiting for the storks in Israel, then "they" had called him back to Bulgaria with the sole objective of killing me.

"Sikkov had pretty advanced weapons. How do you explain that?"

"You're holding the answer in your hands. Sikkov was a United Nations security agent, and so had access to UN weaponry."

"Why did he have a UN passport?"

"It's a handy passport to have. You no longer need a visa to cross borders and you avoid the usual checks. The United Nations sometimes grants this sort of favour to those of our agents that travel a lot. It's a sort of perk."

"So One World has close ties with the UN?"

"Very much so. But we remain independent."

"Does the name Max Böhm mean anything to you?"

"Is he German?"

"No, he's a Swiss ornithologist. He's quite famous in your country. And what about Iddo Gabbor?"

"No."

Nor did the names of Milan Djuric or Markus Lasarevich ring any bells. I asked another question:

"Do your teams perform serious operations, such as organ transplants?"

Christian shrugged.

"Our equipment isn't sophisticated enough."

"You don't even run tests on tissue, to establish possible compatible donors?"

"You mean HLA? (I noted down the term in my notebook.) No, not at all. But then again, we might. We do lots of tests on our patients. But why would we analyse their tissue type? We haven't got the right equipment for operating."

I asked my last question:

"Apart from Sikkov's death, have there been any other unusually violent incidents? Acts of cruelty not normally perpetrated by the Intifada?"

Christian shook his head.

"We've got enough on our plate as it is."

He stared at me as though he had never seen me before. Then, breaking into a nervous laugh, he said:

"Your eyes are scaring me! You know, I think I preferred you when you were mute."

CHAPTER 27

Two days later, I set off for Jerusalem. On the way, I thought over my new plan. I was more determined to follow the storks than ever, but I was now going to change direction. Sikkov's presence in Israel proved that my enemies knew the path I was taking. Therefore, I decided to break that logic by joining the storks of the west. There were two advantages to this initiative: firstly, it would throw my pursuers, at least for a time; secondly, the western storks, which were presumably already nearing the Central African Republic, would lead me directly to the smugglers.

At about 4 p.m., I arrived in a totally deserted Ben-Gurion Airport. A plane was leaving for Paris in the late afternoon. I got some change and headed for a phone box.

Firstly, I called my answering machine. Dumaz had phoned several times. He was now worried and talked about issuing an international missing person notice. It was normal that he was fretting. A week ago, I had promised to phone him back the next day. Through his various messages, I followed the progress that he had made. Dumaz had gone to Antwerp and said he had discovered things of "capital importance". He must have found traces of Max Böhm in the diamond exchanges.

Wagner, too, was troubled by my silence and had left several messages. He was closely following the storks' path and said that he had faxed a summary of them to my home. There was also a call from Nelly Braesler. I dialled the number of Dumaz's direct line. After eight rings, the inspector answered and sounded startled to hear my voice.

"Louis! Where are you? I thought you'd been killed."

"I nearly was. I became a Palestinian refugee."

"In a camp?"

"I'll tell you all about it later, in Paris. I'm coming back this evening."

"So you're dropping the investigation?"

"Not at all. I'm about to relaunch it."

"What have you found out?"

"Many things."

"For instance?"

"I can't tell you by phone. Wait for my call this evening, then fax me. Okay?"

"Okay, I . . ."

"Till this evening, then."

I hung up and called Wagner. The scientist confirmed that the eastern storks were heading for Sudan. Most of them had already successfully crossed the Suez Canal. I then asked him about the ones in the west, explaining that I now wanted to follow the other migration route. I made up some more reasons, saying that I was impatient to see them in the savanna and to observe their behaviour and how they fed. Ulrich consulted his computer and gave me the information. The birds were now crossing the Sahara. Some of them had already forked off towards Mali and the Niger delta, while others were heading for Nigeria, Senegal and the Central African Republic. I asked Wagner to fax me the satellite map and a list of exact locations.

It was time to check in. I had carefully stripped down my Glock and placed its two metal parts – the barrel and breech – in a sort of small greasy tool box which Christian had given me. On the other hand, I had abandoned my stock of cartridges. At the check-in desk, a man from the Israeli tourist board was waiting for me. He was a friendly sort, and quite openly admitted that he had followed me all the way from Balatakamp. He asked me to follow him and I had the agreeable experience of walking straight through passport control and customs without the slightest check or question. "We want to spare you the usual annoyance of Israeli regulations," my guide explained. He apologized once more for that dreadful "accident" at Balatakamp and wished me a good flight. In the departure lounge, I silently cursed myself for not having brought along my 45mm cartridges.

We took off at 7.30 a.m. In the plane, I opened the book that Christian had given me, *Paths of Hope*, in which Pierre Doisneau told his story. I skimmed through the six-hundred-page doorstopper. The book was relatively well written and crammed with good intentions. For example: "The faces of the sick were pale. They gave off a soft, sad light, which had the acrid, melancholy colour of sulphur. That morning, I realized that the children were all flowers, all sick flowers, and it was my job to nurse them and return them to health."

Or: "The monsoon approached. And, with it, the inevitable hordes of miasma and diseases. The town was going to turn red and the streets would summon up death. Never mind which neighbourhood. Never mind which form it took. The spectacle of human pain was going to spread and languish along the sodden pavements. As far as the feverish confines of humanity, where the darkness of the flesh is given up to the blindness of the night."

Or else: "Khalil's face was scarlet. He was biting his blanket and holding back his tears. He did not want to cry in front of me. And, from the depths of his pride, the child even smiled at me. Suddenly, he coughed up some blood. And I knew that it was the dew that sometimes precedes the endless shadows, marking his arrival in the next world."

The style was ambiguous. The images and phrasing conjured up a strange fascination. Doisneau transfigured Calcutta's suffering and, in a way, gave it a disquieting beauty. All the same, I knew that the book's success was really down to that French doctor's solitary destiny, and the way he had affronted the Indian people's implacable misfortunes. Doisneau hid nothing: the horror of the slums, the millions living like rats in filth and sickness, the abject existences of those that survive by selling their blood or their eyes, or by pulling rickshaws.

Paths of Hope was a black-and-white book. On the one hand, there was the unbearable daily suffering of the many. On the other, the lone man who cries "no!" and cures the people of their pain. According to him, Bengalis had been able to preserve genuine dignity in the face of agony. The public liked this sort of story about "pride in suffering". I closed the book. It had taught me nothing. Except perhaps that One World and its founder were absolutely irreproachable.

At about midnight, the plane touched down. I went through customs at Roissy-Charles-de-Gaulle Airport and, in the bright night, took a taxi. I was home.

CHAPTER 28

It was almost 1 a.m. by the time I got back to my apartment. I stumbled across a pile of mail, picked it up and then checked each room to see if anybody had broken in during my absence. I went into my study and called Dumaz. The inspector immediately faxed me back a five-page document.

I read straight through it, without bothering to sit down. Firstly, Dumaz had evidence that Max Böhm used to go to Antwerp. He had shown a portrait of the ornithologist around the diamond exchanges. Several people recognized old Max and clearly remembered his regular visits there. Since 1979, he had gone there to sell his diamonds each year at exactly the same period, between March and April. Some dealers had even joked with him and asked if he had a "diamond tree" which blossomed in springtime.

The second part of the fax was even more interesting. Before setting off for Belgium, Dumaz had asked the CSO – the huge uncut diamond purchasing group based in London, that controls eighty to eighty-five per cent of the world's overall diamond production – to send him a complete list of all the managers, engineers and geologists who had worked in mines in the east and west of Africa from 1969 to the present. On his return, he had patiently studied this long list and, besides Max Böhm, had found two other names that were familiar to him.

The first was Otto Kiefer. According to the CSO, "Papa Grenade" was still in charge of several diamond mines in the Central African Republic and, in particular, of Sicamine. Now, Dumaz was convinced that this Czech played a vital role in smuggling out the stones. The second man opened up unexpected horizons. In the list covering South Africa, Dumaz had noticed a name that rang bells – Niels van Dötten, a man who had worked with Max Böhm from 1969 to 1972 and who was now one of the principal heads of the mines in Kimberley. Niels van Dötten was also the Belgian geologist who had gone into the depths of the jungle with Böhm in August 1977. Guillard, the French engineer whom Dumaz had questioned, thought that Dötten was Flemish. His name and accent had deceived him. Dötten was neither Flemish nor Dutch. He was an Afrikaner.

This vital discovery showed that Böhm had remained in close contact with a South African diamond specialist from the beginning of the 1970s. What is more, for some mysterious reason van Dötten had joined up with Böhm in the Central African Republic in August 1977. After Böhm's "resurrection" in 1978, the two of them must have got back in touch. Van Dötten was the man in the east – the one who "loaded" the South African storks with diamonds he had removed from the mines he managed – while Kiefer was the man in the west.

Just before Dumaz's fax, I had found one from Wagner which had been sent that afternoon. It contained a satellite map of Europe, the Middle East and Africa, on which the itineraries the storks had taken were clearly marked, along with their future routes. On the map of Europe, at the top of the network, I wrote "Max Böhm", the brains behind the system. Midway, in the centre of Africa, I wrote "Otto Kiefer". And in the extreme south-east, "Niels van Dötten". On the satellite map, the paths of the storks ran between these names, linking the three points together. The system was perfect. Infallible.

I called Dumaz.

"Well?" he asked as soon as he heard my voice.

"It's perfect," I said. "Your information confirms what I've discovered."

"Now it's your turn to tell me what you've found out."

I gave him a brief summary – the use of the storks, the diamonds, Sikkov and his accomplice and the mysterious involvement of One World. Finally, I informed Dumaz of my intention to go to the Central African Republic. The inspector was speechless. Then, after a minute or so, he managed to ask:

"Where are the diamonds?"

"Which ones?"

"The ones from the east, which disappeared with the storks."

This question bugged me. I had mentioned neither Iddo nor Sarah. Dumaz was highly intrigued by that missing fortune. I decided to lie.

"I don't know," I said bluntly.

Dumaz sighed.

"We're starting to get out of our depth here."

"What do you mean?"

"I always thought that Max Böhm was involved in smuggling African merchandise. But only as an amateur. The enormity of the system takes my breath away."

"And so?"

"I spoke to some people at the CSO. For years they have suspected that smuggling has been going on, and that Max Böhm played a central role in it. But they never succeeded in pinpointing the method – the stork network that you have uncovered. You've done a great job, Louis. But now it's time to hand over to the specialists. Let's call the CSO."

"No, let's make a deal. Give me ten days, the time to go to the Central African Republic and come back – then we'll pass the entire affair over to the CSO and Interpol. Until then, not a word to anybody."

Dumaz hesitated, then said:

"Ten days, okay."

"Listen," I continued. "I have a job for you. A new person has entered into this business. A woman. Her name's Sarah Gabbor. She became involved quite by chance, she now has the diamonds and is going to try to sell them in Antwerp. Can you try to find her?"

"Is she one of Max Böhm's accomplices?"

"No. She's simply going to try to shift the stones."

"A lot of them?"

"A few."

My irrational lack of trust had made me lie to Dumaz again.

"What does she look like?"

"Very tall and slim. She's twenty-eight, but looks older. She's blonde, with shoulder-length hair, dark skin and absolutely stunning eyes. Her face is rather angular, and unusual. Believe you me, Hervé, people won't forget her once they've seen her."

"The stones are uncut, I suppose."

"That's right. They come from Böhm's network."

"How long has she been trying to sell them?"

"She probably started four or five days ago. Sarah is Israeli. So she'll go to see the Jewish dealers. Go back and see the ones you questioned."

"And what if I find her?"

"You approach her cautiously and tell her that you're working with me. Don't mention the diamonds. Just persuade her to lie low until I get back. Okay?"

"Okay."

Dumaz seemed to ponder this for a few seconds, then he said:

"Suppose I find this Sarah. What can I do to convince her that we really are working together?"

"Tell her I'm wearing her Glock over my heart."

"Her what?"

"Her Glock. G. L. O. C. K. She'll understand. One last thing," I added. "Don't be fooled by Sarah's appearance. She's slight and beautiful, but she's also dangerous. She's an Israeli, you understand? A trained soldier, used to handling guns. Beware of her every move."

"I see," Dumaz said off-handedly. "Is that all?"

"I asked you for information concerning One World. I didn't find any in the fax."

"I came up against some serious obstacles."

"Meaning?"

"One World gave me a detailed map showing its centres throughout the world. But they refused to give me a list of the members of the 1001 Club."

"As a policeman, you could . . ."

"I don't have a warrant, or any official backing. What's more, One World is a real institution here in Switzerland. It wouldn't do for one insignificant cop to start bothering them about a case where there is not an iota of proof. To be honest, it's beyond my powers."

I found Dumaz exasperating. He was losing his touch.

"Could you at least fax me the map?"

"The minute you hang up."

"Hervé, I'm leaving as soon as possible for the Central African Republic. Tomorrow, or the next day. I won't contact you. It's too complicated. In about ten days, I'll be back with the last keys to this enigma."

I bade Dumaz farewell and hung up. A few seconds later, the fax machine started to hum. It was the map of OW centres. There were currently about sixty camps scattered across the world, about a third of which were permanent. The rest moved about as required. There were centres in Asia, Africa, South America and Eastern Europe, concentrated in areas wracked by war, famine or poverty. For example, there were over twenty in the Horn of Africa. Bangladesh, Afghanistan, Brazil and Peru had a further twenty or so. But, among that varied distribution, I noticed two clear paths. An "eastern" itinerary going through the Balkans, Turkey, Israel, Sudan, and then South Africa. And a far shorter "western" route running from the south of Morocco (the Polisario front), then via Mali, Niger, Nigeria and the Central African Republic. I laid this map over Wagner's one. The camps corresponded to the storks' migration routes and could be used as bases for the birds' sentinels, such as Sikkov.

That night, I hardly slept. I phoned to inquire about flights to Bangui. An Air Afrique flight was leaving the following evening at 11.30 p.m. I reserved a first-class ticket – once more courtesy of Max Böhm.

My destiny was closing in around me. I was alone again. Headed for the kernel of this mystery, and the still-smoking ashes of my own past.

IV
The Depths of the Jungle

On the evening of 13 September, when the glass doors in Roissy-Charles-de-Gaulle opened beneath the Air Afrique ensign, I realized that I was already in darkest Africa. Tall women swaggered in their brightly coloured robes, serious-looking Blacks dressed in diplomatic suits watched over their cardboard luggage, giants in turbans and pale jellabas holding wooden canes were waiting under the departure boards. Many flights to Africa leave at night. And, that evening, there was a huge crowd waiting at the counters.

I checked in, then took the escalator up to the departure lounge. That day, I had completed my equipment by buying a small waterproof rucksack, an oilcloth cape (it was the middle of the rainy season in Central Africa), a light cotton bed sheet, walking shoes made of a synthetic material that dried rapidly and an impressive-looking knife with a jagged blade. I had also procured a light tent, for one or two people, in case I had to sleep out, and had added to my first-aid kit a supply of treatments for malaria and diarrhoea, plus an anti-mosquito spray. Also in my luggage was some survival food – marzipan, cereals, self-heating meals – which would allow me to avoid having to dine off grilled monkeys or antelope kebabs. Finally, I had brought along a Dictaphone and some 120-minute cassettes to record any possible interrogation sessions.

We boarded at about 11 p.m. The plane was half empty, and the passengers were all men. I noticed that I was the only White. The Central African Republic did not seem to be a tourist destination. The Blacks made themselves comfortable, then conversed in some unknown language, full of lumpy syllables and sharp intonations. I guessed that they were speaking Sango, the Republic's national language. Occasionally they broke into a French that was full of hollows and bumps, of sententious tags and heavily rolled r's. I immediately fell in love with that unexpected parlance. It was the first time that I had heard a language being spoken as much by its sonority as by the words themselves.

At midnight, the DC 10 took off. My neighbours opened their attaché cases and produced bottles of whisky and gin. They offered me a glass. I refused. Outside, the night was radiant and seemed to be surrounding us with a strange halo. My neighbours' conversation rocked me. I soon fell asleep.

At 2 a.m., we stopped over at Ndjamena in Chad. All I could see through the window were the vague contours of an ill-lit building at the end of the runway. The acrid heat filtered almost hungrily into the plane through the open door. Outside, pale figures floated around in the darkness. We took off again. Ndjamena had been as furtive as a vision.

At five in the morning, I awoke with a start. Daylight was shining above the clouds. It was a vibrant grey light, an iron glacis casting reflections that scintillated like mercury. The plane shot down at an eighty-degree angle through the clouds. We crossed layers of black, blue and grey that left us in total darkness.

Then, suddenly, Africa appeared.

An endless forest spread out before my eyes. It was an emerald sea, huge and undulating, becoming ever clearer as we descended. Little by little, the dark green lightened into a variety of shades. I saw its dishevelled locks, its fluffy crests, its effervescence of treetops. The rivers were yellow, the earth blood-red and the trees shook like shards of freshness. Everything was vibrant, sharp and luminous. In that seething life, darker patches, areas of rest, were marked out with languid water-lilies or tranquil meadows. Tiny shacks appeared in the jungle. I imagined the people that lived there and belonged to that exuberant nature. I imagined the watery existence, the iron mornings with animal calls whistling in their ears, the earth giving way under their feet, leaving the imprint of their slow trudging. During the entire time we spent landing, I remained there, my mouth gawping in astonishment.

I do not know exactly where the Tropic of Cancer lies but, on leaving the plane, I knew that I had crossed it and was now near the Equator. The air was a pure blast of fire. The sky had a uniform and totally pure clarity, as though it had been washed clean by the morning rains. Above all, I was overwhelmed by the smells. Slow, heavy odours, tenaciously biting, forming a strange mixture of excessive life and death, of birth and decay.

The arrivals hall was a simple block of solid concrete, undecorated and unfinished. In the middle stood two small wooden counters, behind which armed soldiers checked our passports and vaccination certificates. Then we passed through customs: a long moving pavement, which was out of order, where we had to open all of our luggage (my Glock was still in separate pieces in my two bags). The soldier drew a cross on the luggage with some damp chalk, then motioned me on. I found myself outside, among a crowd of voluble families come to pick up their brothers or their cousins. The humidity got worse and it felt as if I was moving into the heart of an infinite sponge.

"Where are you going, boss?"

A tall Black with a stiff smile was barring my way. He was offering me his services. Off the cuff and just for the hell of it, I said: "I'm from Sicamine. Take me to the usual hotel." I was bluffing, but the name of the mine acted as an "open Sesame". The man whistled between his fingers, calling over a mob of children who immediately picked up my luggage. He kept repeating to them "Sicamine, Sicamine" to make them work faster. One minute later, I was on my way to Bangui in a dusty yellow taxi whose chassis was bouncing off the ground.

Bangui looked nothing like a town. It was more of a large village, composed of odds and ends. The houses were made of wattle with corrugated iron roofs. The road was beaten earth, a scarlet track flanked by numerous passers-by. Under the smooth sky, I drank in the duality of African colours. Black and red. Flesh and earth. The morning downpour had saturated the ground, and the road was dotted with gleaming puddles. The men were elegant in their short-sleeved shirts and sandals. They walked with nonchalant valour in the rising heat. But, above all, there were women. Tall straight beanstalks, backs arched, as beautiful as goddesses, carrying bundles on their heads as a flower carries its petals. Their necks were like graceful collars, their faces radiated sweetness and firmness and their long feet, black above, pale below, were mind-blowingly sensual. Under that apocalyptic sky, those elegant, proud figures were the finest spectacle that I had ever seen.

"Sicamine, loadsa money!" my guide joked next to the driver. He rubbed his index finger against his thumb. I smiled and nodded. We had arrived in front of the Novotel. A building of grey roughcast, with wooden balconies, in the shadow of some immense trees. I tipped the young Black in French francs and entered the hotel. I paid for one night in advance and changed five thousand French francs into CFA francs – enough to organize my trip into the jungle. I was taken to my room, which was on the ground floor, beside a large interior patio containing a swimming pool amid an exotic garden. I shrugged. It was the rainy season and that patch of turquoise water now looked like a village pond.

My room was pleasant, spacious and bright. The decor was anonymous, but the colours – brown, ochre and white – seemed to me for some unknown reason to be typically African. The air conditioning purred. I had a shower and changed. Deciding to start my inquiries at once, I rummaged through the drawer of the desk and discovered a national telephone directory, a slim volume of about thirty pages. I dialled the number of Sicamine's head office.

I spoke to an executive director called Jean-Claude Bonafé. I told him that I was a journalist and that I wanted to write a piece about Pygmies. It had come to my attention that some of the company's mines lay on the territories of the Aka Pygmies. Could he help me visit the region? In Africa, you can count on solidarity between Whites. Bonafé immediately offered to lend me a car to drive as far as the edge of the forest, then provide me with a guide he knew. But he also warned me that I should absolutely avoid trespassing on Sicamine property. The general manager, Otto Kiefer, lived out there and he was "an awkward customer". In conclusion, he added in a confidential tone: "In fact, if Kiefer knew I was helping you, then I'd be in deep water."

Bonafé then invited me to come to his office that morning to prepare the excursion. I accepted and hung up. I made some other calls round Bangui's French community. It was Saturday, but apparently everybody was at work. I spoke to mine managers, heads of sawmills and people at the French embassy. All of those uprooted French, worn out and emptied by the tropics, sounded pleased to speak to me. By discreet questioning, I managed to obtain a clear idea of the general situation and, in particular, draw a full portrait of Otto Kiefer.

The Czech managed four mines scattered across the far south of the country, at the beginning of the great equatorial forest which spreads across the Congo, Zaire and Gabon. He was now working for the government of the Central African Republic. Unfortunately, everybody agreed that the veins were drying up. The country no longer produced high-quality diamonds, but they continued digging anyway. Personally, I had a different idea about the reason for this lack of valuable gems, of course.

Without exception, everybody I talked to confirmed that Kiefer was violent and cruel. He was now old, about sixty, but more dangerous than ever. He had set up home in the depths of the jungle in order to watch over his men more closely. Nobody suspected that Kiefer was behind a diamond smuggling network. The real reason why he remained in the darkness of the forest was to have a free hand, to make off with the uncut gems and send them to his friend Böhm by means of the storks.

I resolved to find Kiefer in the jungle and confront him there. Or else, according to how things turned out, to follow him until he went off looking for the storks. Even though Böhm was dead, I felt sure that he would not abandon their system of couriers. The storks had not yet reached the Central African Republic. I thus had eight days in which to trap Kiefer in the heart of his mines. It was eleven o'clock. I slipped on my safari jacket and went to meet Bonafé.

CHAPTER 30

Sicamine's head office was to the south of the town. It took about fifteen minutes to go there by taxi, along the red avenues that branched out beneath the massive trees. Right in the middle of Bangui, genuine patches of forest land could be found, criss-crossed with huge crimson ruts, or else overgrown ruined buildings, looking as though they had been pulverized by a herd of elephants.

The offices had been set up in a sort of wooden ranch, in front of which some Range Rovers were parked, speckled with laterite – or African earth. I gave my name at reception. A broad woman then insisted on escorting me along a corridor with ill-fitting wooden tiles. I followed her supple swagger.

Jean-Claude Bonafé was a plump, balding little fifty-year-old White. He was wearing a sky-blue shirt and trousers of unbleached linen. At first sight, he looked just like any other French company manager. Except for the gleam of utter madness in his stare. He seemed consumed from within, eaten up by torment, chock full of volleys of laughter and painful ideas. His eyes shone like panes of glass and his long bevelled teeth rested on his lower lip in a perpetual smile. He still had not admitted defeat by the tropics. He was struggling against tropical decay by applying himself to details, adding personal touches and wearing Parisian aftershave.

"It's a real pleasure to meet you," he said at once. "I've looked into your project and picked a guide you can trust. He's one of my employees' cousins, and comes from the Lobaye."

He sat down behind his desk, which was a block of undressed timber scattered with African sculptures, then pointed a manicured hand at a map of the Central African Republic which was pinned on the wall behind him.

"In fact," he said, "the best-known part of the Republic is the south, because the capital Bangui is there and this is where the dense forests begin, which are the source of all its wealth. It is also the territory of the Mbakas, the true masters of the country. Bokassa belonged to that tribe. The region you want to visit is even farther to the south, beyond Mbaïki."

Bonafé indicated a huge patch of green on the map. There was no sign of there being any roads, tracks or villages. Nothing, except green. Infinite forest.

"Here," he went on, "is where our mine is. Just above the Congo. It is the territory of the Aka Pygmies. The 'Tall Blacks' never venture there. They're terrified of the place."

An idea formed in my mind. Kiefer, the lord of darkness, was better protected there than by a huge army. The trees, animals and legends were his bodyguards. I took off my jacket. It was sweltering in there. The air conditioning was not working. I glanced over at Bonafé. His shirt was drenched with sweat. He pressed on:

"As for me, I adore Pygmies. They're an exceptional people, full of joy and mystery. But the forest is even more exceptional." His eyes were lit with delight, his teeth like smashed bottles opened in beatitude. "Do you know how that world works, Monsieur Antioch? The Greenwood draws its energy from the light. And this light arrives, drop by drop through a canopy." Bonafé formed his chubby fingers into a roof, then lowered his voice, as though confiding a secret. "If a tree falls, crash! Then the light filters in through the hole. The vegetation captures the rays, grows rapidly and immediately plugs the gap. It's fantastic. On the ground, the fallen tree then fertilizes the earth for the next generation. And so on and so forth. It's a marvellous forest, Monsieur Antioch. An intense, seething, rapacious world. An independent universe with its own rhythms, own rules and own inhabitants. Thousands of different species of vegetation, invertebrates and vertebrates live there!"

I looked at Bonafé's grotesque waxy face, stuck onto his broad shoulders. He had struggled in vain, and was now melting, fading away into the torpor of the tropics.

"And is the forest . . . dangerous?"

Bonafé sniggered.

"Oh yes, indeed it is," he replied. "Pretty dangerous. Especially the insects. Most of them carry diseases. There are mosquitoes that transmit endemic forms of malaria, which are extremely resistant to quinine, or dengue, otherwise known as break-bone fever. There are *fourroux*, whose stings provoke quite unbearable itching, ants which destroy everything in their path, and filaria which inject filaments into your arteries that completely block them. Then other tough little horrors, such as jiggers which eat into your toes or vampire flies that suck your blood. Or even a special sort of worm that hatches out under your skin. I had a few of them on my head. I could feel them digging, scratching and moving under my scalp. It is quite common to spot one with the naked eye, wriggling across the eyelid of the person who is talking to you. (Bonafé laughed. He looked taken aback by his own conclusions.) So, yes, the forest is dangerous. But accidents can happen anywhere. So don't you worry, Monsieur Antioch. The brush is marvellous, absolutely marvellous . . ."

He picked up his phone, said something in Sango, then asked me: "When do you intend to leave?"

"As soon as possible."

"Do you have authorization?"

"What authorization?"

Bonafé's eyes widened, then he chuckled once more. Clapping his hands together, he repeated: "What authorization? What authorization?" His face was running with sweat. Still chuckling away to himself, he took out a silk handkerchief, then explained:

"You can't leave here without ministerial authorization. Every track, every village is watched by the police. What do you expect? After all, this is Africa, and we are still governed by a military regime. What's more, there have been troubles recently. Strikes. You'll have to apply for authorization from the Ministry of Information and Communications."

"How long will that take?"

"At least three days, I'm afraid. Especially as you will now have to wait until Monday to lodge the application. As for me, I can speak up for you to the Minister. He's a mulatto and a friend of mine. (It sounded as though those two facts were inextricably linked.) We shall then accelerate the procedure. But I shall need some passport photographs of you and your passport itself. As soon as you receive the document . . ."

I regretfully gave him what he asked for, including two photos from a now useless visa for Sudan.

There was a knock at the door. A huge Black came through it. His face was round with a pug nose and bulging eyes. His skin looked like leather. He was about thirty and dressed in a mostly blue jellaba.

"Gabriel," Bonafé said, "I'd like to introduce you to Louis Antioch. He's a French journalist and wishes to go into the brush to research an article about the Pygmies. I think you'll be able to help him."

Gabriel stared at me. Then Bonafé said:

"Gabriel comes from the Lobaye region. All of his family lives on the edge of the forest."

The Black continued to stare at me. His protruding eyes were lit with a smile. Bonafé went on:

"Gabriel will take your papers to the Ministry. One of his cousins works there. As soon as your authorization is ready, I'll lay on a Range Rover for you."

"Thank you very much."

"Don't thank me. The car will be of little use to you. The forest starts twenty miles beyond Mbaïki. No more roads."

"And so?"

"And so you will have to continue on foot as far as our mines. It's about a four-day march."

"So you haven't laid roads to your mines?"

Bonafé snorted.

"Roads! (He turned towards the Black.) Roads, Gabriel. (Then back towards me.) That's a good one, Monsieur Antioch. You have no idea of the jungle you are going to be up against. It takes that vegetation only a few weeks to wipe out the slightest trace of any track. We long ago gave up trying to lay roads through that tangle of creepers. Anyway, in case you didn't know, diamonds are not a particularly heavy load. There's no need for lorries or any special equipment. However, we do have a helicopter which regularly performs a shuttle service. But we can't charter it out just to you."

A smile flickered over his lips, an eel slithering into murky waters.

"What's more, once you reach the depths of the jungle, you won't be able to count on our men. Miners work hard. And Clément, our foreman, is senile. As for Kiefer, I've already warned you about him. Steer clear of him. So, go round our mine and head for the Mission."

"The Mission?"

"Even deeper in the forest, an Alsatian nun has set up a clinic, where she nurses and teaches the Pygmies."

"She lives alone there?"

"Yes. She comes to Bangui once a month to supervise the loading of her supplies. We let her use our helicopter. Then she vanishes again with her porters for a month. If you're looking for a quiet existence, then look no further. It's impossible to imagine a more isolated place. Sister Pascale will point out the more interesting Aka camps to you. How does all that sound?"

The intensity of the jungle, a nun protected by Pygmies, Kiefer in the heart of darkness: the madness of Africa was beginning to take control.

"I have one last request."

"Fire away."

"Could you procure some 45mm bullets for an automatic pistol?"

He gave me a side-on glance, as though trying to gauge my real intentions. Then he peered across at Gabriel.

"No problem."

Bonafé slapped both of his hands on the desk, then turned towards the Black.

"Do you understand, Gabriel? You're going to take Monsieur Antioch to the edge of the forest. Then ask your cousin to guide him to the Mission."

The Black nodded. His eyes were still fixed on me. Bonafé had spoken to him like a primary teacher talking to his pupils. But it seemed to me that Gabriel was bright enough to run rings round both of us. His intelligence hovered in the stifling heat, like a wily insect. I thanked Bonafé then returned to the subject of Kiefer.

"It seems rather odd for your managing director to have set up shop in the middle of nowhere like that."

Bonafé smirked once more.

"That just depends on your point of view. The mining of diamonds requires extremely close surveillance. And Kiefer is someone who knows and controls everything."

I risked another question:

"Did you know Max Böhm?"

"The Swiss guy? No, not personally. I arrived here in 1980, after he had left. He was the head of Sicamine before Kiefer. Is he an acquaintance of yours? Do forgive me, but everybody here thinks that Böhm was even worse than our Czech. Which is really saying something. (He shrugged.) But that's the way it goes, my friend. Africa makes men cruel."

"Why did Böhm leave Africa?"

"I have no idea. I think he had health problems. Or problems with Bokassa. Or both. Really, I don't know."

"Do you think Mr Kiefer is still in touch with him?"

That was one question too many. Bonafé gave me a searching look, his eyes seeming to concentrate on digging out what was really on my mind. I forced a smile onto my face and stood up. On the doorstep, Bonafé slapped me on the back and repeated:

"Don't forget, old chap, not a word of all this to Kiefer."

I decided to walk back under the shade of the tall trees. The sun was high. In places, the mud was already dry and flaking away like a purple pigment. The heavy tops of the trees swayed slowly as the wind soughed through them.

Suddenly, I felt a hand on my shoulder. I turned round to discover Gabriel standing there with a broad grin on his face. He immediately said, in his steady voice:

"Boss, you're as interested in Pygmies as I am in cacti. Now, I know someone who can tell you about Max Böhm and Otto Kiefer."

My heart stopped beating.

"Who?"

"My father. (Gabriel lowered his voice.) My father was Max Böhm's guide."

"When can I see him?"

"He'll be in Bangui tomorrow morning."

"Ask him to go to the Novotel. I'll be expecting him."

CHAPTER 31

I had lunch in the shade of the hotel's terrace. The tables were positioned around the swimming pool and, below the tropical plants, I was served fresh fish from the river. The Novotel seemed deserted. Its few guests were European businessmen, who rushed through their deals with only one thought in mind – the return flight. But I liked the hotel. The wide terrace covered with pale stones and plants had the melancholy charm of abandoned colonial residences, where the vegetation had sculpted rivers of creepers and lakes of wild grasses.

While enjoying my thread-fin, I watched the gardener being lectured by the hotel manager. He was a young Frenchman with a greenish tinge, who seemed to be at the end of his tether. He was trying to straighten a rose plant, which the Black had crushed by mistake. Without the dialogue, the scene was decidedly burlesque. The White's irritation, his wild gesticulations, and the Black nodding his head automatically with a contrite air. It was like a scene from a silent movie.

He then came straight over to welcome me to his hotel, while trying to fathom out the obscure reason for my coming to the Central African Republic. I noticed that he twitched when he saw the scar on my lip. I told him about my ideas for an article. He then told me the story of his life. He had volunteered to manage the

Bangui Novotel. According to him, it was a necessary career move. He seemed to be suggesting that if you could manage something here, then you could manage anything anywhere. Then he launched into a long tirade against the incompetence of the Africans, their carelessness and their innumerable faults.

"I have to keep everything under lock and key," he explained, shaking the huge bunch of keys he had on his belt. "And don't be taken in by their neat appearance. That's the fruit of a long struggle."

The manager's "struggle" had resulted in the pink short-sleeved shirt, topped off by a bow tie, which all the staff wore to great comic effect.

"As soon as they leave the hotel," he went on, "they go back barefoot to their huts and sleep on the floor!"

The manager had the same expression as Bonafé. They were worn down, strangely corroded by a root that had grown up inside their bodies and was feeding off their blood.

"By the way," he said in conclusion. "You haven't got too many lizards in your room, have you?"

I replied that I hadn't, then froze him out with a long silence.

After lunch, I decided to consult the documents I had brought from Paris concerning diamonds and heart surgery. I rapidly flicked through the information about diamonds: mining methods, classification, carats etc. I now knew enough about the main links in Böhm's network. Technical data and specialist comments were not going to teach me much more.

So I turned to my heart surgery file, which contained extracts from medical encyclopaedias. Its history was truly epic, written by daredevil pioneers. I went back in time:

"... The true beginnings of heart surgery go back to Philadelphia and Charles Bailey. His first operation on a mitral valve dates back to the end of 1947. It was a failure. The patient bled to death. However, Bailey was sure that he was on the right track. But his colleagues attacked him, calling him a madman, or a butcher. Bailey waited and thought things over. In March 1948, he performed an apparently satisfactory valvotomy in Wilmington Memorial Hospital. But the patient died three days later because of a mistake made in intensive care. To carry out his scheme, Bailey had to become a quack surgeon and operate only in hospitals that would tolerate his work. On 10 June 1948, Charles Bailey had to operate on two strictured valves in one day. The first patient died of a heart attack before the end of the operation. Scared that he would not be allowed to proceed, Charles Bailey dashed to the other hospital before news of the failure spread. Then a miracle happened: the second operation was a success. Mitral valve surgery had at last been born."

I continued reading, paying especial attention to the first heart transplants.

"Contrary to popular belief, it was not Christiaan Neethling Barnard, the South African surgeon, who, on 3 December 1967, performed the first heart transplant on a man. Before him, in January 1960, a French surgeon, Pierre Sénicier, grafted a chimpanzee's heart into the thorax of a sixty-eight-year-old patient who was in the final stages of irreversible cardiac insufficiency. The operation was successful. But the new heart only worked for a few hours."

I browsed on:

"One of the greatest dates in the history of cardiac surgery remains the heart transplant performed by Professor Christiaan Barnard in Cape Town in 1967. The technique of this operation, which was soon to be repeated in the United States, Great Britain and France, had been perfected by an American, Professor Shumway, and is accordingly called the 'Shumway method' . . . The patient, Louis Washkansky was fifty-five years old. In a period of seven years, he had suffered three myocardial infarctions, the last of which had left him in a state of terminal cardiac insufficiency. During the entire

month of November 1967, a team of thirty surgeons, anaes-
thetists, doctors and technicians was permanently on hand in
Groote Schuur Hospital, in Cape Town, awaiting the operation whose date and time were to be decided by Professor
Christiaan Barnard. This decision was made during the night
of 3rd/4th December. A young woman aged twenty-five
had just been killed in a car accident. Her heart would replace
Louis Washkansky's defective one. He survived for three
weeks, before dying of pneumonia. The huge quantity of
immuno-depressive drugs that he had taken to stop the graft
from being rejected had so weakened his system of defence
that he was unable to fight against the infection."

All that open flesh and manipulations on organs was making
me feel sick. However, I was sure that Max Böhm had his part in this
story. He had worked in South Africa from 1969 to 1972. I dreamt
up some unlikely explanations for his transplant. Maybe he had
met Christiaan Barnard in Cape Town, or else some doctors in his
department. Perhaps he had gone back there after his attack in 1977.
Or else, for some reason that escaped me, he knew that one of those
doctors capable of performing a transplant was in the Congo in
1977. But such ideas were too improbable. Nor did they solve the
"miraculous" nature of Max Böhm's physical tolerance. I then came
across a passage dealing with just that problem of tolerance:

"In the field of heart surgery, the surgical problems have been
solved and the remaining difficulties are immunological ones.
For, except in the case of identical twins, the donor's organ,
even if coming from a close relation, will be recognized by
the receiver as being different and there will be phenomena of
rejection. It is thus always necessary to treat the receiver with
immuno-depressors to limit the extent of this rejection. The
usual treatments (azathioprine, cortisone) are non-specific
and thus create risks, particularly of infection. More recently,
in the 1980s, a new product has appeared: ciclosporine. This
substance, derived from a Japanese fungus, removes a large

number of rejection phenomena. Patients thus have a far greater life expectancy and transplants have become more widespread. Another way to limit rejection is, of course, to choose a donor who is as compatible as possible. The most favourable solution is to select a sibling, or close relative, who, though not being a twin, has the same four HLA histo-compatibility antigens as the receiver. We are here referring to non-vital organs, such as the kidney. Otherwise, the organ is removed from a corpse and, by long-distance exchange, attempts are made to achieve the most compatible combinations possible. But there are over twenty thousand different HLA groups."

I closed the file. It was 6 p.m. Outside, night had already fallen. I got up and opened the bay window in my room. A wave of heat suffocated me. It was the first time that I had confronted the heat of the tropics. This climate was not an ancillary detail, but an additional factor. It was violence attacking your flesh, a weight that dragged your heart and body down into uneasy depths that are hard to describe – a softening-up of the being, in which the flesh and organs seem to melt and dissolve slowly in their own juices.

I decided to take an evening stroll.

Bangui's long avenues were empty and the few buildings, crude and blotched with mud, looked even more naked than in daylight. I headed for the river. The banks of the Ubangi were silent. The ministries and embassies slept their dreamless sleep. Barefoot soldiers stood guard. In the darkness near the water I made out the naked tops of the trees along the riverside. Sometimes, further down, a slapping could be heard in the water. I imagined some huge animal, half wild-cat half fish, slithering through the damp grass, attracted by the smells and noises of the town.

I walked on. Since arriving in Bangui, an idea had been plaguing me. This wild country had, during my childhood, been "my" country. An island in the jungle where I had grown up, played, learnt to read and write. Why had my parents buried themselves in the most obscure region of Africa? Why had they sacrificed everything, fortune, comfort and tranquillity for this patch of forest?

I never thought about my past, nor my dead parents and the history of my existence. My family did not interest me. Nor did my father's vocation, nor the devotion of my mother, who had left everything to follow her husband, nor even that brother, two years my elder, who had been burnt to death. No doubt, such indifference was a shelter. Something I often compared to the numbness of my hands. All along my arms the skin reacted normally then, further down, I could feel no precise sensations. As though an invisible wooden bar had severed my hands from the world of feelings. The same sort of phenomenon affected my memory. I could remember up until the age of six. Thereafter, there was nothing, an absence, death. My hands had been burnt. My soul, too. And my flesh and spirit had healed over in the same way, owing their recovery to forgetfulness and insensibility.

I suddenly stopped. I had left the riverbank and was now walking along a large, poorly lit avenue. I looked up and examined the street name on the sign that was hung up on the railings. I shuddered from head to toe. Avenue de France. Without realizing it, my feet had irresistibly led me to the scene of the tragedy. The place where my parents had been massacred by a horde of crazed killers on New Year's Eve, 1965.

CHAPTER 32

The next morning, I was having breakfast under a sunshade when a voice asked me:

"Are you Monsieur Louis Antioch?"

I looked up. A man aged about fifty was standing in front of me. He was short, stocky and was wearing a khaki shirt and trousers. He gave off an aura of unquestionable authority. I remembered Max

Böhm's heavy build and dress sense. The two men were alike. Except that the person talking to me was as black as an English umbrella.

"I am indeed. And who are you?"

"Joseph Mkonta. Gabriel's father, from the Sicamine."

I got to my feet at once and offered him a chair.

"Oh yes, of course. Please sit down."

Joseph Mkonta did as he was asked, linking his hands over his belly. His head shrinking into his shoulders, he glanced around in curiosity. He had a flat face, wide nostrils and rheumy eyes that seemed veiled with tenderness. But his lips were pursed in a grimace of disgust.

"Can I offer you anything? Tea? Coffee?"

"Some coffee, please."

Mkonta was also sizing me up, out of the corner of his eye. The coffee arrived. After a few standard civilities about the country, the heat and my flight, Joseph abruptly got down to the subject in hand.

"You're looking for information about Max Böhm?"

"Exactly."

"Why are you interested in him?"

"Max was a friend. I met him in Switzerland, just before he died."

"Max Böhm is dead?"

"A month ago. From a heart attack."

This news did not seem to surprise him.

"So the little time-piece finally gave up."

He fell silent, thought for a moment, then asked:

"What do you want to know?"

"Everything. His activities in the Central African Republic. His daily life. Why he left."

"Is this an investigation?"

"Yes and no. I just want to learn more about him, posthumously. That's all."

Mkonta looked suspicious.

"Are you a policeman?"

"Not at all. Everything you say will remain strictly between you and me. You have my word on that."

"Are you ready to be a little generous?"

I stared at him questioningly. Mkonta pouted.

"With a few bank notes, I mean."

"All that depends on what you can tell me," I replied.

"I knew old Max well . . . "

After a few minutes spent negotiating, we arrived at a suitable price. He then became more voluble. The words rolled out like marbles across the carpet.

"Max Böhm was a strange customer, boss . . . Round here, nobody called him Böhm . . . He was Ngakola . . . the father of white magic."

"Why was he called that?"

"Böhm had powers . . . Hidden beneath his hair . . . His hair was completely white . . . It grew straight up towards the sky . . . Like a bouquet of coconuts, see? . . . And that's what made him so strong . . . He read in everybody's soul . . . He unmasked the diamond thieves . . . Always . . . No one could resist him . . . No one . . . He was a strong man . . . Really strong . . . But he was on the side of the night."

"What do you mean?"

"He lived in the shadows . . . His spirit . . . His spirit lived in the shadows."

Mkonta sipped at his coffee.

"When did you first meet Max?"

"In 1973 . . . Before the dry season . . . Max Böhm arrived in Bagandu, my village, by the edge of the forest . . . He'd been sent by Bokassa . . . He'd come to supervise the coffee plantations . . . At that time, bandits were pillaging the crops . . . It took Böhm just a few weeks to dissuade them."

"How did he manage that?"

"He caught one of the thieves, beat him up, then dragged him into the village square . . . There, he grabbed a punch, one of the tools we used to plant the seeds . . . Then he pierced both his eardrums."

"And then?" I stammered.

"And then . . . people stopped stealing the coffee in Bagandu."

"Was anybody with him?"

"No, he was alone . . . Max Böhm wasn't afraid of anybody."

Torturing a Mbaka, all on his own on the village square. There was certainly nothing lily-livered about Böhm. Joseph went on:

"Then the next year, Böhm came back . . . This time it was to inspect the diamond mines . . . Still on Bokassa's behalf . . . The veins extended way beyond the SCAD, a big sawmill on the edge of the forest . . . You know the deep jungle, boss? No? Believe me, its really dense . . . " Joseph formed the canopy with his broad hands. His r's rolled like a cavalry charge. "But Böhm wasn't afraid . . . Böhm was never afraid . . . He wanted to go south and was looking for a guide . . . I knew the forest well, the Pygmies too . . . I even spoke Aka . . . So Böhm chose me."

"Were there any Whites working in the mines?"

"Only one . . . Clément's his name . . . He's completely mad and he married an Aka . . . He had no authority . . . It was total chaos there."

"And the mines were producing valuable stones?"

"The most beautiful diamonds in the world, boss . . . You just had to lean down and look in the creeks . . . That's why Bokassa sent Böhm . . ." He laughed sharply. "Bokassa loved precious stones!"

Joseph drank another sip of coffee, then looked at my croissants. I passed him the plate. With his mouth full, he continued:

"That year, Böhm stayed four months . . . At the beginning he played at nigger beating . . . Then he reorganized the mine and changed the techniques . . . Everything then went smoothly, believe you me . . . When the rainy season started, he went back to Bangui . . . Then, every year, he returned at the same time . . . For a 'surveillance trip', as he put it."

"That's when he used the cable cutter?"

"You know that story, do you, boss? . . . It was all really exaggerated, in fact . . . I only ever saw him do it once, in the Sicamine camp . . . And it wasn't to punish a smuggler, but a rapist . . . A bastard who'd assaulted a little girl then left her for dead in the jungle."

"What happened?"

Mkonta's grimace of disgust sharpened. He took another croissant.

"It was horrible. Really horrible. Two men held the killer down on his stomach, with his legs in the air . . . He was looking at us like a

182

trapped animal . . . He was giggling, like he didn't understand . . . Then Ngakola arrived with his huge pliers . . . He opened them then closed them with a clack on the rapist's heel . . . He screamed . . . A second snip, and it was over . . . His tendons had been cut . . . I saw his feet, boss . . . I couldn't believe it . . . They were dangling from his ankles . . . With bones sticking out . . . Blood everywhere . . . Clouds of flies . . . And the silence of the village . . . Max Böhm was standing there . . . Not saying a word . . . Blood all over his shirt . . . His face was white and covered with sweat . . . I'll never forget that, boss . . . Then, without a word, he turned the man over with his foot, brandished his pliers, then snapped them shut on the rapist's groin."

A vein was twitching in my throat.

"Böhm was that cruel?"

"He was definitely hard . . . But, in his own way, he was meting out justice . . . He was never sadistic or racist."

"So Max Böhm wasn't racist? He didn't hate Blacks?"

"Not at all. Böhm was a bastard, but no racist. Ngakola lived with us and respected us. He spoke Sango and loved the forest. Not to mention the *chagatte*."

"The what?"

"The *chagatte*. Fucking. Böhm loved Black women."

Joseph then waved his hand up and down, as though the very idea had scorched him.

I pressed on:

"Did Böhm steal diamonds?"

"Steal diamonds? . . . He'd never have done anything of the sort. I've told you, Max was a just man."

"But he supervised Bokassa's thefts, didn't he?"

"He didn't see things like that . . . He was obsessed by order and discipline . . . He wanted the camps to work without a hitch . . . After that, he didn't care less who got the diamonds, or where the money went . . . It just didn't interest him. To his mind, that was just peanuts."

Had Max Böhm disguised what he was up to that successfully, or had he started smuggling later on?

"Joseph, do you know why Max Böhm was so keen on orni-thology?"

"Birds you mean? Course I do, boss. (Joseph burst out laughing, a sabre flashing across his face.) I used to go with him to watch the storks."

"Where?"

"To Bayanga, to the west of the Sicamine. Thousands of storks go there. They feed off the crickets and other little animals." Joseph laughed again. "But the inhabitants of Bayanga used to feed off them! Böhm couldn't stand that. So he got Bokassa to open a national reserve. Suddenly, several thousand hectares of forest and savanna were declared untouchable. I've never been able to understand things like that. The forest belongs to everyone! But, then, around Bayanga, the elephants, gorillas, antelopes and gazelles became protected. And the storks, too."

So, he had managed to have his storks protected. Was he already planning to use them as couriers? At least the exchange seemed clear enough. The diamonds for Bokassa. The storks for Böhm.

"Did you know Max Böhm's family?"

"Yes and no . . . We never saw his wife . . . She was always ill . . ." Joseph grinned broadly. "A real white woman! . . . Böhm's son was different . . . He sometimes came with us . . . He never said anything . . . He was a dreamer . . . He strolled around in the forest . . . Ngakola tried to educate him . . . He made him drive the Range Rover, go hunting, supervise the prospectors in the mine . . . He wanted to make a man of him . . . But that young white kid just stayed there, daydreaming, terrified . . . He was useless . . . But what was extra-ordinary was how much they looked like each other . . . Philippe Böhm and his father were identical, boss . . . Same build, same cropped hair, the same melon head . . . Max Böhm hated his son."

"Why?"

"Because he was timorous. Böhm couldn't stand that."

"What do you mean?"

Joseph hesitated, then leant over and whispered:

"His son was like a mirror, see? A reflection of his own fear."

"You've just said that Böhm was frightened of nobody."

"Nobody, except himself."

I stared into Mkonta's rheumy eyes.

"His heart, boss. He was frightened of his heart." Joseph put his hand on his chest. "He was scared that things would stop working inside . . . He kept checking his pulse . . . In Bangui, he spent his life in the clinic."

"There's a clinic in Bangui?"

"A hospital reserved for the Whites. The Clinique de France."

"Is it still there?"

"Yes and no. Now it's open to Blacks and our local doctors work there."

I moved on to the vital question.

"Did you take part in Böhm's last expedition?"

"No. I'd just moved to Bagandu. I'd stopped going into the forest."

"Do you know anything about it?"

"Only what people told me. At Mbaïki, that journey has become a legend. It's still called by its code name, PR 154, from the plot of land the prospectors were going to study."

"Where did they go?"

"Far away beyond Zoko . . . Over the Congo border."

"And?"

"On the way, Ngakola got a telegram which had been brought to him by a Pygmy . . . His wife had just died . . . The news came as a shock . . . His heart gave out . . . He collapsed."

"Go on."

Joseph's grimace was now so pronounced that his lips were turning up.

"Go on, Joseph."

He hesitated a moment longer, then sighed.

"Thanks to his secret pact with the forest, Ngakola was resurrected . . . Thanks to magic and the Panther that steals our children."

I remembered what Guillard had told Dumaz. Mkonta's version tallied with the engineer's. It was enough to terrify anybody witless.

A journey into the heart of darkness, a horrific mystery, in torrential rain, and that diabolic hero, the white-haired man, who had risen from the dead.

"I'm going into the forest, to follow Böhm's trail."

"That's a bad idea. This is the middle of the rainy season. The diamond mines are now managed by a single man, Otto Kiefer. A murderer. You're going to walk a very long way and take pointless risks. All that for nothing. What do you intend to do there?"

"I want to find out what really happened in August 1977. How did Max Böhm survive his attack? The spirit world is not a good enough explanation."

"You're wrong. What are you going to do?"

"I'm going to avoid the mines and pay a call on Sister Pascale."

"Sister Pascale? She's almost as tough as Kiefer."

"I've been told of a Pygmy camp, called Zoko. I mean to stay there and use it as a base for my explorations. I'm going to ask discreet questions to the men who were already working in the creeks in 1977."

Joseph shook his head then poured himself some coffee. I looked at my watch. It was after 11 a.m. It was Sunday and I had no idea how I was going to spend the day.

"Joseph," I asked. "Do you know anybody who works at the Clinique de France?"

"One of my cousins."

"Can we go there now?"

"Now?" Mkonta was enjoying his coffee. "I have to visit my family on Kilometre 5, then . . ."

"How much?"

"Another ten thousand."

I swore with a smile, then slipped the money into his shirt pocket. Mkonta winked, then put down his cup.

"Let's go, boss."

CHAPTER 33

The Clinique de France lay on the banks of the Bangui. The river rolled smoothly in the dazzling sunlight. It could be glimpsed between the undergrowth, black, huge and still. It looked like thick treacle in which some fishermen and their pirogues had become trapped.

We walked along the bank just where I had strolled the day before. The path was bordered with pastel-coloured trees. On the right stood the massive ochre, red and pink ministry buildings. On the left, near the river, wooden shacks snuggled into the grass, left behind by the usual sellers of fruit, cassava and knick-knacks. Everything was quiet. Even the dust had given up rising in the light. It was Sunday and, as elsewhere in the world, that day was cursed in Bangui.

Finally, the clinic appeared – a square two-storey block with a deserted air. Its colonial architecture could be seen in its stone balconies, decked with ornamentation and off-white roughcast. The entire building was being eaten up by laterite and vegetation. The claws of the forest and reddened footprints led up to its walls. The stone seemed swollen, as though bloated with humidity.

We went into the garden. The surgeons' white coats were drying on the trees. They were blotched with dark, scarlet stains. Joseph noticed the expression on my face. He burst out laughing.

"That's not blood, boss. It's earth. Laterite. It never washes out."

He stood aside to let me in. The vestibule of rough concrete and decrepit lino was totally empty. Joseph knocked on the desk. Several long minutes went by. Finally, there appeared a tall man in a white coat, striped with red stains. He joined his hands, bowed and said in an unctuous tone:

"How can I help you?"

"Is Alphonse Mkonta here?"

"No one's here on Sundays."

"What about you, are you no one?"

"I'm Jésus Bomongo."

He leant even further down and added in his sugary voice:

"At your service."

"My friend here would like to have a look at the medical records going back to the days when there were only Whites here. Is that possible?"

"Well, it would be more than my job's worth to . . . "

Joseph winked pointedly at me. I went through the motions of haggling, and then paid over another one thousand CFA francs. Joseph left me there. I followed my new guide down a concrete corridor that was plunged into darkness. Then we went up some stairs.

"Are you a doctor?" I asked him.

"Only a nurse. But round here, that comes down to much the same thing."

After going up three flights, another corridor opened up, lit by daylight that filtered through the openwork patterns. A strong smell of ether filled the air. The rooms we went past contained no patients, just a chaotic jumble of equipment: wheelchairs, long metallic rods, pink sheets and pieces of beds propped up against the walls. We were in the attic. Jésus produced a bunch of keys and unlocked the creaking, off-centre metal door.

He stayed in the doorway.

"The files are all stacked up over there any old how," he explained. "After the fall of Bokassa, the owners fled. The clinic was closed for two years, then we opened it again to treat the local people. We have our own doctors now. You won't find that many files. Not a lot of Whites were treated in Bangui. Only in emergencies, when it was impossible to transfer them. Or else for minor ailments." Jésus shrugged. "African medicine is a mess. Everyone knows that. And it's not the witch doctors who are going to make it any better."

With these parting words, he turned on his heel and vanished. I was alone.

The room where the records were stored contained only some tables and a few scattered chairs. The walls were darkened by long, black, damp patches. Distant cries buzzed in the air. I found the records I wanted in an iron cabinet. Its four levels were crammed with yellow files, eaten through by the damp. I flicked through some of them, and realized that they were not in any order. I pushed some tables together, then stacked the various piles on top. There were fifteen of them, each consisting of several hundred files. I wiped off the sweat that was dripping down my face and started picking through them.

Bending over the tables, I pulled the first sheet of each file towards me. They contained the name, age and nationality of each patient. Then came the condition and any medicine that had been prescribed. I thus glanced through several hundred files. Names of Frenchmen, Germans, Spaniards, Czechs, Yugoslavs, Russians and even Chinese ran on endlessly along with the illnesses that had turned these frail foreigners into feverish wrecks. Malarial diarrhoea, allergies, sun stroke, venereal diseases etc. There then followed the names of the drugs, which were always the same, then, more unusually, a repatriation demand to the embassy concerned was stapled onto the file. The hours passed. So did the piles. At seven o'clock, I had completed my search. Not once had I come across the names of Böhm or of Kiefer. Even here, old Max had wiped out every trace of his past.

Footsteps echoed behind me. It was Jésus come to see how I was doing.

"So?" he asked, stretching out his neck.

"Nothing. I haven't found the slightest trace of the man I'm looking for. But I know that he came to this clinic regularly."

"What's his name?"

"Böhm. Max Böhm."

"Never heard of him."

"He used to live in Bangui during the 1970s."

"Böhm . . . That's a German name, isn't it?"

"Swiss."

"Swiss? The man you're looking for is Swiss?" Jésus giggled and slapped his hands together. "A Swiss. You should have told me at once. There's no point looking here. Switzerland's medical files are kept elsewhere."

"Where?" I asked impatiently.

Jésus looked put out. He remained silent for a few seconds, then brandished his long, turned-up index finger.

"The Swiss are a serious bunch, boss. Never forget that. When the clinic closed in 1979, they were the only country to worry about their nationals' medical records. Above all, they were concerned about their citizens maybe going home carrying African germs. (Jésus raised his eyes to the ceiling with consternation.) So, they wanted to make off with all the files. The government refused. You understand. The patients may have been Swiss, but the illnesses were African. This all went on for quite some time."

"And then?" I interrupted in exasperation.

"Ah, I can't really tell you that, boss. It's the confidentiality of the entire medical profession that's at stake and . . . "

I slipped another one thousand CFA franc note into his hand. He returned a broad grin and immediately went on:

"The files are kept at the Italian embassy."

There was one chance in a hundred that old Max had not known about that move. Jésus continued:

"The embassy janitor is a friend of mine. His name's Hassan. The Italian embassy is at the other side of town and . . . "

I crossed Bangui in a clapped-out taxi going at full speed. Ten minutes later, we stopped in front of the steps outside the Italian embassy. This time, I did not bother to haggle. I found Hassan – a little man with frizzy hair and mauve bags under his eyes – pushed a five thousand franc note into his pocket and dragged him down to the basement. Before long I was sitting in a large lecture hall, looking at four metal drawers that had been placed in front of me – the medical records of all the Swiss citizens who had been to the Central African Republic between 1962 and 1979.

They were filed neatly in alphabetical order. Under the letter "B", I found the files dealing with the Böhm family. The first one belonged to Max. It was extremely thick and contained a mass of prescriptions, tests and electrocardiograms. As early as 16 September 1972, the year of his arrival in the country, Max Böhm had gone to the

Clinique de France for a complete check-up. The head doctor, Yves Carl, had immediately prescribed a treatment, which was directly imported from Switzerland, and advised him to take it easy and avoid strenuous efforts. In his confidential memo, Carl had written in biro in a slanting hand: "Myocardial insufficiency. To be followed closely." The latter sentence was underlined. Then, every three months, old Max had gone back for his prescriptions. As the years went by, the doses had increased. Max Böhm was a condemned man. The file ended in July 1977, when new drugs were prescribed in massive doses. The following month, when Böhm went into the jungle, his heart was a mere shadow of itself.

Irène Böhm's records started in May 1973. The file began with some medical tests that had been made in Switzerland. Dr Carl had then simply followed the patient, who was suffering from an infection of the Fallopian tubes. The treatment had lasted for eight months. Madame Böhm was cured, but the record stated: "Sterility". She was then thirty-four. Two years later, Dr Carl identified another condition. The file contained a long letter to a doctor practising in Lausanne, saying that it was urgent that further tests be made. Carl did not mince his words: "Possible cancer of the uterus". There then followed a diatribe against the means put at the disposal of hospitals in Africa. In conclusion, Carl asked his colleague to talk Irène Böhm into spacing out her trips to the Central African Republic. That was the last document contained in the file. It was dated 1976. I knew the rest. In Lausanne, tests revealed that the growth was cancerous. She had then preferred to stay in Switzerland, trying to cure her illness while keeping her husband and son in the dark. She died a year later.

The nightmare became more tangible with Philippe Böhm's records; the first mention I had found of the ornithologist's son. During his first months there, he had contracted fevers. He was ten. The following year, he had been given a long treatment against diarrhoea. Next came amoebae. A case of dysentery was nipped in the bud, but young Philippe contracted a liver abscess. I glanced through the prescriptions. Between 1976 and 1979, his health improved. Visits to the clinic became less frequent and the results of tests were encouraging. The adolescent was then fifteen years old. However, his file ended on a death certificate dated 28 August 1977. A postmortem report was stapled onto it. I removed the wrinkled sheet of paper, written in a conscientious hand. It was signed: "Dr Hippolyte Mdiaye, of the University of Medicine, Paris." What I read convinced me that, up until then, I had remained on the edges of the nightmare.

Postmortem Report : Mbaïki Hospital, Lobaye
28 August 1977
Subject: Böhm, Philippe.
Sex: Male.
White, Caucasian.
1.68 metres, 78 kilos.
Naked.
Born 8/9/62 in Montreux, Switzerland.
Died on about 24/8/77 in the depths of the jungle, forty kilometres from Mbaïki, a subprefecture of Lobaye, Central African Republic.
The face is intact, except for traces of scratches to the cheeks and temples. Inside the mouth, some teeth are broken, and others merely chipped, probably owing to some huge jaw spasm (no sign of exterior bruising). The neck is broken.

The frontal face of the thorax reveals a deep, perfectly central wound, running from the left clavicle to the navel. The entire length of the sternum has been severed longitudinally, thus revealing the thorax. We also noticed numerous scratch marks, covering all of the torso and in particular adjacent to the main wound. Both upper limbs have been amputated. The fingers of the left hand are broken, and the index and ring fingers of the right hand have been torn off.

The thoracic cavity reveals the absence of the heart. At the level of the abdominal cavity, we can observe the lack of, or mutilations to, several other organs, such as the intestines, stomach and pancreas. Near the body, fragments of organs were discovered bearing animal bite marks. No sign of haemorrhaging in the thoracic cavity.

Extremely broad gash (seven centimetres) to the right of the groin, reaching the hip bone. The penis, testicles and flesh around the top of the thighs have been torn off. Numerous traces of scratch marks around the thighs. Lacerations to the external faces of the right and left thighs. Multiple fractures to both ankles.

Conclusion: Philippe Böhm, a young Swiss citizen, was attacked by a gorilla during the PR 154 expedition, near the border with Congo, where he had accompanied his father, Max Böhm. The scratch marks leave no room for doubt. Certain other mutilations on the victim's body are also typical of the animal. Gorillas habitually tear off the external faces of their victims' thighs, then crush their ankles to stop them from escaping. It seems that the ape responsible for this attack, an old male who had been wandering through that region for some weeks, was later killed by a family of Aka Pygmies.

NB: The body is to be transported to the Clinique de France, Bangui, this afternoon. I enclose a copy of my report and the death certificate addressed to Dr Yves Carl. 28 August 1977, at 10.15.

Time came to a stop. I looked up and stared round that huge empty hall. Despite the sweat pouring down my face, I was icy cold. Philippe Böhm's postmortem report was identical to Rajko Nicolich's. In a period of thirteen years, two people had been murdered and their hearts stolen, and the crime explained away by an animal attack. But, over and beyond that terrifying discovery, I now understood the root of Max Böhm's hidden destiny – what had happened in the shades of the jungle during expedition PR 154. His own son's heart had been transplanted into his body.

CHAPTER 34

It does not always help to sleep on your thoughts. On that Monday 16 September, I woke up in a state of delirium. The night had been one long torment, haunted by Philippe Böhm's suffering. I was totally devastated by the fact that Max Böhm had survived by sacrificing his son and I now felt more convinced than ever that my quest for diamonds coincided with a deeper pursuit for a group of extraordinary murders – linked to Max Böhm by a blood pact.

I drank my tea on the balcony of my bedroom. At half past eight, the telephone rang. It was Bonafé.

"Antioch? I've done you quite a favour. I was able to contact the minister this weekend and your authorization is sitting on the general secretary's desk even as we speak. You can go straight along and pick it up. I'll put one of our cars at your disposal at two o'clock this afternoon. Gabriel will drive. He'll tell you what you should take with you in terms of food, gifts, equipment, and so on. One last thing: he'll also give you a box containing a hundred cartridges. Be discreet on that point, will you? Good luck."

He hung up. So, the time had come. The forest was waiting for me.

A few hours later, I was in a five-door Peugeot 404, which had replaced the Range Rover I was to have had, being driven by Gabriel who was sporting a T-shirt marked: "AIDS. I protect myself. I wear condoms." On the back was a map of the Central African Republic slipped inside a condom.

As soon as we left Bangui, an army camp barred the way. A group of slovenly soldiers, with evil grins and dusty machine-guns, ordered us to stop. They explained that they were going to "check our ID papers, then search our vehicle in the official way". Gabriel at once went inside their hut, clutching my passport and authorization. Two minutes later, he re-emerged. The roadblock was lifted. African bureaucracy moves in mysterious ways.

The countryside now had a fluorescent gleam to it. Trees and creepers swarmed over the tarmac track as far as the eye could see.

"It's the Central African Republic's only properly made road," Gabriel explained. "It goes to Berengo, Bokassa's old palace."

The temperature had fallen and the breeze made by our speed was laden with sweet, elegant scents. We passed by some haughty individuals, who were walking beside the asphalt with a grace that Blacks alone possess. Once more, the beauty of the women took my breath away. So many tall solitary flowers, walking supply through the high grasses.

Thirty miles farther on, another roadblock appeared. We were entering Lobaye province. Gabriel negotiated our passage again. I got out of the car. The sky had darkened. Huge violet-coloured clouds were crossing it. In the trees, flocks of birds were twittering, as though sensing an approaching storm. The air was wracked with teeming agitation. Beside some parked trucks, men were drinking elbow to elbow along a makeshift bar, while, on the ground, women were selling all sorts of merchandise.

Most of them were offering brightly coloured live hairy caterpillars, which were wriggling around at the bottom of large bowls. Squatting down over their harvest, the women were trying to drum up trade by calling out shrilly: "It's caterpillar season, boss. The season of life, of vitamins . . ."

Suddenly, the storm broke. Gabriel suggested having some tea at his Muslim brethren's place. So we sat down on the veranda and I had my first cup of real tea, in company with men in white jellabas who were wearing their characteristic skullcaps. For a few minutes, I looked on, listened and admired the rain. This get-together, with its unexpected intimacy, left me with a feeling of friendship, of charm and well-being.

"Gabriel? Do you know a doctor in Mbaïki called Mdiaye?"

"Of course I do," Gabriel replied. "He's president of the prefecture. We'll have to pay him a courtesy call. What's more, Mdiaye has to sign your authorization."

Half an hour later, the rain stopped. We set off again. It was four o'clock. From the glove compartment, Gabriel produced a plastic bag full of dark, squat bullets. I immediately loaded sixteen of them into my magazine, then slid it into the grip of my Glock 21. Gabriel made no comment, but just watched me out of the corner of his eye. There was nothing surprising about carrying an automatic pistol in the jungle. On the other hand, it was the first time that he had seen such a light weapon, that clicked together in such a quiet, fluid way.

Mbaïki appeared. It was a set of earth shacks with corrugated iron roofs, spaced out into small ill-assorted neighbourhoods, on the side of a hill. At the top, sat a large faded blue residence.

"Dr Mdiaye's house," Gabriel murmured.

Our car drove up to the gate.

We entered a chaotic garden, full of twisting creepers and massive leaves. Some children immediately came into view. With smiling faces, they were observing us from behind the trees. The house was like a colonial memory. It was very large, topped off by a long roof of rusted metal, and could have been magnificent, but it seemed to be letting itself die under the relentless rain and scorching sun. Torn curtains stood in place of the doors and windows.

Mdiaye was waiting on the steps, his eyes red.

After the customary greetings, Gabriel launched into a long preamble, punctuated with "Mr President, sir" and complicated explanations concerning our excursion. With a distant expression on his face, Mdiaye listened. He was small, with limp shoulders, and he wore a sodden boater on his head. His face was hazy and his stare even more so. The man we were confronted with was an example of an incorrigible African drunk, who was already fairly tipsy. He finally invited us in.

The large room was plunged in shadows. Water trickled down the walls, whispering in the darkness. Slowly, very slowly, Mdiaye took a biro out of a drawer to sign my authorization. Behind the curtain over another doorway, I could make out the rear courtyard, where a plump Black woman with oblong breasts was preparing a seething mass of caterpillars. She was sticking the larvae onto sharpened twigs, then gently laying them down onto the hot coals. Children were running and leaping around her. Mdiaye still had not signed.

He was speaking to Gabriel:

"The forest is dangerous at this time of year."

"Yes, president."

"There are wild animals. The tracks are in a bad state."

"Yes, president."

"I don't know if I can allow you to leave like that . . . "

"No, president."

"How could I help you if you had an accident?"

"I don't know, president."

Silence fell. Gabriel had adopted the eager stare of a good boy at school. Mdiaye got round to the main point.

"I'll need some money. A deposit, so that I can help you if need be."

This masquerade had gone on long enough.

"Listen, Mdiaye," I said. "There's something important I have to tell you."

The doctor looked round at me. He did not seem to have noticed I was there.

"Something important?"

His stare floated away across the room.

"In that case, let's have a drink."

"Where?"

"At the café. Just behind the house."

Outside, a light languid rain was falling. Mdiaye led us into a dive, with a floor of beaten earth and tables that were up-turned crates. He ordered a beer. Gabriel and I had a soft drink. The doctor laid his weary eyes on me.

"Tell me all about it," he said.

I went straight to the point.

"Do you remember Max Böhm?"

"Who?"

"Fifteen years ago, a White who used to supervise the diamond mines."

"If you say so."

"A big man, hard and cruel, who terrorized the workers and who lived in the forest."

"No, that doesn't ring any bells."

I banged on the table. Our glasses bounced. Gabriel looked at me with astonishment.

"You were young then, Mdiaye. You'd just qualified as a doctor. You signed the postmortem report of Max's son, Philippe Böhm. You can't have forgotten that. The kid had been dismembered, his body covered with lacerations and his heart had disappeared. I know all of this from your own certificate, Mdiaye. I have it here with me, signed with your name."

The doctor did not respond. His red stare was fixed on me. He felt for his glass, without taking his eyes off me. He lifted his beer to his lips and slowly sipped at it. I moved my jacket to reveal the grip of my gun. The other customers left.

"You said that he'd been attacked by a gorilla. I know you were lying. On the 28th of August 1977, you covered up a murder, presumably for money. Answer me, you two-bit quack!"

Mdiaye turned round, examined the patch of sky through the doorway, then lifted his drink to his lips again. I took out my Glock and struck him round the face with it. He slumped backwards and crashed against the corrugated iron wall. His hat flew off. Shards of glass were stuck in his flesh. Through his split cheek, a pink gum could be made out. Gabriel tried to hold me back, but I pushed him away. I grabbed Mdiaye then shoved my gun up into his nostrils.

"You bastard," I screamed. "You whitewashed a murder with your lies. You covered up for the killers of a child and . . ."

Mdiaye limply waved his arm.

"All right . . . all right, I'll talk."

He looked over at Gabriel then slowly said:

"Leave us."

My guide scurried away. Mdiaye leant back on the corrugated iron. I whispered:

"Who found the body?"

"Several . . . several people did."

"Who?"

The drunk did not answer. I tightened my grip.

"Some Whites . . . a few days before . . . "

I gave him some slack, but with the barrel of my Glock still in front of his nose.

"An expedition . . . They were looking for seams of diamonds in the forest."

"I know. It was expedition code number PR 154. I want their names."

"There was Max Böhm, his son Philippe, and then another White, an Afrikaner. I don't know what he was called."

"Is that all?"

"No, there was also Otto Kiefer, Bokassa's right-hand man."

"Otto Kiefer was also there?"

"Yes, he was."

I suddenly saw a further link. Max Böhm and Otto Kiefer were as much bound together by the events of that savage night as by their diamond business. The doctor wiped his mouth. Blood was pouring down onto his shirt. He went on:

"The Whites passed by Mbaïki, then headed for the SCAD."

"And then?"

"I don't know. A week later, the tall White, the South-African, came back on his own."

"What was his explanation?"

"There were no explanations. He went back to Bangui. And we never saw him again. Ever."

"What about the others?"

"Two days after that, Otto Kiefer turned up. He came to see me at the hospital and said: 'I've got a customer for you out in the van.' It was a body, for Christ's sake, the body of a White, with his torso ripped open. His guts were pouring out all over the place. It took me a while before I recognized that it was Max Böhm's son. Kiefer told me: 'It was a gorilla that did it. Now you do the postmortem.' I started to shake all over. Kiefer screamed at me. He said: 'Just do the damned postmortem, and remember – it was a gorilla that did it.' I started work in the operating theatre."

"And?"

"An hour later, Kiefer came back. I was scared to death. He walked over to me and asked: 'Finished yet?' I told him that it wasn't a gorilla that had killed Philippe Böhm. He told me to shut it and then took a wad of bank notes out of his pocket – crisp new five-hundred franc notes. He started to stuff them into the corpse's open chest. Christ, I'll never forget the sight of all that money swimming in his guts. While still ramming more notes inside, the Czech said, : 'I'm not asking you to go around telling stories, only to confirm that it was a fucking gorilla attack.' I wanted to answer back, but he'd already gone. He'd left two million French francs in that gaping wound. I got the money back and cleaned it. Then I wrote up the report just as he'd asked."

My blood was burning in my veins. Mdiaye was still staring at me with ghastly eyes. I pointed my gun back at his face and whispered:

"Tell me about the body."

"The wounds were . . . too fine. There were not scratch marks, as I wrote in the report. They were cuts from a lancet. No doubt about that. And then there was the missing heart. When I looked inside the thoracic cavity, I immediately noticed how the arteries and veins had been excised. A real professional job. I realized that the young White's heart had been stolen."

"Go on," I said, my voice shaking.

"I closed up the body and finished my report. 'A gorilla attack.' The case was closed."

"Why didn't you come up with something simpler? Like malaria, for example?"

"Impossible. Dr Carl in Bangui was going to see the body."

"Where is this Dr Carl?"

"Dead. He died of typhus two years ago."

"How did the story of Philippe Böhm end?"

"I don't know."

"Who do you think carried out that murderous operation?"

"No idea. But it was definitely a surgeon."

"Did you ever see Max Böhm again?"

"No, never."

"Have you ever heard of a clinic in the jungle, over the Congolese border?"

"No."

Mdiaye spat out some blood, then wiped his mouth with the back of his sleeve.

"We never go that way. There are panthers, gorillas, spirits . . . It's the realm of the night."

I released my grip. Mdiaye slumped to the floor. Some men and women had rushed over. Not daring to go inside, they were grouped round the windows. In the crowd, Gabriel was mumbling:

"We'll have to take him to hospital, Louis. Or fetch a doctor."

Mdiaye picked himself up on an elbow.

"What doctor?" he sneered. "I'm the doctor."

Full of disdain, I stared at him. He was spitting out a stream of blood. I spoke to the Blacks who were observing this sad spectacle.

"Look after him, won't you!"

Then Mdiaye broke in.

"What about the diesel?" he gurgled.

"What diesel?"

"Who's going to pay for the petrol, and the electricity for the hospital?"

I threw a bundle of CFA franc notes into his face, then turned on my heel.

CHAPTER 35

We drove for some hours along a bumpy mud track. The sun was setting. A sort of dry rain, formed of dust, was beating on our windscreen. Finally, Gabriel asked me:

"How did you find out about that business with the White?"

"It's an old story, Gabriel. And I'd rather not talk about it.

Whatever you think, I'm here to write an article about Pygmies. That's my sole objective."

A wide path, bordered by shacks, opened out in front of us. Then the SCAD village loomed into sight. In the distance, to the right, lay the sawmill. Gabriel slowed down. We passed through a mass of men and women, covered with red dust, who brushed against the car's bodywork with a dry hiss. These violent colours and sensations were wearing me out.

At the end of the village, we reached some rough concrete buildings. Gabriel told me:

"This is Sister Pascale's former clinic. You can sleep here tonight, before heading off into the jungle tomorrow morning."

The small block-houses contained camp beds, covered with plastic and hung with tall mosquito nets – and good enough for a reasonably comfortable night. Further on, the red track continued, surrounded by the depths of the forest until it became a green wall. All that could be seen in that abyss was the path winding onwards.

Gabriel and a few others unloaded our equipment. Meanwhile, I studied the map of the region that Bonafé had given me. In vain. There was no road leading in the direction I wanted to take. The SCAD was the last named location, just before the dense forest that spread out over three hundred miles to the south. The sawmill's village seemed poised on the edge of a huge precipice of creepers and vegetation.

When I raised my eyes, I saw that some strange men had surrounded us. They were no more than four and a half feet tall. They were dressed in rags, filthy T-shirts and torn tops. Their skin was a light caramel colour and they were smiling at us sweetly. Gabriel immediately offered them some cigarettes. They giggled in return. The tall Black introduced us:

"Here are the Akas, boss. Pygmies. They live nearby in Zoumia, a village of huts."

Then some women appeared. They had bare breasts, round bellies and their heads were crowned with circles of leaves or cloth. They carried their children in slings and were laughing louder than the men. They, too, accepted the cigarettes and lit up enthusiastically. All of the women had very short hair. Some of them looked incredibly elaborate. One had the teeth of a saw drawn on her neck. Another, two grooves along her temples, while her eyebrows had been picked out into dotted lines. On all of their skins could be seen the marks of swollen scars, curling around in arabesques and fine patterns. One detail froze the blood in my veins. All of the Pygmies' teeth were sharpened into points.

Gabriel introduced me to his cousin, Beckés, who was going to be my guide as far as Zoko. He was a tall slender Black, in Adidas sports gear, who never took off his sunglasses. He exuded a disarming calmness. Grinning, he told me to meet him the next morning, at the same place, at seven o'clock – and that was that.

Gabriel followed him. He wanted to have a "family dinner" at the SCAD. I asked him to be back at the clinic by 8 p.m. at the latest. He nodded, winked, then wished me good luck. My guts tightened as I listened to the sound of his Peugeot pulling away.

Soon, darkness fell. A woman prepared dinner. I consumed my serving of manioc – a sort of greyish glue smelling of excrement – then decided to sleep on the roof of the clinic. Under the stars, I slipped inside my cotton sheet. Then, with my eyes wide open, I waited for sleep to come. In a few hours' time, I was going to discover the forest for myself. The Greenwood. For the first time since my adventures had begun, I had to admit that I was afraid. My fear was as persistent as the dull gnashing of teeth from unknown animals that were wishing me good night from the depths of the jungle.

CHAPTER 36

At seven o'clock the next morning, Beckés appeared. We drank some tea together. His French was very limited, punctuated by long silences and many a thoughtful '*bon*'. However, he knew the jungle to the south extremely well. According to him, the track that lay in front of us had been dug out by the sawmill's bulldozers and went on only for about three-quarters of a mile. After that, we would have to take narrower paths. In this way, it would take us a three-day hike to reach Zoko. I agreed without having the slightest idea what such a marathon would entail.

Our team formed up. Beckés had recruited five Pygmies to be our porters. Five scruffy little men, smoking and grinning, who seemed willing to follow us into the depths of the shadows. He had also taken on a cook called Tina, a young, distinctly attractive Mbaka. She swaggered along in her twisted robe, with a huge cooking pot on her head, containing her kitchen utensils and personal belongings. She was continually laughing. This expedition seemed to delight her.

I handed out some cigarettes and explained the main idea of the trip. Beckés translated my words into Sango. I spoke only of the Zoko part of my expedition and made no mention of the rest of my plan. From the Pygmy village, I was counting on making my own way to Otto Kiefer's mines, which were just a few miles further to the south-east. I repeated that the entire journey would take only a week, then I stared up the reddish track. That rope of earth seemed to go on for ever through the monstrous tangle of trees and creepers. Our troop set off.

The jungle was a real graveyard, a mixture of vibrant existence and utter annihilation. Everywhere the worm-eaten trunks, fallen trees and smell of decay resembled the final flickering of a life of excess. Walking through that forest meant manoeuvring through that eternal agony, those melancholy odours, that rancorous out-growth of mosses and creeks. Sometimes, the sun broke through. It splashed over the heady mass of leaves and creepers, which seemed to awaken, writhing round at its touch, like thirsty souls come to drink at that stream. The forest then became a phantasmagoric vivarium, an upsurge of growth that was so powerful and hurried that you could almost hear it slithering beneath your feet.

Nevertheless, I did not feel at all claustrophobic. The forest was also an immense ocean, spanning out endlessly. In the high interwoven creepers, in the hanging gardens, the myriad of leaves, that massive lacework that still resembled our European forests, there was an extraordinary sense of freedom. Despite the cries, despite the trees, the jungle gave the impression of being a huge open space. Of course, that solitude was a mere mirage. Not one inch of it was uninhabited. Life seethed and swarmed everywhere.

According to Beckés, each animal occupied a specific territory. A clearing created by a fallen tree was the porcupine's habitat. Inextricable undergrowth overladen with creepers was where antelope dwelt. As for open clearings, birds nested and sang there during the day, despite the rain.

Sometimes, when a raucous cry or a hissing was heard that was louder than the others, I asked Beckés:

"What's that cry?"

"Its the Ant."

"The ant?"

"It's got wings, a bill and it walks on the water. (He shrugged his shoulders.) It's the Ant."

Beckés had a particular way of looking at the equatorial forest. Like all Mbakas, he thought that the jungle was inhabited by spirits, powerful invisible forces which had covert alliances with the wild animals. In fact, people from the Central African Republic do not speak about animals in the way a European might. In their beliefs, they are superior beings, at least the equals of mankind, who are to be feared and respected, and are supposed to have hidden desires and parallel powers. Thus, Beckés always spoke of "the" Gorilla in hushed tones for fear of annoying "it", recounting how, in the evening, the Panther could smash a glass in a lamp just by looking at it.

The rains started on the first day. It was a relentless downpour, which became an integral part of the journey, just as the trees, the bird calls or our own fever did. These torrents had no cooling effect and simply slowed us down – the earth subsided, forming deep ruts where we walked. But everyone continued, as though the wrath of the sky could not reach us.

In this deluge, we ran into some Mbaka hunters, carrying narrow baskets on their backs in which they kept their game: gazelles with ochre hides, monkeys curled up like babies, or silver anteaters with crackling scales. These tall Blacks exchanged cigarettes and a smile with us, but their faces looked distinctly worried. They were in a hurry to get back up north to the forest rim before nightfall. Only the Akas had the courage to stay in that darkness and brave the spirits. But our group was heading south, like a walking blasphemy.

Each evening we pitched camp out of the rain. At 6 p.m., night fell abruptly and the fireflies lit up, tirelessly swerving around the trees. We ate a little later, sitting grouped around the fire, and emitting the eating noises of wild beasts.

I did not converse, but thought about the secret aim of my journey. Then I went into my tent and stayed there, sheltered, listening to the raindrops flopping down onto the double canvas roof. At moments like that, I rolled up in the silence and considered the tragic turn my adventure had taken. I thought about the storks, about the countries I had crossed like a meteor, about that wave of violence that was rising around my feet. It felt as though I were swimming up a river of blood, whose source I was about to discover – the place where Max Böhm had stolen his son's heart, where three men, Böhm, Kiefer and van Dötten, had made a diabolical pact based on diamonds and storks. I thought of Sarah, but with neither remorse nor sadness. In other circumstances, the two of us might have decided to build a life together.

But, I must admit that I also thought about our cook, Tina. As we travelled onwards, I could not stop myself from glancing at her furtively. Her profile was sublime, a straight neck finishing in a short chin before opening out into wide glorious jaws and thick sensuous lips. Her eyes sparkled below her domed forehead. On her closely cropped head, little plaits stood up like the horns of an antelope. On several occasions, she caught me staring at her. She then burst out laughing and her mouth blossomed like a crystal flower to murmur:

"Don't be frightened, Louis."

"I'm not frightened," I would reply in a firm voice, before turning my attention back to the bumpy path.

On the third day, we still had not seen any sign of a Pygmy camp. The sky was now a distant memory and our limbs were beginning to stiffen like iron bars with fatigue. More than ever I had the impression of going straight down a deep well in the earth, of burying myself in the very flesh of the vegetation, with no hope of return.

However, near the end of the afternoon of 18 September, we came across a burning tree. A red furnace in that ocean of plant life. It was the first sign of a human presence since our departure. Some men had apparently decided to burn this massive trunk, before it collapsed under the weight of the rain. Beckés turned back through the downpour and said, with a smile on his lips: "We've arrived."

CHAPTER 37

Zoko camp stood in the middle of a large, perfectly circular clearing. Huts of leaves and laterite shacks surrounded the main central area, which was as naked as a desert. Oddly enough, the ground, walls and domes of leaves did not display the same green and red colours as the forest, but a harsh ochre, as though the very essence of the jungle had been rubbed away. Zoko was a gouged-out breach amid the confusion of the vegetable kingdom.

There was a scene of great agitation. Women were returning from their gathering expeditions, carrying heavy woven hods full of fruit, seeds and roots. From other directions, the men appeared with monkeys, gazelles and long nets slung across their shoulders. Heavy blue smoke hung around the huts, before whirling into spirals and rising up above the centre of the camp. The rain had just stopped and in that murky atmosphere I noticed families gathered in front of their huts feeding the fires.

"A Pygmy technique," Beckés whispered. "To chase away insects."

Songs rose up. Long sharp, almost Tyrolese wails, sonorous vibrations in which the human voice becomes that infinitely sensitive string, which had already welcomed us at the moment when we had found the burning tree. The Akas used this method to communicate over a distance, or simply to express their delight.

A tall Black walked over to us. It was Alphonse the primary school teacher, the "owner" of the Zoko Pygmies. He insisted that we make ourselves comfortable before nightfall in a neighbouring clearing, which was smaller and contained a canopy about ten yards long. His family was already camping there. I pitched my tent nearby, while my companions were weaving leaf mattresses. For the first time in two days, we were dry. Alphonse never stopped talking, going on about "his" fiefdom and pointing out from afar each part of the Pygmy camp.

"What about Sister Pascale?" I asked.

Alphonse raised his eyebrows.

"The clinic, you mean? It's at the other end of the camp, behind the trees. I wouldn't advise you to go there this evening. The nun's in a bad mood."

"A bad mood?"

Alphonse spun round and simply repeated:

"An extremely bad mood."

The porters kindled the fire. I went over to them and sat down on a tiny bowl-shaped stool. The blaze crackled and gave off a strong smell of damp grass. The plants imprisoned in the flames seemed to be burning unwillingly. Abruptly, night fell. It was a night full of damp clearings, cool breezes and bird cries. In my deepest being, I felt a sort of call, a whisper, like an opening in my heart. I raised my eyes and understood this novel sensation. Above us, the clear sky was studded with stars. I had not seen it for four days.

That was when the drumming started.

I could not resist smiling. It was so unreal, yet at the same time so predictable. In the depths of the jungle, we were hearing the world's heart beat. Beckés got to his feet and grumbled:

"There's a party over there, Louis. We'd better go."

Behind him, Tina chuckled and shook her shoulders. A minute later, we were standing on the edge of the esplanade.

In the half-light, I could see Aka children dashing left, right and centre. Little girls, in front of the earthen shacks, tying up their waists in raffia skirts. Some boys had got hold of some assegais and were trying out a few dance steps then stopping in hysterical laughter. The women were coming back from nearby groves, their hips ringed with leaves and branches. Meanwhile, the men stared at this agitation with amused faces, smoking the cigarettes that Beckés had given them. And still the drumming went on, keeping up the mounting fever.

Alphonse ran over with a storm lantern in his hand.

"You want to dance with Pygmies, boss?" he whispered in my ear. "Follow me."

I did as I was asked. He set down a small bench near the huts, then positioned the lantern in the middle of the clearing. In this way, the bodies of the little ghosts could clearly be seen. Their saraband of fire and joy was tearing through the darkness.

The Akas were dancing in two separate arcs. The men on one side, the women on the other. A dull chant rose up from their circling:

"*Aria mama, aria mama . . .*"

The mingled mantra, raucous and deep, was occasionally pierced by a burst of children's voices rising up through the din:

"*Aria mama, aria mama . . .*"

In the lamplight, I first saw the round-bellied women dance past. Their supple legs. Their bouquets of leaves. Immediately afterwards, the men appeared. In that petrol gleam, those caramel bodies turned red, bronze, then ashen. The raffia skirts rustled in a counter-beat, wrapping their thighs in a shimmering veil.

"*Aria mama, aria mama . . .*"

The beating of the drum intensified. The drummer was bent over his instrument, a cigarette between his lips. His neck raised like an eagle, he was hammering with all his strength. I contained a shudder. His eyes, absolutely white, were glimmering in the dark. Alphonse laughed:

"He's blind, that's all. They make the best musicians."

Then other drummers joined him. The rhythm intensified again, filled with echoes and counter-beats, until it was a vertiginous, irresistible song of the earth. More voices rose up, forming a unison around that continuum:

"*Aria mama, aria mama . . .*"

Their magical fluorescence gleamed under the starry sky.

The women passed once more in front of the lamp in a straight line, each one holding the hips of the woman in front of her, following the beat. They seemed to be cajoling the rhythm, slipping inside and out of it. Their bodies belonged to the shaking of the drums, as an echo belongs to the cry that sets it off. They had become pure resonance, a vibration of flesh. The men returned, squatting down, hands on the ground, backwards and forwards like seesaws, suddenly becoming beasts, spirits, elves.

"What are they celebrating then?" I yelled over the drumming.

Alphonse peered round at me. His face was hidden in the shadows.

"Celebrating? This is a wake. One of the southern families has lost a daughter. Today, they are dancing with their Zoko brothers. That's the custom."

"What did she die of?"

Alphonse shook his head and shouted into my ear:

"It was horrible, boss. Really horrible. Gomoun was attacked by the Gorilla."

A red veil fell across my eyes.

"What are people saying about the accident?"

"Nothing much. It was Boma, the camp elder, who found the body. Gomoun hadn't gone home that evening. So the Pygmies organized a search party. They were afraid that the forest had got its revenge."

"Its revenge?"

"Gomoun didn't respect the traditions. She refused to get married. She wanted to go on studying with Sister Pascale in Zoko. The spirits don't like being made fools of. That's why the Gorilla attacked her. Everyone knows that. The forest got its revenge."

"How old was Gomoun?"

"Fifteen, I think."

"Where did she live exactly?"

"In a camp to the south-east near Kiefer's mines."

The thundering hides were filtering into my senses. The blind man was going crazy, his milk-white eyes glittering in the darkness. I shouted:

"Is that all you can tell me? You don't know anything else?"

Alphonse pulled a face. His white teeth stood out against his pink throat. He waved my questions away.

"Forget it, boss. This is an evil story. Extremely evil."

The teacher made a move to stand up. I gripped his arm. Sweat was pouring down my face.

"Think hard, Alphonse."

The Black exploded:

"What do you want, boss? You want the Gorilla to come back? It tore off Gomoun's arms and legs. It wiped out everything in its path. Trees, creepers, the earth. You want it to hear you? To crush all of us as well?"

He leapt to his feet in a fury, taking his lamp with him.

The Pygmies kept on dancing, now imitating a huge caterpillar. The blind man's drum accelerated. And my heart with it. The names and the dates of that series of murders ran through my mind in letters of suffering. August 1977: Philippe Böhm. April 1991: Rajko Nicolich. September 1991: Gomoun. I felt certain that the young girl's heart had been removed. A detail sprang into my thoughts. Alphonse had said: "It wiped out everything in its path. Trees, creepers, the earth." Twenty days before, in the forest of Sliven, the gypsy who had found Rajko said: "There must have been one hell of a storm the day before. Because, all around, the trees had been blown flat, their leaves were all over the place."

Why hadn't it occurred to me before? The murderers travelled by helicopter.

CHAPTER 38

At 5 a.m., dawn broke. The forest echoed with muffled cries. I had not slept a wink all night. The Akas had concluded their ceremony at about two in the morning. After that, I had lain in the shadows and the silence, under the canopy of leaves, watching the last embers casting their rosy glints through the darkness. I no longer felt the slightest bit afraid. Just extremely weary and strangely calm, almost secure. As if I had approached so near to an octopus that its tentacles could not reach me any more.

The first raindrops of the day fell. A slight hammering to begin with, then a denser, more regular drumming. I got up and walked over to Zoko. Fires were already burning in front of the huts. I noticed a few women who were repairing a long net, presumably to be used during that day's hunting trip. I crossed the central area then, behind the shacks, came across a large concrete structure topped with a white cross. It was completely surrounded by flowers and a vegetable garden. I headed towards the open door. A tall Black blocked my path, hostility gleaming in his eyes.

"Is Sister Pascale up yet?" I asked.

Before the man could answer, a voice burst out from inside:

"Come in. Don't be afraid."

It was an authoritarian voice, which expects no questions. I obeyed it.

Sister Pascale was not wearing a veil. She was simply dressed in black, with a matching pullover and skirt. Her severe grey hair was short. Despite the numerous wrinkles, her face had the timeless quality of rocks and rivers. Her icy blue eyes were like steel shards sticking up from prehistoric silt. Her shoulders were broad and her hands huge. Just a glance at her was enough to convince me that she was capable of confronting the dangers of the jungle, terrible diseases and savage hunters.

"What do you want?" she asked, without looking at me.

She was sitting down and patiently buttering some bread over a bowl of coffee.

The room was practically empty. There was just a sink and a fridge against the far wall. A wooden crucified Christ stared down in torment.

"My name's Louis Antioch," I said. "I'm French. I've travelled thousands of miles in order to find the answers to certain questions. I think you may be able to help me."

Sister Pascale kept on buttering her bread. The slices were limp and damp, due to the unsuitable storage conditions. I looked at her dazzling whiteness which, here in the depths of the jungle, seemed like an improbable treasure. She caught me staring at her.

"Sorry. I'm failing in all my duties. Please sit down and share my breakfast."

I grabbed a chair. She peered round at me with an expression of pure indifference.

"What questions might they be?"

"I want to know how young Gomoun died."

This clearly did not take her aback. Picking up the scalding coffee pot, she asked:

"Coffee? Or would you prefer tea?"

"Tea, please."

She gestured towards the servant who was standing in the shadows, and addressed him in Sango. A few seconds later, I could smell the bitter scent of some anonymous Darjeeling. Sister Pascale returned to the subject.

"So, you are interested in the Aka people, are you?"

"No," I replied, blowing into my cup. "I'm interested in violent deaths."

"Why?"

"Because several victims have been killed in the same way in this forest. And elsewhere, too."

"Are you pursuing wild animals?"

"Wild beasts, more like."

The rain was still tapping above our heads. Sister Pascale dunked her slice of bread in her coffee. It softened on contact then, with one swift bite of her teeth, the nun snapped off the part that was about to fall. She did not seem at all surprised about what I was saying. But her words contained a strange irony. I decided to break this game of innuendoes.

"Let's be clear about one thing, Sister. I don't believe a word of that story about a gorilla. I have no experience of the jungle, but I do know that gorillas are pretty rare in this region. I think that Gomoun's death belongs to a series of murders I am currently investigating."

"I have no idea what you're talking about, young man. Can you start by explaining who you are and what brought here? We are over ninety miles from Bangui. You had to walk for four days to reach this God-forsaken spot. My instincts tell me that you are not in the French army, nor are you a mining engineer, nor even an independent prospector. If you want me to help you, then you had better explain yourself."

I briefly summed up my inquiries. I told her about the storks and the various "accidents" that had dotted my route. I spoke of the death of Rajko, torn to pieces by a wild bear. I mentioned the fatal gorilla attack on Philippe Böhm. I described the circumstances of these deaths, comparing them with what had happened to Gomoun. I did not mention the theft of hearts. Nor did I talk about the system for smuggling diamonds. All I wanted to do was draw the sister's attention to all those coincidences.

She was now staring at me with incredulity in her blue eyes. The rain was still beating down on the corrugated-iron roof.

"Your story doesn't hang together. But never mind. What do you want to know?"

"What do you know about how Gomoun died? Have you seen the body?"

"No. She was buried a few miles from here. Gomoun came from a family of nomads that travels around further to the south."

"Did they tell you about the state of the body?"

"Do we really have to talk about this?"

214

"It's essential."

"One of her legs and one of her arms had been torn off. Her torso was covered with wounds and cuts. Her chest was gaping open and her rib cage completely crushed. Wild animals had started to eat her innards."

"What animals?"

"Warthogs and wild-cats probably. The Akas told me about scratch marks on her neck, breasts and arms. Who knows? The Pygmies buried the poor girl in their camp, then left the place for good, as is their custom."

"There were no other traces of mutilation on the body?"

Sister Pascale was still clutching her bowl. She hesitated, then dropped it. I noticed that her hands were now trembling slightly. She lowered her voice.

"Yes, there were . . . Her vagina was wide open."

"You mean that she had been raped?"

"No. I'm talking about a wound. The ends of her vagina seemed to have been widened by scratch marks. The lips were severely lacerated."

"Was the inside of the body intact? I mean, had any specific organs disappeared?"

"I told you. Some organs had been half eaten. That's all I know. The poor girl was coming on fifteen. God have mercy on her soul."

The nun fell silent. I pressed on:

"What sort of teenager was Gomoun?"

"Extremely studious. She followed my lessons attentively. The girl had turned her back on Aka traditions. She wanted to continue her studies, go to town, and work with the Tall Blacks. Recently, she'd even refused to get married. So, the Pygmies think that the spirits of the forest had sought their revenge. That's why they danced for such a long time last night. They wanted to make it up with the forest. As for me, I can't stay here any more. I'm going back to the SCAD. People are saying that it was my fault Gomoun died."

"You don't seem particularly upset, Sister."

"You don't know the forest. Here, we co-exist with death. It

215

strikes regularly and blindly. Five years ago, I was teaching in Bagu, another camp not far from here. In two months, sixty of its one hundred inhabitants had died. A TB epidemic. A disease that had been 'imported' by the Tall Blacks. In the past, the Pygmies lived secluded from germs, protected by the bell jar of the dense forest. Today, they are being massacred by diseases brought in from the outside. They need people like me. They need health care and medicine. I just do my job and try not to think too much."

"Did Gomoun often go walking alone in the forest? Did she wander away from the camp?"

"She was a loner. She liked going off along the jungle paths with her books. Gomoun adored the forest, its odours, its noises, its animals. In that sense, she was a real Aka."

"Did she ever go near the diamond mines?"

"I've no idea. Why ask me that? Still on your absurd murder hypothesis! Who on earth could have anything against a young Aka girl who'd never stepped out of the jungle?"

"Sister, it's time I told you a little more. I mentioned Rajko's murder, in Bulgaria. And also that of Philippe Böhm, in this very country, in 1977. Those two killings had something particular in common."

"What was that?"

"In both cases, the murderers removed the victim's heart, using standard surgical techniques."

"What utter rubbish. Such operations are inconceivable in a natural environment."

Sister Pascale remained calm. Her eyes were still blue and gleaming, but her lashes were trembling rapidly.

"And yet, that is precisely what happened. I met the doctor who carried out the postmortem on that gypsy in Bulgaria. There's no doubt about the excision. The killers have incredible resources at their disposal, which allow them to operate in perfect conditions absolutely anywhere."

"Do you know what that means?"

"Yes, it means they have a helicopter, electricity generators, a pressurized tent, and no doubt other equipment as well . . . Nothing insurmountable about all that."

"So?" the missionary asked. "You think little Gomoun . . . "

"I'm practically certain."

She shook her head, in an off-beat rhythm with the raindrops drumming on the roof. I looked away and stared through the doorway at the vegetation. The forest seemed drunk on rain.

"I haven't finished, Sister. I've already mentioned the 'accident' that took place in the Central African Republic in 1977. Were you already here at that time?"

"No, I was in Cameroon."

"In August that year, Philippe Böhm was found dead in the jungle, a little further south in the Congo. His death was just as violent, just as cruel and his heart had vanished, too."

"Who was he? A Frenchman?"

"He was the son of Max Böhm, a Swiss who used to work in the diamond mines not far from here. You must have heard of him. The boy's body was transported as far as Mbaïki, where a postmortem was carried out in the hospital. It was decided that he had been 'attacked by a gorilla'. But I have proof that his death certificate was faked, and that certain vital pieces of evidence were concealed which would have shown that the operation was a human one."

"How can you be so sure?"

"I found the doctor who performed the postmortem. A local practitioner called Mdiaye."

The nun laughed.

"But Mdiaye's a drunk!"

"He didn't drink at that time."

"Where's all this leading us? What did Mdiaye tell you about the operation? How could he see that it had been done by humans?"

I leant over and whispered:

"A sternotomy. Lancet marks. Perfect excision of the arteries."

I paused for a moment and observed her. Her grey skin was twitching. She raised a hand to her temple.

"My God . . . why such horror?"

"To save a man, Sister. Philippe Böhm's heart was transplanted into his own father's body. A few days before, Max Böhm had had a terrible heart attack . . ."

"But that's monstrous . . . impossible . . ."

"Believe me, Sister. Four days ago, I talked Mdiaye into telling me the truth. His version fits with what I was told in Sofia about Rajko. Both reports tell the same story of a murderous, sadistic frenzy. But a strange sort of sadism, because it apparently also helps to save people's lives. Gomoun was one of these murderers' victims."

Her hand on her brow, Sister Pascale was shaking her head.

"You're mad, completely mad . . . You have no proof at all as regards Gomoun."

"That's right, Sister. And that's where you come in."

The missionary stared at me wildly. I immediately asked:

"Do you have any knowledge of surgical techniques?"

She was still staring at me, uncomprehendingly. She replied:

"I've worked in war hospitals, in Vietnam and Cambodia. What do you mean?"

"I want to exhume the body and carry out a postmortem."

"You're crazy."

"Listen, Sister, I have to check my hypothesis. You're the only person who can help me. You alone can tell me if any organs have been extracted from Gomoun's body using surgical techniques, or if she was attacked by an animal."

The missionary clenched her fists. Her eyes were glinting with a metallic light, steel eyeballs beneath flesh and blood lids.

"Gomoun's camp is too far away. It's inaccessible."

"We'll get a guide."

"No one will take us there. And no one will allow you to desecrate her grave."

"We'll operate together, Sister. Just you and me."

"There's no point. In the forest, bodies decompose extremely quickly. Gomoun was buried about seventy-two hours ago. As we speak, her body is no more than a ghastly mass of worms."

"Even the present state of the body cannot conceal the precise incisions of a surgical instrument. A quick glance will be enough. We'll triumph together, Sister. The awful truth against vain suppositions."

"Remember who you are talking to, my son."

"I haven't forgotten, Sister. The corruption of dead flesh is nothing in comparison with the greatness of truth. Are not the children of God lovers of light?"

"Don't blaspheme!"

Sister Pascale stood up, her chair scraping shrilly. Her pupils were now mere slits in her slate-grey features. In a distant voice, she said:

"Let's go. Now."

She spun round abruptly and called out something in Sango to the Black, who ran over at once and started busying himself around. Then she removed a silver crucifix on a metal chain from her pullover, kissed it and muttered a few words. When the Christ fell back down again onto her chest, I noticed that the lateral bar of the cross was bent downwards, as though the weight of suffering had warped the very instrument of execution. I, too, got to my feet, then staggered. I had eaten nothing since the previous day, nor had I slept. My cup of tea was still there, completely full, on the table. I gulped it down. The Darjeeling was lukewarm and viscous. It tasted of blood.

CHAPTER 39

We walked for several hours. Sister Pascale's servant, Victor, led the way opening up a path with his machete. Behind him came the missionary, upright in her khaki cape. I was at the rear, resolute and single-minded. Swiftly and silently, we were heading due south. We zig-zagged, slid and clambered along. Old tree trunks and twisted roots, rocks full of holes and sticky branches, clumps saturated with water and leaves like knife blades. The rain kept up. We passed through those shining spikes, just as soldiers march past terrifying bayonets on their way to the front. The creeks multiplied. We sank up to our waists in the dark water, with a sensation of being drawn down into it forever.

No cries, no presence interrupted the half-day's march. The forest animals remained hidden, totally invisible under the leaves or in their burrows. We met only three Pygmies. One of them was wearing a camouflage shirt, with black and ochre stripes, which he had picked up God alone knew where. A narrow band of fuzzy hair crossed his scalp, like a Mohican. The one in front was holding a smoking ember under his shirt as well as a closed cylindrical basket of woven leaves.

Sister Pascale spoke to him. It was the first time that I had heard her speak the Aka language. Her deep voice echoed with its characteristic "hmm-hmms" and long suspended vowels. The Aka opened his basket and handed it to the missionary. They exchanged some more words. We were standing there in the rain, which seemed to be beating down on us as though we were targets. The branches of the trees dipped down under the violence of the drops, and torrents were running down the dark trunks.

Without looking at me, the missionary murmured:

"Honey, Louis."

I leant over the basket to see a gleaming honeycomb full of bees protecting their hidden stores. I looked up at the man. He grinned back at me with his sharpened teeth. Stings covered his shoulders. For an instant, I imagined him climbing up a tree through a din of buzzing, then slipping in between the leaves to affront the fury of the nest. I imagined him plunging his hand into the crack in the bark, feeling around inside the swarm to remove a few sweet pieces of honeycomb.

As though following my thoughts, the Aka offered me a lump of it, dripping with honey. I broke a piece off, then put it to my lips. At once, my throat filled with an exquisitely heavy, deep odour. The pressure of my tongue made a heady nectar spurt out from the papery hexagons. It was so smooth and sweet that I immediately felt a sort of drunkenness, deep in my stomach, as though my innards had suddenly grown tipsy.

Half an hour later, we reached Gomoun's camp. The vegetation had been transformed. There was no longer that inextricable tangle that we had crossed up until then. Here, the forest seemed airy and disciplined. Slender black trees made a near perfect symmetry as far as the eye could see. We stepped into the camp. There were just a few huts, placed beside the trees in no apparent order. And a feeling of intense solitude. Oddly enough, that totally empty, totally motionless area of leaves reminded me of Böhm's house, when I had searched through it on the day before setting off. Another place inhabited by death.

Sister Pascale stopped in front of a small hut. She said a few words to Victor, who produced two spades wrapped up in old cloths. The missionary pointed at a mound of freshly turned earth behind the domed hut.

"It's there," she said.

Her voice was barely audible in the splashing rain. I dropped my rucksack and picked up one of the spades. Mute and trembling, Victor watched me. I shrugged my shoulders and started digging up the red earth. It felt as if I was sliding a blade into the side of a man.

I worked on. Sister Pascale spoke to Victor again. Apparently, she had not told him what the aim of our expedition was. I kept digging. The crumbling earth put up no resistance. In a few minutes, I had reached a depth of eight inches. My feet were sinking in the humus, full of insects and roots.

"Victor!" the nun yelled.

I looked up. The Mbaka did not move, eyes starting out of his head. He was glancing rapidly from me to her, and back again. Then he spun round and ran off at full tilt.

Silence closed over us. I went on with the job. I heard her pick up the other spade. Without raising my eyes, I murmured:

"Please, let me do it, Sister."

I was now at waist height in the hole. Worms, centipedes, beetles and spiders swarmed around me. Some of them fled, startled at the violence of my thrusts. Others clung onto my trousers, as though trying to stop me from wreaking more havoc. The smell of the earth filled my mind. My spade was slapping on a pool of mud. I dug on, ever downwards, not thinking about what I was looking for. But then, my spade hit something solid, bringing me back to my senses. I heard my companion's pale voice:

"It's bark, Louis. You're there."

I hesitated for a fraction of a second, then scraped the earth away with the edge of my spade. A piece of wood appeared. The red, cracked surface was slightly swollen. I threw the spade out of the pit and tried to lift up the bark with my bare hands. At the first attempt, my hands slipped off it and I tumbled down into the mud. Sister Pascale, by the edge of the grave, put out her hand towards me.

"Leave me alone!" I yelled.

I tried again. This time, the bark definitely began to give. The rain was flooding into that gaping hole and was beginning to fill it up. Suddenly, the wood came away. I had been pulling so hard that I now fell backwards once more, the coffin lid spinning through 360° and landing on my head. I felt a strange softness. For a second, I mentally examined that unexpected touch then screamed with all my strength. It was the sensation of Gomoun's skin, her little body.

I stood up and forced myself to calm down. The girl's corpse lay in front of me. The poor thing was dressed in a shabby little flowery dress and a threadbare tracksuit top. My heart ached at such poverty. But I was surprised at her almost immaculate beauty. Her family had carefully cleaned up her wounds before burying her. Only a few scars could still be seen around her hands and naked ankles. Her face was intact. Her closed eyes had large brownish bags round them. I was also surprised by the truth of that cliché – how alike sleep and death are, two drops of the same brown ink. The chill in my feet brought back the urgency of the situation to me.

"Your turn now, Sister!" I shouted. "Come down here. The rain's filling up the grave."

Sister Pascale had taken off her cape and was standing near the edge, fiddling with her crucifix. Her metallic hair and grey face were gleaming in the rain, making her look like an iron statue. Her eyes were staring fixedly at the corpse. I yelled again:

"Quick, Sister! We haven't got much time."

She didn't move. Her body twitched spasmodically, as though receiving electric shocks.

"Sister!"

The nun pointed at the grave then stammered automatically:

"My God, she's . . . she's going . . . "

I looked down at my feet and pushed myself back against the wall of mud. Streams of rain had got under the girl's dress. One of her legs was now floating in the water, a yard away from her body. Her right arm was beginning to detach itself from her shoulder, pulling aside the collar of the tracksuit top and revealing a white bone.

"Jesus Christ." I murmured.

I waded through the red flood and pulled myself up to the surface. Then I lay down on the ground and slipped my hands under the girl's armpits. She had lost one of her arms, which was thumping against the tree bark. The cloth of her dress was slipping through my fingers. I was screaming furiously.

"Help me, Sister! For Christ's sake, help me!"

The woman did not budge. I looked up. Waves of electricity were now flowing through her body. Her lips quivered. Suddenly, I heard her voice.

" . . . *Lord Jesus, You who wept at the grave of Your friend Lazarus, dry our tears, we beg You . . .* "

I plunged my arms once more into the mud and pulled harder at the child's body. Under the pressure, the mouth opened and a flood of worms spewed out. The little Aka was now no more than a flask of skin, protecting millions of carrion. I threw up a spray of bile, but did not release my grip.

" . . . *You who have brought the dead to life again, grant eternal life to this our sister, we beg You . . .* "

I pulled again and dragged the girl to the surface. Gomoun had lost one of her lower limbs and her right arm. Soaked in laterite, her dress flapped over her orphan hip. I picked the nearest hut, grabbed the torso and dragged it over to the shelter of leaves.

" . . . *You blessed our sister in the waters of baptism, give her now in plenitude the life of God's children, we beg You . . .* "

In the darkness, I laid the little body down on the dry earth. The roof was so low that I had to advance on all fours. I leapt outside to grab Sister Pascal's bag, before returning under the dome. Then I got out her equipment – surgical instruments, rubber gloves, white-paper coats, a storm lantern and, for some reason, a car jack. I also found some green-paper masks and several bottles of water. Everything was in one piece. Trying not to look at Gomoun, who had insects pouring out of her mouth, eyes and nose, I laid it all out on a plastic sheet. Her soaked dress was bulging up over her stomach. Thousands of desecrators were teeming beneath it. The smell was unbearable. In a few minutes' time, we would be through.

" . . . *You fed her with Your body, receive her at the table of Your kingdom, we beg You . . .* "

I went out again. Sister Pascale was now standing, singing out her prayer. I grabbed her by both her arms, shaking her violently to awake her from her mystic catalepsy.

"Sister!" I yelled. "For Christ's sake, wake up!"

She jumped so violently that I lost my grip on her then, after about a minute, she said "yes" with a blink of her eyelids, and I helped her back to the hut.

I lit the storm lantern and hung it on the network of branches. Its milky glare blinded us. I placed a mask over the nun's face, put a white-paper coat on her, then slipped the rubber gloves over her fingers. Her hands had stopped shaking. Her colourless eyes were looking down at the girl. Her breathing puffed out the layer of paper. With a curt gesture, she told me to give her the surgical instruments. I did so. I, too, had put on a paper coat, mask and gloves. Sister Pascale picked up the scissors then cut through Gomoun's dress so as to reveal her torso.

A wave of disgust flowed over me once more.

The little Aka's chest was now a big, variegated, incredible wound. One of her tiny breasts had almost been severed. All of her right side, from her armpit to the start of her groin, bore deep lacerations, the edges of which were darkened and fissured like ghastly lips. Above that, a point of bone could be seen sticking out from her stump. But, worst of all, in the centre was the long, main incision, cleanly crossing the upper part of the thorax. In that nightmare vision, the skin on each side was palpitating slightly, as if the chest had been invaded by some new, crawling, terrifying life force.

But all of that was nothing in comparison with the girl's genitalia. The almost hairless vagina was a gaping slit going up to the navel, revealing brownish folds in its depths, crawling with worms and insects with gleaming carapaces. I was about to faint, but then another detail of the horror came home to me. What I had before me was an exact replica of one of Böhm's photographs. A link. Another link that was tying together dead flesh and darkness.

"What are you doing, Louis? Pass me the jack!"

Her voice was muffled behind the mask. I stammered back:

"The . . . the jack?"

The nun nodded. I gave her the tool. She put it down beside her, then said:

"Help me."

She had just seized the left side of the central incision with both hands, while pressing firmly down on the sternum. My nerves numb, I did the same on the right side and, together, we pushed in both directions. When the wound was open, the nun slid the jack inside, being careful to wedge the two ends against the edges of the bone. She then immediately started to turn the mechanism, and I saw that little body open out over an organic abyss.

"Water!" she screamed.

I gave her one of the bottles. She poured out the entire litre. A veritable flood of creatures streamed out. Without a moment's hesitation, Sister Pascale plunged her hands into the body and felt around what was left of the adolescent's organs. I looked away. She poured most of another litre over it, then asked me to redirect the beam of the lantern. After that, she pushed her hand into the dead girl's thorax up to her wrist. She leant over, until her face was almost touching the wound. She fished around inside for a few seconds more then suddenly pulled back, elbowing the jack out of the way. The two sides of the thorax immediately closed, like the wings of a beetle.

The nun sat back, shaken by a final spasm.

She pulled off her mask. Her skin was as dry as a snake's scales. She stared at me with her grey eyes then said:

"You were right, Louis. They operated on her. Her heart's been removed."

CHAPTER 40

We got back to the clearing of Zoko at about 7 p.m. The sun was already setting. After we had changed out of our oil coats and drenched shoes, Sister Pascale made some tea and coffee with-out saying a word. At my request, she agreed to draw up a death certificate, which I immediately pocketed. It was not worth much – Sister Pascale was not a doctor. But it was still a sworn statement.

"Would you mind answering a few more questions, Sister?"

"Go ahead."

Sister Pascale had recovered her calm. I went straight ahead.

"How many helicopters are there in the Central African Republic that could land here, in the middle of the jungle?"

"Only one. Otto Kiefer's. The man who runs the Sicamine."

"Do you think that the men working there are capable of commit-ting such an atrocity?"

"No. Gomoun was operated on by professionals. The Sicamine boys are just brutes, barbarians."

"Do you think that, if they were paid well, they could have aided and abetted such an operation?"

"Yes, maybe. They have no scruples. Kiefer should have been

locked up long ago. But why do that? Why bother to attack a little Pygmy girl in the middle of the jungle? And why in such conditions? Why mutilate the body like that?"

"That's my next question, Sister. Is there any way of knowing the HLA groups of Zoko's inhabitants?"

Sister Pascale stared straight into my eyes.

"You mean their tissue groups?"

"Exactly."

The nun hesitated, wiped her hand over her forehead, then murmured:

"Oh, my God . . . "

"Answer my question, Sister. Is there any way?"

"Yes, yes there is."

She got to her feet.

"Follow me."

She picked up an electric torch then walked over to the door. I followed her. Outside, night had fallen, but the rain still persisted. The purring of a generator could be heard in the distance. Sister Pascale took out her keys and opened the door of a structure that abutted onto the clinic. We went inside.

There was a strong smell of antiseptic in the room, which must have measured a mere four yards by ten. In the darkness, I noticed two beds to the left. In the middle, lay some medical equipment – an x-ray machine, a physioguard and a microscope. On the right, a computer lay on a makeshift table amidst a muddle of cables and other grey contraptions. The beam from her torch played over the IT equipment, which included several CD Roms. I could not believe my eyes. There was the possibility of stocking huge quantities of data there. I also noticed a scanner for analysing images, then entering them into the computer's memory. But the most astonishing item was the mobile phone connected to the machine. From this shack, Sister Pascale could communicate with the entire world. The contrast between the rough concrete room, lost in the jungle, and the sophisticated equipment it contained astonished me.

"There are many things you don't know yet, Louis. Firstly, this is not some forgotten African mission with limited means. On the contrary. Zoko clinic is a pilot project, whose capacities we are currently testing, with the help of a humanitarian organization."

"Which organization?" I stammered.

"One World."

I was speechless. My heart skipped several beats.

"Three years ago, our community signed a contract with One World. The association wanted to begin working in Africa and asked if they could benefit from our experience on this continent. They offered to provide us with modern instruments, give technical training to our sisters and whatever medicines we needed. All we had to do was stay in touch with their centre in Geneva, send them the results of our tests and occasionally give hospitality to their doctors. Our mother superior agreed to this unilateral deal. This was in 1988. From that moment, things went very quickly. Budgets were voted through. The Zoko mission was equipped. Some men from One World arrived and explained how to use it all."

"What sort of men?"

"They don't believe in God, but they have just as much faith in humanity as we do."

"And what exactly is all this equipment?"

"Most of it is for analyses. To take x-rays and run medical tests."

"What sort of tests?"

Sister Pascale laughed shrilly. As though a stylus had scratched her metal face. Then she murmured:

"I really don't know myself, Louis. All I do is take blood samples and perform biopsies on various subjects."

"Then who carries out the analyses?"

The missionary hesitated then, her eyes lowered, she whispered:

"It does."

She was pointing at the computer.

"I put the samples in the programmed scanner, which carries out various tests. The results are automatically entered into the computer, which draws up an analytical chart of each patient."

"Who is this sort of test done on?"

"Everyone. It's for their own good, do you see?"

I wearily nodded, then asked:

"Who sees the results?"

"The centre in Geneva. Via the mobile phone and the modem, they regularly consult the computer files and draw up statistics regarding the health of Zoko's Pygmies. They can pick up risks of epidemics, the evolution of parasites, that sort of thing. It's basically preventive medicine. But, in an emergency, they can send us the necessary drugs extremely quickly."

The perfidious nature of this system horrified me. Sister Pascale quite innocently took organic samples. Then the computer software carried out the required tests. The programme obviously analysed, among other things, each Pygmy's HLA group. Finally, the data was consulted by the HQ in Geneva. The inhabitants of Zoko made a perfect stock of humans, whose precise tissue characteristics had been recorded. In the same way, other "subjects" had no doubt also been analysed in Sliven and Balatakamp. And this technique was presumably used in each camp belonging to One World, which thus possessed a terrifying pool of living organs.

"What personal contact do you have with One World?"

"None. I send my orders for drugs via the computer. I also enter the vaccines and treatment I administer. Then I communicate, via modem, from time to time with a technician who takes care of the maintenance of the equipment."

"You never speak with any of the OW management?"

"Never."

The missionary fell silent for a few seconds, then resumed:

"Do you think there is a connection between Gomoun's death and these tests?"

I hesitated before entering into any explanations.

"I cannot be certain, Sister. The system I have in mind is so incredible . . . Do you have Gomoun's file?"

Sister Pascale rummaged through a metal drawer. A couple of seconds later, she handed me an index card. I read it in the light of the torch. It contained Gomoun's name, age, village of origin, height and weight. Then there were some columns. On the left, dates. On the right, the treatment she had received. My heart sank at the sight of these trivial events that had marked the ordinary life of a young forest girl. Finally, at the bottom of the card, I found what I was looking for. Printed in tiny characters was Gomoun's HLA group: A^w 19,3 − B 37,5. A shiver ran across my skin. Without any doubt, these initials and figures had cost the young Aka her life.

"Answer me, Louis. Have these tests got anything to do with the girl's death?"

"It's too early to say, Sister. Far too early . . ."

Sister Pascale's eyes were glistening like needle points. From the expression on her face, I gathered that she had finally understood the cruelty of this system. A nervous tic played across her lips again.

"It's impossible . . . impossible . . ."

"Calm down, Sister. Nothing's certain and I . . ."

"No, shut up . . . it's impossible."

I backed out, then ran through the rain towards the camp. My companions were having dinner around the fire. The smell of manioc floated beneath the canopy. They invited me to sit down. I ordered our immediate departure. Such an order was unheard of. Tall Blacks are terrified of darkness. However, my voice and expression showed that I was in no mood for a discussion. Beckés and the others grudgingly did as they were told. The guide stammered:

"Where . . . where are we going, boss?"

"To see Kiefer. At the Sicamine. I want to grab that Czech before dawn."

CHAPTER 41

We walked all night. At four in the morning, we had nearly reached Kiefer's mines. I decided to wait for the sun. We were all exhausted and drenched to the bone. Without bothering to find shelter, we settled down beside the track. Squatting, with our heads down, we fell asleep. I felt a fatigue bearing down on me that I had never known before. A dazzling burst of darkness, that shattered me, then deserted me, as if burying me in a heap of cinders.

At five o'clock, I woke up. The others were still asleep. I moved off at once towards the mines on my own. All I had to do was follow the old path, which had been dug out by the miners. Trees, creepers and undergrowth were biting into the road, forming delicate illuminations, leafy gargoyles and frescoes of roots above it. At last, the track widened out. I took my Glock out of its holster, checked the magazine, then slipped it back under my belt.

A handful of men, submerged in a long creek, were digging at the soil with their bare hands, then filtering the earth through a large sieve. It was patient labour, smelly and damp. The miners started work at dawn, with weary eyes and slow gestures. Their dark stares expressed nothing but fatigue and brutishness. Some of them were coughing and spitting into the brackish water. Others were shivering and making an incessant slapping noise. All around, the high vault of leaves opened out, like a nave of trees, onto the bird calls and the clicking of wings. The golden light rose higher, brightening as I watched, already singeing the tips of each leaf and breathing flames into the tiny spaces between the branches and creepers.

Further upstream, an encampment of shacks could be seen. Thick smoke rose from the iron chimneys. I headed on towards Otto Kiefer's lair.

It was another red, muddy clearing, ringed by hovels and canvas tents. In the middle, a long plank had been laid on some trestles. Around it, about thirty workers were drinking coffee and eating manioc. Some of them were leaning over a radio, trying to listen to Radio France Internationale or Radio Bangui, despite the din from the generators. Swarms of flies fluttered over their faces.

Fires blocked the entrances to the tents. Monkeys were being roasted in the flames, their fur sizzling and giving off a revolting smell of leathery meat. All around, men were trembling feverishly. Some of them had accumulated layers of jackets, pullovers and plastic sheets, all full of holes and tangled into a mass of folds. They were wearing worn-out shoes – sandals, boots or moccasins – that were coming apart like a crocodile's jaws. Others were almost naked. I noticed one slender man, wrapped up in a turquoise African robe, whose head was decked with a sort of woven Chinese cone. He had just slit an anteater's throat and was carefully collecting its blood.

There was a paradoxical atmosphere there. A mixture of hope and despair, of impatience and nonchalance, of exhaustion and nervous energy. All of the men belonged to the same lost dream. Fixed on their desires, they spent their lives feeling blindly through the scarlet mud. I glanced round the camp once more. There was no sign of any vehicles. These men were the forest's hostages.I went over to the table. A few eyes were slowly raised. One man asked:

"What do you want, boss?"

"Otto Kiefer."

The man nodded over to a corrugated iron shack, with a sign that read "Management". The door was ajar. I knocked and went inside. I was totally calm, my hand clutching the grip of my Glock.

There was nothing terrifying about the sight that met my eyes. A tall man, whose pallor was reminiscent of the cold gleam of a skeleton, was busy repairing a video recorder, which was positioned on an ancient wood and metal television. He looked about sixty. He was wearing the same sort of hat as me – a khaki cap, with metal-ringed air holes – and a grey sweater. The holster on his belt was empty. His bony face was long and pockmarked. His nose was straight and his lips thin. He looked over at me. His washed-out blue eyes were empty.

"Hi. Whatcha want?"

"Are you Otto Kiefer?"

"I'm Clément. You know anythink about videos?"

"Not really. Where's Otto Kiefer?"

The man did not answer. He leant back down over his machine and murmured:

"Maybe I need a screwdriver."

I repeated:

"Do you know where Otto Kiefer is?"

Clément was playing round with the controls and checking the lights. After a while, he pulled a face. I was seized by terror. His teeth had been sharpened into points.

"Whatcha want with Kiefer?" he said, without looking up.

"I just want to ask him a few questions."

The old man mumbled:

"Definitely need a screwdriver. I reckon I've got the necessary over here."

He walked round me, then went behind a metal desk covered with damp papers and empty bottles. He opened the first drawer. I immediately leapt over and slammed it shut on his fingers. Then I pressed as hard as I could on his outstretched arm. His wrist snapped. Clément made no reaction. I pushed this madman down onto the damp metal. His broken hand was clutching a Smith and Wesson 38. I snatched it away from him. He took the chance to bite my hand with his pointed teeth. I felt not the slightest pain. I hit him round the face with his gun, grabbed him by his sweater and hauled him up until he was standing next to a calendar illustrated with a topless girl. Clément grimaced once more. Between his teeth, he still had the scraps of flesh he had torn off my hand. I rammed the 38 into his nose. This was turning into a habit.

"Where's Kiefer, fuckface?"

The man whispered between his bleeding lips.

"I'm not telling you anythink, asshole."

I smacked him in the mouth with the gun. His teeth flew everywhere. I squeezed his throat. Blood oozed from his lips, dripping down onto my clenched hand.

"Cough, Clément, and in two minutes I'm out of here. I'll leave you to your mines and your loony life as a white Pygmy. Where's Kiefer?"

Clément wiped his mouth with his good hand and mumbled:

"He ain't here."

I tightened my grip.

"Where is he?"

"I dunno."

I banged his head off the wooden wall. The pin-up's breasts wobbled.

"Out with it, Clément."

"He's . . . He's in Bayanga. West from here. About twelve miles . . ."

Bayanga. That fitted. It was the name of the plains Mkonta had mentioned. Each autumn, migrating birds gather there in thousands. The storks must be back. I yelled:

"He's gone to see his birds?"

"His birds? What birds?"

The vampire was not putting it on. He obviously knew nothing about the system. I asked:

"When did he go?"

"Two months ago."

"Two months? Are you sure?"

"Yeah."

"By helicopter?"

"Course."

I was still throttling the old reptile. His wrinkled skin was puffing up in search of oxygen. I felt disorientated. This information did not correspond to what I had foreseen.

"And you've had no news from him since?"

"Nope . . . None."

"And he's still in Bayanga?"

"I dunno."

"What about the helicopter? It came back about a week ago, didn't it?"

"Yeah."

"Who was on board?"

"Dunno. Didn't see a thing."

I banged his head against the wall. The pin-up slid down to the floor. Clément coughed, then spat out some blood. He repeated:

"I swear it. I didn't see a thing. We . . . we just heard the helicopter. That's all. They didn't land at the mine. I swear it!"

Clément knew nothing. He participated neither in the diamond smuggling system, nor in the theft of hearts. In Kiefer's opinion, he was obviously worth no more than the mud that stuck to his arse. But I still kept asking.

"What about Kiefer? Was he on board?"

The old prospector laughed, showing his set of sharpened teeth. He whined:

"Kiefer can't go with nobody no more."

"Why not?"

"He's sick."

"Sick? What are you on about, for Christ's sake?"

Shaking his old body, the reptile repeated:

"Sick. Kiefer's sick. Very, very sick."

Clément was choking on his blood-soaked laughter. I released my grip and let him slide down to the floor.

"What's wrong with him, you old fool?"

He glanced up at me, with a crazy look in his eyes.

"AIDS. Kiefer's got AIDS."

CHAPTER 42

I ran back at full speed through the forest until I found Beckés, Tina and the others. I dressed my hand, then told them that we were moving again. To Bayanga, this time. We set off due west along a broader track. The journey took ten hours. Ten hours of silent, breathless, crazed marching. We stopped just once, to finish the cold leftovers of manioc. The rain had started again. An incessant downpour, which we no longer noticed. Our drenched clothes stuck to our skins, making progress more difficult. However, we did not slow down and, at eight that evening, Bayanga loomed into view.

All that could be seen were distant lights, scattered and wavering. A smell of manioc and oil hung in the air. My legs could hardly carry my weight. My heart was full of a stabbing anxiety, like the backwash of a bad dream.

"We'll sleep in the villas belonging to Kosica, a logging company that closed down." Beckés said.

We walked through the ghost town then crossed a plain of reeds. The path rolled around incessantly. Suddenly, the track widened out, then opened onto a huge savanna. In the darkness, the only thing visible about it was its immensity. We had reached the western rim of the forest.

We came across some villas. They were widely spaced out, so that they seemed to have nothing to do with one another. Suddenly, a Black holding an electric torch barred our way. He said something to Beckés in Sango, then guided us towards a vast residence flanked by a short veranda. Three hundred yards away, stood another house, with a few lights on. The man with the torch lowered his voice and explained:

"Watch out for that villa. A monster lives there."

"A monster?"

"A Czech called Otto Kiefer. A terrible man."

"He's sick, isn't he?"

The Black pointed the beam of his torch at my face.

"Yes. Very sick. With AIDS. You know him?"

"I've heard of him."

"That White is a pain in the arse, boss. He's been dying for too long now."

"So there's no hope?"

"Course there isn't," the man replied. "But that doesn't stop him from still running the place. He's a dangerous animal. Extremely dangerous. Everyone knows him round here. He's killed God knows how many Blacks. And now he always keeps grenades and automatic weapons with him. He's going to blow the lot of us up. But we're not going to let him get away with it. I for one have got a gun and . . . "

The Black hesitated. He was a bundle of nerves.

"Does this Czech live on his own?"

"A woman looks after him. A Mbati. She's sick, too."

The Black came to a halt, shone his torch on me again then asked:

"It's him you've come to see, isn't it boss?"

The night was as heavy as a warm syrup.

"Yes and no. I'd just like to pay him a visit. That's all. An old friend of his sent me."

The Black lowered his torch and sighed.

"You've got weird friends, boss. Nowadays, nobody wants to sell us meat here any more. They're talking about burning everything when Kiefer dies."

Beckés carried the bags into the house. Tina had vanished into the darkness. I paid the Black and asked him one more question:

"What about the storks? The black and white birds? Do they settle far from here?"

The Black opened his arms towards the plain.

"The storks? They land right here. We're at the heart of their territory. In a few days' time, there'll be thousands of them. On the plain, by the river, around the houses. Everywhere. So many you can scarcely walk!"

My journey was over. This was the final destination of the storks, of Louis Antioch and of Otto Kiefer, the last link in that chain of diamonds. I bade the man farewell, picked up my bag and went into the house. It was quite big and furnished with low tables and wooden armchairs. Beckés pointed out my bedroom to me, to the right at the end of the corridor. I entered my sanctuary. In the middle, a tall capacious mosquito net hung over the bed. Its folds of tulle addressed me: "Are you coming, Louis?"

Everything was black. I recognized Tina's voice.

"What are you doing here?" I asked breathlessly.

"I'm waiting for you."

She burst out laughing, her bright teeth slicing through the dark cloth of night. I smiled back at her, then slid beneath the mosquito net with the realization that destiny, once again, was giving me a reprieve.

CHAPTER 43

With a few rapid movements, I unwound her robe. Her breasts jutted out like dark torpedoes. I pushed my mouth into her fuzzy acrid sex. I did not know what I was looking for. Oblivion, tenderness, or some delicious regret. Her skin quivered. Her slender thighs opened on the empire I was profaning. A voice above me was speaking in Sango, then long fingers lifted me up, grabbing my hips to position me precisely in the heart of the shadow. Then slowly, very slowly, I entered between Tina's thighs.

Her tight body was sharp, moulded with muscles and grace. Seemingly distant, it played as it wanted with its sweetness and strength. Tina knew how to reach me. She bore me away with deep, sudden movements I had never known before. Her hands uncovered my secrets, feeling out the most sensitive areas of my flesh. Bathed in sweat and fire, I concentrated on her, running my lips under her dark armpits, her mouth with those savage teeth, and her hard vibrant breasts. Suddenly, far too quickly, an abrupt wave rose in me and an explosion of pleasure faded straight away into pain. At that moment, images flew though my mind, as though tearing my soul away. I saw Gomoun's body, crawling with insects, Sikkov's scorched throat, Marcel's face covered with blood, my childhood mosquito net crackling into flames. A few seconds later, everything had vanished. And pleasure invaded my veins again with its foretaste of the tomb.

Tina had not peaked. She was gripping onto my body hair, licking, sucking, nibbling my armpits and my sex, running her soft bright tongue over my skin, until her arched body stiffened in an animalistic fury. I was no longer hard enough for her. Groaning, Tina tore the bandages off my wounded hand and pushed my fingers into her sex, so pink and vibrant that it seemed to shine in the darkness. Contorting rhythmically, she reached her climax while the blood from my freshly reopened wound ran down her thighs. There was an explosion of aromas, delicious bitter perfumes, the smell of the girl's acute pleasure. Tina slumped backwards onto the sheets, like a fallen flower of delight, destroyed by its own nectar.

I did not sleep that night. In the pauses that Tina granted me, I could not stop thinking. I reflected on my destiny's hidden logic, the incessant crescendo of emotions, of sensations and of splendour that was being offered to me as my life became more violent and more dangerous. There was a strange symmetry: stormy skies, Marcel's friendship, the caresses of Sarah and Tina echoed with the horror at the train station, the violence in the Occupied Territories and Gomoun's desecrated body. All of these events formed the opposite sides of the same road, along which I was travelling and which would take me, whether I wanted or not, to the end of my existence. There, where man cannot stand any more, where he accepts death because he feels, over and above his consciousness, that he has seen enough. Yes, that night under the mosquito net, I admitted the possibility of my own death.

Suddenly, I heard a noise. For several seconds, the same light, obstinate echo was repeated, like a myriad reflections in the morning air. I knew that clacking and humming well. I looked at my watch. It was six in the morning. Dawn was dimly peeping through the glass blinds. Tina was asleep. I walked over to the window, opened its glazed slats and looked outside.

They were there. Soft and grey, standing on their scrawny legs. Having landed in one rush, they now covered the plain, surrounding the bungalows, congregating along the river banks or striding between the sharp reeds. I realized that the moment had come.

"Are you going?" Tina whispered.

By way of reply, I went back under the mosquito net and kissed her face. Her stiff tresses stood out against the pillow and her eyes shone like fireflies in the subdued light. Her body faded into the shadows. And it was as if desire had finally found its place in the depths of that darkness. Anonymous, secret, but vertiginous for he who could make it his. Never had it hurt me so much not to be able to run my hands over that long voluptuous body to feel its flesh and its delicious traps, its rises and falls, its magical forms.

I got up, dressed and, having checked that my Dictaphone was still working properly, slipped it into my pocket. While I was putting on my holster, Tina came over to me and wrapped her long arms around me. I realized that we were now acting out a scene that had been repeated for thousands of years, under every latitude and in every language. The warrior's departure.

"Go back under the mosquito net," I murmured. "Our scents are still there. Find them again, my little gazelle, and keep them. So that they remain forever in your heart."

Tina did not immediately grasp what I meant. Then her face lit up and she bade me farewell in Sango.

Outside, the sky was alight in a humid dawn. The tall grasses glistened and the air had never seemed so pure. Thousands of storks milled about, as far as the eye could see. White and black. Black and white. They were thin, exhausted, had lost a lot of their feathers, but they looked happy. After six thousand miles, they had arrived at their destination. I was alone, confronted with this last step, alone to face Kiefer, one of the living dead who knew the last details of the nightmare. I checked the magazine of the Glock 21 once again, then set off. The Czech's house stood out clearly against the waters of the river.

CHAPTER 44

Noiselessly, I climbed up the steps of the veranda. When I entered the main room, I discovered the Mbati woman who was snoring, curled up on a wooden settle. Her heavy face was wallowing in a graceless sleep. Her cheeks bore long scars, which gleamed in the early light. Around her, some children were sleeping on the floor under blankets full of holes.

A corridor opened out to the left. I was struck by how similar this house was to the one I had just left. Kiefer and I shared the same lodgings. I walked on cautiously. Hundreds of lizards were crawling along the walls, staring at me with their dry eyes. An abominable stench hung in the air. I pressed on. My intuition told me that the Czech slept in the same room as mine – the last on the right at the end of the corridor. The door was open. I looked inside. It was bathed in darkness. Under a tall mosquito net stood an apparently empty bed. Some translucent flasks and two syringes lay on a coffee table. I took a couple more steps into the mausoleum.

"What are you doing here, man?"

I shivered. The voice had sprung out from behind the mosquito net. But it was barely a voice. More of a whisper, a hissing full of saliva and hollow tones, which scarcely formed intelligible words. I realized that the voice would stay with me until the grave. It then added:

"You can't harm a man who's already dead."

I approached. Like a terrified child, my trembling hand clutched the Glock. Finally, I made out the form that lay behind those folds of cloth. I could not stop a feeling of disgust rising up from the depths of my soul. The disease had turned Kiefer into a textbook case. His flesh was no more than a piece of limp skin draped over his body. He was bald, had no eyebrows, nor any other trace of body hair. Black blotches and dry scabs stood out here and there on his forehead, neck and forearms. He was wearing a white shirt, stained with dark traces, and was sitting up in his bed like a man who had passed beyond death.

I could not see the features of his face. All I could guess at were his eye sockets, two hollows containing eyes that were burning like sulphur. One trait alone was clear: his dry black lips on his smooth skin. They opened onto swollen gums that were even blacker. At the back of that orifice gleamed a few yellow teeth. Such was the monster that was addressing me.

"Got any smokes?"

"No."

"You bastard. What the fuck are you doing here?"

"I . . . I want to ask you a few questions."

Kiefer burst into a salivating chuckle. A trickle of brown spittle dripped onto his shirt. He took no notice. With difficulty, he said again:

"Right, I know who you are. You're the little shit who's been fucking up our business for the last two months. We reckoned you'd be on the other route. In Sudan."

"I had to change my plans. I was becoming too predictable."

"And you've come here to unearth old Kiefer, is that it?"

I did not answer. Discreetly, I turned on the Dictaphone. Kiefer's breathing was a wheezing of bass notes, gliding over waves of saliva. It was like the cry of an insect drowning in a swamp. Seconds ticked by. Kiefer went on:

"What do you want to know, my boy?"

"Everything," I replied.

"And why should I tell you?"

In a neutral tone, I answered:

"Because you're a tough guy, Kiefer. And like all tough guys, you respect certain rules. The rules of combat, for example. The victor's rights. I killed a Bulgarian in Sofia, who was working for Böhm. In Israel I killed Miklos Sikkov, another of his henchmen. In Mbaïki, I shook up Mdiaye a bit, who told me about what you asked him to write fifteen years ago. I smashed Clément's teeth, and I trailed you to here, Kiefer. So it looks like I'm the victor. I know how you smuggle diamonds using storks. I also know that you've been looking for the stones that vanished last April. I know how your network was organized. I also know that you killed Iddo Gabbor in Israel, because he had uncovered your system. I know a lot of things, Kiefer. And, this morning, I've got you in my sights. Your diamond smuggling days are over. Max Böhm is dead and you haven't got long for this world. I've won, Kiefer, and that's why you're going to talk."

The whistling kept on. In the darkness, it sounded as though Kiefer was snoring. Or else, that he was a menacing snake, hissing as it lay in wait for its prey. Finally, he said:

"Okay, kid. Let's make a deal, you and me."

Riddled with disease and with a gun on him, Kiefer was still playing the smart guy. As he presented his position, a slight Slavic accent could be heard beneath his bile.

"If you know so much, then you must know they call me 'Papa Grenade' round here. Beside me, under the sheet, I've got a nice warm grenade that's just ready to blow. So, this is the way it goes. Either I spill the beans this morning and, as a thank you present, you kill me straight afterwards. Or, you don't have the balls for it, and I blow us both to hell. Now. You're giving me a great chance to get it over with, kid. It's too hard to do it on my own."

I swallowed. Kiefer's infernal logic was too much for me. He was going to die in a few days anyway, why did he want to commit suicide via my Glock? I answered:

"You're on, Kiefer. When you're through, you're through."

The dying man sneered. Black pus oozed out from his lips.

"Right. So, listen good. Because you won't hear many stories like this one. It all started in the 1970s. I was Bokassa's right-hand man. At that time, there was plenty of work to be done. From thieves to ministers, everyone was on the make. I did my dirty work well and was well rewarded. Life was great. But Bokassa was starting to go totally nuts. There was the business with the two Martines, the sliced-off ears, the thirst for power, things were starting to look nasty . . .

"In spring 1977, Bokassa offered me another job. I was to work with a Swiss guy called Max Böhm. I knew him vaguely. He was pretty efficient, except that he kept trying to right wrongs. He wanted to have a clean pair of hands, even though he was up to his neck in coffee swindles and diamond smuggling. That year, Böhm had discovered a lode of diamonds the other side of Mbaïki."

Surprised, I butted in:

"A lode?"

"Yeah. In the forest. Böhm had come across some villagers who were finding superb diamonds all along the creeks. He'd called in a geologist he knew, an Afrikaner, to check out the discovery and start mining there. Böhm was clean, but Bokassa didn't trust him. He'd got it into his head that the Swiss was going to double-cross him. So

I was put in charge of the expedition, with Böhm and the geologist. A bloke called van Dötten."

"Expedition PR 154."

"Exactly."

"And then?"

"Everything went as planned. We headed down due south, beyond the SCAD. On foot, in the pissing rain, in the mud, with a dozen porters. We reached the lode. Böhm and the gay did their tests."

"The gay?"

"Van Dötten was a homo. A big Afrikaner poofter who loved Black ass and little workers. You want a diagram, kid?"

"Go on, Kiefer."

"The two of them worked together for several days. Prospecting, extracting, analysing. Böhm's initial conclusions were confirmed. The lode was stuffed full of diamonds. And exceptional diamonds at that. Small, but absolutely pure. Van Dötten even reckoned that the yield would be enormous. That evening, we drank to the health of the mine and to our reward. Then a Pygmy appeared from nowhere with a message for Böhm. That's how it works in the forest. The Akas are our postmen. The Swiss read the letter and collapsed straight down into the mud. His skin was puffed out like an inner tube. He was having a heart attack. Van Dötten ran over. He pulled off Böhm's shirt and massaged his chest. Meanwhile, I picked up the bit of paper. It was the announcement of Madame Böhm's death. I didn't know he even had a wife. But the son caught on at once. He started going crazy and sobbing like the baby he was. He had no place there, in those swarms of mosquitoes and creeks full of leeches.

"Everyone started to panic. Just remember where we were, kid. Three days' march from the SCAD and four from Mbaïki. And anyway, nobody and nothing was going to save Böhm now. He was a condemned man. All I wanted to do was get the hell out of there and find somewhere quiet. The porters fixed up a stretcher. We packed. But then Böhm came round. He didn't see things the same way we did. He wanted us to go further south. He said he knew a clinic just across the Congolese border. There was a medic there. The

only medic on earth who could save him. He was crying and screaming that he didn't want to die. His son was propping him up and
van Dötten was feeling sorry for himself. Jesus Christ! I just felt like
dumping the lot of them there, but the porters were quicker than
me. They pissed off without saying a word.

"So I had no choice. I had to carry the stretcher and put up
with the kid who was still bawling his eyes out about his mother. We
gave the father some drugs, then set off, me, van Dötten and the
two Böhms. The last chance convoy. But the craziest thing about
it, kid, is that after a six or seven hours' march, we found the clinic.
Incredible! A large residence, slap bang in the middle of the jungle.
With a lab thrown in and niggers running round everywhere in
white coats! I immediately smelt that the place wasn't kosher. There
was something decidedly odd about it all. Then he showed up. A
big fellow, about forty, and handsome with it. Fuck me! Right in the
middle of the jungle there was this guy, looking like an oil magnate,
who calmly says to us: 'What appears to be matter?'"

My head was beginning to throb. A low humming that rose
ever higher as my nerves jangled. It was the first time anybody had
mentioned this doctor. I asked:

"Who was he?"

"Dunno. No one told me. But I caught on at once that him and
Böhm had known each other for ages, and that the Swiss guy had
obviously already seen him in the forest. Probably during some
other expedition. He was yelling on his stretcher of leaves. He was
pleading for this medic to save him, to do something, anything,
he didn't want to die. A smell of crap was starting to waft about.
Böhm had shat himself. I never could stand Böhm, kid, believe me.
But seeing him in a state like that did get to me a bit. Fuck it! We
were tough guys, boy. Fucking White Africans! But the forest was
starting to eat us up raw. So then the medic leant down and
whispered: 'You're ready to do anything, Max? *Really anything?*' He
had a soft voice. He sounded like something right out of a high
society gossip column. Böhm grabbed hold of his collar and
murmured back: 'Save me, Doc. You know what's wrong with me.

So save me. This is your chance to show what you're capable of. We've got diamonds. A real fortune! They're further north, up in the jungle!' It was crazy! The two of them were chatting like old pals. But the weirdest thing is Böhm was talking to him like he was a heart specialist. But what was a heart specialist doing in the middle of the jungle?"

Kiefer came to a halt. Slowly, daylight was seeping into the room. The Czech's face expressed his terror. His black gums were glistening in the shadows. His cheekbones were jutting out, as though they were about to slice through the skin that covered them. I suddenly felt extremely sorry for this killer with his grenade. Nobody on earth deserved to rot away like that. Kiefer picked up his story again.

"So, then the medic spoke to me. He said: 'I'm going to have to operate.' 'What, here?' I went. 'You crazy or something?' 'We don't have any choice, Mr Kiefer,' he answered. 'Help me move him.' Suddenly I realized that he'd used my name. That he knew all three of us, even van Dötten. We carried old Max inside the house, into a big tiled room. Some sort of air conditioning was purring away. It looked just like an operating theatre. Sterile and everything. But there was like this distant smell of blood that was getting right to my guts."

Kiefer was describing the slaughter house in Böhm's photographs. One by one, the pieces of the puzzle were sliding into place. I staggered under the shock. I felt for a chair and slowly sat down on it. Kiefer sneered:

"Feeling a bit off colour, son? Make yourself comfortable, 'cos the best is yet to come. In the first sterile room, we had to have a shower and change. Then we went into another room, where there was the operating theatre itself, separated off by a glass panel. It contained two spanking new metal tables. We laid down Böhm on one of them. The medic was putting on his best bedside manner and old Max seemed calmer. After that, we went back to the first room, where the son was waiting for us. The surgeon says to him softly: 'I'm going to need you, kid. To take care of your dad, I'm going to have to take some of your blood. There's no danger. You won't feel a thing.'

246

Then he turned towards me and declared: 'Leave us, Kiefer. This operation is delicate and I must now prepare the patients.' So leave them I did. My head was spinning. I didn't know where I was. Outside, it was pissing down. I found van Dötten again. He was trembling like a leaf. I wasn't feeling too hot either. Then hours went by. Finally, at two in the morning, the doctor came out again. He was covered with blood. His face was haggard and white as a sheet. His veins were twitching all over the place. When I saw that, I said to myself 'Böhm's dead'. But then, he broke out in a nasty grin. His eyes sparkled in the light from the petrol lamps. He said: 'Max Böhm is out of danger.' Then added: 'But I couldn't save his son.' I stood up. Van Dötten was holding his head in his hands and mumbling: 'Oh, my God . . . ' I screamed: 'What do you mean? What the fuck have you done? What have you done to the kid, you fucking butcher?' I rushed inside the clinic before he'd had time to answer. It was a real maze, with white tiles everywhere. Finally, I found the operating theatre again. An A-rab with an AK-47 was guarding the door but, through the glass panel, I could see signs of the carnage.

"The tiles were red. The walls were dripping with blood. The two tables were soaked in it. I would never have believed that a human body had so much blood in it. The whole place stank of death. I was fucking glued to the spot.

"At the far side of the room, in the darkness, I made out Max Böhm, who was sleeping peacefully under a white sheet. But, nearer to me, I saw Böhm junior. He was an explosion of blood and guts. You know my reputation, kid. I'm not afraid of death and I've always liked hurting people, specially niggers. But what I now had in front of me was more than I could take. The body was lacerated all over. There were wounds I couldn't even describe. The kid's chest was open, from his throat to his belly button. His guts were all half sticking out and hanging down over his stomach.

"You didn't have to be Einstein to work out what the surgeon had done. He'd ripped out the kid's heart and transplanted it into the father's body. You had to be a genius to pull a thing like that off in the middle of the jungle. But what I was looking at was not a genius's work. It was the work of a loony, a fucking Nazi, or God knows what. I just couldn't stand it, man. For the last fifteen years there hasn't been one night when I haven't thought about that mutilated body. I leant further over, face against the glass. I wanted to see Böhm junior's face. His head was turned at an impossible angle. 180°. I saw that his eyes were wide open in terror. The kid was gagged. I realized that the fucker had done that to him while he was still conscious, without any anaesthetic. I took out my gun and went back outside. The medic was waiting for me with four towel-heads armed to the teeth.

"They pointed the storm lanterns at me. I was dazzled. I couldn't see a thing. I just heard the medic's plummy voice as it drilled into my brains: 'Be reasonable, Kiefer. One move, and I'll have you shot like a dog. You are now an accomplice to the murder of a child. That means the death sentence in both the Congo and the Central African Republic. But if you follow my instructions, no harm will come to any of us, and we may even become extremely rich . . . ' The medic then told me what I had to do. I was to take the son's body to Mbaïki and cook up an official version of his death with a Black doctor. That would already earn me a few thousand. Then there would be an even more lucrative business in the future. I didn't have any choice. I strapped Philippe Böhm's body onto a stretcher and headed off with two porters towards the SCAD. I left old man Böhm with the loony. Van Dötten had split. I got back to my van and drove to Mbaïki with the kid's corpse. This whole business was so revolting that I hoped the jungle would swamp over the medic and wipe out that nightmare."

So, on that terrible night, Böhm, Kiefer and van Dötten had unwittingly sold their souls to the devil. It had never occurred to me that another person was giving the three of them their orders. Since that night in August 1977, they had been under his command. The point of the lump of titanium on Böhm's new heart was now clear: it was material evidence, the doctor's 'signature', the object that made the murder concrete and allowed the surgeon to control Böhm and, indirectly, the two others as well.

"I know what happened next, Kiefer," I said. "I questioned Mdiaye. You dictated his report to him, then went back to Bangui with the body. And then?"

"I made up some bullshit to tell Bokassa. I told him that a gorilla had attacked us, how young Böhm had got himself killed and how old Max had gone home to Switzerland, via Brazzaville. It was all dead suspect, but Bokassa didn't give a damn. All he was worried about was whether we'd found any diamonds. His coronation was in three months' time. And he was looking for stones everywhere. For his 'crown'. In complete secrecy, a prospecting team was sent to the jungle. I was in charge. By October, extraordinary diamonds were being dug up. They were packed straight off to Antwerp to be cut."

"When did you next see Böhm?"

"A year and a half later, in Bangui. I couldn't believe my eyes. Old Max had withered away. He moved slowly and cautiously. His short cropped hair was even whiter than ever. We found a quiet spot by the Oubangui and had a chat. The town was starting to get too hot for comfort. The student riots had started."

"What did Böhm tell you?"

"He wanted me to be part of the craziest scheme I'd ever heard of. This is more or less what he said: 'Bokassa's reign is over, Kiefer. He'll be dethroned within a few weeks. Nobody knows the Sicamine's real potential, except you and me. And you're in charge of the operation. You control your men and run your stock, right? Now, we all know how things work in the forest. What's to stop you from keeping the best stones? No one's ever going to come to check exactly what the creeks have produced.' Böhm, Africa's righter of wrongs, was talking me into becoming a diamond thief. There was no two ways about it. His 'operation' had made a new man of him. 'For me,' he went on, 'Africa is finished. I can't come back here. Ever again. But I could be at the receiving end of your stones in Europe and sell them in Antwerp. What do you reckon?'

"I thought it over. Smuggling diamonds is the biggest temptation when you've got a job like mine. You spend all day up to your neck in shit, watching endless treasures slipping through your fingers.

But I also knew the risks. So I said: 'What about the couriers, Böhm? Who's going to transport the diamonds?' Then Böhm answered: 'That's just it, Kiefer. I've got some couriers. Some couriers that nobody will ever notice or arrest. Couriers that don't take planes, boats, or any other known means of transport, that never pass through customs and are never searched.' I looked at him without saying a word. So he asked me to go with him to Bayanga, in the west, where he'd introduce me to his 'smugglers'.

"All I could see on the plain were thousands of storks, which were about to take off for Europe. Böhm lent me his binoculars and pointed out a stork which had a ring round its leg. He said: 'I've been looking after storks for twenty years now. When they go back to Europe in March, I welcome them, feed them, and ring their chicks. For twenty years, I've been studying their migration, their life cycles, all sorts of things like that which have fascinated me since I was young. Today, my studies are going to be of unexpected use to us. Look at that bird.'

"He pointed out a ringed bird. 'Imagine just for a moment that I place one or more uncut diamonds inside the ring. What will happen? In two months' time, the diamonds will arrive in Europe, in a specific nest. Like clockwork. Storks always return each year to exactly the same nest. If we extended this method to all the ringed storks, we could deliver thousands of stones without any risk. In spring, I visit the birds and pick up the diamonds. Then all I have to do is go and sell them in Antwerp.'

"Suddenly Böhm's plan didn't sound so crazy. I asked: 'What would my part be?' He replied: 'You pocket the best diamonds during the mining season. Then, you come here to Bayanga, you slip the diamonds into the birds' rings. I'll give you a rifle and some knockout shots. You're a good shot, Kiefer. A job like that would only take you a couple of weeks at most. And you'll be paid ten thousand dollars a year.' This was peanuts in comparison with the profits a scheme like that could make. But our Swiss friend explained that he wasn't the only one involved in the business. And I grasped what was going on.

"It hadn't been his idea. The project had been cooked up by that surgeon, that jungle medic. We were in it up to our necks and now he could force us to carry out the scheme. The same system was being set up in the east, with van Dötten in my role in South Africa. We were pawns in someone else's game, yet we were going to be extremely rich. 'Count me in,' I said. You know the rest. The project worked like a charm. Every year, I loaded a good thousand small diamonds into the birds' rings. Everything was going perfectly, in the west and the east, till April . . ."

Kiefer stopped. His lips made a sucking noise, then his entire body arched up, as though in the throes of some terrible pain. Then he slumped back down and glanced up at me from his hollow black eye sockets.

"'Scuse me, kid. It's time for my little feed."

Kiefer grabbed a syringe and one of the flasks from off the table, removing a dose of morphine in a phial. He prepared his injection in a few swift gestures. He seized a strap of brown rubber, then stiffened his left arm and rolled up his sleeve. His arm was dotted with dark, granular blotches, like dried blood scabs forming strange atolls on a milky sea. With an expert hand, he strapped himself up, syringe between his teeth. His veins swelled at once. Kiefer examined each of them with the point of the needle, in search of the best line of attack. Suddenly, he pushed the syringe in. Still concentrating on what he was doing, he curled up under the effect of the drug. His bald head passed through a sunbeam and gleamed with a white dazzle, like a fluorescent stone. His bony joints rippled under his skin. Seconds ticked past. Then Kiefer relaxed. He laughed to himself, then his head turned in the shadows.

My mind was still on his closing words. Yes, I did know the rest. In April, the eastern storks had not returned. Böhm had panicked and sent out his henchmen. The two of them had retraced the storks' path, but found nothing. All they did was kill Iddo, who was the only person who could have told them what had happened. Later, Max Böhm had had the idea of sending me out on the same route, with the two Bulgarians on my tail, with instructions to kill me if

I got too "inquisitive". So he had packed me off to be killed in the hope that I would uncover a scrap of vital evidence. The unanswered question now was: why me? Maybe Kiefer could help. As though reading my mind, he asked me:

"What I don't get, kid, is why you were following those birds."

"I was following Böhm's orders."

"Böhm's orders!"

Kiefer's laugh was long and glutinous – a horrible, fractured hissing – and some more black strands fell down onto his shirt. He repeated:

"Böhm's orders! Böhm's orders!"

I yelled over his gurgling:

"I don't know why he chose me. I had no knowledge of ornithology, and wasn't part of your set-up. So Böhm seems to have sent me out to get you, like a bloodhound surrounded by murderers."

Kiefer sighed.

"All that doesn't matter much any more. We were fucked, anyway."

"What do you mean?"

"Böhm's dead, lad. And without him, the system falls to pieces. He was the only one who knew the nests and the numbers. He carried that off to the grave with him. And damned us, too. Because we know too much and are of no further use."

"Who do you mean by 'us'?"

"Me, van Dötten and the two Bulgarians."

"Is that why you're hiding out in Bayanga?"

"Yup. I did a runner. But no sooner had I got here, than the disease broke out. One of life's little ironies, son. AIDS at sixty, makes you laugh really."

"What about van Dötten?"

"I don't where he is. Stuff him."

"Who's after you, Kiefer?"

"The system, or the medic, I dunno. We belonged to some bigger set-up, something international, get me? But I've been stuck in this shit-hole for the last ten years. I couldn't tell you a thing about all of that. Böhm was the only contact I had."

"Does the name One World mean anything to you?"

"Not much. They've got a mission, near the Sicamine. A nun who looks after the Pygmies. It's not exactly my ball game."

Operations without anaesthetic and the theft of hearts were definitely not Kiefer's department. But still, I pressed him:

"Sikkov had a United Nations passport. Is it possible that, without you being aware of it, he was working for One World?"

"Yeah, that's possible."

"Do you know about the murder of a gypsy called Rajko Nicolich, in Sliven in Bulgaria, last May?"

"No."

"And the killing of Gomoun, a little Pygmy from Zoko, near the Sicamine, just ten days ago?"

Kiefer sat up.

"Near the Sicamine?"

"Don't play the innocent with me, Kiefer. You know damn well that the medic came back to the Central African Republic. He even used your helicopter."

Kiefer slumped back down and murmured:

"You really are well informed, aren't you, my little fellow? Ten days ago, Bonafé sent me a message. The doc was back in Bangui. I suppose he was looking for his diamonds."

"His diamonds?"

"This year's collection. The stones have got to take wing one way or the other." He sneered. "But the doc didn't find me."

I decided to bluff.

"He didn't find you because he wasn't looking for you."

The Czech sat up again.

"What are you on about?"

"He didn't come here for the diamonds, Kiefer. In his mind, money is only the means to an end. It's of secondary importance."

"So why did he come to this pit full of niggers?"

"He came here for Gomoun, to extract a little Pygmy's heart."

He spat.

"Bullshit!"

"I saw the girl's body, Kiefer."

The Czech seemed to be thinking.

"He didn't come for me . . . Well fuck that, then. I can now die in peace."

"You're not dead yet, Kiefer. And you've never seen this doctor again?"

"No, never."

"You don't know his name?"

"No, I tell you."

"Is he French?"

"He speaks French, that's all I know."

"Without an accent?"

"Without an accent."

"What does he look like?"

"Tall, thin face, starting to bald, grey hair. An expression like stone."

"Is that all?"

"Leave it out, kid."

"Where is this doctor hiding, Kiefer?"

"Someplace somewhere."

"Did Böhm know where the medic was?"

"Yeah, I reckon so."

My voice quavered:

"Where?"

"I dunno."

I stood up and pushed away the chair. The heat had invaded the room, heat that could melt iron bars. Kiefer's voice creaked:

"We made a deal, fuck-face."

I stared into his eyes.

"I haven't forgotten."

I extended my arm and took the safety catch off the Glock. Kiefer wheezed:

"Fire, you asshole."

I hesitated a moment longer. Suddenly, I saw the shape of the grenade beneath the sheet, with the Czech's finger curled round the ring. I put my hands together and fired once. The mosquito net flapped. With a dull noise, Kiefer was blown apart, spraying the net with his black blood and brains. Outside, I heard the storks reacting, and taking off rapidly.

A couple of seconds later, I pulled aside the folds of tulle. Kiefer was no more than an empty corpse stretched out on the pillow, a mess of blood, skin and bits of bone. The grenade, still intact, was glued down to the folds of the sheet. I noticed some tiny diamonds and iron rings, which were scattered around in that human hash. I left the fortune where it was, but took one of the metal rings.

I went out into the corridor. The Mbati woman, who had woken up with a start, was running towards me and gesticulating, her kids at her heels. Through her tears she was laughing: the monster was dead. I elbowed my way past. On the walls, the lizards were still scampering about, like some ghastly green moulding. I leapt outside. The sun stopped me in my tracks. Dazzled, I staggered down the steps then dropped my Glock onto the scarlet earth.

It was all over – it was all beginning.

Far away, in the tall grasses, Tina was running towards me.

V

An Autumn in Hell

CHAPTER 45

Four days later, as dawn broke, I was back in Paris. It was 30
September. My spacious flat now seemed small and cramped. I was
no longer used to circumscribed spaces. Picking up the mail that
had accumulated over two weeks, I went to my study to listen to
the messages on my answering machine. I recognized the voices of
friends and acquaintances, all rather put out that I had been away
for several weeks. There was no message from Dumaz. His silence
struck me as being odd. The other surprise was a further call from
Nelly Braesler. In twenty-five years of remote-controlled upbringing
she had never contacted me so often. Why this sudden concern?

It was six o'clock in the morning. I ambled about my apartment,
feeling rather giddy. It seemed unreal to be back there alive, in
comfortable surroundings, after everything I had just been through.
Images of the final days in Africa flickered into my mind. Beckés
and I on the plain, burying Otto Kiefer's corpse, which was still
wrapped up in its gory mosquito net – and still with its diamonds.
The problems with the Bayanga gendarmerie, where I had explained
that Otto Kiefer had committed suicide using an automatic pistol
that he kept under his pillow. The farewell to Tina, whom I had
embraced one last time on the bank of the river.

My trip to Africa had cast both light and darkness on my
investigations. Otto Kiefer's confession rounded off the diamond
smuggling business. Two of the main players were dead, while van
Dötten was presumably hiding out somewhere in South Africa.

Sarah Gabbor was still on the run, perhaps after managing to sell her diamonds. She would now be extremely rich, but also in danger. Killers were surely already on her heels. This was the only loose end left in the diamond affair – the rest of that business involving winged couriers was well and truly over.

But there remained the "African doc", the person who had started the whole operation.

For at least fifteen years, a man had been extracting hearts, operating without anaesthetic on innocent victims scattered across the world. The organ smuggling hypothesis was obvious, but several details led me to believe that the truth was more complex. Why was this surgeon so sadistic? Why did he make such a precise selection across the entire planet, whereas the illegal procurement of body organs could operate perfectly in any one of the countries concerned? Was he looking for a specific tissue group?

For the moment, I had just two solid leads.

First: the "medic" and Max Böhm had met in the equatorial forest between 1972 and 1977, during the latter's excursions. Therefore this surgeon had lived in the Congo or the Central African Republic – and presumably not always in the depths of the jungle. I could get his name by applying to both countries' immigration control and hospitals. But how to obtain this information without any official standing? I could also question European heart specialists. A surgeon capable of carrying out a heart transplant in the middle of the jungle in 1977 was certainly an exceptionally gifted wielder of the scalpel. It must surely be possible to discover the identity of such a virtuoso, someone who was a native French speaker and who had exiled himself in the middle of Africa. I immediately thought of Dr Catherine Warel, who had carried out Böhm's postmortem, then helped Dumaz during his investigation.

The second lead was One World. The murderer made use of this massive system of tests and data to locate his victims throughout the world. When in action, he used helicopters, sterile tents and other logistic methods associated with field hospitals. To be able to do that, he had to occupy a senior post there. So I needed to be able to consult OW's organization chart. By putting this information beside the African findings, a name might spring out. But there, too, I was up against my lack of any official status. I had no power, nor specific mission. Dumaz had warned me: it is no easy matter to attack a world famous humanitarian organization.

At a deeper level, my own inquiries were now stagnating. I was shattered, wracked with remorse and cornered into a solitude that had never seemed more profound. If I was still alive, then that was thanks to a sort of miracle. I simply had to go to the police and obtain their help before confronting the organ trafficking.

7 a.m. I called Hervé Dumaz's home number. No answer. I made some tea, then sat down in my living-room, thinking dark thoughts. On the coffee table, I looked through the pile of mail – invitations, letters from university colleagues, learned journals and daily news-papers. I picked up some recent copies of *Le Monde* and flicked through them absent-mindedly.

A few seconds later, in a daze, I was reading this article:

MURDER AT THE DIAMOND EXCHANGE

On 27 September 1991, a murder was committed on the premises of the famous Beurs von Diamanthandel in Antwerp. In one of the upper rooms of the Diamond Exchange, Sarah Gabbor, a young Israeli, armed with an Austrian-made Glock automatic gun, shot dead Hervé Dumaz, a Swiss Federal Inspector. The young lady's motives are not yet known, nor the source of the quite exceptional diamond that she was intending to sell that day. At nine o'clock, on the morning of 27 September 1991, everything seemed normal at Beurs von Diamanthandel. The offices opened, the security measures were applied and the first vendors arrived. It is here, and in Antwerp's other Exchanges, that twenty per cent of the world's production is bought and sold, that which escapes the control of De Beers' South African empire.

At about 10.30 a.m., a tall blonde young woman, carrying a leather handbag, went up to the first floor and entered the main room. She approached one of the dealers and offered to sell him a white envelope full of dozens of rather small, but absolutely pure, diamonds. The buyer, who is also Israeli (and who wishes to remain anonymous) recognized her. For the last week, she had been going there every other day to sell a similar quantity of diamonds, which were always of the same high quality.

But, that day, another person intervened. A man aged about thirty went over to the woman and whispered something in her ear. She immediately spun round and produced an automatic handgun from her bag. Without any hesitation, she fired. The man collapsed, killed outright by a bullet in his forehead.

Threatening the security guards, who had rushed into the room, the young woman then attempted to make her escape. She backed away, remaining extremely calm. But she did not know about the Exchange's sophisticated security system. When she reached the elevators on the first-floor landing, sheets of bullet-proof glass suddenly rose up around her, blocking her exit. Trapped, she then heard the traditional announcement requesting her to drop her gun and give herself up. She did so. Immediately, the Belgian police poured into the closed-off area through the lifts and arrested her.

Since then, Beurs von Diamanthandel's security team and Belgian police officers specializing in diamond smuggling have been examining the footage of the murder which had been filmed by the video cameras. Nobody can see any reason for this sudden outbreak of violence. The identities of the two protagonists have merely deepened the police's doubts. The victim was a Swiss Federal Inspector called Hervé Dumaz. This young officer, aged thirty-four, was posted to the Montreux police headquarters. What was he doing in Antwerp, given that he had taken two weeks' holiday? And why, if he intended to arrest the young woman, had he not informed the Exchange's security forces?

The woman's identity adds to this mystery. Sarah Gabbor, a young kibbutznik aged twenty-eight, came from the Beyt Shean region, near Galilee, just by the Jordanian border. For the moment, nobody knows how this young woman, who worked in a fish farm, had come into possession of such a fortune in diamonds . . .

I crumpled the page in a fit of rage. So, violence had broken out again. More blood had flowed. Despite my advice, Dumaz had decided to play it his way. He had threatened Sarah, like some clumsy cop. She had not hesitated for a moment about gunning him down. Dumaz was dead and Sarah in prison. The only comfort to be drawn from this gory epilogue was that my young lover was now safe.

I stood up and went into my study. Automatically, I stood behind the window and pulled the curtain aside. The gardens of the American Centre, which is just beside my block, had been mown flat. The clumps and thickets had been replaced by the dark furrows of bulldozers. Only a scattering of trees had been saved. I absolutely had to see Sarah again. This would be my first real chance to enter into contact with the international police.

CHAPTER 46

The morning crackled by like a brush fire. I made some phone calls – international directory enquiries, embassies, law courts – then had to send several faxes in order to obtain what I wanted: official authorization allowing me to see Sarah in Ganshoren women's prison in the suburbs of Brussels. By about noon, I had done everything I could. I had hinted that I possessed some information which might cast new light on this case. It was double or quits: either they would believe me, then the consequences of what I had done would be out of my hands, or they would think I was mad and refuse my request. I then tried international directory enquiries again. A few seconds later, I was dialling the twelve-figure number of the hospital in Montreux where the postmortem had been carried out on Max Böhm's body on 20 August. I asked for Dr Catherine Warel. About a minute later, I heard an energetic "hello?"

"This is Louis Antioch, Dr Warel. Maybe you remember me."

"No," she replied.

"We met just over a month ago in your clinic. I'm the person who discovered Max Böhm's body."

"Oh right, the ornithologist."

I was not sure if she was speaking about me or about Böhm.

"Exactly. Dr Warel, I am in urgent need of additional information – related to that death."

I heard the metal clink of a lighter being flicked open.

"Go ahead. If I can help in any way ... "

I was about to launch off, but then realized that what I was going to say would sound totally ridiculous.

"I can't speak on the phone. I'd like to see you, as soon as possible."

Catherine Warel was a cool lady. Without any hesitation, she replied:

"Well, how about this afternoon? There's a flight from Orly to Lausanne around lunchtime. I'll be expecting you in the clinic at around three o'clock."

"I'll be there. Thank you, doctor."

Before leaving, I phoned up Dr Djuric in Sofia. After fifteen minutes of unsuccessful attempts, I at last heard the ringing tone. About seventeen rings later, a sleepy voice answered, in Bulgarian:

"Yes?"

It was Milan Djuric's voice. He must have been taking a nap.

"This is Louis Antioch, doctor. The stork man."

After a few seconds' silence, the deep voice answered:

"Antioch? You have been much in my thoughts since we first met. Are you still investigating Rajko's death?"

"Now more than ever. And I think I've found out who the killer is."

"You've . . ."

"Yes, or at least I'm on the right track. Rajko's murder is part of a perfectly organized system, whose real motives remain a mystery to me. But there's one thing I'm sure of – the network covers the entire planet. Other similar murders have occurred in other countries. And, to stop this massacre, I need your help."

"Go on."

"I need to know Rajko's HLA group."

"That's simple. I still have my postmortem report. Hang on a minute."

I heard drawers being opened and a rustling of paper.

"Here it is. According to the international code, his was HLA A^w 19,3 – B37,5."

My chest tightened. It was the same group as Gomoun's. This could certainly not be a coincidence. I stammered:

"Is this group rare, or does it have any special characteristics?"

"I've no idea. This isn't my field. In any case, there's an infinite number of tissue groups and I don't see why . . ."

"Do you have access to a fax?"

"Yes. I know the director of a health centre and . . . "

"Could you fax me your postmortem report today?"

"Of course. What's going on?"

"Note down my number first, doctor."

I gave him my personal phone and fax numbers, then went on:

"Listen, Djuric. There's a surgeon who's stealing hearts all over the world. In the depths of Africa, I personally witnessed the postmortem of a little girl whose body was in a similar state to Rajko's. The man I'm talking about is a monster, Djuric. He's a savage beast, but I also believe that he works according to his own personal logic. Follow me?"

His deep voice boomed into the receiver:

"Do you have his identity?"

"Not yet. But you were right, he's a brilliant surgeon."

"What nationality is he?"

"French, perhaps. Certainly a native French speaker."

The dwarf seemed to think for a moment, then he asked:

"What are you going to do now?"

"Keep looking. I'm expecting some vital information any moment now."

"You haven't informed the police?"

"Not yet."

"There's something I'd like to ask you, Antioch."

"What's that?"

Interference crackled across the line. Djuric raised his voice:

"When you came to see me here in Sofia, I told you that your face seemed familiar."

As I did not respond. Djuric pressed on:

"I thought about that resemblance for some time. I think you look like a doctor I knew in Paris. Do you have any medical practitioners in your family?"

"My father was a doctor."

"Was he also called Antioch?"

"Yes, of course. Sorry, Djuric, but I'm pressed for time."

The dwarf went on:

"Did he work in Paris during the 1960s?"

My heart was leaping up into my throat. Once more, the mention of my father had made me feel vaguely uneasy.

"No. My father always worked in Africa."

Djuric's far-off voice resonated:

"Is he still alive? Is your father still living?"

There was a further outbreak of crackles. I finished this conversation off by answering in a jolting voice:

"He died the last day of 1965. In a fire. With my mother and brother. Dead. All three of them."

"And was that the fire in which your hands were burnt?"

I slammed my palm down onto the phone and cut him off. Talk of my parents always gripped me with uncontrollable fear and panic. And I did not understand what he was driving at. How could he have known my father in Paris? Djuric may have studied at the Rue des Saints-Pères but, in the 1960s, he was only a child.

11.30 a.m. I grabbed a taxi and headed for the airport. During the flight, I read some other newspapers. Most of them contained further brief articles about the diamond murder, but without proffering any new information. What most interested them were the diplomatic complexities of such a case, with the murder of a Swiss policeman by an Israeli woman in a Belgian town. They quoted the Swiss and Israeli ambassadors in Brussels, who expressed their "consternation" and their "desire to see the reasons for this unfortunate incident brought to light as rapidly as possible".

In Lausanne, I rented a car and drove off towards Montreux. I was still feeling bugged by the questions Djuric had asked me. The confused state of the situation weighed down on me, while at the same time I was dreading the drastic direct action that I was now going to have to take. What is more, my memories of Africa still hovered around me. That sparkling night with Tina, the tangling of the Bayanga tracks, the glittering of the rain – but also Gomoun's body, Otto Kiefer's face, the coordinated horror of the destinies of Max Böhm, his son and Sister Pascale. And that surgeon forever lurking in the background. Faceless and nameless.

Dr Warel was expecting me at the clinic. There she was once more with her blotchy face and her strong French cigarettes. I did not beat about the bush:

"Doctor, after Max Böhm's death, you helped Inspector Dumaz undertake certain research."

"That's correct."

"I was also working with him. And I now need some information."

The woman twitched nervously. She lit a cigarette, took a drag and then asked:

"You're not a police officer, so what do you think gives you the right?"

I answered without pausing for breath:

"Max Böhm was a friend of mine. Now that he's dead, I'm looking into his past. Certain details are of vital importance."

"Why doesn't Inspector Dumaz just call me himself?"

"Hervé Dumaz is dead, doctor. Shot dead in circumstances that are not unrelated to the death of Max Böhm."

"What?"

"Go and buy a newspaper, doctor. You'll see if I'm telling the truth."

Catherine Warel hesitated for a moment. After a few seconds, sounding less sure of herself, she asked:

"And what's your role in all of this?"

"I'm going it alone. Sooner or later, the police will get onto the case. Will you help me?"

A cloud of smoke blew out from her lips. She finally replied:

"What do you want to know?"

"I'm sure you remember that Max Böhm had had a heart transplant. It looked as though the operation had been done over three years ago. But you found no record of it in Switzerland or elsewhere. Nor did you find out which doctor was treating Böhm."

"That's correct."

"I think I've found a lead that may take us to the surgeon. He's an extraordinary person. Terrifying, in fact."

"What do you mean?"

"This man is a virtuoso heart surgeon, but he's also a dangerous murderer."

"Listen, Monsieur Antioch, I don't know whether I should be wasting my time listening to you. Do you have any proof for all of this?"

"Some, yes. Since our first meeting, I've travelled across the world and pieced Böhm's life together. For example, I've discovered the circumstances behind his heart transplant."

"And?"

"It was performed in central Africa in 1977. His son's heart was transplanted into his body. The lad was killed for that very reason."

"My God . . . you're not serious?"

"Do you remember, doctor, how extraordinarily compatible the receiver's body and the organ were? Do you also recall that capsule of titanium? The surgeon deliberately 'signed' his operation with that lump of metal. So as to keep Max Böhm under his control."

Catherine Warel lit another cigarette. Her nerves were still holding. She asked:

"Do you know who he was?"

"No. But he's still at work in various parts of the globe. For some reason that I do not yet understand, he's been stealing and will continue to steal hearts torn out of living bodies anywhere on earth. The means at his disposal are infinite."

"You're talking about smuggling body organs?"

"I don't know. My intuition tells me that there's another explanation. The man's mad. And unbelievably cruel."

Warel exhaled.

"Meaning?"

"He operates without anaesthetic."

The doctor lowered her head. Her cigarette moved from one clenched fist to the other. Finally, she took a note pad out of her white coat and asked:

"How . . . how can I be of help?"

"In August 1977, this surgeon was working near the border between the Congo and the Central African Republic. At the time, he had some sort of clinic in the middle of the equatorial forest. I think he was already in hiding – but there must be some trace of his presence there. He needed equipment, drugs, and so on. I'm sure that you'll be able to find who it was. Remember, he's an expert, a man capable of carrying out a heart transplant in the middle of the jungle at a time when, as you yourself put it, there were not that many successful operations."

Catherine Warel jotted down the main lines. She then asked:

"What about his nationality?"

"He's a native French speaker."

"Do you know when he moved to Africa?"

"No."

"Do you think he's still there?"

"No, I don't."

266

"Do you have the slightest idea where he may be now?"

"I think he works for One World."

"The humanitarian organization?"

"I think he uses the association's administrative structure to carry out his fiendish experiments. Dr Warel, I'm telling the truth, believe me. Each day is a new nightmare. And he's still at work, you understand? Perhaps, even as we speak, he's torturing an innocent kid somewhere in the world."

In a gruff voice, she answered:

"There's no need to start laying it on. I'll make a few phone calls. I may be able to get the information you need by this evening. Or tomorrow, at the latest. But I'm not promising anything."

"Do you think you could get hold of a list of doctors that work for One World?"

"That would be difficult. One World is a closed universe. But I'll see what I can do."

"If I'm right, doctor – and if the murderer hasn't changed his name – the two sets of information should fit together. Please, be as quick as you can."

Warel stared at me with her dark eyes. We were standing in the corner of a small corridor of gleaming linoleum. Tense but confident, I stared back at her. I knew she would not inform the police.

CHAPTER 47

I arrived back home in Paris at about 10 p.m. I had received no answers from any of the embassies or law courts, nor any message from Dr Warel. But Djuric had faxed me his postmortem report on Rajko. I took a boiling hot shower, then cooked some scrambled eggs with salmon and potatoes. I made some brown, smoky Russian tea and, hoping that sleep would come, I slipped into bed with my Glock at hand's reach. At about 11 p.m., the phone rang. It was Catherine Warel.

"So?" I asked.

"Nothing for now. Tomorrow morning I should receive a complete list of all the French or French-speaking doctors who had practised in central Africa between 1960 and 1980. I also contacted a few old friends who might be able to give me more precise information. As for One World, there's no way to get a list of their doctors. But all hope isn't lost yet. I know a young eye specialist who's just been taken on by them. He's promised to help."

A complete failure. And time was running out. I hid my disappointment.

"Very good, doctor. Thanks for trusting me."

"Don't mention it. I've been around a bit, you know. But never before have I heard of anything like this."

"I'll tell you everything . . . When I understand it myself."

"Take care of yourself. I'll call back tomorrow."

My mind blank, I hung up. I was going to have to wait.

It was not yet dawn when the phone rang again. I picked it up and blinked at the time on my quartz clock. It was 5.24.

"Yes?" I growled.

"Is that Louis Antioch?"

It was an extremely deep voice, with a heavy oriental accent.

"Who's speaking?"

"This is Itzhak Delter, Sarah Gabbor's lawyer."

I sat up in bed.

"What can I do for you?" I said clearly.

"I'm calling you from Brussels. I hear that you phoned the embassy yesterday. You wanted to visit Sarah Gabbor, is that right?"

The man cleared his throat. His voice resonated like the body of a double bass.

"You must understand that, in the present situation, that would be rather difficult."

"I have to see her."

"May I ask what your relationship is with Miss Gabbor?"

"A personal one."

"Are you Jewish?"

"No."

"How long have you known her?"

"About one month."

"You met her in Israel?"

"In Beyt Shean."

"And you think that you have important information for us?"

"Yes, I think so."

He seemed to pause for thought. Then his deep voice streamed on:

"This is an extremely complicated business, Mr Antioch. And rather an embarrassing one. I mean for the state of Israel and for the other governments involved. Our theory is that Sarah Gabbor's reflex action merely reflects the tip of the iceberg. The visible part of a larger, international smuggling network."

"Reflex action" to describe a Glock bullet in the middle of the forehead. Delter certainly had a way with euphemisms. He went on:

"The police force of each country is looking into this case. For the moment, the information is completely confidential. I cannot promise you that you'll be able to visit Sarah Gabbor. On the other hand, I think it would be a good idea if you came to Brussels – so that we could have a little talk. We can't speak about all of this on the phone."

I grabbed a note pad.

"Give me your address."

"I'm at the Israeli embassy, 71 rue Joseph-II."

"Could you repeat your name?"

"Itzhak Delter."

"Well, Delter, let's be clear about one thing. If I can help you, I will. But on one condition: that I get to see Sarah Gabbor."

"That isn't up to us. But we'll do our utmost to get permission. If the investigators think that such a meeting might help their inquiries to run more smoothly, then there won't be any problem. In my opinion, it all depends on how much you cooperate and what you have to tell us."

"No, that's not the way it's going to be. Sarah first, then my statement. I'll be in Brussels around midday."

Delter's sigh was like the purring of a reactor.

"We'll be expecting you."

A few minutes later, I had showered, shaved and dressed. I was wearing the grey silk Hackett suit with mother-of-pearl buttons that I kept for special occasions. I booked a hire car and called a taxi to take me to the agency.

I had over 30,000 francs left of the sum Böhm had given me. To which was added my monthly allowances of 20,000 francs, which I had received in August and September. Seventy thousand francs in all, which was enough for me to organize all the trips I needed in order to catch the "doc". Furthermore, I still had a wad of car hire vouchers and first-class plane tickets, which were easily exchangeable.

As I closed my front door, a wave of adrenalin ran through me.

CHAPTER 48

At nine o'clock, I was driving up the northbound autoroute towards Brussels. The sky was criss-crossed with dark lines, like a menacing network of power cables. As the kilometres shot by, the landscape changed. Red-brick buildings appeared, as though they were blood clots scattered across the countryside. I had the impression of descending into the lower strata of some dark, endless depression. Despair seemed to flourish here, amid the weeds and the railway lines. At noon, I crossed the border. An hour later, I was driving through Brussels.

The capital of Belgium struck me as being dull and lifeless. A shrivelled version of Paris, drawn by a gloomy artist. I found the embassy without any difficulty. It was a typical example of modern architecture – grey concrete and sharp balconies. Itzhak Delter was waiting for me in the lobby.

He looked like his voice – a six foot three giant ill at ease in his suit. With his craggy features, aggressive jaws and blond crewcut, he was more reminiscent of a soldier in mufti than a wily lawyer, well used to hard diplomatic cases. So much the better. I preferred dealing with a man of action. We were not going to waste any time with useless chitchat.

After the standard body search, Delter led me into a small anonymously furnished office. He asked me to take a seat. I refused. Standing facing each other, we spoke for a few minutes. The lawyer was a good head taller than me but, concentrating on my anger and my secrets, I felt sure of myself. Delter told me that he had obtained permission for me to visit Sarah Gabbor. In turn, I explained that I was in possession of several pieces of evidence concerning the diamonds which would acquit her, at least of having any direct role in the smuggling.

Delter looked sceptical and asked me a few more questions before we left for the prison. I refused to answer. He clenched his fists and his jawbones stood out under his skin. A few seconds later, he calmed down and smiled.

"You're a tough one, Antioch. Come on. My car's downstairs. We have an appointment at Ganshoren Prison at two o'clock."

On the way, Delter quite openly asked me if I was Sarah's lover. I ducked the question. Once again, he asked me if I was Jewish. I shook my head. He seemed obsessed by the notion. Delter then stopped trying to question me. He told me that Sarah Gabbor was an extremely awkward "client". She refused to speak to anyone, even to her lawyer. He then admitted that, when she had heard I was coming to Brussels, she had expressed a desire to see me. I suppressed a frisson. So, despite everything, our love was not yet a thing of the past.

The western suburbs of Brussels might easily have been called "De Profundis". It was a journey through the heart of sadness and boredom. The brown houses made up a strange cloud of dark, gleaming organs, as though solidified in their own coagulated blood.

"We're there," said Delter, braking in front of a huge edifice, its gate framed by square granite columns. Two women, armed with sub-machine guns, were on guard. Above them, the words "Tribunal des Femmes" were engraved in the stone.

We were announced. A few seconds later, a woman of about fifty came to meet us, a nasty suspicious expression printed on her face. She introduced herself: Odette Wilessen, the prison governor. Staring at me with the eyes of a bird of ill omen, she repeated, in a strong Flemish accent:

"Sarah Gabbor has agreed to see you. In fact, she's in solitary confinement until further notice, but Monsieur Delter and the investigating magistrate both think that it would be a good thing for you to visit her. She's a difficult prisoner, Monsieur Antioch. I don't want any additional problems. Please remember who you are and where you are."

We stepped inside and found ourselves in a small garden.

"Wait for me here," Odette Wilessen commanded.

We waited beside a stone fountain. The silent, starchy atmosphere was rather reminiscent of a convent. What is more, there was no outward sign that we were inside a prison. We were surrounded by classic-style grey buildings, with no bars on their windows. The governor returned, with two warders dressed in blue, who both stood a good eight inches taller than her. Odette Wilessen asked us to follow her. We walked down a tree-lined path, then a door opened.

At the end of a long corridor, a tall glass-paned doorway stood in the interior of the building. Broad flat bars, which were sky blue, ran through the thick dirty glass. I now understood why the prison had been hitherto invisible. It was a building inside the building. A block of iron and bolts, ringed round with stone. We walked over to the gate. The governor signalled to a woman on the other side, who unlocked it. There was a clicking noise. We then entered a different sort of space, confined, misty, pierced by blinding white strip-lights.

The corridor continued. The sky-blue paint had been daubed over everything – the bars on the narrow windows, halfway up the walls, the locks and fuse boxes. Here, daylight was a scarce commodity, and those blank strip-lights were presumably on all year, day and night. We followed the warders. The place was wrapped in heavy, total silence, as though pressurized from the depths of the ocean.

At the end of the corridor, we had to turn right, slide in another key and open another door. I went past a door, the upper half of which was made of glass. Women's faces appeared. They were busy working on tiny sewing machines. Their stares converged on me. I, too, observed them for a few seconds, then continued on my way with my head down. Without realizing it, I had stopped in order to examine those imprisoned creatures, to try and read the traces of their past misdemeanours on their faces, like birth marks. More doors followed with different activities going on behind them – computing, pottery, leatherwork, and so on.

We advanced further. Between the flat, flaking bars, I caught glimpses of a grey, dreary sky. The dark walls surrounded an open-air courtyard of cracked tarmac, with a volleyball net stretched across the middle. The leaden sky looked like an extra wall. There, women were coming and going, arm in arm, smoking cigarettes. Once more, their eyes fell on me. The gazes of hurt, humiliated, wounded souls. Dark deep stares, reflecting a sharpened desire, mixed with hatred. "Come on," one of the turnkeys said. Itzhak Delter tugged on my sleeve. More locks and more metallic clicks followed.

At last we reached the visiting room. It was large and even darker and dirtier. The area was divided in half lengthwise by a series of glass panels. Their wooden frames and the tables at either side were also covered in that same sinister blue paint. The architect of the prison must have decided to add this delicate touch to his block-house. Our group came to a halt on the threshold of the room. Odette Wilessen turned towards me.

"This visit is an exceptional one, Monsieur Antioch. I repeat, Sarah Gabbor is a dangerous woman. Don't stir her up, please, just don't stir her up."

With a nod, Odette Wilessen pointed out the way to me. I walked alone beside the empty compartments, my heart pounding as I advanced past the glass partitions. Suddenly, I noticed that I had passed a shadow. Feeling my legs give way, I walked back. I slumped down onto a chair facing the window. On the other side, Sarah was looking at me, her face expressionless and grim.

CHAPTER 49

My kibbutznik's hair was now short. Her blonde mop had become a straight delicately smooth cut. Under the strip-lights, she seemed paler. But her cheekbones still stood out proudly beneath her eyes. She was definitely the same beautiful, tenacious wild thing that I had met amongst the storks. She picked up the telephone.

"You're looking like shit, Louis."

"You're looking great, Sarah."

"Where did you get that scar on your face?"

"It's a souvenir from Israel."

Sarah shrugged.

"That's what you get for nosing around."

She was wearing a baggy, blue short-sleeved shirt. I wanted to kiss her, to lose my lips in the contours of her body, devour its harsh light outline. There was a moment of silence. I asked:

"How are you, Sarah?"

"So-so."

"I'm pleased to see you."

"You call this seeing me? You don't seem to have any idea of what's going on here."

I slid my hand under the table to check if there were any hidden mikes.

"Tell me everything, Sarah. From the moment you disappeared in Beyt Shean."

"You came here to wrangle that out of me for them?"

"No, Sarah. It's nothing like that. They allowed me to see you only when I promised to give them some information which will get you off."

"What are you going to tell them?"

"Everything that will prove that you played a very minor role in this diamond smuggling business."

She shrugged again.

"Sarah, I came here to see you. But also to find out. You owe me the truth. It could still save the two of us."

She burst out laughing and stared at me icily. Slowly, she extracted a packet of cigarettes from her pocket, lit up, then began:

"All this is your fault, Louis. Just get that into your head. All of it, you understand me? That last evening in Beyt Shean when you told me about the rings on the storks, you put me in mind of a few details I had ignored till then. After Iddo's death, I'd tidied away all his stuff. His bedroom, but also his 'laboratory', as he used to call that shack where he nursed his storks. When shifting his equipment, I'd uncovered a small trap-door under a cage. Hundreds of blood-stained metal rings were hidden there. At the time, I paid no attention to the disgusting things. But, through respect for his memory and his passion for ornithology, I left the canvas bag where I'd found it, under the trap-door. Then I forgot all about it.

"Much later, when you explained your idea about there being a message hidden in the rings, it all fell into place. I remembered Iddo's bag and suddenly understood. Iddo had discovered what you were looking for. That's why he'd armed himself and used to disappear all day. He'd been shooting down the storks and collecting the rings.

"That evening, I decided to leave you in the dark. I waited patiently till dawn, so as not to arouse your suspicions. Then, when you'd set off for Ben-Gurion Airport, I went back to the shed and dug out those lumps of metal. With some pliers, I opened one of the rings. Suddenly, a diamond dropped down into my hand. I couldn't believe my eyes. I immediately opened another ring. It contained several, smaller stones. I repeated the procedure ten times over. Each time, I found more diamonds. The miracle just kept happening. I tipped up the bag and screamed in joy: it contained at least one thousand rings."

"So?"

"So, I was rich, Louis. I had the means to make a break, to forget the fish, the mud and that kibbutz. But, first of all, I wanted to be sure. I packed a small bag, selected a few guns and took the bus to Netanya, the diamond capital."

"I trailed you that far."

"As you can see, that didn't do much good."

I did not respond, so Sarah went on:

"There, I found a jewel cutter who bought one of the diamonds. He ripped me off, but he was incapable of hiding the extraordinary quality of the stone. The poor old guy! His emotions were written all over his face. So, I was in possession of a fortune. I was so deliriously happy at that moment that I didn't weigh up the situation, and I didn't think about those loonies who had been smuggling diamonds using storks as their carriers. All I knew was that they had killed my brother and were still after the diamonds. I hired a car, then headed for Ben-Gurion Airport. Once there, I took the first flight to Europe. Then I travelled on for a while and hid the diamonds somewhere safe."

"And then?"

"A week went by. Independent producers generally sell their gems in Antwerp. So I now had to go there and play it carefully. Discreetly, and rapidly."

"Were . . . were you still armed?"

Sarah could not resist smiling. She pointed her index finger at me and cocked an imaginary pistol with her thumb.

"Mr Glock followed me everywhere."

For a fleeting moment, I thought "Sarah's mad".

"I decided to flog the lot off in Antwerp," she went on. "In envelopes of ten to fifteen stones, every other day. The first day, I picked out an old Jew, a bit like the cutter in Netanya. I got 50,000 dollars in a few minutes. Two days later, I went back and changed my contact. 30,000 more. The third time, while I was opening the envelope, I felt a hand on me and heard: "Don't move. You're under arrest." I felt a barrel in my back. I lost my head, Louis. In a flash, I saw all my hopes reduced to nothing. I saw my money, my happiness, my freedom vanish. Holding the Glock, I turned round. I didn't want to shoot him. All I wanted to do was get the upper hand on this shitty little cop who thought that he was going to stop me in my tracks. But the idiot was pointing a 9mm Beretta at me, with the safety catch off. I had no choice. I fired once, straight at his forehead. The guy just flopped down onto the floor, with half his skull missing." Sarah laughed morbidly. "He hadn't even touched the trigger. Keeping my gun on the diamond dealers, I picked up my stones. They were terrified. I suppose they thought I was going to rob them. I backed out of the room. For a moment, I thought I was going to get away with it. That's when the glass panels came down. I was stuck there like I was in a fucking aquarium."

"I read all that in the papers."

"The story doesn't stop there, Louis."

Sarah nervily stubbed out her cigarette, as in control as ever.

"The man who tried to arrest me was a Swiss Federal Agent called Hervé Dumaz. This rather complicated matters for the Belgian authorities. A Swiss policeman, murdered in Belgium by an Israeli. Plus a fortune in diamonds with a murky past. The Belgians started grilling me. Then my lawyer, Delter, had a go. After that, a Swiss delegation showed up. I didn't tell them anything, of course. Not to any of them. But I started thinking. How come an obscure inspector from Montreux had followed me to Antwerp, given that nobody knew I was in Belgium? I then remembered the 'strange cop' you had told me about and I figured that it was you who had sent Dumaz after me, while you continued on the trail of your storks and smugglers. I worked out that it was you, you mother-fucker, who'd put that policeman on my track."

I went pale and stammered:

"You were in danger. Dumaz was supposed to protect you till I got back."

"Protect me?"

Sarah's laughter was so raucous that one of the warders came over to us, gun in hand. I made a sign to her to back off.

"Protect me?" Sarah repeated. "So you still haven't worked out who Dumaz was? That he worked with the smugglers you were after?"

These last words tolled heavily inside me. My blood froze. Before I was able to reply, Sarah went on:

"Since they started interrogating me, I've learnt a lot about those diamonds. Much more than I could ever tell them. Delter came here once with an Austrian Interpol officer called Simon Rickiel. They tried to make me cooperate by telling me a few highly interesting stories. In particular, the one about Hervé Dumaz, the corrupt cop who made a nice little income on the side doing extremely dubious security work for even more suspect companies. After I'd whacked him, several witnesses recognized Dumaz. They said that each spring Dumaz came to Antwerp with Böhm when he sold his stones – ones just like mine, small but of an incredibly high quality. Do I need to go on?" Sarah laughed again and lit another cigarette. "I've known a few suckers in my life, but never one like you."

My heart was beating fit to bust. Everything suddenly became clear: the speed at which Dumaz had obtained information about old Max, the fact that he was sure that the whole thing was about diamond smuggling, the way he had insisted on my going to the Central African Republic. Hervé Dumaz knew Max Böhm, but he did not know how the system worked. So he had used me as an unwitting assistant to find the missing diamonds and discover how the network operated. I felt so sick I could hardly speak.

"I want to help you, Sarah."

"I don't need your help. My lawyer will get me released." She laughed. "I'm not frightened of Belgians, nor of the Swiss. We're the best, never forget that, Louis."

Silence fell once more. A few seconds later, Sarah whispered:

"Louis, we never talked together . . ."

"Sorry?"

Her voice was slightly husky.

"Do storks bring babies in your country?"

At first, I did not understand her question. Then at last I answered:

"Yes Sarah, they do."

"Do you know why people say that?"

I wriggled on my seat and cleared my throat. Two months ago, when preparing for my travels, I had read about this very subject. I told Sarah the old Germanic legend according to which the goddess Holda had chosen the stork as her messenger. In a damp dark place, that goddess kept the souls of the dead as they fell from the sky with the rain. She then reincarnated them into babies' bodies and told the storks to carry them to their new parents.

I also explained that throughout Europe and the Middle East, this orange-billed bird was credited with this virtue. Even in Sudan they were supposed to bring children. But there, they worshipped the black stork, which placed black babies on the roofs of their huts. I told her a few more tales, interspersing some charming and affectionate additional details. It was a moment of pure love, as brief as it was eternal. When I had finished my lecture, Sarah murmured:

"Our storks have brought us only violence and death. It's a shame, I wouldn't have been averse to the idea."

"What idea?"

"Having children. With you."

Emotion spread across my heart in tentacles of fire. I leapt to my feet and pressed my two burnt hands against the glass panel.

"Sarah!" I yelled.

My wild woman lowered her eyes and sniffed. Then suddenly she stood up and whispered:

"Get out, Louis. Get out of here."

But she was the one who ran away, without looking back. Like a modern-day Eurydice in a hell of sky-blue wood.

CHAPTER 50

"I want to see Simon Rickiel."

Itzhak Delter frowned. His anvil jaws half opened:

"Rickiel? The Interpol man?"

"Yes," I replied. "He's the person I'd like to talk to."

Delter rolled his shoulders. I could hear the rustling of his jacket. We were in the garden of Ganshoren Prison.

"That's not the way things were planned. You're supposed to talk to me. I'm the person most directly interested in your statement. I need to weigh up how useful it will be in my client's defence."

"You're not following me, Delter. I'm not double-crossing you. By talking, all I want to do is stop Sarah from getting a heavy sentence. But this is a case of international proportions. My statement should also be given to someone from Interpol, who knows what's going on."

Smiling, I emphasized the last words. Delter pulled a face. In fact, the purpose behind my request was to stop him from being able to manipulate my statement. From what Sarah had told me, this Rickiel clearly knew a lot. Storks or no storks, Böhm had obviously been in the international police's firing line for quite some time. By speaking in front of an officer, I would be preaching to the converted. Delter boomed in his deep voice:

"Don't fuck about with me, Antioch. No one pulls a fast one on a lawyer of my calibre."

"Spare me the threats and call up Rickiel. I'll tell everything, to both of you."

Delter headed off towards the granite gate. We took his car then crossed the suburbs through a fine drizzle until we reached Brussels. The lawyer did not say a word during the journey. Finally, we stopped in front of a huge black building, dating back to the last century and squeezed in between two clock towers. The façade was dotted with high windows, their lights already on. Armed guards stood unflinchingly under the rain in their bullet-proof jackets.

We went up a wide staircase. On the second floor, Delter turned down an interminable labyrinth of corridors, with alternating squeaky parquet and threadbare rugs. He seemed at home there. Finally, we entered a small standard model police office: filthy walls, sickly lamp, metal furniture and pre-war typewriters. Delter spoke for a few minutes with two men in shirt-sleeves, who were almost as hefty as he was, and who each had a 38 Magnum in a shoulder holster. I wondered what sort of jacket could possibly conceal such monsters.

The men glanced at me gloomily. One of them went behind a desk and asked me the usual questions: surname, first name, date of birth, married or single and so on. He then wanted to take my fingerprints. Cheekily, I held up my hands, with their pink, smooth and anonymous flesh, in front of him. This took him aback a little. He murmured an apology, then dived into another office. Meanwhile, Delter, too, had disappeared.

I waited for a long time. Nobody was civil enough to explain exactly what I was waiting for. I stayed sitting there, brooding over my remorse. The visit to Sarah had shattered me. My mistakes – and their consequences – spun round in my mind and I was incapable of coming up with a single argument in my defence. Crime is a career, whether you are a practitioner or an investigator, and it requires intuition and patience. To be efficient, it was not enough just to be suicidal.

Delter reappeared. A curious character was with him, a small man with a crumpled face, the upper half of which was glazed with a pair of extremely thick spectacles. His frail frame was wrapped up in a turtle-neck sweater with a zip fastener and a heavy pair of corduroy trousers. The best thing about him were his shoes. He was wearing thick-soled sports shoes with high tongues. Real rapper's models. Finally, on his belt, half-hidden in the folds of his sweater, could be seen an automatic hand gun – a Glock 17, 9mm parabellum, exactly the same as Sarah's.

Delter bowed slightly and introduced us.

"This is Simon Rickiel, Louis. An Interpol officer. As far as our case is concerned, he's our main contact." He turned towards the little fellow. "Simon, I'd like to introduce you to Louis Antioch, the witness I mentioned."

The fact that the lawyer had used my first name implied that he had decided to play along. I stood up, bowing slightly in turn, and keeping my hands behind my back. Rickiel treated me to a fleeting smile. His face was cut in two: his lips arched up, while the upper half remained motionless, as though trapped in a fish tank. I had not imagined that international police officers would be like this.

"Follow me," the Austrian said.

His office was unlike the other rooms. The walls were spotless, the parquet dark and polished. A large wooden desk stood in the middle, weighed down with state-of-the-art computer equipment. I noticed a Reuter's agency terminal – which broadcasts in real time all the news in the world – and a second terminal which flashed up other sorts of news, presumably to do with Interpol.

"Take a seat," Rickiel commanded, sliding behind his desk.

I did so. Delter sat down slightly away from us. Without beating about the bush, the Austrian then summed up the situation:

"Well, Delter has told me that you wish to make a voluntary statement. It seems that you might be in possession of information that could throw light on this case and perhaps alleviate the charges against Sarah Gabbor. Is that correct?"

Rickiel was speaking in French, without the slightest trace of an accent.

"Absolutely," I replied.

The policeman paused. His head was slouched down between his shoulders, his arms crossed on his desk. The computer screens were reflected in his glasses, like a set of fairy lamps. He went on:

"I've been through your file, Monsieur Antioch. And your profile is decidedly atypical. You say that you're an orphan. You aren't married and you live alone. You're thirty-two, but you've never had a job. Despite all that, you have an opulent lifestyle and live in an apartment on Boulevard Raspail in Paris. You explain this comfortable situation through the great interest shown in you by your adoptive parents, Georges and Nelly Braesler, rich landowners in the Puy-de-Dôme region. You also say that you lead a solitary, sedentary existence. However, you've just travelled halfway round the world in rather an adventurous manner. I've checked certain details. Traces of you can still be found, particularly in Israel and in the Central African Republic, and in a quite remarkable way. One last paradox: you dress like a dandy, yet you have a fresh scar running across your face – not to mention your hands. Exactly who are you, Monsieur Antioch?"

"A traveller lost in a nightmare."

"What do you know about this business?"

"Everything, or just about."

Rickiel chuckled between his shoulders.

"That sounds promising. Could you, for example, tell us where the diamonds found on Sarah Gabbor came from? Or why Hervé Dumaz attempted to arrest her without first informing Beurs van Diamanthandel's security guards?"

"No problem."

"Very good. Go ahead, we . . ."

"Just one second," I cut him off. "I'm going to talk without a lawyer or protection and, what is more, in a foreign country. What guarantees can you offer me?"

Rickiel laughed again. His eyes were cold and still amid all that flashing equipment.

"You speak as though you were the guilty party, Monsieur Antioch. All of that depends on how involved you are in this business. But I can assure you that, as a witness, you will not be bothered by administrative difficulties. Interpol is used to working on cross-border cases with mixed nationalities. What then happens depends on the countries concerned and can become more complicated. Speak, Antioch, and we'll sort that out later. For the moment, we want to listen to you as an off-the-record witness. No one will write down or record what you say. No one will add your name to any file. Then, according to the importance of your information, I'll ask you to repeat what you told me to other people in our department.

You will then become an 'official witness'. In any case, I can guarantee that if you have neither killed nor stolen, you will leave Belgium a free man. How does that sound?"

I swallowed and mentally blacked out my own murders. I summed up the main events of the past two months. I told it all, removing from my bag as the story progressed various articles that fleshed out my narrative: Max Böhm's index cards, Rajko's little notebook, Djuric's postmortem report, the diamond Wilm had given me at Ben-Gurion Airport, Philippe Böhm's death certificate, the statement signed by Sister Pascale, Otto Kiefer's taped confession. As an epilogue, I laid on the desk the first exhibits that I had found in Switzerland: Max Böhm's photographs, and the x-ray of his heart with the appended titanium capsule.

My statement lasted over an hour. I did my best to explain the twofold intrigue – the "diamond thieves" and the "heart thieves" – and how those two networks were interconnected. I was also careful to situate each of our roles, especially that of Sarah, who had become involved in the story despite herself, and that of Hervé Dumaz, the crooked cop who had exploited me and would almost certainly have shot Sarah once he had got his hands on the jewels.

Observing the reactions of my two interviewers, I came to a halt. Rickiel's glassy stare was examining the exhibits on his desk. He was smiling fixedly. As for Delter, his jaws had almost come loose. Silence eased down over my words. Finally, Rickiel said:

"Wonderful. Your story's quite wonderful."

My face burnt red.

"You don't believe me?"

"Oh, about eighty per cent of it. But there are numerous points that will have to be checked, or even proved, in what you have told us. What you call 'proof' is purely relative. A gypsy's scribblings, the conclusions of some nun who isn't a doctor and one single diamond are more like vague clues than solid evidence. As for your cassette, we'll listen to it, but I'm sure you know that this sort of recording cannot be used in evidence before a court of law.

That leaves us with a possible statement from Niels van Dötten, your South African geologist."

I had an irresistible desire to smash the little policeman's spectacles for him. But, deep down, I also admired how coolly he had taken all of this. My adventure would have flabbergasted anybody else, but Rickiel was just sitting there evaluating it, weighing it up, examining each facet of the story. The officer went on:

"Thanks, anyway, Antioch. This has cleared up a number of points that had been bugging us for some time. Dumaz's murder really came as no surprise to our department, because we had suspected that diamond smuggling was going on for at least the last two years, and we had a good deal of circumstantial evidence. We knew the names: Max Böhm, Hervé Dumaz, Otto Kiefer and Niels van Dötten. We knew the network: the Europe / Central African Republic / South Africa triangle. But we lacked the essential: the runners, i.e. the proof. We had been watching the main players in this system for two years. None of them ever directly took the routes the diamonds travelled along. Today, thanks to you, we know that they were using birds. It may sound incredible but I've seen many similar systems, believe me. Congratulations, Antioch. You are both highly tenacious and very brave. If you ever get bored with storks, come along and see us. I'll have a job for you."

The way this conversation was going left me speechless.

"Is . . . is that all?"

"No, of course it isn't. This is merely our first interview. Tomorrow, we'll take down most of your statement in writing. The investigating magistrate should also listen to you. Your evidence might allow us to send Sarah Gabbor back to Israel while she's awaiting trial. You have no idea how much crooks want to serve their sentences in their own country. We spend all our time transferring prisoners. So much for the diamonds . . . As for your mysterious doctor, I'm far more sceptical."

I stood up, my face burning.

"Don't you understand, Rickiel? The diamond smuggling is over. It's all washed up. Meanwhile, a loony surgeon is still stealing body organs across the globe. The madman is relentlessly pursuing some hidden goal. That's a certainty. He has all the necessary means at his disposal. So, the only urgent thing we have left to do is trap the fucker. Arrest him before he kills again and again in order to carry out his experiments."

"Let me be the judge of what is and isn't urgent," Rickiel barked back. "Stay in your hotel this evening in Brussels. My men have reserved a room for you at the Wepler. It's not a luxury hotel, but it's comfortable enough. I'll see you again tomorrow."

I banged my fist on the desk. Delter leapt to his feet, but Rickiel did not budge. I yelled:

"Rickiel, a monster's walking the earth! He's killing and torturing children. You could put out a wanted notice, check your terminals, analyse thousands of different crimes, contact the entire planet's police forces. Do something, for Christ's sake!"

"Tomorrow, Antioch," the policeman murmured, his lips quivering.

I slammed the door as I left.

CHAPTER 51

A few hours later, I was still chewing over my anger in my hotel room. In many ways, I had been outwitted. I had given a lot of information to ICPO-Interpol and received practically nothing in return – at least, not regarding my own investigations. My only consolation was that my statement was going to play a decisive role in Sarah's defence.

Otherwise, that evening had been a series of blind alleys. I called my answering machine: no messages. I called Dr Warel: no answer.

At 8.30, the phone rang. I snatched at the receiver. The voice I heard surprised me:

"Antioch? This is Rickiel. I'd like to have a word with you."

"When?"

"Now. I'm downstairs, in the hotel bar."

The Wepler's bar had a dark pink carpet and was rather more reminiscent of an alcove set aside for earthly pleasures. I found Simon Rickiel in a leather armchair, wrapped up in his baggy sweater. He was gingerly nibbling at some olives, a glass of whisky in front of him. I wondered if he still had his Glock with him – and if he would be quicker on the draw than me.

"Sit down, Antioch. And stop acting the hard guy. You've done enough to prove yourself."

I took a chair and ordered some China tea. For a few seconds, I watched Rickiel. His face was still distorted by his convex glasses, like the image in a mirror that was half misted over.

"I've come to congratulate you once more."

"Congratulate me?"

"You know, I'm quite experienced when it comes to crime. I can appreciate the value of your investigation. You did a great job, Antioch. Really you did. I wasn't joking just now when I offered you a job."

"That's not the only reason you're here, I suppose?"

"No. I understood how disappointed you were this afternoon. You think that I didn't pay enough attention to your story about a murderous surgeon."

"Exactly."

"I couldn't. At least, not while Delter was there."

"Why not?"

"That part of the case doesn't concern him."

The waiter arrived with my tea. Its heavy pungent odour suddenly reminded me of the humus of the jungle.

"So you believe what I told you?"

"Yes." Rickiel continued to toy with his olives with the point of a cocktail stick. "But, as I told you, this aspect of the case requires a thorough investigation. What is more, you're going to have to play it straight with me."

"Sorry?"

"You haven't told me everything. People don't uncover stories like this with impunity."

A sip of tea allowed me to conceal how worried I was. I decided to play it dumb.

"I don't see what you mean, Rickiel."

"You don't? Very well. This afternoon we mentioned Max Böhm, Otto Kiefer and Niels van Dötten. They were hardened criminals, but they were also in their sixties and so rather inoffensive, wouldn't you agree? But these men were under protection. There was Dumaz, but there were also others. Who were far more dangerous. I have a few names up my sleeve. Shall we see if they ring any bells?"

Rickiel grinned ironically, then swallowed an olive.

"Miklos Sikkov."

A punch in the liver. I forced my mouth open.

"Never heard of him."

"Milan Kalev."

Presumably Sikkov's accomplice. I mumbled:

"Who are they?"

"Travellers. People like you, though a lot less lucky. They're dead. Both of them."

"Where?"

"Kalev's body was found in Bulgaria in the suburbs of Sofia on the 31st of August, his throat had been slit by a piece of glass. Sikkov died in Israel on 6th September in the Occupied Territories. Sixteen bullets in his face. Both cases have been abandoned. The first murder was committed while you were in Sofia, Antioch. And the second, while you were in Israel, in exactly the same place – Balatakamp. Which is rather a strange coincidence, is it not?"

I repeated:

"I've never heard of these people."

Rickiel started playing with his olives again. Some German businessmen had just come into the bar. There were outbreaks of raucous laughter. The cop's lips glistened as he went on:

"I have a few more names, Antioch. What do you know of Marcel Minaüs, Yeta Iakovic and Ivan Tornoï?"

The victims of the Sofia train station massacre. Raising my voice slightly, I declared:

"Really, these names mean nothing to me."

"How odd," said the Austrian. Then he sipped at his whisky, before continuing:

"Do you know what made me want to work with Interpol, Antioch? It's not because I love taking risks. Nor was it a desire for justice. It was my passion for languages. I've been fascinated by them ever since I was a child. You probably don't realize how important foreign languages are in the world of crime. Right now, FBI agents in the USA are working night and day to master the various dialects of Chinese. It's the only way they'll be able to pin anything on the Triads. Anyway, it so happens that I speak Bulgarian. (Another grin.) So I read the paper signed by Dr Milan Djuric with the greatest attention. It was rather instructive, terrifying even. I also studied a Bulgarian police report concerning a massacre that occurred in the train station in Sofia on the evening of the 30th of August. The work of a pro. During that slaughter, three innocent people were killed, the ones I just mentioned – Marcel Minaüs, Yeta Iakovic and Ivan Tornoï. Ivan's mother made a statement, Antioch. She was positive that the killers were aiming at a fourth man, a Caucasian who answers your description. A few hours later, Milan Kalev died in a warehouse, stuck like a pig."

I gave up trying to drink my Lapsang.

"I still don't see what you're on about," I stammered.

Rickiel abandoned his olives and stared at me. His whisky tumbler was reflected in his spectacles, setting off reddish sparks of fire.

"Kalev and Sikkov were known to us. Kalev was a Bulgarian mercenary – some sort of quack – who liked torturing his victims with a high-frequency lancet. No blood, no traces, just extreme, finely tailored agony. Sikkov was an army instructor. In the 1970s, he trained Idi Amin's forces in Uganda. He specialized in automatic weapons. They were an extremely dangerous double-act."

Rickiel remained silent for a moment, then dropped his bomb:

"And they were working for One World."

I feigned astonishment.

"What? Mercenaries working for a humanitarian organization?"

"Such people can be of use. To protect supplies or guarantee the personnel's security."

"Where is all this leading us, Rickiel?"

"To One World. And to your vast theory."

"Well?"

"You think that Max Böhm lived, or survived perhaps I should say, in the power of one man: the brilliant surgeon who had saved him from certain death in August 1977, isn't that so?"

"Precisely."

"In your opinion, this doctor exploited Böhm via One World. Which explains why the old man left his entire fortune to that organization, am I right?"

"You are."

Rickiel plunged his hand into his huge sweater and pulled out a thin file, from which he plucked a typewritten sheet of paper.

"In that case, I should like to tell you of certain factors that corroborate your version."

I was so astonished that I was speechless.

"I, too, have investigated this organization. One World is extremely secretive. It is difficult to get any precise information regarding the true extent of its activities, how many doctors work for it, and how many contributors it has. But, when it comes to Max Böhm, I've unearthed several curious facts. Max Böhm paid most of his ill-gotten gains to OW. Every year he 'contributed' several hundreds of thousands of Swiss francs to the organization. But these figures are incomplete, in my opinion. Böhm used several banks including, of course, some numbered accounts. So it is difficult to get an exact idea of how much money was really being made over. But one thing is sure: he belonged to the 1001 Club. I suppose you know the system. But what you don't know is that, when the club was set up, Böhm contributed one million Swiss francs – almost a million dollars. This was in 1980 – two years after the beginning of the diamond smuggling."

I was amazed. Suddenly everything clicked. My mind whirled. So, old Max gave his earnings to One World and not directly to the "doc". Either the organization then paid the Monster or, more simply, it financed the surgeon's "experiments" in its own name. Rickiel went on:

"You told me that Dumaz didn't succeed in finding out where Böhm was treated. There was no trace of the ornithologist in clinics in Switzerland, France or Germany. I think I know where he had highly secret tests done on his transplanted heart. At the One World centre in Geneva, which has highly efficient medical equipment at its disposal. Once again, Böhm had to pay a high price for this little 'favour'."

I attempted to drink some tea. My fingers were trembling. There was no doubt about it, Rickiel was right.

"But what does that prove, in your opinion?"

"That One World has something to hide. And that your 'doc' occupies a highly responsible position there, which allows him to hire people like Kalev and Sikkov, to fund his own experiments and to sell his services to the world's most precious heart patient – the man who tamed the storks."

Rickiel had played a close game. When I had seen him that afternoon, he already knew more about One World than about the diamond smuggling. As though reading my mind, he went on:

"Before meeting you, Antioch, I knew about the curious links between Max Böhm and One World – but I had no idea that it was all about hearts. The murders of Rajko and Gomoun belong to a far longer series. Since our interview, I've made a computer search. Thanks to our terminals, I was able to launch an investigation into all murders or violent accidents over the last ten years where the victim's heart was missing. You can imagine how much computer data there is in the member countries of ICPO. But, the particular characteristic of the removal of the heart speeded things up. The list came out at eight o'clock this evening. It is far from exhaustive, given that your 'thief' generally operates in poor or developing countries, where we often have no data. But this list will be sufficient.

It sends shivers down your spine. Take a look."

I crushed my cup. Scalding tea spilled over my numb hands. I snatched the list from Rickiel. It was a record of that heart thief's evil deeds:

21/9/91. Name: Gomoun. Pygmy. Sex female. Born some time in June 1976. Died 21/9/91 near Zoko in the Lobaye province of the Central African Republic. Circumstances of death: accident / gorilla attack. Characteristics: numerous mutilations / disappearance of heart. Blood group: B Rh$^+$. HLA type: Aw $_{19,3}$ – B $_{37,5}$.

22/4/91. Name: Rajko Nicolich. Gypsy. Sex male. Born some time in 1963 in Iskenderun, Turkey. Died 22/4/91 in the 'clearwater' forest near Sliven, Bulgaria. Circumstances of death: murder, case unsolved. Characteristics: mutilations / disappearance of heart. Blood group: O Rh$^+$. HLA type: Aw $_{19,3}$ – B $_{37,5}$.

3/11/90. Name: Tasmin Johnson. Hottentot. Sex male. Born: 16 January 1967 near Maseru, South Africa. Died 3/11/90 near the Waka mine, South Africa. Circumstances of death: wild animal attack. Characteristics: mutilations / disappearance of heart. Blood group: A Rh$^+$. HLA type: Aw $_{19,3}$ – B $_{37,5}$.

16/3/90. Name: Hassan al Begassen. Sex male. Born some time in 1970 near Jebel al Fau, Sudan. Died 16/3/90 in the irrigated farmlands of Village Nb 16. Circumstances of death: wild animal attack. Characteristics: mutilations / disappearance of heart. Blood group: AB Rh$^+$. HLA type: Aw $_{19,3}$ – B $_{37,5}$.

4/9/88. Name: Ahmed Iskam. Sex male. Born: 5 December 1962 in Bethlehem, Occupied Territories, Israel. Died 4/9/88 at Beyt Jallah. Circumstances of death: political assassination. Characteristics: mutilations / disappearance of heart. Blood group: O Rh$^+$. HLA type: Aw $_{19,3}$ – B $_{37,5}$.

The list went on like this, covering several pages, until 1981, when computer records began. It could be supposed that, in reality, the series was far longer. Several dozen children or adolescents, male or female, had been tortured somewhere in the world and the only point they had in common was their HLA type: Aw $_{19,3}$ – B $_{37,5}$. The precision of this system was breathtaking. What I had suspected on discovering the similarity between Gomoun's and Rajko's groups was here confirmed over and over again. Rickiel gave voice to my thoughts:

"You see? Your animal is no organ smuggler. Nor is he interested in dangerous experiments. His desire is far more precise. He's looking for hearts that belong to the same tissue group all over the world."

"Is . . . is that all?"

"No, I've brought you something else."

Rickiel rummaged around inside his sweater, then produced a black plastic bag. I understood the point of his baggy pullovers. They allowed him to conceal just about anything he wanted. He laid an object on the table. Another wave of astonishment. The bag contained some 45-calibre Glock magazines, wrapped up in a silvery adhesive band. I looked quizzically at the Interpol officer.

"I thought some fresh supplies might come in handy. This 'stock' has been wrapped up in a leaded adhesive, which cancels the effects of x-rays in airports. Your weapon is no mystery to me, Antioch. Polymer guns are the traveller's new armament, especially terrorists. Sarah Gabbor also used a Glock, a 9mm parabellum. And don't forget Sikkov's little 'accident': sixteen 45 cartridges in the face."

I stared down at the magazines. At least one hundred and fifty 45 bullets, and the same number of promises of death and violence. Simon Rickiel concluded, in a neutral tone of voice:

"As I told you, ICPO-Interpol is used to investigating complex cases. We can also, when necessary, delegate responsibilities in order to save time. I'm sure that you're capable of unmasking the heart thief. And long before us, given that we have to sort out the diamond business, check your statement, find van Dötten, and so on. I lied to you earlier. Your statement this afternoon was recorded on DAT and immediately transferred onto our computer. I have it here, in my pocket. Sign it and disappear. You're alone, Antioch. And that's what's playing in your favour. You can infiltrate One World and get the bastard. Find him, find the man who inflicted such horrible torture on Rajko, Gomoun and all those other victims. Find him, then do what you want with him."

CHAPTER 52

When I returned to my bedroom, a red light was flashing on my telephone. I grabbed the receiver and called reception.

"Louis Antioch, here. Room 232. Have I had any messages?"

A thick Belgian accent answered:

"Monsieur Antioch . . . Antioch . . . Let me see."

I heard the gentle clicking of a computer keyboard. In my bent forearm, my veins were beating visibly under my skin, as though with a life force of their own.

"A Dr Catherine Warel telephoned at 21.15. You weren't in your room."

I was furious.

"I did ask for any calls to be put through to me in the bar!"

"The rota changes at nine o'clock. I'm sorry, but your request was not passed on."

"Did she leave a number where I can call her?"

The voice dictated Catherine Warel's home number. I immediately dialled its ten figures. The phone rang twice and then I heard the doctor's gravelly voice:

"Hello?"

"Antioch, here. What's new?"

"I have the information you wanted. It's incredible. You were absolutely right all along. I got a list of Francophone doctors who worked in the Central African Republic or Congo during the last thirty years. There is one name that could be your man. But what a name! It's Pierre Sénicier, the true precursor of heart transplant techniques. A French surgeon who transplanted an ape's heart into a man for the first time in 1960."

My entire body began to shake feverishly. Sénicier. Pierre Sénicier. In my mind, I could see, written in dark letters, that encyclopaedia entry that I had read in Bangui: " ... in January 1960, a French surgeon, Pierre Sénicier, grafted a chimpanzee's heart into the thorax of a sixty-eight-year-old patient who was in the final stages of irreversible cardiac insufficiency. The operation succeeded. But the new heart only worked for a few hours."

Catherine Warel went on:

"The story of this true genius is well known in the medical world. At the time, the transplant he'd carried out was much talked about, then Sénicier completely disappeared. The word was that he had had problems with the Medical Association. He was suspected of having carried out forbidden experiments and of illegal dabblings. Sénicier and his family took refuge in the Central African Republic. There, he is supposed to have become a do-gooder. The Blacks' saviour. A sort of Albert Schweitzer, if you want. So, Sénicier could be your man. But, there's something that doesn't fit ... "

"What's that?" I murmured hoarsely.

"You did say that Max Böhm was operated on in August 1977?"

"That's correct."

"You're sure about the date?"

"Positive."

"Then, it can't have been Sénicier who carried out the operation."

"Why?"

"Because, in 1977, he was dead. At the end of 1965, on New Year's Eve, he and his family were attacked by some prisoners who had been released by Bokassa during his coup d'état. They all died – Pierre Sénicier, his wife, and their two children – in the fire that destroyed their villa. I didn't know about that myself, and ... Are you still there, Louis? ... Louis? ... Louis?"

CHAPTER 53

When summer arrives in the Arctic, the pack-ice cracks and opens up, almost unwillingly, to reveal the dark waters of the Bering Sea.

That is how I felt at that moment. Catherine Warel's devastating revelation had rounded off my adventure's infernal circle. Only one person could now enlighten me about my sinister past: Nelly Braesler, my adoptive mother.

With my foot down, I was driving towards the centre of France. Six hours later, as night began to fade, I passed by Clermont-Ferrand then looked for the turning to Villiers, a few miles further to the east. The clock on my dashboard read 5.30 a.m. At last, the little village appeared in my headlights. I meandered around it until I found the Braeslers' house, then pulled up beside the wall of an enclosure.

Dawn was coming up. The countryside, reddened by autumn, looked like a petrified forest in flames. Everywhere, an indescribable calm reigned. Tall grasses grew up from the dark canals, and naked trees scratched at the smooth grey sky.

I entered the courtyard of the manor, a U-shaped ring of stone. On my left, I spotted Georges Braesler, who was already up and shuffling around among the cages containing noisy, ash-grey birds. He had his back to me, and so could not see me. Silently, I crossed the lawn and slipped into the house.

Inside, everything was made of stone or wood. Large windows, hewn from the rock, gave out on to the gardens. Oak furniture was everywhere, giving off a strong smell of wax. Cast iron candelabra threw their angled shadows on the stone floor slabs. There was a rigidity from the Middle Ages here, an odour of blindly cruel nobility. I had entered a timeless refuge. A den for ogres greedily hanging on to their privileges.

"Who are you?"

I turned round to discover Nelly's thin frame, her narrow shoulders and her chalky face languid from drink. The old woman recognized me at once and had to lean back against the wall, stammering:

"Louis . . . What are you doing here?"

"I want to talk to you about Pierre Sénicier."

Nelly staggered over towards me. I noticed that her slightly blue-rinsed wig was askew. My adoptive mother had doubtless not slept a wink and was already drunk. She repeated:

"Pierre . . . Pierre Sénicier?"

"Yes," I said in an off-hand way. "I think I've reached the age of reason, Nelly. The age of reason and of truth."

The old woman lowered her eyes. I saw her eyelids quiver slightly then, quite unexpectedly, her lips form a smile. She murmured: "The truth . . . ," then walked with a more decisive step towards an occasional table, covered with a large selection of carafes. She poured out two glasses of spirits and handed me one.

"I don't drink, Nelly. And anyway, it's far too early."

She insisted:

"Sit down and drink, Louis. You're going to need it."

I obeyed without further argument. I selected an armchair by the fire, then started shaking again. I gulped down some whisky. The heat from the alcohol did me good. Nelly sat down facing me, against the sunlight. She laid the carafe of whisky on the floor beside her, then downed her glass in one. She refilled it immediately. Her colour and her assurance had returned. She began her tale:

"Some things can never be forgotten, Louis. Things that are engraved on our hearts, as though on the marble of our tombstones. I have no idea where you heard Pierre Sénicier's name. I have no idea what exactly you have found out. And I have no idea how migrating storks have brought you here, to unearth the best-kept secret in the world. But all of that doesn't matter. Nothing matters any more. The time for the truth has come, Louis, and perhaps the time for my liberation.

"Pierre Sénicier belonged to an upper middle-class Parisian family. His father, Paul Sénicier, was one of the most distinguished magistrates of his time and moved successfully from one regime to another. He was an austere man, silent and cruel, a man to be feared, who saw the world as a frail construction under his powerful fist. At the turn of the century, his wife gave him three sons in quick succession, three boys destined for the most brilliant futures, but who turned out to be degenerate 'runts' with sterile minds. The father was furious, but his wealth allowed him to save face. Henri, the eldest, a hunchback half-wit, was sent to look after the 'châteaux': three dilapidated manor houses in Normandy. Dominique, physically the strongest, joined the army and climbed the ranks thanks to a good deal of string-pulling. As for Raphaël, the youngest, who was the least stupid and most cunning, he became a priest. He acquired a parish in some distant diocese, not far from Henri's properties, then he, too, disappeared into oblivion.

"By then, Paul Sénicier had lost all interest in his first three children. He cared only for his fourth son, Pierre, who was born in 1933. Paul Sénicier was then fifty. His wife, who was not much younger, gave him this child *in extremis*; then she died, as though having fulfilled her final duty.

"Pierre was clearly a blessing. This extraordinary child seemed to have acquired all the gifts and powers of that degenerate bloodline. His old father concentrated all his efforts on his son's education. He personally taught him to read and write, and he followed the development of his intelligence very attentively. When Pierre reached the age of puberty, Paul Sénicier hoped that he would follow him and become a magistrate. But his son wanted a medical career. The father accepted this decision. He felt that a true vocation had been marked out in the child's character. He wasn't wrong. By the age of twenty-three, the young Sénicier was already a renowned surgeon, specializing in heart surgery.

"It was at this period that I met Pierre. He was much talked about in our little circle of children from rich, idle and arrogant families. He was tall, handsome and austere. His whole body resonated with a curious silence. I remember how we used to organize so-called 'rallies': stuffy parties, during which we locked ourselves away together like timid creatures made anaemic by our own solitude. The girls wore their mothers' dresses and the boys put on old starched dinner jackets. During those parties, we girls were all on the lookout for one man: Pierre Sénicier. He already lived in the adult world of responsibilities. But when he was there, the party was transformed. The lights, dresses, drinks, everything seemed to dance and sparkle for him."

Nelly paused, then refilled her glass.

"I was the one who introduced Pierre Sénicier to Marie-Anne de Montalier. Marie-Anne was a close friend of mine. She was blonde and slim, with constantly dishevelled hair, as though she had just got out of bed. But the most striking thing about her was her pallor: she was white, transparent, there's no other word for it. Marie-Anne came from a rich French colonial family who had moved to a remote region of Africa during the nineteenth century. Word had it that, to avoid corrupting themselves with Blacks, they had intermarried, which explained their present anaemia.

"When Marie-Anne set eyes on Pierre, it was love at first sight. At once, I vaguely regretted having introduced them. However, their destiny was now fixed. Before long, Marie-Anne's passion became an obsession, a latent anxiety that cut her off from the rest of the world. As the days went by, she became filled with a deep light that made her all the more beautiful. Pierre and Marie-Anne married in January 1957. During the reception, she whispered to me: 'I'm lost, Nelly. I know that. But it was my own decision.'

"It was at this time that I met Georges Braesler. He was older than me, he wrote poetry and screenplays. He wanted to travel as a diplomat, 'like Claudel or Malraux', as he used to say. In those days, I was quite pretty, carefree and frivolous. I saw my old acquaintances less and less often and kept in touch only with Marie-Anne, who wrote to me regularly. That is how I found out about the true nature of her husband Pierre Sénicier, to whom she had just given a son.

"In 1958, Sénicier held an important post in the heart surgery unit at La Pitié. He was twenty-five. He had a brilliant career in front of him, but was irresistibly drawn to evil. Marie-Anne told me about this in her letters. She had delved into his past and discovered some terrifying skeletons in his cupboard. While still a student, Sénicier had been caught practising vivisection on young cats. The horrific screams echoing around the dome of the university and the sight of those little bodies writhing in agony was such that the witnesses could scarcely believe their eyes. Later, he had been suspected of despicable acts on abnormal children in a public hospital in Villejuif. Inexplicable wounds, burns and lacerations had been discovered on educationally subnormal youngsters.

"The Medical Association threatened to strike off Sénicier but then, in 1960, a great event occurred. A first. Pierre Sénicier managed to transplant a chimpanzee's heart into a human body. The patient survived for only a few hours but, on a technical level, the operation had been a success. Those terrible suspicions were forgotten. Sénicier became a national hero, hailed by the scientific world. At the age of twenty-seven, he even received the Légion d'honneur from Charles de Gaulle in person.

"One year later, old Sénicier died. In his will, he left most of his property to Pierre, who used the money to open a private clinic in Neuilly-sur-Seine. It took only a few months for his Clinique Pasteur to become a well frequented establishment, to which rich VIPs from all over Europe came to be treated. Pierre Sénicier was at the peak of his glory. He then turned to humanitarian work. He built an orphanage in the gardens of the clinic, to lodge young orphans or else to help in the education of poor children, especially gypsies. His recent fame allowed him to gain rapid access to state funding, as well as private sponsors and charities."

I heard a tinkling sound – the carafe against the glass – then the gurgling of liquid. A few seconds of silence, then Nelly clicked her tongue. In my mind, these events were now taking form, rising up around me in a wave of darkness.

"And that's when it all went wrong. The tone of Marie-Anne's letters changed. She stopped writing friendly chitchat and started scribbling terrifyingly incoherent rants." Nelly sneered. "At first, I thought that my old friend had gone mad. I just couldn't believe what she was telling me. According to her, Sénicier's institution was a centre of unimaginable barbarity. Her husband had set up an operating theatre in the basement, locked and bolted, where he practised the most horrible experiments on the children: monstrous grafts, transplants without anaesthetic, countless tortures.

"At the same time, complaints from gypsy families were piling up. The police decided to search Clinique Pasteur. For the last time, Sénicier's contacts and influence were to save him. He was warned of the police intervention, and set fire to his property. They just had time to save the children from the upper storeys and the patients from the clinic. He had avoided the worst. Officially, at least. For nobody came out alive from his underground laboratory. Sénicier had bolted the door of his chamber of horrors and let the grafted children burn.

"A brief investigation concluded that the fire had been accidental. The children who survived were handed back to their families or sent to other homes. The case was closed. Marie-Anne wrote to me again saying that – how ironic – her husband was 'better' and that they were leaving for Africa to help and treat the Black inhabitants. At that moment, Georges was given a diplomatic post in South-East Asia. He persuaded me to go with him. This was in November 1963. I was thirty-two."

Suddenly, a light came on in the hall. An old man in a cardigan appeared. Georges Braesler. In his arms he was holding a large heavy bird with muddy plumage. Its grey feathers were spilling out onto the floor. He moved as though he were going to come into the room, but Nelly stopped him:

"Go away, Georges."

He did not seem at all surprised by her aggressive tone. Nor by the fact that I was there. Nelly screamed:

"Go away!"

The old man turned and moved off. Nelly had another drink and belched. A strong smell of whisky filled the room. Daylight was beginning to seep into the house. I could now see Nelly's wrecked face.

"In 1964, after one year in Thailand, Georges was transferred once more. Malraux, who was a close friend, was Minister of Culture at the time. He knew Africa well and sent us to the Central African Republic. He told us that it was 'an incredible, fantastic country'. The author of *La Voie royale* was absolutely right, but he was ignorant of one vital point. It was there that Pierre and Marie-Anne Sénicier were living with their children.

"It was rather strange to meet up again. But we were soon close friends once more. Our first dinner together was perfect. Pierre had aged, but seemed calm and relaxed. He had readopted his soft, distant manner. He spoke of the fate of African children, riddled with disease, which he was doing his utmost to cure. He seemed a million miles from the horrors of the past and I began to have doubts again about Marie-Anne's revelations.

"However, I slowly began to understand that Sénicier was still definitely mad. He was furious about being in Africa. He couldn't endure the fact that he'd had to put a stop to his career. He, who had pulled off sensational unheard-of feats, was now reduced to being a common-or-garden practitioner, in paraffin-fuelled operating theatres where the corridors stank of manioc. Sénicier just couldn't stomach that. His anger transformed itself into a stubborn vengeance directed against himself and his family.

"For example, Sénicier considered his two sons to be case studies. He'd drawn up extremely precise biotypes for each of them, analysed their blood groups, tissue types, taken their fingerprints, and so on. He then put them through atrocious psychological experiments. During certain dinner parties, I witnessed traumatic scenes which I shall never forget. When the food arrived at the table, Sénicier leant over his two boys and whispered: 'Look hard at your plates, children. What do you suppose you're eating?' Some scraps of brownish meat were swimming in the sauce. Sénicier started to dab at them with the tip of his fork. 'Which animal do you think you're eating this evening? A little gazelle? A little pig? A monkey?' And he carried on fiddling with the slimy pieces of meat which glistened in the uncertain electric light, until tears started to flow down the two terrified boys' cheeks. Sénicier went on: 'Unless it's something else. No one knows what the niggers eat round here. Maybe tonight it's . . . ' The children ran away in panic. Marie-Anne remained unmoved. Sénicier sneered. He wanted to convince his children that they were cannibals – that, each evening, they ate human flesh.

"The children grew up in pain. The elder one became utterly neurotic. In 1965, at the age of eight, he became fully aware of his father's monstrousness. He became stiff, silent, insensitive and, paradoxically, the favourite. He was now the apple of Pierre Sénicier's eye, and his father loved him with all his strength and all his cruelty. This warped logic meant that the little boy had to put up with more and more, until he was irrevocably traumatized. What was Sénicier after? I never found out. But his son became aphasic, incapable of any coherent course of action.

"A few days after Christmas that year, the boy decided to act. He tried to commit suicide, as people do in Africa, by swallowing tablets of nivaquine which, when taken in large doses, has irreversible effects on the human body – and especially on the heart. Only one thing could save the boy now: a new heart. Do you grasp the secret logic of Pierre Sénicier's destiny? After pushing his own child into attempting suicide, he, the brilliant surgeon, was now the only person who could save him. At once, Sénicier decided to carry out a heart transplant, as he had done five years before on a sixty-eight-year-old man. He had managed to install an operating theatre in his residence in Bangui, which was relatively sterile. All he needed now was the essential ingredient: a compatible heart in perfect working order. He didn't have to look very far. His two sons had almost perfectly compatible tissue. In his madness, the surgeon decided to sacrifice the younger one in order to save the elder. This was on New Year's Eve, 1965. Sénicier set everything up and prepared his theatre. In Bangui, the atmosphere was rising. People were drinking and dancing all over town. Georges and I had organized a reception at the French embassy. All the Europeans were invited.

"Just when the surgeon was about to carry out the operation, History caught up with him. That night, Jean-Bedel Bokassa led a coup d'état and occupied the town with his soldiers. There were some clashes. There was pillaging, arson and murder. To celebrate his victory, Bokassa freed the prisoners from Bangui gaol. New Year's Eve turned into a nightmare. In the overall chaos, something particular took place.

"The freed prisoners included some of the parents of Sénicier's recent victims. For he had started carrying out his cruel experiments once more. Fearing reprisals, the doctor had managed to get these people locked up under various pretexts. So, once freed, they headed straight for Sénicier's house to get their revenge. At midnight, Sénicier was settling the final details of the operation. Both children had been anaesthetized. The electrocardiograms were working. Their blood circulation and temperatures were being recorded and catheters had been placed. That's when the prisoners burst in. They broke down the fences and invaded the estate. Firstly, they killed Mohamed, the steward, then they shot his wife Azzora and their children with Mohamed's gun.

"Sénicier heard the cries and the din. He went back to the house to fetch his Mauser, which he used when out hunting. The attackers, despite their numbers, were powerless when faced with Sénicier. He shot them down, one by one. But the most important part was happening elsewhere. Marie-Anne had seen her younger boy being taken off by her husband and, making the most of the confusion, she went inside the operating theatre. She tore out the tubes and the cables, then wrapped her younger son up in a hospital sheet. Clutching him, she ran through the town where all hell was breaking loose. She arrived at the French embassy, where the panic was at its height. All the Whites were hiding inside, not knowing what was going on. Stray bullets had wounded several of us and the gardens were on fire. That's when I saw Marie-Anne through the embassy windows. She quite literally emerged from the flames, wearing a blue-striped dress that was stained with red earth. She was carrying a little wrapped-up body in her arms. I ran outside, thinking that the child had been wounded by the soldiers. I was completely drunk, and Marie-Anne's form was dancing in front of my eyes. She yelled: 'He means to kill him, Nelly! He wants his heart, do you understand?' It took her only a few seconds to tell me everything: the elder boy's botched suicide, the need for a heart transplant, her husband's scheme. Marie-Anne was panting, squeezing that little sleeping body. 'He's the only one who can save his brother. We've got to make him vanish. Totally.' As she spoke, she seized the inanimate child's hands and pushed them into a burning shrub. Then she repeated her action, after looking at those little palms that were on fire. 'No fingerprints, no name, nothing! Take the plane, Nelly. Vanish with him. He must no longer exist. Never. For anybody.' And she left that bundle of nerves and suffering at my feet, on the red earth. I'll never forget her figure when she staggered away, Louis. I knew that I'd never see her again."

Nelly fell silent. I raised my burnt hands up in front of my tear-drenched face. I stammered:

"Oh, my God, no. . ."

"Yes, that child was you, Louis. Pierre Sénicier is your father. The infernal chaos of New Year's Eve 1965 was your second birth. Fortunately, you have no recollection of it. That night, it was announced that the Sénicier family had all died in the fire in their villa, which was completely untrue. They had escaped, but I didn't know where. Marie-Anne convinced her husband that you had died in the fire. Pierre managed to keep the other son alive and perform a heart transplant, presumably in a hospital in the Congo. The child rejected the organ shortly afterwards, but the surgeon had succeeded in making the first heart transplant on his own flesh and blood. Other operations followed. Since that date, Sénicier has been stealing hearts and transplanting them into his surviving son, who has been on his death bed for the last thirty years. And he's still looking, Louis. He's tracking down hearts across the entire globe. He's looking for *your* heart, the organ that will be totally compatible with Frédéric's body."

My hands were clasping my face, tears were choking me.

"No, no, no . . . "

Nelly went on in a neutral tone:

"That night, I followed Marie-Anne's instructions. Georges and I chartered a plane and we fled. Once back in Paris, I looked after you. I invented a new identity for you." Nelly burst out laughing. "We were about to be sent to Turkey, to Antakya. I found it amusing – amusing in a sinister way, I should say – to call you Antioch, the former name of the town where we were going to stay. I had no problem having the new identity papers made. Georges knew people who were well placed in the government. You became 'Louis Antioch'. You had no fingerprints any more. On your identity card, the prints are those of a little drowned boy, whose hands Georges made use of one cold February night in the Paris morgue. We rewrote your story, Louis. You were the son of a family of charitable doctors who had died in a fire in Africa. You alone had survived. That's how we 'created' you from scratch.

"I then contacted the nanny who had brought me up. We paid her to take care of your upbringing. She never knew the truth, either. As for us, we disappeared. It was too dangerous. You have no idea of your father's intelligence, tenacity and cunning. Far from us, and far from his past, Louis Antioch had nothing to fear. All I had to do was play at being a distant fairy godmother, and make your life as easy as I could. In all that time, I've made just one mistake: sending you to Max Böhm. For he knew your story. I'd told him everything one day when I needed support. I thought he was a friend, an old 'African' like Georges and me. I now realize that Max also knew Sénicier and, for some reason that escapes me, sent you out on this mission so that you could wreak revenge on your own father."

Through my tears, I screamed:

"But who is Sénicier now? Who is he, for Christ's sake? Speak, Nelly. I beg of you. What name is he hiding under?"

Nelly emptied her glass in one swig.

"He's Pierre Doisneau, the founder of One World."

VI
Calcutta, conclusion

CHAPTER 54

4 October 1991, 10.10 p.m. local time.

That my fate must be sealed in Calcutta seemed perfectly and irrevocably logical. Only the stagnating hell of that Indian city could provide a dark enough context to suit the ultimate violence of my adventure.

As I stepped off the Air India plane, damp, nauseous odours rose up, like the last breath of the monsoon. Once more, the tropics were opening their burning gates to me.

I followed the troop of other travellers, large ladies in bright saris, little dry men in dark suits. In Dhaka, the final stop-over, I had finally left behind the world of tourists who were off to see Kathmandu, and was surrounded by Bengali passengers. Once again, I was alone amid the Indians returning home, and the missionaries and nurses devoted to good causes. I was getting used to this.

We entered the airport building, its ceiling dotted with slowly revolving fans. Everything was grey. Everything was humid. In one corner of the room, a scrawny labourer was digging into the deeper levels of the earth with a pickaxe. Beside him, some children were hiding their faces, exhibiting pockmarked chests. Calcutta, the mortuary town, greeted me none too profusely.

Three days before, on leaving the Braeslers' residence with my tears and fears wiped away, I got back into my car, drove through the countryside and returned to Paris. That very day, I went to the Indian consulate, in order to obtain a visa to Bengal, in the east of India.

"As a tourist?" the little lady asked, looking at me suspiciously. I replied "yes" and nodded. "And you're going to Calcutta?" I nodded once more, without saying a word. The woman took my passport and declared: "Come back at the same time tomorrow."

In my study that day, not a single thought, not a single idea disturbed my consciousness. Sitting on the parquet, I simply waited for the hours to pass by, looking at my small travelling bag and my fully loaded gun. The next morning, at 8.30, I was back in possession of my passport, stamped with an Indian visa, and heading straight for Roissy airport. I had my name down on all of the waiting lists for flights that could take me nearer to my final destination. At 3 p.m., I took off for Istanbul, then on to Bahrein in the Gulf. After that, I flew to Dhaka in Bangladesh, my last stop-over. After thirty-four hours of flights and endless waiting, I at last reached Calcutta, the Communist capital of East Bengal.

I took a taxi – a 1950s Ambassador, which is the standard car in Bengal. I gave the address of a hotel that had been recommended to me: the Park Hotel on Sudder Street, in the European quarter. After driving for ten minutes past grassy meadows, the heavy heat suddenly flooded down over the Bengali capital.

Even at that late hour, Calcutta was crawling with people. In the dusty night air, thousands of figures stood out: men in short-sleeved shirts, their faces drowned in the shadows, women in multi-coloured saris, whose naked bellies vanished into the darkness. I could not distinguish any faces, just the splashes of colour on the foreheads of the girls, or the black and white stares of some passers-by. Nor could I make out the shop fronts, or the architecture of the houses. I was advancing through a dark tunnel, whose sides seemed to consist entirely of brown heads and scrawny arms and legs. The crowds surged everywhere. Cars bumped into one another, horns blaring, while the trams with barred windows forced their way through the hordes. From time to time, a noisy procession appeared. Haggard creatures, dressed in red, yellow and blue, banging percussion instruments and playing pervasive melodies in the acrid smoke of incense. A death. A wake. Then the heaving throng closed in again. Lepers approached, brushing past the car, tapping on the windows. In that chaotic night Calcutta's main curiosity could also be seen: the rickshawallahs, those men of burden who drag their passengers through the town, galloping on their spindly legs, walking on the torn-up asphalt, breathing in car fumes as they go.

But the people were nothing in comparison with the smells: unbearable stenches that wandered in the air like violent crazed animals. Vomit, mould, incense, spices. The night smelt like a gigantic rotten fruit.

The taxi turned down Sudder Street.

At the Park Hotel, I gave a false name and converted two hundred dollars into rupees. My room was on the first floor, at the end of a staircase that was open to the sky. It was small, dirty and it stank. I opened the window, which looked out over the kitchens. It was unbearable. I closed it again at once and locked the door. For some time, I had been incessantly sniffing and coughing. My throat and nostrils were caked with a blackish substance and the folds in my shirt were full of the same disgusting pollution. Half an hour in Calcutta and I had already been poisoned.

I had a shower. The water seemed as filthy as everything else. Then I changed. After that, I gathered together the various parts of my Glock. Slowly and surely, I reassembled it. I placed sixteen bullets in the magazine, then slipped it into the grip. Fixing my holster on to my belt, I then covered it with my cotton jacket. I looked at myself in the mirror. A perfect embassy secretary or envoy from the World Bank. I unlocked my door and went outside.

I took the first side turning I found, an overpopulated alley with neither a roadway nor pavement, just a covering of decaying asphalt, on the edges of which crouching beggars peered up at me with pleading eyes. Indians, Nepalese and Chinese approached me to suggest changing my dollars. Tiny shops, whose windows were mere holes in the rubble, opened up revealing nauseating interiors. Tea, poppadums, curry. Smoke wafted across the shadows. Finally, I came across a wide square, on which stood a covered market.

Numerous braziers glistened there. Faces floated around them, faceted with golden reflections. Hundreds of people were sleeping on the ground. Bodies piled up under the blankets, prostrate in a profound slumber. The asphalt was damp and gleamed here and there with a feverish shimmer. Despite the horrendous poverty, despite the unspeakable stench, that vision was flamboyant. In it, I recognized the particular texture of nights in the tropics. That blackness, that blue and grey, pierced by gold and fire, misted over by fumes and aromas, and which seems to reveal the hidden seed of reality.

I pushed on further through the night.

I turned, branching off, not worrying about the direction I was taking. Now I was wandering through the covered market, which contained narrow badly paved alleyways, covered with rotten and stale food. From time to time, the half-open doors partly revealed huge rooms, where ant-men were carrying and pulling immense crates in the crude light of the electric lamps. However, here the city became less agitated. Crouching in front of their unlit workshops, Bengalis were listening to radios. Some barbers were wearily shaving heads. Other men were playing a strange game – some sort of table tennis – in what must have been an abattoir during the day, to judge by the streams of blood on the walls. And rats everywhere. Huge, powerful rats, freely coming and going like dogs. Sometimes an Indian noticed one at his feet, nibbling a lettuce leaf. He then pushed it away with his foot, as though it were a pet.

I walked for hours that night, trying to tame the city and its terror. When I found my way back to the hotel, it was 3 a.m. As I walked down Sudder Street, I breathed in once more that smell of poverty and spat up some more soot.

A grin flickered over my face.

Yes, Calcutta was definitely the ideal place.

To kill or to die.

CHAPTER 55

At dawn, I had another shower and got dressed. I left my room at half past five and questioned the Bengali who was dozing in the hotel lobby – a wooden counter on a raised dais, surrounded by a scanty garden. The Indian knew of just one One World centre, near Howrah bridge. I couldn't miss it. There was a permanent long queue outside. "But always beggars and incurable cases," he added with a look of disgust. I thanked him, thinking that contempt was an unaffordable luxury in Calcutta.

The sun was still rising hesitantly. Sudder Street was grey, made up of decrepit hotels and greasy fast food places, offering combinations of English breakfasts and chicken tandooris. A few rickshawallahs were napping on their wagons, while hanging on to their horns. A half-naked man with an eye missing offered me a *chai* – tea flavoured with ginger and served in stoneware cups. I drank two scalding and over strong doses then went my way in search of a taxi.

Five hundred yards further on, some old Victorian palaces, now cracked and colourless, rose up at either side of the street. At their feet, hundreds of bodies dotted the pavements, curled up beneath filthy rags. A few lepers, with no fingers or faces, spotted me and approached. I walked on more quickly. Finally, I reached Jawaharlal Nehru Road, a huge avenue bordered with ruined museums. All along it, beggars were offering attractions. One of them, in the lotus position, was facing a hole dug out in the asphalt. He slipped his head inside, covered it completely with sand, then raised up his body backwards, knees pointing at the sky. Anybody who appreciated this trick could reward him with a few rupees.

I hailed a cab and set off due north towards Howrah bridge. The sun was coming up over the town. The rails of the tramways glistened between the weed-covered paving stones. The traffic was not heavy yet. There were just some men running along the road and silently pulling huge trolleys. On the pavements, dark hobbledehoys were washing in the gutters. They were spitting up mucus, scraping their tongues clean with steel wires then dousing themselves with waste water. Further on, children were carefully picking their way through some piles of half-burnt rubbish, as the ashes fluttered away in the wind. Old women were defecating under the bushes and groups were beginning to form up in the streets, pouring out of the houses, the trains and trams. As the heat rose, Calcutta sweated people. We drove on through the streets and avenues, where I also spotted the inevitable temples, the bony cows and sadhus with a touch of colour on their foreheads. India: horror embracing the absolute in a kiss of darkness.

The taxi reached Armenian Ghat, beside the river. The One World centre stood in the shadows of a motorway bridge. It consisted of a canvas canopy that ran the length of the pavement among the itinerant pedlars, propped up on metal supports. Beneath it, pale Europeans were opening boxes of medicines, setting up barrels of drinking water and sharing out food parcels. The centre was spread over a good thirty yards – thirty yards of nourishment, health care and devotion. After that came the endless queue of the sick, the lame and the skeletal.

I sat down discreetly behind an ear-cleaner's shack and waited, observing the work of these apostles of a better world. I also watched the Bengalis as they walked off to work or to their inescapable poverty. Before starting the working day, perhaps they had sacrificed a goat to Kali, or gone swimming in the oily waters of the river. The heat and smell were giving me a migraine.

Finally, at 9 a.m., he appeared.

He was walking alone, a worn leather bag round his wrist. I summoned all of my strength to get to my feet and examine him in detail. Pierre Doisneau / Sénicier was tall and thin. He was wearing pale cotton trousers and a sleeveless shirt. His face was like stone. His forehead protruded from his grey curly hair and he wore a harsh smile on his face that was kept in place by aggressive jawbones that stood out clearly from beneath his skin. Pierre Doisneau. Pierre Sénicier. The heart thief.

My hand instinctively went for my Glock. I had no precise plan in mind and simply intended to observe what went on. More and more urchins arrived. Pretty blonde girls in day-glo shorts were helping the Indian nurses, handing them dressings and drugs with angelic application. Lepers and sickly mothers paraded before them, taking their rations of pills or food, waggling their heads in gratitude.

It was 11.15 a.m., and Pierre Doisneau / Sénicier was preparing to leave.

He closed his bag, smiled around at his neighbours then vanished into the crowd. I followed him at a good distance. There was no way he would ever spot me in that sea of humanity. On the other hand, I could easily pick out his tall figure from as far away as fifty yards. We walked on for twenty minutes. The "doc" did not seem to fear reprisals. What did he have to fear? In Calcutta he was a true saint, a man everyone adored. And that crowd around him made for the best protection imaginable.

Sénicier slowed down. We had reached a more affluent looking area. The streets were wider, the pavements less dirty. As we arrived at a crossroads, I noticed an OW centre. I, too, slowed my pace and kept at a distance of about two hundred yards from him.

At that time of the day, the heat was overwhelming. Sweat was pouring down my face. I took shelter in the shade, near a family that looked as if they had lived on the pavement for ever. I sat down next to them and asked for some tea, playing at the tourist who likes to experience a little poverty.

Another hour went by. I scrutinized Sénicier's every move as he carried out his humanitarian labours. The sight of that man, whom I knew to be a murderer, playing at the Good Samaritan took my breath away. I tasted to the full his ambivalent nature. I realized that at every moment in his life, whether plunging his hands into entrails or treating a leper woman, he was equally sincere. In the throes of the same mad attraction for bodies, illness and flesh.

This time, I changed tactics. I waited for Sénicier to leave before going over and chatting to some of the European women who

313

were acting as nurses. It took me half an hour to discover that the Doisneau family lived in a huge mansion, the Marble Palace, which had been given to them by a rich Brahmin. The doctor was intending to open a clinic there.

I rushed off. An idea had suddenly occurred to me: wait for Sénicier in the Marble Palace and gun him down on his home turf. In his operating theatre. I caught a cab and headed towards Salumam Bazaar. After half an hour spent in the crowds, in narrow streets with the horn constantly rammed down, the taxi burst into a bustling souk. As the car advanced, it knocked into the stalls or caught on the women's saris. Insults rained down and the sun exploded in scattered shards, gleaming through the hordes of people. The neighbourhood seemed to be growing increasingly dense and narrower, like a tunnel in an ant-hill. Then suddenly, a huge park opened up in which, among a grove of palm trees, stood a large residence with white pillars.

"Marble Palace?" I yelled at the driver.

The man turned round and nodded, smiling at me with all his steel teeth.

I paid him and leapt out. My eyes refused to believe what they were seeing. Behind the high railings, peacocks and gazelles wandered around. The way into the park was not even closed. There was neither a janitor nor a security guard to stop me. I crossed the lawn, went up the steps and entered that palace of a thousand varieties of marble.

I happened upon a large, airy grey room. Everything was made of marble, marble that altered its colours and textures, with pinkish veins, blue filaments, dark compact slabs, creating a mixture of weight and icy beauty. But, above all, the room was full of hundreds of white, elegant statues – sculptures of men and women in the renaissance style, as if they had been lifted from a Florentine palace.

I crossed that forest of busts. Their calm, ghostly eyes seemed to follow me. At the other end, some doors opened out onto a patio overlooked by an iron balcony. I walked on into the courtyard. Tall façades, pierced by finely carved windows, surrounded me. Marble Palace formed a gigantic enclosure around that island of cool serenity. This patio was its heart, the true reason for its having been built. The windows, the stone guard-rails and the carving on the columns had nothing to do with any Indian tradition, nor even with Victorian architecture. Once more, I had the impression that I was strolling through an Italian renaissance palace.

The garden consisted of tropical plants that grew between the marble flagstones. Fountains shimmered in the breeze. This unreal place exuded a shadowy atmosphere, a calm solitariness, something like the sweet dream of a deserted harem. Here and there, stood more statues, casting their curves and their bodies into the occasional rays of sunlight that managed to enter. Were we really still in Calcutta, in the midst of indescribable chaos? Some soft bird cries rang out. I slipped down the covered walkway that ran alongside the patio. At once, I noticed some large wooden cages hung up along the walls, containing white birds.

"They're crows. White crows. They're unique. I've been breeding them here for years."

I turned round. Marie-Anne Sénicier was standing in front of me, just as I had always imagined her, her white hair pulled back into a large bun above her colourless face. Only her purplish lips stood out, like a cruel bloody fruit. My eyes misted over, my legs almost gave way. I tried to speak, but instead I collapsed on the steps and spewed my guts up. I went on coughing and spitting up bile for what seemed like a long time. Finally, I murmured through my aching throat:

"I'm . . . I'm sorry . . . I . . ."

Marie-Anne cut my agony short:

"I know who you are, Louis. Nelly rang me. This is a strange way to meet again. (Then she added, in a softer tone:) Louis, my little Louis."

I wiped my mouth – I had also spat up blood – then dried my eyes. My real mother. My emotions were crushing me and I was incapable of speaking. It was she that continued, in her absent tone of voice:

"Your brother's sleeping there at the end of the garden. Do you want to see him? We'll have some tea."

I nodded in agreement. She tried to help me up. I pushed her hands away and got to my feet unaided, then opened the collar of my shirt. I headed for the centre of the patio and pushed aside the plants. Behind them, there were some sofas, cushions and a silver tray with a steaming copper teapot on it. On one of the sofas, a man in an Indian tunic was asleep. He was completely bald and his face was as white as plaster; the wrinkles looked as if they had been dug out by a minuscule chisel. His posture was that of a child, but he seemed even older than the marble surrounding him. The stranger looked like me. He had the same decadent face, the high forehead and weary eyes sunk into their sockets. But his body was totally unlike my own hefty build. Beneath his tunic, his limbs appeared to be scrawny, his waist slim. A large dressing could be seen, covering his chest, its cotton fibres protruding above the embroidered neckline. Frédéric Sénicier, my brother, the eternal transplant patient.

"He's asleep," Marie-Anne whispered. "Shall we wake him up? The last operation went very well. That was in September."

Little Gomoun's face suddenly sprang into my mind. My guts were being wrenched apart.

Marie-Anne added, as though the rest of the world did not exist:

"He's the only person who can keep him alive. You understand that?"

Softly I asked:

"Where's the theatre?"

"What theatre?"

"Where he operates."

Marie-Anne did not reply. A few inches away from her, I felt her old woman's breath.

"Downstairs, in the cellar. Nobody's allowed to go down there. You have no idea . . ."

"What time does he go there in the evening?"

"Louis . . ."

"What time?"

"At about eleven."

I was still looking at Frédéric, the aged child, whose breast was rising and falling irregularly. I could not take my eyes off the dressing that puffed up his tunic.

"How can I get inside his laboratory?"

"You're mad."

I had calmed down again. It felt as though my blood were now coursing in long regular waves through my veins. I turned round and stared at my mother.

"Is there any way I can get into his goddam operating theatre?"

My mother lowered her eyes and mumbled:

"Wait for me here."

She crossed the patio then came back a few minutes later, clutching a bunch of keys in her hand. She opened the ring and, with a look of lost sweetness, gave me just one. I grabbed it, then simply said:

"I'll be back this evening. After eleven."

CHAPTER 56

Marble Palace at midnight. As I went down the steps, a heavy pungent stench greeted me. It was the smell of death, the pure essence of darkness so strong that it seemed to be seeping into my pores despite myself. Blood. Torrents of blood. I pictured ghastly landscapes. A dark red backdrop on which passed a parade of rosy crests, thinned vermilion and brown scabs.

At the bottom of the stairs, I found the door to the cold chamber locked with an iron bolt. I used my mother's key. Outside, it was pitch black. But the figure that slipped down the staircase had not escaped me. The animal was returning to its lair. The heavy door swung open. Glock in hand, I entered my father's laboratory.

A soothing coolness enveloped my body. At once, I drank in the terrible nightmare around me. I was walking straight through Max

Böhm's photographs. In that tiled room, lit by strip-lights, lay a veritable forest of corpses. Bodies hanging from meat hooks, the sharpened metal piercing cheeks, facial cartilage, eye sockets, until the points gleamed evilly in the air. All of these bodies were Indian children. They swayed gently, creaking softly on their pivots, displaying their unimaginable wounds: open rib cages, cuts zig-zagging through their flesh, dark holes torn out in their joints, bones jutting out. And blood. Blood everywhere. Dried torrents that seemed to coat and varnish their torsos. Motionless streams that traced out curling patterns on the mounds of their skin. Splashes of ink staining their faces, chests and groins.

The cold and the terror made my hair stand on end. I had the feeling that my hand was going to fire the gun of its own accord. I placed my index finger along the barrel, in combat posture, and forced myself to go on, eyes wide open.

In the middle of the room, heads were piled up on a tiled block. Narrow faces twisted by agony, frozen into their dying expressions. Under their eye sockets, long blue bags hung down, deepening their suffering. All of these heads had been sliced off cleanly at the base of the neck. I walked past this butcher's stall. At the end, I found a pile of limbs. Little arms and thin legs, with dark skin, lay strewn together in an abominable tangle. A slight coat of frost covered them. My heart was beating like a terrified beast. Suddenly, beneath that ghastly mess, I noticed some genitals. Little boys' penises that had been sliced off at the root. Girls' ruddy vulvas positioned there, like fleshy fish. I bit my lips to stop myself from screaming. A warm sensation flooded my throat. I had just reopened my scar.

I listened attentively, my every sense alert, and moved on. One room followed another in a variety of horror. Scraps of bloody tissue nestled in little coffins. Pieces of bodies swaying slowly in the frosty atmosphere. I saw gleaming scanners, hung in the air, revealing incomprehensible monstrosities. Something like Siamese hearts, a spontaneous generation of livers and kidneys, coagulated together in one body, as though at the bottom of a flask. The further I went, the colder it got.

Finally, I reached the last door. It was not locked. My chest aching from my beating heart, I slowly opened it. It was the operating theatre, completely empty. In the centre, surrounded by glass shelves, stood the table under a convex lamp that gave off a white light. There was nobody on it. Nobody was to be tortured that evening. I leant forwards and peered inside.

Suddenly, a rustling sound made me turn round. At the same moment, I felt an intense burning sensation in the nape of my neck. Dr Pierre Sénicier was on top of me, a syringe stuck in my flesh. Roaring, I leapt back and pulled out the needle. Too late. My sensations were already clouding over. I raised my gun. My father put his hands up, as though he was afraid, but he kept coming at me and talking to me in his soft voice:

"You wouldn't shoot your own father now, would you, Louis?"

He came slowly towards me, forcing me back. I tried to raise the Glock, but I had no more strength in my wrists. I bumped into the operating table and forced my eyes open. For a split second, I had fallen asleep. The white light was throwing me into oblivion. The surgeon went on:

"I'd given up all hope of ever experiencing this moment, my son. We're going to start again just where we left off, so long ago, and then the two of us will save Frédéric. Your mother just couldn't contain her emotion. You know what women are like ... "

At that moment, I heard the dull thud of the door of the cold chamber and hurried footsteps. Through the icy mists, my mother appeared, her fingernails stretched out towards us. Her face was entirely covered with needles and blades. I staggered. With what was left of my strength, I pointed the Glock at my father and pressed the trigger. I heard a metal click through my mother's screams, who was now only a few inches from us. I realized that the gun had jammed. In my mind's eye, I saw Sarah again, teaching me how to shoot. I pulled back the breech and pushed the bullet out. I was reloading when I heard a ghastly "no". It was not my mother's voice, nor my father's. It was my own voice screaming as the monster was slicing his wife's head off with a glistening metal scythe. My second "no" died in my throat. I dropped the Glock and fell backwards through a crashing of glass. Gunshots rang out. My father's body exploded into a thousand pieces. I thought I was hallucinating. But, when I hit the ground, I saw the upside-down image of Dr Milan Djuric, the gypsy dwarf, standing on the steps, a Uzi machine-gun in his hands. It was still smoking from the volley of redemption he had just fired.

CHAPTER 57

When I came to, the smell of blood had gone. I was lying on a wicker-work sofa in the inner courtyard of the palace. I was aware of the hazy light of early morning and I could hear the crows croaking in the distance. Apart from their soft cries, the place was totally silent. I was still not quite sure what had happened, then a friendly hand gave me a cup of tea. Milan Djuric. He was in shirt sleeves, covered in sweat, with his Uzi on his shoulder. He sat down next to me and, with no preamble, told me his story in his deep voice. I listened, drinking my ginger infusion. His voice soothed me. It offered me a terrible, but at the same time reassuring echo of my own destiny.

Milan Djuric was one of my father's victims.

In the 1960s, Djuric had been a typical gypsy child, living on the wastelands around Paris. A free and happy nomad. His only problem was that he was an orphan. In 1963, he was sent to the Clinique Pasteur in Neuilly. He was then ten years old. As soon as he arrived, Pierre Sénicier injected staphylococcus into his kneecaps, in order to infect his legs. As an experiment. The operation occurred a few days before the final fire – the "purification" carried out by the surgeon who was about to be unmasked. But, despite his infirmity, Djuric managed to escape the flames by crawling along the lawns. He was the only survivor of the experimental laboratory.

For a few weeks, he was carefully looked after in a Paris hospital. Finally, he was told that he would live, but that the infection would stop him from growing normally. Djuric had become an "accidental dwarf". He then realized that he was doubly different and doubly excluded. Both a gypsy and deformed.

The little boy then received a grant from the state. He concentrated on his studies, read widely, perfected his French, also learnt Bulgarian, Hungarian, Albanian and, of course, improved his knowledge of Romany. He studied the history of his people, discovering their Indian origins and the long journey that had taken them to Europe. Djuric decided to become a doctor and to practise in the Balkans, where millions of gypsies could be found. He became a brilliant, hard-working student. At the age of twenty-four, he completed his studies and successfully passed his hospital entrance examination. He also joined the Communist Party in order to be able to emigrate behind the Iron Curtain more easily and join his people. Never did he try to find that sadistic doctor who had done him so much harm. On the contrary, he made a virtue of wiping out all recollection of his stay in that clinic. His body was there to remember for him.

For fifteen years, Milan Djuric cared for the Roms with patience and enthusiasm, driving around the countries of Eastern Europe in his Trabant. He was sent to prison on several occasions. He confronted all sorts of accusations, and always survived. As the gypsies' doctor, he looked after his own people, those whom no other practitioner would touch, unless it was to sterilize the women or draw up anthropometric charts.

Then came that rainy day when I knocked at his door. In many ways, I was a visitor from hell. Firstly, I forced him to delve once more into Rajko's murder. Then, strangely, my physical appearance reminded him of forgotten terror. At that moment, he was incapable of saying where that impression of *déjà vu* came from. But, during the following weeks, my face returned to haunt him. Little by little, it came back to him. He put a name and a context to my features. He understood what I did not yet know: the bloodline that linked me to Pierre Sénicier.

When I called him after returning from Africa, Djuric questioned me. I refused to answer. He became even more convinced. He also realized that I was nearing my objective: a confrontation with the devil. He took the plane to Paris. There, he spotted me as I was returning from my visit to the Braeslers, on the morning of 2 October. He followed me to the Indian embassy, talked someone into revealing my destination, then also asked for a visa for Bengal on his French passport.

On the morning of 5 October, he was still dogging me, this time near the One World centre. He recognized Pierre Doisneau / Sénicier and trailed me to the Marble Palace. He knew that the time had come for the confrontation. For me. For him. And for the "doc". But, that evening, he failed to enter the Marble Palace in time. When he did manage to get inside, he had lost my scent. He walked past the columns, the cages of crows, went up the stairs on the patio, searched each room and finally found Marie-Anne Sénicier who had been wounded, then locked up. Her husband had tortured her to find out why she was so emotional. Djuric freed her. She said nothing – her jaws were pocked with a multitude of bleeding points – but she ran off in the direction of the cellars. She realized that I had fallen into a trap. When she reached the laboratory, Djuric was still clambering down the marble steps. The rest will remain forever printed on my soul. Pierre Sénicier's attack, the blind blade slicing through my mother's neck, and my gun powerless to wipe out that monster. When Djuric appeared and fired his Uzi, I thought I was dreaming. Yet, before passing out, I knew that my guardian angel had snatched me from my father's clutches. An angel no taller than a hydrant, but whose avenging fire had engraved on those tiled walls the final epitaph to the entire adventure.

It was 6 a.m. I, too, told my story. When I had finished, Djuric made no comment. He got to his feet and told me about his immediate plans. All that night, he had worked on closing down the laboratory. He had anaesthetized the few children that were still alive, then injected them with large doses of anti-septics. He had helped those deformed victims to flee, hoping that they would find their place in this capital of the damned. Then he had discovered my brother, Frédéric, who had died in his arms, calling out for his mother. Finally, he had gone back into the cellars to pile the bodies up in the main room, ready to be burnt. He was waiting for me to light the bonfire and watch over the flames. "What about the Séniciers?" I asked, after a long pause.

Djuric calmly replied:

"Either we burn their bodies with the others, or we take them to Kali Ghat on the banks of the river. There, they will be cremated according to Hindu tradition."

"Why them and not the children?"

"There are too many of them, Louis."

"Let's burn Pierre Sénicier here, and take my mother and brother to Kali Ghat."

From that moment on, everything was heat and flames. The tiles exploded in that furnace, the smell of roast meat swirled in our heads as we fed that hell fire with corpses. My burnt hands allowed me to work nearer the flames. As I pushed loose limbs back into the fire, my mind was empty. The heavy smoke billowed out through air vents in the patio. We fully realized that it would attract the servants and wake up the neighbours. They would come to put out the fire and evaluate the damage. In the back of my mind, I thought of that fire in the clinic, from which little Milan had escaped, despite his atrophied legs. I thought of Bangui, when my mother had sacrificed my hands to save my life. Djuric and I were both sons of fire. And here we were burning the last link with our infernal origins.

Immediately afterwards, we took a five-door saloon from the garage, and slid the bodies of Marie-Anne and Frédéric in the back. As I drove, Djuric directed me through the streets of Calcutta. Ten minutes later, we reached Kali Ghat. The quarter was crossed by a narrow interminable road, which ran alongside some small confluents of the river, full of green stagnant water. Brothels replaced the workshops of religious sculpture. Everything seemed asleep.

I was driving automatically, staring at the dull sky which could be seen behind the roofs and electricity cables. Suddenly, Djuric stopped me. "It's there," he said, pointing at a stone fortress on our right. The surrounding wall was topped by several turrets shaped like sugar loaves, carved with ornamentations and sculptures. I parked the car while Djuric went inside. I immediately followed him and found myself in a vast courtyard covered with cropped grass.

In the four corners, wood faggots were smouldering. Around them, skeleton-like men were looking after the fires, pushing the embers into a compact mass with long sticks. The flames gave off a pale glow and thick clouds of black smoke. I recognized the smell of burnt flesh and noticed a hand drop out from one of the braziers. One of the men coolly picked this human debris up and put it back into the flames. Exactly as I had done, a few minutes before. I looked up. The stone turrets rose up in the grey dawn. I realized that I did not know any prayers.

At the back of the courtyard, Djuric was speaking with an elderly man in fluent Bengali. He gave him a thick wad of rupees, then came back towards me.

"A Brahmin is coming," he explained. "A ceremony will take place in an hour's time. They will then scatter the ashes over the river. It will all be just as it is for real Indians, Louis. We can do no better than that."

I nodded and said nothing. I watched the two Bengalis who had just lit a large log, on which lay a body dressed in white. Djuric followed my stare, then said:

"These men are Doms, the lowest caste in the Indian hierarchy. They alone are allowed to handle the dead. Thousands of years ago, they were singers and jugglers. They are the ancestors of the Roms, Louis. My ancestors."

We carried Marie-Anne Sénicier's head and body and Frédéric's remains all wrapped up in a surgical sheet. Nobody would see that they were Westerners. Djuric spoke to the old man once more. This time he talked more loudly and threatened him with his fist. I understood nothing. We left immediately afterwards. Before getting into the car, Djuric yelled something at the old boy again, who nodded his head with a look of fear and hatred. As we drove away, Djuric explained:

"Doms have a tendency to be economical with wood. When the bodies are half burnt, they give them to the vultures in the river and sell the rest of the faggots. I didn't want that for Marie-Anne and Frédéric."

I was still staring at the road in front of me. Dark tears were flowing down my cheeks. Later, when we took the plane to Dhaka, I still had the taste of burnt flesh in my mouth.

Epilogue

A few days later, in Calcutta, a cortège of several thousand people paid homage to Dr Pierre Doisneau and his family, who had died in the tragic fire in his laboratory. Their deaths were little talked about in Europe. Pierre Doisneau was a legend, but a distant, unreal one. Now, although he is dead, his work goes on. More than ever, One World is expanding and doing its good deeds. The media have even mentioned the possibility of Pierre Doisneau being posthumously awarded the 1992 Nobel Peace Prize.

In every respect, Simon Rickiel dealt with the diamond smuggling affair with a masterful touch. On 24 October 1991, the Cape Town police discovered Niels van Dötten, a terrified effeminate old man hiding out in one of the town's residential suburbs. The Afrikaner, now no doubt reassured by the successive deaths of his accomplices and master, freely confessed to all his crimes. He explained the network's basic structure, giving names, places and dates. Thanks to Simon Rickiel, I was even allowed to read his statement myself and noticed that van Dötten had brushed over the role of Pierre Sénicier, who had been blackmailing the three smugglers.

Today, Sarah Gabbor is in prison in Israel. She is in a camp where the prisoners work outside, as they do in a kibbutz. In some ways, she has thus gone back to square one. She has not yet been tried and, given the recent revelations, her case is looking more hopeful.

I have written several letters to her, which have remained unanswered. In her silence, I can read that pride and strength of character which so fascinated me when I was in Israel. Nobody has yet found the beautiful kibbutznik's money and diamonds.

As for the mystery of the hearts, it has never been mentioned in any official documents. Only Simon Rickiel, Milan Djuric and I know the truth. And we will carry the secret to our graves.

When Milan Djuric left me, he simply said: "We should never see each other again, Louis. Never. Our friendship would only open old wounds." He gripped my hand and squeezed it as tightly as he could. That brave man's handshake shattered forever the complex I had about my deformity.